LANDSLIDE

DAVE DOUGHERTY

About the Author

Dave Dougherty is an author who lived from 1979 to 2001 in El Paso, and is intimately familiar with the region and chili cooking, being often a participant at chili cook-offs. He was a Professor in the Business Department, and headed up the Computer Science – Business Option Program from 1979 to 1984 at the University of Texas, El Paso. He holds advanced degrees from Colorado School of Mines and Case Western Reserve University and advanced to candidacy for a PhD at both Case Western Reserve and the University of Maryland. He is a Registered Professional Engineer. Dave has authored over twenty academic papers and a number of books, primarily history, including *A Patriot's History Reader: Essential Documents for Every American, A Patriot's History of the Modern World, Volumes I and II, Starve The Beast!,* and now *Landslide.*

Table of Contents

Preface

This is a work of fiction. The places are real with the exception of Mac Frazier's Bar-D ranch and the property with the well. Certain actual personalities in the El Paso/Las Cruces area are mentioned in the context of local color but without involvement in the fictional story. The Fraziers and Prescotts are fictional, as well as all characters connected directly with them in their activities. Any resemblance of actual persons to the Fraziers, Prescotts, and other characters involved with the Bar-D or well operation is strictly accidental and unintentional.

The annual chili championship cook-off at Terlingua is an actual event, and Taranchili is the name formerly used by Gary and Georgann Thompson of El Paso, Texas, for their competitive chili. Like the fictional Hamms, they featured a large Mexican red-legged tarantula as their mascot, and their showmanship stories formed the basis for the Hamm's chili cook-off participation.

Various El Paso and Las Cruces establishments figuring in this tale are real, including the Great American Land & Cattle restaurant, Casa Jurado, and others. No denigration of any actual locality is intended—quite the contrary, those real sites were included because of their excellence and the cultural impact they lend to the story.

The El Paso/Las Cruces area is a unique jewel in American geography, well worth a visit by travelers. The clash of cultures and the area's location, sometimes described as *between* the United States and Mexico, have ramifications reaching far beyond the area's geographic limits. Generally, the interplay between Anglos and Hispanics—almost always referred to simply as "Mexicans"—is harmonious, but the language used is often like that in this work. Anglos (a designation that also includes blacks) and Mexicans tend to inter-marry and carry on relationships freely and without stigma in

1

local society, a situation often not prevalent in other communities. The Mac Frazier character does not reflect even a small minority, as his attitudes are carried to an extreme due to his injuries. It is hoped this story will give the reader some insight into a micro-culture which many might otherwise never know exists.

The date of this story is 1986, although the setting could just as easily be 2015. That should mean something to our politicians.

Chapter 1—Valentine's Day

It was a beautiful day in the desert, clear and cool, giving Stuart unlimited sight for miles. He topped a small hill with his Blazer, following the sandy track and the Rio Grande Valley spread out before him. In the distance was the seven-foot-high cyclone fence, the well, and buildings that were his objective. The enclosure was a postage stamp of private property surrounded by BLM land, just north of the Bar-D's northern fence and alongside a flood control dam.

The front gate was padlocked, but the rear entrance leading onto Bar-D property was wide open. Stuart drove in and parked beside the well. The cattle pens were empty, no vehicles were parked anywhere, and the house trailer looked deserted. The trailer was weathering from lack of maintenance, and a distinct air of decay had settled over the miscellaneous structures. Had Stuart not known better, he would have thought the site was abandoned and in process of being reclaimed by the desert.

He concentrated on the task ahead. There were several fresh sets of tire tracks, and the diesel pump looked oily and recently used. The desert breeze pierced his windbreaker, but the sun was warm—as usual for February. A perfect day for football. A snow bird would call the weather "fresh." Stuart called it invigorating and beautiful.

He strode across the crushed stone loading area, wanting to ignore the white dust that coated his beige Tony Lamas. He tried the door to the trailer. It was unlocked. The owners weren't afraid of trespassers.

The inside was filthy and looked like it had been the venue of non-stop stag parties. The stench of stale beer, booze, unwashed dishes and glasses almost gave him nausea. Tostada chips were strewn about on the kitchen counter, and salsa was spilled on the linoleum floor. Sacks of empty beer cans were piled against a couch. No rats scurried about, but Stuart kept his eyes open just the same. He half-expected to find some passed-out drunk in the bedroom. If anything, the bedroom was a bigger mess than the living area, and its unmade bed spoke volumes about its use.

Stuart couldn't imagine the Aztec goddess participating except as some kind of ringmaster with a whip. She probably used prostitutes from El Paso or Juarez. In that case she might not show up. He might have to wait several nights for his chance at her. Stuart ignored such thoughts and went to work. If he had to wait a month, he would wait.

The trailer abounded in hiding places, and Stuart selected spots to cover the entire inside. He stashed dynamite charges under the kitchen sink, the bathroom's washbasin, under the large bed, and behind a couch. In each case, he bracketed the sticks with gasoline cans, a setup he had tested on his property east of the Franklin Mountains. The explosion and fire had been awesome enough from a single placement, but here he was using four. Three extra cans went on the roof for added insurance. They were clearly visible to anybody who looked, but in the mess and disorder, particularly at night, he doubted they'd be noticed.

The storage sheds and pens were easy. There was trash everywhere, and Stuart hid the dynamite and gasoline cans under sacks of feed, hay bales, and various items where they would be most destructive. He placed charges in the wellhead and its diesel pump, and even buried two in the sand where the tanker would park to take on water. There were still three extra bundles, and Stuart buried them where tracks indicated vehicles were usually parked by the trailer. Satisfied with himself, he drove out the open gate and headed for the Great American Land & Cattle Company restaurant. He wanted a full stomach for the evening's activities, and there were hours to kill before his guests showed up.

Time was a luxury which rarely permitted Stuart to stop and contemplate his legacy. From dawn to dusk, his energy was concentrated on the mundane mechanics of his businesses. He was the sole heir to the extensive Prescott holdings in southern New Mexico, and was often referred to as "the man who owns half of Doña Ana County." That was an exaggeration, but he wielded enormous influence in the county, both politically and economically.

It was a good thing, because with his short and unimposing build, sandy hair and brown eyes, Stuart knew he was not a man who impressed the ladies on sight.

At GALACCO Patty Duncan was singing her country-western songs in the long barroom, and Stuart settled back to be entertained after polishing off a sixteen-ounce sirloin. He requested "Landslide," remembering how Mac and he had listened together so long ago. Sooner or later, landslides brought everybody down.

The restaurant was crowded and it seemed like everyone in the Upper Valley was there. Stuart would have preferred to spend the time listening to Patty, but there were hands to shake and obligatory schmoozing to perform. All the time, he was smiling to himself thinking of what he was about to do that night.

When Patty sang "Someday Soon," he knew it was time to leave. "Crazy Blue Eyes" would follow and he didn't want to think any more about Mac, his blue eyes, or the past.

He covered the distance from the restaurant to the Bar-D property in about ten minutes. He drove his Blazer along the desert escarpment's access road until he came to the arroyo leading to Mac's tin mine. The scrub mesquite there hid his Blazer from prying eyes, and he walked along an obscure path to the crest of a low hill immediately south of Mac's fence line. Stuart settled where he could readily observe the well, trailer, and all approaches. The evening was turning colder, and he began to shiver. He wished he hadn't consumed those Harvey Wallbangers in GALACCO's bar, and wondered if alcohol made his blood more susceptible to cold.

Mac would have done this without becoming chilled. He had been hot-blooded but handled dangerous situations as if ice water flowed in his veins. And Mac wouldn't have gone to Dallas to find someone to rig the transmitter on the ground. He would have done it himself.

Stuart smiled at his own lack of mechanical aptitude. At least he knew how to arrange things. It only required money and grit, and he had plenty of both. He had practiced with the transmitter in Dallas, setting off fireworks on demand. The equipment was surprisingly simple, made with off-the-shelf components obtainable in any electronics store. That was good, because any recovered fragments would be untraceable. Mac would have been proud.

5

Thinking about his friends brought tears to his eyes, and the cold increased his discomfort. He hoped his guests would show up and that tonight wasn't going to be an off-night. Mac was usually home by eleven, and Stuart's watch already showed a quarter past ten.

He scooted a few feet back down the hill and stood up to relieve himself. As he buttoned up, two cars showed up on the road to the entrance gate. A watched pot never boils, Stuart reminded himself. The cars halted while someone unlocked the gate and headed for the trailer.

He resumed his position behind the transmitter, just as yellow lights headed in from the west. Three vehicles followed Mac's fence line, sinister in the gloom and moving like a weaving snake from the underworld. Crap. Did they have radios to coordinate their timing? That might interfere with his transmission or set off his charges prematurely.

Lights in the trailer snapped on. Four people stood in the floodlit area outside the door. One was a woman whose long blond hair was whipping around her face in the evening breeze.

It had to be her. No one else had that body.

Just to be sure, he picked up his binoculars. Bingo. The Aztec goddess. Looking more expensive and elegant than he remembered. Completely out of style for the desert, she was wearing high heels and a coat more appropriate for the Metropolitan Opera. And oblivious to the danger.

It was a shame those shapely legs and beautiful face hadn't been given to someone more deserving. Now they would be wasted.

The other three were Hispanic males, hardly a surprise considering what Stuart had heard. He wondered which one was her current lover, or if all three received favors according to her moods. One was older, bald, with a large mustache, and the goddess stood closer to him than the others. When she pointed to the gate, one of the younger men immediately trotted over and held it open for the incoming vehicles.

In the lights, Stuart could see her Mercedes parked over one of his buried charges. Behind it was a dark van, and both vehicles were going to become smoking wreckage in a few minutes. The three new additions parked haphazardly between the trailer and well, and Stuart soon counted nine individuals standing in the light.

For two or three minutes nothing happened, but then the sound of an approaching truck drew the attention of those in the compound. A tank truck passed through the front gate and circled around by the well to face out the way it had entered.

Two men mounted the tanker while the remaining men unloaded the vehicles and carried tote boxes to the truck driver and the goddess. They stood together checking the boxes, then handed them up to the men who had unscrewed the cap over the central access port.

It took probably twenty minutes to load the tanker. The two men dismounted and everyone stood around the goddess checking the paper work. The van's side door slide open and another female emerged. The goddess was providing another young Anglo with blond hair and a stunning figure for sexual services.

A few minutes later, everyone followed the other girl into the trailer. Eleven people must make quite the crowd inside with all that filth.

With his quarry inside, it was time for Stuart to act. The girl had been in there for several minutes, and each passing second increased the chance that one of his bombs would be discovered. There was absolute quiet until he switched on the transmitter with a loud click. His face flushed in spite of the cold, and he suddenly realized he wasn't breathing. He took a deep breath and looked at the green button.

This time green didn't mean life.

Chapter 2 - July, The Previous Year

The blazing New Mexico sun was raising dust devils like desert geysers as Stuart Prescott hung on to the Jeep's roll-bar for dear life. His best friend, Mac Frazier, wheeled his well-worn Jeep along the sandy track that passed for a road, oblivious to Stuart's discomfort or the danger of nosing into soft sand and risking a roll-over. Guardians along the narrow gauntlet—hostile mesquite bushes—leaned inward and clawed fiercely at the metallic interloper, screeching and grating their protest. Away from the intruding men and their machine the desert was quiet, stirred only by an occasional roadrunner.

Mac was driving too fast to spot the geckos and rattlesnakes Stuart knew were eyeing the jeep's transit. The Bar-D's trails were ugly scars on the face of nature, a beauty no longer able to adequately protect herself behind the outdated armor of cactus, yucca, and thistles. These centuries-lasting disfigurements were an indignity, signifying defeat but not surrender.

The Apaches who once inhabited this region adapted to its unrelenting harshness by becoming more fearsome than nature herself. They searched out her hidden resources and survived through a nomadic existence to terrorize lesser tribes and wanna-be settlers. Spanish colonists and Mexicans threaded their way northward and built small towns along rivers in relatively fertile flood plains, but attempts to reach outward and extract remote treasures ended miserably in confrontations with their unmerciful opponents. It remained for Stuart's and Mac's ancestors, the much-abused Scotch-Irish, to conquer the land and subdue its inhabitants.

They were perhaps the most efficient human predators the world ever knew, those Scotch-Irish frontiersmen. Constantly moving westward in a futile attempt to remain self-governing, they

8

automatically assumed the white man's burden after Mexico suspended its feeble efforts to defeat the desert savages.

In deadly campaigns marked by utter mercilessness on both sides, the Scotch-Irish Anglos ripped Texas from Indian hands and broke the warlike spirit of North America's fiercest combatants, the recently arrived Comanches and Kiowas. New Mexico and Chihuahua fell like over-ripe peaches to the likes of Kit Carson and Colonel Doniphan. Mac and Stuart were descendants from these fearless frontiersmen, but facing greatly changing times. The renewed Mexican invasion that started after World War II was threatening to send them the way of the Indians.

The friendship between Stuart and his childhood buddy Mac spanned the gulf of wealth. Stuart possessed all the money he could use, while Mac was faced with the constant problem of sheer survival. Stuart was an astute businessman, Mac the romantic cowboy. Ranching was no longer the path to wealth, and Mac was hurting. New Mexico had been over-grazed toward the end of the nineteenth century, and the advent of modern conveniences had not rendered ranching life significantly easier or more profitable. Only water could do that, but the life-giving fluid was scarce and becoming scarcer.

Although a resident of New Mexico, Mac considered himself a southwestern Anglo, probably fitting the stereotype of a Texas cowboy to city dwellers east of the Mississippi. His ranch lay in that tiny segment of New Mexico immediately west of El Paso that was often placed in Mexico by careless cartographers. The Rio Grande turned almost due north after passing between Juarez and El Paso, and formed the border between Texas and New Mexico for about fifteen miles. Mac's Bar-D spread lay wholly on the desert escarpment west of the river, midway between Anapra on the border with Mexico and Anthony, a town bifurcated by the Texas-New Mexico line where the Rio Grande became a wholly New Mexican River.

The area of New Mexico adjoining the tip of Texas lay in Doña Ana County, the largest and second most populous county in the state. Its seat was Las Cruces, forty-three miles north of El Paso, and considered by many Texans as little more than an El Paso suburb. This attitude incensed Stuart, and like most New Mexicans, he spent more time in bucolic Las Cruces than in the geographically more convenient environs of El Paso.

From the Bar-D ranch house to downtown El Paso was twenty-two miles, enough to cloak the spread in splendid isolation. Sometimes it was comforting to know a half million people lived only a few miles away, but two or three times that number filled the teeming streets of Mexico's Ciudad Juarez. The Rio Grande was hardly more than a concrete-channeled ditch between the two cities, and border control was a constant bone of contention.

Stuart wasn't a rancher, but sometimes lived the lifestyle vicariously through working with Mac. Not that their circumstances made any difference; they told each other everything and trusted each other implicitly. They were partners, and called each other, "podge," the local rendition of "partner." Mac was tall, well-built, and a lady-killer; everything Stuart wasn't. Offsetting the fiery and impulsive Mac, Stuart was even-tempered and logical. They were *kumpas,* the local corruption of *"compa"* for *"compadre."* Even as educated Anglos, the men frequently employed such Tex-Mex words in every-day conversation.

This morning had started as usual for Mac with an argument. His wife, Mary Lou, had wanted to enter the La Union volunteer fire department's annual chili cook-off, but Mac's financial condition made every cook-off a strain. His chili-cooking partner Norm was floating most of their expenses, and Mac didn't like owing anyone.

Some days Mac's debts looked overwhelming, particularly to his banker who was becoming increasingly nervous. Stuart had bailed him out on occasion, but the last several years had been one disaster after another; drought, falling cattle prices, all of last year's foals dying, and a wife tired of ranching. Stuart had come over to act as peacemaker, but found a new issue in play—Mac's dog Magic was missing. Next to Stuart, Magic was Mac's best friend, and according to Mac, a far better friend than his independent-minded wife.

As Mac drove, he held forth about Mary Lou.

"I'm not sure a wife can be a friend," he said. "The terms might be mutually exclusive. A man can talk to a friend about everything and anything, but not to a wife. One way or the other, she's always part of the problem. Particularly when money is scarce."

Mac's marital relationship was becoming increasingly intolerable, and he didn't know how to put it back on track. Neither did Stuart. Last night, they drank together at the Great American

10

Land & Cattle restaurant. They'd sat in the bar listening to Patty Duncan sing western songs that reminded him how he expected a western woman to be. Mary Lou had fit his image in the beginning, but not now. Patty sang Stuart's favorite song, "Landslide," before closing, and it seemed to Mac he was caught in a similar situation as the song.

"Early on, we used to go riding with only our boots and hats on," Mac said. "Mary Lou would get so hot, she'd practically rip my donkey off."

"Any place in the house where you haven't made it?" Stuart asked.

"Nope, nor even twice. We used to go for records, like ten times a day or fifty times a week. Now it's more like once a week, and I practically have to get on my knees and beg."

"Yeah, Ermie's like that but it's more like once a year. After our third kid, she decided she'd had enough. Won't use birth control, so we practice abstinence."

"That's what marrying a Catholic will get you, podge."

He may not miss Mary Lou, but he sure did his dog. The wolf-like German Shepherd hadn't come home last night or shown up this morning. And Mary Lou was no help. She announced in no uncertain terms that it wasn't her job to look after his stupid hound.

So here Stuart was, holding on while the Jeep careened across the landscape, wishing he was back making land deals or collecting money from his convenience stores.

Wily and desert-smart, Magic had been with Mac since being weaned. He stuck to Mac like glue and never spent a night more than an arm's length away. Stuart wished he had a dog like Magic, but his wife didn't like dogs. If the truth be known, his wife Ermie was why he spent so much time with Mac at the Bar-D—it allowed him to get away from her and all of his relatives.

Mary Lou tolerated Stuart as friendly competition for Mac's time. She also tended to put him down because he was short. She and Stuart were the same height and she was one of those women who had to look up to men to respect them. At any rate, it was his idea to scour the countryside for Magic—getting away from the ranch would do both of the men good.

Mac said that a large, frequently wet arroyo on the northern edge of the ranch was Magic's favorite place to roust jackrabbits. For the last two months, his Bar-D cattle had been grazing the south range, and Mac hadn't been north of number three tank for some time. Rainfall had been heavy during the last week of June, and good grass was plentiful south of the county road which split his holdings. It was certainly enough to support his reduced herd after loan demands forced him to convert much of his stock into cash. They headed toward the arroyo on Mac's hunch, not knowing what they expected to find.

Mac's hunch proved barren, but ten minutes later they noticed vultures circling an arroyo farther east. Only two were in the sky, but as they approached, several more burst into flight from around something on the ground.

Stuart grabbed Mac's shotgun and tried his luck. Three shells, three misses. Stuart cursed his poor marksmanship while Mac stopped Rover on the trail. They descended into the broad, steep-sided gully on foot.

Magic lay alongside the arroyo's hard-packed sand which could be used by wide-tracked vehicles as a good road in dry weather. His belly was already torn open by the carrion-eaters, but the mess of Magic's head indicated a gunshot.

Mac crouched down and examined the wound with almost professional detachment. "It must have been made by at least a .30 caliber weapon," he said to Stuart. "Why would anyone want to shoot an old, harmless dog? A good friend like Magic?"

Stuart couldn't think of a reply and instead scoured around like a detective looking for evidence.

Black-brown fur was scattered among the cactus and brush, already covered with large desert flies and attracting beetles. In a few days, Magic would have been fully re-introduced into the food chain.

Mac knocked down a huge orange-winged tarantula hawk that buzzed his head. Actually, it was officially a desert wasp, looked like a four-inch long black ant, and was relatively harmless. Except to tarantulas.

There were no cartridges to be seen, so they decided the perpetrator had used a .38 or .45 caliber revolver. There were several sets of large tire tracks in the arroyo's sand, relatively deep, indicating heavy vehicles. The light but steady breeze had already smoothed over what might have been footprints, but Magic could just as easily have been shot from a Jeep or truck. With mounting anger, Mac collected Magic's remains in a trash bag. Then they followed the tracks eastwards along Mac's northern fence line and onto BLM land that Mac leased.

Mac's ranch frequently acted as a thoroughfare for coyote-led groups of illegals. It was within hiking distance from El Paso and Juarez but beyond the area heavily watched by border patrol units. The nearest town was La Union, east and slightly south in the Rio Grande valley, and Stuart assumed these tracks would lead east to Interstate 10. The Bar-D had experienced several thefts over the years which Mac attributed to wetbacks, but never anything like this. Magic was getting old, and no longer formidable. It couldn't have been a two-legged coyote, because a shot would attract attention. Magic was probably killed for sport.

Stuart blinked as Mac topped a steep hill and the wide Rio Grande valley spread out before them. They could see and hear the heavy truck traffic on Interstate 10 across the river. Scrub was sparse and the largest bushes were not over four feet high. The earthen flood control dam north of them contained nothing but dry sand as usual, but what they saw on the far side of the BLM land brought them to a dead stop.

Chapter 3

Bordering the BLM land was a small enclosure of about six acres containing a dilapidated trailer and several small structures. The tracks skirted the dam and went directly through a locked gate on the compound's western side.

"How long has this been here?" Stuart asked. The weird compound was hidden from I-10, and Stuart hadn't been up in this area for years.

"Don't know," Mac said, shaking his head. "Never seen it before."

A power line stretched from La Union into the fenced property. Stuart counted utility poles. There were fourteen, and the standing charge from El Paso Electric was nine hundred dollars per pole. Running electricity in had cost more than the scruffy trailer was worth. And the Cyclone fence must have cost twenty thousand and looked like it belonged around the federal penitentiary at La Tuna.

Mac drove around to the Rio Grande side and stopped again. A newly-built private road led up to an industrial style gate, but what caught their attention was its heavy-duty construction. Access roads in the area were built cheaply from indigenous materials such as caliche, sand, dirt, or gravel, but some contractor had outdone himself to provide a first-class entrance and drive. This road was comprised of crushed stone, fully capable of supporting the heaviest trucks allowed on New Mexico highways. The only place Stuart had seen the same type of stone was at ASARCO. There it was used in the smelter's yard and work areas where dense compaction was required. The gate wasn't any less imposing. Built of heavy pipe on wheels for ease of operation, its posts were set in concrete, and the padlocked chain rivaled anything Stuart had ever seen.

They approached the gate, stopped again and surveyed the compound. Inside the fence they could see a livestock pen holding four cows. Which made no sense at all.

Almost immediately a Mexican emerged from the trailer and drove to the front gate on a three-wheel ATV. Bright red, it was one of the fun but dangerous types not usually found on ranches like Mac's. It could easily tip over and was usable only in relatively flat terrain. It definitely could not be used outside the compound. The Mexican was dressed in jeans, boots, and the obligatory straw hat, but was hardly a working cowboy.

"Kin I help you?"

Stuart sucked in his breath with surprise. He knew the region's accents, and the Mex was from somewhere north, maybe Colorado. Nothing went through his nose, and there was no hint of the usual Tex-Mex whine. He was almost six feet tall, fairly slender, and unusually handsome for a Mexican. The rider remained astride his ATV and met their gaze without flinching.

Mac hopped out of Rover and walked to the gate.

"Not really," he said. "My dog was shot west of here, and I was checking out my fences. Haven't been up at this corner for months and didn't know all this existed."

"It's been here for two months." The Mexican didn't bother turning off his motor to make conversation easier. "Surprised you hadn't noticed."

Definitely no trace of a Hispanic accent, Stuart decided. The guy exuded authority and was no casual ranch hand, but neither was this a ranch.

"Looks like somebody came in through your west gate," Mac said. "I followed those tracks from where my dog was shot. You wouldn't know anything about that, would ya?"

"Nope, not a thing. Went out last night to that hill over there when it thundered to check on where it was raining, that's all." The Mex pointed to the hill west of the compound.

"Didn't rain last night."

"Nope, wasted my trip. Sorry I can't be more help."

"Yeah." Mac returned to his jeep and Stuart watched the Mexican ride back to the trailer. There was nothing to be gained here, and their opponent was not about to be intimidated. That was unusual in itself. Mexicans were normally polite and eager to please Anglos, even making up stories if necessary. This one felt no need to give them the time of day. Nor were his clothes dirty or dusty as if he'd been working.

"That guy's not from around here," Stuart said.

"Tell me something I don't know," Mac said. "So what's going on?"

The Bureau of Land Management's flood control dam afforded them a better view of the Mexican's property. In addition to the trailer and animal pens, they could see an open shelter for vehicles and two small utility sheds. The crushed stone driveway was circular and a large parking area west of the trailer allowed semi-trailers to be turned around inside the fence. To Stuart's practiced eye the most unusual feature was a well in the parking area about sixty feet from the trailer. It was a huge installation, grossly out of proportion to the postage stamp enclosure. He would have thought it was some natural gas or oil pipeline station, but he knew the closest pipeline belonged to El Paso Natural Gas some miles to the north. The well piping looked to be at least six inches in diameter, the casing much larger, and the pump easily out-classed the valley's irrigation diesels. Its capacity had to be enormous.

Stuart wondered if the well reached down into the Mesilla Valley Bolson for pure Deming water or if it merely drew from the shallow Rio Grande level. Either way it required a permit, and the county wasn't issuing permits for agricultural purposes. Not while the El Paso water suit made its tortuous way to the Supreme Court. Mac's new well applications were held up like everyone else's, so how had this one gotten approval? Nobody had asked him to help grease any skids.

Mac pointed out a line of suitcases hugging what little shade remained alongside the trailer's living room. Stuart counted the suitcases. There were at least a dozen. That was the answer to the site's purpose—the Mexican was running illegals through the Bar-D for transport somewhere to the north. The trailer was probably full of transients at that very moment. It had to be stifling inside even with two window units going full blast. A lone door split the trailer into halves, and its windows indicated a bath and maybe two bedrooms in the northern half, and a combination kitchen, dining area, and living room in the other.

"Illegals," said Mac.

Stuart agreed. It was the only way things made sense. The ATV rider was no low-life coyote, however. Probably working the next leg and waiting on transportation.

Stuart wondered how they were shipping the wetbacks out. Obviously trucks, but under what cover? There was a good answer, no doubt. The whole operation was highly organized and professional from what he had seen. And the well indicated excellent political connections.

"Well, first things first," said Mac. "Magic needs proper attention. The Mexican and his network of coyotes and whatever can wait."

Mac and Stuart drove back onto his range with little conversation. Someone connected with the trailer was responsible for killing Magic and had to pay.

"You going to take them on?" Stuart asked.

"Whatever I do will have to be done carefully. Don't know how many I'm up against. And they clearly have better political connections than I do." Mac looked almost accusingly at Stuart as he said that.

"Must be at the state level, then," Stuart said, defending himself. "I couldn't have gotten that well approved."

Mac nodded. Stuart had seen Mac like this before. Someone was going to get hurt. The only question was who and how many. He hoped one would not be Mac.

Chapter 4

The trash bag threatened to bounce out as Mac steered through sand and rocky ledges, but Stuart kept a hand on it until Mac turned Rover onto the ranch house road.

The ranch house came into view as they crested a low ridge formed eons ago by a rogue basaltic lava flow. The plateau between Mac's ranch and Las Cruces had once seen considerable volcanic activity, and lava flows added an element of geologic interest to an ordinary landscape. Typical for the area, the Bar-D was ordinary but not without interesting features.

Many older ranch houses in southern New Mexico were adobe, but Mac's was built with double walls of brick for the main structure and clapboard on the attached rear porch. Except for the sheet metal equipment shed and garage, its outlying buildings were wood, now highly desiccated and weathered. The dull metal sheets and large evaporative air conditioning unit spoiled what otherwise could have been a nineteenth-century setting. The house itself was large and spacious inside, but somewhat rambling under its low roof. Nestled behind shady cottonwood trees in a shallow valley, it could have been used in scores of western movies. With its expansive desert backdrop, the ranch fit perfectly with its surroundings.

Usually Magic would announce Mac's arrival when he turned off the county road, but today there was silence. He stopped in front of the garage, pulling the following dust cloud over Rover like a blanket.

Stuart hopped out, hoping his presence would help keep Mac's temper under control.

"Crap, no one to greet me," Mac said.

"Mary Lou's probably busy making chili paste," Stuart offered.

18

Her red Honda Prelude was providing shade in the open garage for one of her cats and obviously hadn't moved since last night. So Stuart knew she was home. Chiles were stacked on the rear patio, and a large aluminum cooker simmered on their outdoor fireplace. Various kitchen implements were scattered about in Mary Lou's usual unorganized fashion.

Chili cook-offs were currently Mary Lou's passion. The chiles were boiled and squeezed outside before being blended into one cup bags of chile pulp for cook-offs. It was fun, but came with a caveat: sometimes the cook would forget and touch himself with chile-stained fingers while going to the bathroom. It was worse for a female, but in either case, it was an experience to be avoided. Mac had told him about one time when he and Mary Lou had gotten frisky while eating his chili, and he had gone down on her. She practically knocked him unconscious.

"Let's have a Coors," Mac said.

Stuart thought that was a good idea. They entered the kitchen and Mac went straight to the fridge.

"Find Magic?" Mary Lou asked.

"Mexicans shot him," Mac answered. His mood immediately went from bad to worse.

Stuart picked up on the conflict. It wasn't so much what she said, it was how she said it. Total disinterest with an edge of accusation. Of what, he had no idea. He looked over in her direction and sucked in his breath.

Mary Lou was wearing only a halter and cotton shorts which were practically painted on. Very little was left to the imagination. Her body never failed to arouse him. He wanted to pull those shorts down and nail her against the sink. But she was his kumpa's wife, and out of bounds. Stuart wondered why Mary Lou was showing so much skin. She should have assumed he would return with Mac.

*****

Mac had the same impulse when he glanced at his wife, except he wanted to bend her over the sink. But she'd never allow it, and even if she did, he'd pay heavily for the next two months. Last night she'd been unusually cold, letting him use her doggy style without a sound to indicate her interest or displeasure. So what if he had been drinking? She could show a little support once in a while.

Mac opened the fridge and retrieved two cans of beer.

"Little early for that, isn't it?" she said.

Mac's sexual thoughts vanished. Almost instantaneously, they boiled over into rage.

"Woman!" he yelled. "Don't you say shit! Goddamn wetbacks kill my dog, and all you can do is bitch about me drink'n a fuck'n beer."

Mary Lou stood like a statue and eyed him angrily. When she spoke, her tone lowered the kitchen temperature twenty degrees.

"Then drink it outside, big man. Get the hell out of my kitchen."

Stuart took the beer Mac held out to him and scurried outside, but Mac stood his ground, glaring at his wife. He was within an inch of slapping that mouth into obedience. Mary Lou was spoiling for a fight, goading him to say or do something he'd regret. She had destroyed whatever good intentions and humor he had in a single sentence. Mac finally turned on his heel and slammed the screen door as he tromped outside.

*****

Mary Lou didn't enjoy taking Mac on every time he was in a bad mood, but enduring his rage in silence was not her long suit either. There was a mean streak in Mac which might send her to the hospital someday, but so far it hadn't happened. She sometimes wondered what would trigger his resort to violence. Maybe his sexual needs deterred him. As long as he could enjoy her body, he wouldn't damage the goods. But if he thought she was giving it to someone else, she wouldn't trust him for a heartbeat.

Today's conflict was especially stupid. God only knew why Mac had been devoted to his dog, a mangy, lazy critter if there ever was one. Magic and she had never been on particularly good terms, and lately Mac and the hound had been taking sides against her for no reason. That someone killed the dog was good riddance as far as she was concerned.

Like the ranch, Magic wasn't her fault. Regardless of her feelings, she had taken care of Magic when Mac was away or forgot.

The ranch, too. Mac was well on his way to losing it, but she had sacrificed her city life and friends to make a home in the desert where Mac could be happy. All for naught. The only efforts he appreciated anymore were in the bedroom.

She stood at the window as Stuart drove away and watched Mac dig alongside the storage shed. Mac was a fine specimen of cowboy, tall and lean, with rugged good looks that worked wonders on barmaids and waitresses. Already in his middle thirties, he could wear his Levis too tight and make a statement that turned most female heads and dropped their eyes below his belt. Those other women should know him like she knew him. Anything requiring advertising was always flawed.

She pursed her lips thinking about Mac. Actually, his body wasn't flawed in the least. Quite the contrary. Everyone said she was fortunate to have a husband so physically attractive. And they were right. It was an ego trip to be with him and watch other women bite their lips in jealousy. Other women might fatten their husbands to make them unattractive, but not her. Unfortunately, body and looks didn't make a relationship, at least not for the long term. Once the bloom of newness wore off, something else was needed.

Their basic problems were the same as for most couples; differing expectations and money. She now understood that lust, curiosity, and need for security were probably the main reasons why she'd married Mac. He had been an exciting catch, and her friends were green with envy. That was all gone. Only a grim, hardscrabble struggle for existence remained.

Mac seemed indifferent to their financial peril while she was terrified. Losing the ranch would throw her out on the street without resources, probably into some cheap rental. Just like when she was a child. Growing up as an army brat, she had hated the feeling of temporary quarters and assignments. But worst of all, was the lack of money. She and her sisters were frequent visitors to thrift shops, rummaging through cast-offs their friends had discarded, scared they would select an item some classmate might recognize as formerly hers.

It hadn't been a happy family in which she'd grown up. Her father was a strict disciplinarian and brooked no treason in his household. All the daughters rebelled. As the oldest, she bore the brunt of her father's tirades and was blamed for influencing the younger girls. He beat her unmercifully for the slightest infraction, and the bruises on her arms, legs and back remained for weeks.

Her father owned two dogs, and a number of times she received beatings over something she did or didn't do for them. Her worst beating had come as a high school senior when she forgot to feed them before going on a date. Her father was waiting when she returned, and almost put her in the hospital. She fought back, and her mother's intervention probably saved her life. That was some night.

Just thinking about her father invoked terrible memories. Since retiring from the Army he became bald and fat, spending most of his free time watching sports on TV and guzzling beer. She hated her father for his brutality and lack of love. He treated his daughters as property, somewhere below his dogs in value. When she was eleven years old, she was attacked by three older boys coming home from school. Although not technically raped, she had been forced into performing oral sex while they poked and pinched her intimate areas. When she finally broke free and ran home, her father ignored her tears and story, beat her, called her a slut, and said it was her fault for enticing the boys. Then, as now, everything was her fault.

Mac was different, and Mary Lou didn't hate him—at least not like her father. But there was never enough money, and Mac's business sense rivaled a chipmunk's. After spending his life on the ranch, he still didn't understand its simple economics. He inherited it after his mother was killed on Interstate 10, and managed to run it into the ground within a half-dozen years. Now they were down to only two Mexican hands, and debts were mounting steadily.

She needed to do something, but didn't know what.

Chapter 5

Watching Mac remove his shirt in the heat, Mary Lou wondered when she would find the courage to call it quits. What had started as a tidal wave of sexual passion had crashed on the rocks of reality. Over a year ago, she had awakened to the realization that a successful long-term relationship required her to like and respect her partner. Unfortunately, those ingredients were missing in her emotions for Mac. Her relationship with Mac had been a torrid love affair that couldn't be sustained.

There was no longer any communication except in conflict. Instead of desiring Mac's presence or attention, she usually hoped he would be busy somewhere else. She had tried to indicate her feelings in bed, but he persisted in spite of her indifference. So she performed as expected, doing what was necessary to maintain a semblance of peace.

She hadn't always been ambivalent toward sex, even if not obsessed by it like her father believed. Orgasms had come regularly since puberty, but she remained a virgin through high school out of fear she might get pregnant. It was easy to limit her exposure by going steady during her last two years, doing everything but the act itself. It still might have happened, but her boyfriend developed leukemia. She drew away, avoiding him at the end to protect herself from emotional turmoil. Skipping Tommy's funeral had put him out of her mind.

Except for Mac and her father, men were easy to control. Their primary interests were sexual gratification and ego-boosting behavior. Allowing them access to her body was usually sufficient by itself to establish a position of power, but when she showed enthusiasm for their members, they'd practically kill to do her bidding.

In high school it was poor, silly Tommy, thinking his desire for her made him stronger and more manly. Actually it put her in the driver's seat. Control was so simple; a touch here and there, and the car windows fogged up. A little more here, some there, and the world was hers if she'd just relieve him of his embarrassing state. Attaining that goal was simple, and afterward, she would emerge from Tommy's Chevy unscathed, rakishly toss semen-laden tissues into the neighbor's hedge, and march to her door feeling superior and powerful.

Everything changed seconds later. Entering her home, she went from a position of total dominance to complete subservience. There was no question which she preferred.

UTEP had given her the opportunity to break free, and she found a youthful assistant professor in the Education department who was charmed by her vitality and spirit. He invited her to accompany him on an excursion to Mazatlán, and she accepted after some initial trepidation. The trip changed her status from someone who didn't to someone who did, and it was a change for the better. The professor became her mentor, sexually and otherwise, helping and teaching her at every step. Discovering that she possessed an almost total lack of inhibition, Mary Lou indulged herself in every conceivable fantasy.

The unconventional aspects of her relationship and its secrecy made it exciting to Mary Lou. Faculty-student affairs were frowned upon by UTEP's administration and grounds for faculty dismissal. But the benefits more than outweighed the risks. Mary Lou loved being an insider with knowledge of faculty and school problems. Her friends were mere students while she was connected and powerful. And forbidden acts like making love in a professor's office kept her body in a perpetual state of sexual arousal.

After two years of unrestrained hedonism, the ax fell when her professor was denied tenure. Facing unemployment, he asked her to marry him while he looked for a job. That wasn't at all what she wanted. How could he ask her to face the unknown without a job or money? They couldn't live on sex, and she was a long way from graduation. It became time to terminate her zero-potential relationship.

She changed her major to business and found a waitressing job in the evenings. Almost immediately she met Mac, and he took her dancing at the Anthony Gap and other popular local spots. Her distraught academic lover went off the deep end, and things might have turned ugly except for Mac. He warned the pathetic professor to stay away, and she began spending her nights at Mac's ranch.

Following a Vegas wedding she quit UTEP to concentrate on her marriage, produce a family, and live on the ranch. Then the ranch went downhill, Mac's ego became tedious, and everything was her fault.

Mac didn't like the way she gave head, brewed coffee, drove the truck, bit her fingernails, or anything. And then the doctor said she had a tipped uterus and she'd sooner win the lottery than have a child. Bad odds, since there was no lottery in New Mexico.

Mac was furious and took out his frustration on her.

In retaliation, she denied him her active participation in sex.

It could have been otherwise. Mac should have counted his blessings instead. She wore tight jeans better than anyone in the county, and would stack her body up against the best around. Mary Lou knew she wasn't beautiful, but there was no denying her sexual attractiveness. Her breasts were small but perfectly shaped, jutting straight out with a firmness which suggested silicone implants. She was proud they were natural, and loved to watch men's expressions when they discovered that for themselves. Her stomach was flat and muscular, accenting her narrow waist and hips. So what if her calves were a little heavy for her slender frame? In boots, this minor defect disappeared.

Mac didn't realize it, but she could have any of his friends she wished. Several had already indicated their interest, but they weren't worth the risk. Even his best friend Stuart wanted her. She sometimes gave him a show, and had seen him struggle with desire.

Thinking about Stuart amused her. The little guy controlled everything in the valley but he couldn't score in a whorehouse. Oh, the Mexican girls were willing enough, but that was all he could get. Even his wife was Mexican, and Ermie wouldn't rate higher than three on a ten-point scale. It wouldn't take her long to break up Stuart's marriage after she left Mac. Given the opportunity, Stuart would drop his pants and pole-vault into her bedroom without looking back.

As far as she knew on the flip side, Mac hadn't given her cause by playing around. Maybe because times were hard, or he didn't think he could afford a girlfriend. But there were women around who would only require him to show up and be willing. With regard to faithfulness, Mac was a good husband.

Maybe the marriage would work if he'd treat her more like an equal. It was difficult for her to admit a mistake, and divorce was a public admission of failure. As much as her marriage floundered, the thought of divorce was hardly more appealing.

She sighed and reminded herself that marriages were incredibly difficult. It worried her that Mac might be right—their moribund marriage was her fault. She wasn't physically abused, mistreated, or kept barefoot and pregnant. He loved her, and in his own way tried to make her happy. He just wasn't sufficiently sensitive to her needs to make their partnership click.

Like at chili cook-offs—Mac objected to her flirting with other guys. It was all harmless, and letting some good-looking cowboy cop a quick feel did wonders for her morale. She wasn't sleeping with them, and Mac had no right to be jealous. All she wanted was for Mac to realize she was a real person, and someone to be treated as an equal.

On the other hand, she sometimes felt guilty about thinking selfishly. Like now. Mac was upset over losing Magic, and she was concentrating on her own complaints rather than being supportive. It wouldn't hurt to help a little and might even do some good. She poured him a glass of iced tea and went out to join him.

He was almost finished, shoveling the last of the dirt on top of Magic's remains. The mid-day sun was causing him to perspire freely, and Mac took the iced tea with a grunt of thanks.

"Got new neighbors on the north side," Mac said. "Mexicans, and they've fenced in a few acres. I talked to one, and they're involved somehow in shooting Magic."

"Why would anyone kill Magic?"

"Don't know, doesn't make sense. I think they're running illegals across the Bar-D, then shipping them north."

"So who's the 'they' you're talking about?"

"Don't know that either. The guy I talked to didn't gimme his name."

"What makes you think they killed Magic?"

"Tracks. Led right to their doorstep. And he was shot, probably with a revolver."

Mary Lou shuddered and shook her head. "I take it this guy wasn't friendly."

"Like a rattlesnake. And he wasn't from around here, I don't think."

"We should go to Cruces and find out. Check who owns the property. That's public information, isn't it?"

Mac flung the long-handled spade to the ground.

"Rather burn 'em out. Damn Mexicans. Ain't worth a dog. Oughta booby-trap their routes." He thought for a moment. "Yeah, think I will. Need to know who I'm up against."

He handed Mary Lou his empty glass and stomped into the barn. She nodded and trudged sadly back to her chiles. Her peace gesture had gotten lost in the shuffle. His inability to communicate with her was truly awesome. Not once had Mac used the word "we" in their conversation.

Chapter 6

Interstate 10 was lightning fast. Even the female trooper frequently working the Mesquite underpass was missing, and Mac's fuzzbuster was quiet until turning onto Main Street in Las Cruces. The resumption of sixty-five had meant seventy-five in New Mexico, and seat belts weren't required in pickup trucks. Like all wide-open western states, New Mexico just paid lip service to those knee-jerk, bed-wetting liberals inside the Washington beltway.

Sometimes Mac thought the Eastern Establishment promulgated dumb rules simply to aggravate westerners like himself. That crap on landfills, for instance. In the east, there might be some concern over ground water contamination, but not here with the water table out of sight. And the stuff about oil leaking from underground storage tanks at gas stations. Who cared? The oil couldn't contaminate well water in a thousand years, and the ground was worthless for anything anyway. The only ones benefiting from such idiotic edicts were snot-nosed kids from Ivy-League schools who couldn't feed themselves doing honest work.

The BLM lands he sped past reminded Mac of the cancerous Federal Government. He was proud of never having taken a dime in federal largess, even if it was a contributory factor to his financial crisis. His father had worked nifty land-exchange deals with the bureau, and it was only through those swaps that the Bar-D had been put together as a viable entity. Mac's attitude was to stay as far away from the feds as possible.

Easterners usually didn't care much about the west except when they wanted to go skiing. It was mere wasteland to be crossed by high-flying jets carrying elitists between their cultural enclaves in California and the East Coast. Mac wished they'd forget the

28

southwest entirely, but they appeared singularly intent on forcing their welfare state on productive people throughout the country. Washington was moving heaven and earth to turn the United States into a nation of dim-witted consumers manipulated by paternalistic and wealthy aristocrats.

Working men wanted fair trade instead of a North American Free Trade Zone, so Washington opposed them. American businesses wanted sanctions against Japan to eliminate predatory business practices, so the feds supported the Japs. Unemployed workers wanted to restrict immigration, so policy-makers pushed for more liberal immigration laws and amnesty for illegals already here. Mac could list a hundred issues where westerners stood against the politicians of both parties in Congress.

And easterners understood nothing. They thought that citizens of Mexican descent in the southwest favored opening the border. Actually, they were opposed. They had obtained their citizenship following the rules—illegals could do the same.

Well, if easterners could disregard the west and its people, he could ignore federal laws. The Bar-D was still his domain, not some thumb-sucking liberal's in Washington. It was Frazier land, built up by his dad from nothing, and one way or another, that's the way it would remain. Maybe secession was out after 1865, but the sixties had proven that civil disobedience was an honorable alternative.

On the home front, Mac wished he knew how to reach Mary Lou—particularly now when she seemed to be on his side and offering ideas and support. It wasn't that long ago when he'd first spotted her working at Vinton's Great American Land & Cattle Company restaurant. They'd been a terrific pair in the beginning, and for him, it'd been love at first sight. It'd almost been that way for her. One trip in his new Ranger to Radium Springs and the Blue Moon, and he'd snatched her from school for a life in the real world. The Blue Moon was owned by a county commissioner at the time, and meeting local politicians with real stroke was heady stuff for a college kid. The Ranger caused more comment than if they had driven up in a Corvette, and the rednecks treated Mary Lou like royalty. By the time they'd left, there was no question where she would be spending the night—and most likely the rest of her life.

She even looked like a rancher's wife, with deep blue eyes, a terrific ass and body which she flaunted in tight jeans. Her bouncing, shoulder-length light brown hair fell naturally in a carefree shag, blown to the wind as if stepping out of a western movie. Mary Lou was every cowboy's dream. Her angular cowgirl face looked wild and athletic, and her too-large mouth and narrow cheeks gave rise to talk that she could suck a tennis ball through a garden hose.

His wife was the best piece of tail Mac had known, even if deficient in oral skills. In the beginning, she'd screamed and carried on in bed as if she couldn't get enough of him, but now he mostly got the silent treatment. The enthusiasm was gone, and she seemed to be accommodating him like an unavoidable nuisance.

Her silence and avoidance hurt him more than she knew. He loved her dearly and felt a twinge of excitement every time he arrived home. Marriage was permanent, and they couldn't allow this stupid bickering to continue forever. He understood she had needs, but so did he, and they had to agree on some kind of compromise where they could both be satisfied.

There was one sacrifice he had already made—a family. Mary Lou couldn't have kids. Her gynecologist said she had a folded or tipped uterus or something, and her ability to conceive was limited. The good news was she didn't have to use birth control, the bad news was he'd never have sons. He was the last of the Fraziers, and because of Mary Lou, there wouldn't be anyone to inherit the ranch or honor him in his old age.

Mac took the southern entrance into Cruces from I-10 and drove up Main Street past the Borman and Wallace car dealerships. For once the lights were green, and he drove straight to a free parking space in front of the old Doña Ana County Courthouse without stopping.

The white, Spanish-style building housed the sheriff and county administrative offices, but the courts had moved to a new building on the downtown mall. Supposedly the assessor and treasurer were no longer feuding, and the commissioners were tamer and acting like responsible representatives with the county manager. That would change overnight when political campaigning began again.

He entered the assessor's office and presented himself at the worn, wooden counter for assistance.

A tiny, tired-looking blond lady in her middle forties listened to

Mac's request and retrieved the appropriate plat book for the property in question. Within a few minutes, Mac located the parcel number, and the lady brought up its assessment information on her computer screen. It was indeed almost seven acres, and included a well, mobile home, and two small buildings. The mobile home carried a separate parcel ID for tax computations, and there was no mention of a fence or access road.

Hector Castillo, esquire, was listed as sole owner, and his law firm was given as the mailing address for tax billing. Mac thought he knew everyone of importance in town, but he had never heard of Castillo.

"Do you know if this Castillo owns other parcels near me?" he asked.

"We wouldn't have that information, but the treasurer's office would," the lady said. "The system is cross-indexed by name, so tax bills can be combined for all properties owned by the same person."

"How about other stuff? Like usage and purchase date."

"Sometimes we have the date and price paid for a parcel. It helps to determine assessment value if recent enough." The lady keyed over to another screen, then shook her head. "No, this must have been bought a long time ago. There's nothing on purchase date or price."

Mac grinned wryly. Ownership had probably changed within the last few months. Somebody wanted privacy.

"Deeds are filed upstairs with the recorder," the lady said. "They're not always easy to find, but if you have the time, you might find what you're looking for."

"Naw, I'll just try the treasurer." If the information wasn't on her computer, he knew it wouldn't be in the recorder's files. "Can you tell when the assessment was done and who did it?"

She flipped to another screen, and stared at the display.

"Huh. No, I can't. Somebody forgot to enter the data." She pointed at a blank line on her console. "Right here it should give the inspector's name and date of inspection. But it doesn't. Sorry, I don't know what to say."

"That's all right, really don't need it."

He jotted down the parcel number and description while the lady chattered away with directions to the treasurer's office. She was intent on being helpful, and telling her he knew the way would have been impolite. The courthouse was a maze of well-trodden, zigzag hallways with confusing signs. A circular staircase led to the second floor, and in dim light, its uneven steps often proved treacherous to unwary citizens. Access to the basement and a privately-run lunchroom was provided by an ancient and tiny elevator—one so slow that Mac believed he could drive to Anthony before the elevator traveled one floor.

Out of curiosity he scanned other adjacent parcels in the plat book.

"This one doesn't have a windmill on it," he said. Mac pointed to a parcel north of Castillo's.

The lady examined the book and bristled instantly.

"Absolutely it does," she said. "The inspectors wouldn't list a windmill if it didn't exist. You're probably thinking of another piece of property."

"No, believe me, I was just out there this morning, and that land has nothing on it."

"If the inspectors say there's a windmill on it, there's a windmill on it. They don't make these things up."

The once-helpful lady was now hostile. Mac deduced he had over-stayed his welcome, and muttered his apologies and thanks. His interest was Castillo, and he didn't care to fight a court case over somebody's faulty report. It wasn't his property tax that would be excessively high.

The tiny blond glared at Mac as he backed away from her counter. She would have been pretty with her hair down and a smile, but that was too much to ask from somebody spending her days inside adobe walls with computer screens and plat books. All other clerks were bouncy young Hispanic girls, and the office was probably hard on a fading Anglo woman. Her dark roots showed all too clearly, and her sun-dried skin was aging rapidly. Money was probably tight for her, too. His wasn't the only life with hardships. For a moment, Mac felt a kinship of melancholy, then shrugged it off and entered the corridor.

The offices were cool behind the building's thick walls, even if their seemingly random jumble made highly inefficient use of available space. Mac groused to himself over the assessor's information while striding down the tiled hallway. Castillo was probably fronting for Mexican money. Using lawyers as blinds for foreign ownership was common in the county, and a great deal of property was actually owned by Mexican nationals. In both Las Cruces and El Paso, absentee Mexican ownership was a sensitive issue among local residents, but money did the talking. With legions of lawyers specializing in cross-border investments, the area was a popular haven for dollars gained legally or otherwise. Mac snorted when he thought of the flip side—Americans couldn't own real property in Mexico, so why were Mexicans allowed to own property in the U.S.?

A tall, thin Anglo lady in the treasurer's office readily showed Mac a list of Castillo's properties on her computer screen. He was included in a number of partnerships, all with other Hispanic-surnamed individuals, but was always the first name listed. The mailing addresses were invariably identical with his law firm, and Castillo obviously managed those properties from a legal standpoint. There were interesting parcels in Anapra, the southern-most point of New Mexico bordering on El Paso, Santa Theresa, a relatively new development of industrial sites and airport near El Paso, and several trailer courts on the north side of Las Cruces.

Castillo was invested heavily in Doña Ana County, far beyond his means as a Mexican ambulance-chaser. His name was immediately recognized in the treasurer's office because of his many properties, none of which were delinquent in tax payments. The tall lady couldn't give Mac any personal information concerning Castillo, and was apologetic over her unusual lack of knowledge. Castillo apparently kept a very low profile. Mac was hardly surprised after his experience in the assessor's office.

Everything he had found so far was bad. He was up against players that made Stuart look puny, and they seemed to be able to do whatever they wanted in Doña Ana County. Well, his father had faced more formidable opponents and won, so could he. But he was going to have to become invisible. Float like a butterfly and sting like a bee, even if it was just to get revenge for a dog. He wished he hadn't met the Mexican at the enclosure.

Chapter 7

Fat Eddie's was unusually quiet as Mac entered to have a beer for the road. Actually named Eddie's, it received the adjective "Fat" from locals in honor of the previous proprietor. Eddie's included a restaurant Mac had not tried for years, and although located in the Mesilla Best Western on I-10, the bar saw little transient traffic from tourists. A favorite of Mac's because of its excellent munchies and comfortable leather chairs, Fat Eddie's was particularly cozy in cold weather when its fireplace featured a roaring fire, scantily-clad waitresses providing especially fast service, and the singer at the piano bar creating the right ambiance.

He hadn't seen Stuart's Blazer outside, but he was there and sitting alone at a table. Mac wondered if he and Stuart were becoming so alike they naturally frequented the same bars at identical times. He dropped his Stetson onto the chair alongside Stuart's in the dim light, and signaled the bartender for a draft.

"Whatcha doing so far north?" Mac asked. Stuart occasionally imbibed too heavily, and Mac sometimes kept tabs on him or drove him home. "You didn't mention you'd be up here this morning."

"Had business in Mesilla. They won't let me develop my sub-division unless I use traditional Spanish names for my streets." Stuart was sipping a margarita and obviously pissed.

"It's your money, your acreage, your development, but they name the streets?"

"Yep. Typical anti-Anglo bullshit."

Mac shook his head. Stuart walked a tightrope between Anglos and Mexicans every day. His father had produced a number of illegitimate offspring by various Mexican girls in the valley. Stuart had been expected to provide for this unwanted extended family, and

34

most were placed around El Paso and Las Cruces in good jobs. Not surprisingly, many of his half-brothers and sisters worked for him in his various businesses.

Stuart's ruddy complexion and grey eyes appeared almost comical in contrast to the clouds of Mexicans usually around him. Hardly taller than most Mexicans, Stuart was perpetually in motion and often wore out his adversaries in negotiations. His high energy and uncanny sense of timing were the primary factors in his business success, but his lack of height also caused opponents to underestimate him. They did so to their everlasting regret.

Stuart and Mac made an interesting pair. Mac was the last of his line. His grandfather was one of the men killed in Columbus by Pancho Villa, and his father had been struck by lightning in a sudden desert storm. Longevity did not run in his family, and few Fraziers died in bed.

Stuart's family had experienced exactly the opposite fortune. Prescotts sprouted like mushrooms in a damp cave, their numbers enhanced not inconsiderably by the fecundity of Mexican females who joined the clan in each generation. Stuart himself had three kids, two boys and a girl. Bilingual like Mac and Stuart, they would probably follow their father's lead in selecting Mexican spouses.

Mac liked Stuart's wife Ermie in spite of the friction between their two wives. Although she was Mexican with classical endomorphic features, Ermie was unusually light in coloration with brown hair matching Mary Lou's. Stuart's kids had his features with Ermie's complexion, and most people assumed they were full-blooded Anglos.

Born Ermelinda Falcon, Ermie appeared to Mac to be the eternal mother and housekeeper. Stuart would have agreed. Ermie was dutiful, but not a wife in the Anglo-American sense. She would never challenge Stuart, and probably not even correct him or offer her own opinion on anything. In no sense was she Stuart's partner or equal.

"Ever heard of Hector Castillo?" Mac asked.

"Yeah. Don't know him personally, but heard he represents some big Mexican interests. Why?"

"He owns those acres we saw this morning."

"Probably for a relative. Or brother or father of one of his mistresses," Stuart said.

"He a cocksman?"

"Hah. Name me a Mexican mouthpiece who isn't. The only sexual discrimination in a Mexican law firm is when the office girls don't get laid."

"Must be nice to have your own private harem," Mac said.

"Maybe, but it can get expensive. Sooner or later, they want special treatment and presents, sometimes even a house. Remember what my father did. At one time he owned seven houses in the valley, each with a Mexican girl he was keeping."

"Sounds like that was expensive."

"Still is," Stuart said. "So what about Castillo's land?"

"You know everything I know."

"Tell the border patrol then. Let them figure it out. By the way, I forgot to ask, gonna play in the Anthony Invitational?"

"Probably. Mary Lou wants to go and socialize while we hit the links."

Stuart grinned. "She does it real well. You ought to put her in charge of public relations."

Mac frowned. "You know something I don't?"

Stuart looked up in surprise. "I just meant she meets people easily and they like her."

And they don't like me, Mac added to himself. Some deal. Mary Lou had everyone eating out of her hand because of her world-class bod.

"I should divorce her and hire her as my secretary. We'd probably get along better." He grunted in approval of his own half-baked idea. "I could claim her sexual favors then as a condition of employment and not have to put up with all her shit."

Mac's beer arrived, and he switched to talking about their activities in the morning.

"That guy didn't tell me squat, but anybody willing to shoot a harmless old dog doesn't stop with animals."

"No kidding, Sherlock. For fifty bucks, you're a dead man."

"No reason to spend the fifty."

"No reason to kill the dog."

Mac nodded. Stuart's logic was on target as usual. He couldn't think of anything to say.

"Well, if you want to do anything, let me know," Stuart said.

36

"There's strength in numbers, and I'm not looking to pick up your ranch at a government auction."

Mac downed his beer in silence, trying to wish Castillo and his property into oblivion. Most of the land bordering the Bar-D on the Rio Grande side belonged to Stuart, and acquiring Mac's ranch would improve Stuart's holdings considerably. He patted Stuart's shoulder and rose to leave.

"Thanks. Just keep an ear to the ground. As they say, 'Meanwhile, back at the ranch...'"

*****

Stuart watched as Mac paid the bartender and headed to the parking lot. At least Mac could count on his Ranger being there. Fat Eddie's was a safe place to park. As far as Stuart knew, the Best Western had yet to lose a customer's car. In downtown El Paso, Mac wouldn't have an odds-on chance of his Ranger lasting an hour in a parking space that wasn't guarded by a platoon of green berets. El Paso struggled with combating the nation's highest rate of automobile thefts and was losing more every day. Particularly pickup trucks; they seemed to disappear into Mexico as fast as their owners parked them in public places.

This wetback business couldn't have come at a worse time for his buddy. He needed to concentrate on Mary Lou and his failing marriage. Losing the dog could have been a positive event, forcing Mac to confront Mary Lou and listen to her point of view. But not if it diverted his energies to a secondary issue. Money was another serious problem, but not insolvable if Mac would lighten up. Stuart had offered to help, but Mac wanted to make it on his own. It was a self-defeating, bullheaded attitude, and one that might cost Mac his wife.

From the beginning, Stuart had opposed Mac's marrying Mary Lou, but Mac's decision-making apparatus was located down where Stuart's influence couldn't reach. Some poet said the longest distance in the world stretched between a person's head and their heart. Stuart disagreed. In Mac's case, it was between his head and his dick. At least with respect to Mary Lou.

As far as Stuart was concerned, high-strung Anglo chicks were too much trouble for anything but affairs. There was no denying their much greater allure when compared to Mexicans, but that's what made them dangerous. They knew they outclassed brown girls and took advantage of their superior beauty to make demands. Mexican women were exactly the opposite. They counted themselves lucky to have husbands, and allowed their men to have mistresses and girlfriends. He could disappear for months, and Ermie would wait faithfully for his return. No Anglo woman would do that.

In addition to being Anglo, Mary Lou was Scotch-Irish like Mac and himself. Stuart had read they were sometimes referred to as "Amulots" for AMerican-ULster-scOTS, another term for Covenanter descendants in the United States. History told him they were the best of men, a warrior race seeking its place in the sun, but that their women had not kept the faith. Amulot women tended to reject their heritage and their men. All too many chose Hispanics, blacks, and other races, imposing them on their white communities. This "Earth Mother" syndrome gave them license to do things for other races that they wouldn't do for their own kind. Like proving how great white girls were in bed.

Sometimes he considered telling Mac about Mary Lou's behavior with other men, but it wouldn't serve any useful purpose. A man married a woman and had to make his own peace with her. Stuart had watched Mary Lou at cook-offs rub other guys' crotches and let them run their hands inside her blouse. Once she branded a guy's exposed rear end behind their booth with a "Bar-D" stamp, then lifted her halter to let him write on her left breast. Mac didn't see anything because he was busy cooking, and it was probably just as well. Otherwise, someone would have gotten hurt.

Several of his friends had remarked how they could have Mary Lou any time, but were afraid of Mac. If she was actually screwing someone, Stuart didn't know who. But it would happen sooner or later. Somebody who didn't know Mac was going to sample the goodies she flaunted and get caught with his pants down. Hopefully the situation wouldn't rocket beyond Stuart's control, and he'd be able to keep Mac from killing everybody in sight.

There was a violent streak in Mac that couldn't be denied. Forget Mary Lou. It would take all of Stuart's influence to keep Mac from dispatching some of this Mexican mafia that had showed up just over Magic. Mac and the coyote underworld were now neighbors, and that couldn't last.

Chapter 8

Bar-D Brand Chili took first place on Sunday mostly due to Norm's and Mary Lou's efforts. Competition was stiff, and Coyote Chili and Taranchili took second and third place. Norm cooked the diced steak with Mary Lou's chili sauce, while she worked the crowd and branded everyone in sight. Mac sulked in the booth, slowly drinking one Coors after another. He watched his wife show off, two-stepping with any man who sampled their chili, and rewarding the good-looking ones with excessive attention. Her tight jeans and unmistakably bra-less breasts in a short-sleeved shirt did wonders as males of all ages crowded around.

He had probably done the wrong thing when they got up this morning. Mary Lou was excited about the cook-off, and he had taken advantage of her mood. For the first time in months, the sex had been rewarding to both of them, and they had left home in high spirits. Mary Lou kept her high spirits going during the competition, but Mac lost his watching her egg on the guys.

Mac wandered off to sample other chilis and swap stories, knowing there was nothing he could say to Mary Lou without causing a scene. Beer flowed like water in the afternoon sun, and everyone's inhibitions fell by the wayside, including hers. It was better not to look.

Coyote Chili included a taste of pork that wasn't allowed, but its canny cook picked out the pork chunks prior to submitting his sample for judging. Taranchili was traditional diced steak with chili sauce like Bar-D, but featured an unbeatable showmanship gimmick. They displayed a huge Mexican red-legged tarantula that spectators were encouraged to hold and handle. Supposedly, the cook milked the tarantula for its venom and used it to spice up his chili. Whether true or not, it made a great story. And tasters were required to sign a medical release absolving Taranchili of all responsibility for subsequent health problems or heart attacks.

Combined with a previous win and second place, the first place finish qualified Bar-D Brand to compete in the November World Championship Cook-off at Terlingua. Mary Lou was positively ecstatic at the prospect of her first trip to the ghost town near Big Bend, but Mac cursed his luck. Terlingua was a wild and woolly event, and he wasn't looking forward to taking Mary Lou and having to fight off the animals she would attract.

On the drive home Mac ignored the issue of Mary Lou's indecent behavior. He preferred to let her enjoy the high of winning and receiving so much attention. They both had consumed too much beer, and Mac knew better than to start a fight when Mary Lou was half in the bag. She fingered their trophy and talked about expanding her showmanship act for Terlingua—just what Mac didn't want to hear.

She wanted him to let her do things, so he purposely didn't rain on her parade at the cook-off. As his reward she had made him look like a wimp. She wouldn't like it if he chased other women, so why did she play around with other men?

He deposited Mary Lou at the ranch house to bask in her glory, then drove out to check on his herd. He needed to clear his head's beer-induced fuzziness. Dusk was falling, but with visibility still good, he could probably find the main body of steers before becoming engulfed in total darkness.

Nighttime usually fell like a curtain after the sun disappeared behind the horizon, but tonight a layer of clouds was making it difficult for him to judge the remaining minutes of daylight. His vaqueros had moved the herd into the Bar-D's northern range following Magic's demise, and Mac pushed his Ranger hard in the gathering gloom over increasingly invisible sand ruts and rocky trails.

Although he had lived his entire life in this enigmatic area, Mac still marveled at the desert's ability to hide things in what appeared to be a treeless, flat expanse. But it wasn't treeless, and it wasn't flat. Easterners meant tall oaks and maples when they referred to trees, but out here a mesquite tree rarely grew higher than a good-sized bush. Cottonwoods populated bottom land along permanent rivers, but otherwise, trees existed only around springs, man-made wells, and watering holes. Flatness was strictly illusory, especially on Bar-D land. The range was crisscrossed by an infinite number of ridges and arroyos, each swale hiding mesquite thickets and deep sand, and each crest crowned with exposures of rock layers that often jutted out over arroyos and made speedy descents hazardous to the unwary.

Mac scanned the brush and arroyos as he drove, cursing himself for imbibing too heavily at the cook-off. There was no sign of his herd, and Mac began to wonder if his vaqueros had moved it south of the county road. They surely wouldn't have done that without telling him.

Mac shot over a rise and down into a clump of mesquite before he saw the other truck. It was traveling at least as fast as his Ranger, and coming as a blur from the left on an intersecting ranch trail. Larger than a pickup, maybe a flatbed or concrete hauler. It was an apparition, non-descript, neither old nor new, and shouldn't be here on his ranch.

He jerked his head for a second glance. In a flash of comprehension, Mac saw three figures in the heavy vehicle's cab. Brown faces in the dusk, neither smiling nor registering fear. There was no emotion at all, just caricatures carved in stone, staring at him like ghostly hunters drawing beads on a deer. The windshield went dark as Mac's senses registered on his deadly peril. He wrenched his Ranger to the right, but waiting for the resounding smack of metal on tortured metal, knew with certainty it was too late.

A split-second later his front wheels dug into soft sand, and he felt a gigantic shove as the big truck nudged his rear bumper on the passenger side. The Ranger flipped toward the driver's side, and Mac felt himself being thrown out into darkness. Then a monstrous weight descended on his head and chest, blotting out his senses.

*****

It was strange how things changed, Mary Lou thought after Mac left. Last night she'd decided to make this her last cook-off and see a lawyer next week. Mac had brooded in silence since Magic was killed, eliminating the last vestiges of communication in their marriage.

Enough was enough, and she'd considered her decision final.

But in the morning, they'd made love, and it was like four years ago. Then came the cook-off, and Mac returned to acting like a supportive and loving husband. She was feeling amorous again toward Mac, partially for not being a spoil-sport, but also because she wished to celebrate their qualifying win. She changed into a blood-red teddy with crotchless panties from Frederick's of Hollywood and planned to surprise him when he came back. She checked herself in her full-length mirror. He'd never be able to resist her outfit.

Mary Lou looked out at the setting sun, acutely aware of the desert's stark beauty presented daily for her enjoyment. She would miss the freedom afforded her by ranch life if she left; its glorious sun-drenched days and star-filled nights, unhindered breezes, gorgeous flowers and instantaneous coloring after each rain. She loved riding Twister, the palomino mare Mac had given her, especially in mornings when the sun was warm and desert sand still cool from the night before.

In many ways, ranching was hard but rewarding. At least when they weren't beset with financial worries or when Mac was in one of his moods. There was a casualness that appealed to her, too. Often she wore only two articles of clothing, and sometimes only one on hot summer days. During her first summer on the ranch, her penchant for wearing only a loose cotton dress had caused them to make love almost every time Mac entered the house. Those had been good times. Her heart fluttered, and she sighed as she remembered how sex had dominated her life. They had used every excuse and taken advantage of every opportunity. On horseback, in the stock tanks, out on the range, everywhere it struck them, they had done it without qualms or reservations. Life then was an embarrassment of riches.

By ten, Mary Lou was becoming concerned over Mac's failure to return in a reasonable time. He shouldn't have been gone over an hour, and the gaiety and beer-buzz from her afternoon activities had worn off. With her changing mood, she traded in her teddy for jeans and a white T-shirt. She wasn't entirely willing to scratch the evening, and decided to wait up instead of going to bed.

Another hour passed, and when the fireplace clock struck eleven, a thoroughly awake Mary Lou decided it was time to locate her long overdue husband. He had expected to be gone for maybe a half hour, not the entire evening.

The low-lying frame bunkhouse was dark, indicating the two Bar-D vaqueros were either out somewhere or asleep. Either way, Mary Lou wasn't going to enlist their help. She checked the garage for vehicles. Mac's Ranger was missing as expected, and at the ranch at least, nothing looked amiss. Mac generally kept everything well-organized, and only the cook-off gear Mac hastily dumped from the Ranger imparted any sense of disorder.

She ran back to the kitchen with a rising awareness of urgency. She quickly wrote a note explaining her absence and pinned it on her kitchen bulletin board in case Mac returned. She turned to discover her two cats staring at her.

They know. They know that something's wrong. Her subconscious shouted a warning and slapped her for attention. *Trust your animals, they have a sixth sense.*

She fought a sinking feeling in her stomach and hurried out the door.

Mac had named the Jeep Rover for another of his dogs, and normally she drove either her Prelude or the Ranger. Her car would be faster if she went into the valley, and Mary Lou gave a fleeting thought to trying the bars along Doniphan Drive. Then she remembered it was Sunday and everything was closed. The truck must have broken down, and her best chance to find him lay in following the ranch road Mac had taken earlier. She climbed into the Jeep and headed north.

The sky was cloudy with August's usual threat of nighttime thunderstorms, and she blessed Mac for his foresight in installing flood lights behind the Jeep's roll bar. Greatly supplementing her brights, they lit up the surrounding area and reflected the eyes of various animals watching from the brush. The cone of light substantially increased her feeling of security in the open Jeep. It was eerie driving alone in the desert at night, and the floods were security.

She had to find Mac. After all, he would come looking for her if their situations were reversed. He'd do almost anything to help if she needed him. That was one of his good points.

After an hour, Mary Lou was ready to give up. She had traversed much of the northwestern range served by stock tanks three and four and turned back south from the northern fence line. The cool night air was keeping her awake, but she was noticeably tiring. Then as she crested one of the section's innumerable low and rocky ridges, something flashed in the distance. Her lights had reflected off a metal object. Her heart jumped into her throat, and she careened along the track toward where the apparition alternately appeared and disappeared.

She wound around outcrops of lava and limestone, then descended into a wide sandy swale. A block of metal suddenly loomed out of the night. Mac's Ranger lay upside-down in the middle of a shallow arroyo. An icy blast of fear shook her body, snuffing out her breath and causing her cheeks to quiver in spasms. Rover bathed the wreck with light, but there were no signs of life. For a moment she imagined Mac walking home, cursing her for not coming to find him earlier. God, the truck was totaled almost beyond recognition.

She hopped out to examine the smashed Ranger. Facing the badly battered metal, she knew intuitively that Mac couldn't have walked away.

The faded red cab was squashed a least a foot, and both doors had sprung open. An accordion-like piece of metal was all that remained of the pickup's hood, and a faint odor of dirty garage wafted from its engine. The muffler and tailpipe were torn off, and the tailgate was missing.

The world was forebodingly black outside her isolated island of light, and a paralyzing fear threatened to overwhelm her. The friendly chugging of the Jeep's engine was comforting, and she steadied herself against the warm hood to control her weakening legs. *Do something!* she screamed silently to herself. *Don't just stand there and stare!* The sand had already given up its daytime heat, but Mary Lou was sweating profusely.

Talking to herself with every step, she forced her legs into motion. She lurched to the smashed passenger door. The cab was empty. The inside seemed to be in black and white. If there was blood, she couldn't see it.

She stood up straight and looked around. "Mac! Mac!"

The only sound other than the rustling wind was Rover's engine. And there was no sign of Mac in the area of light.

She stepped to the dark side of the upturned Ranger and spotted other truck pieces lying among evil-looking clumps of cactus and mesquite. One solid-looking slab was undoubtedly the missing tailgate, but another form lying in impenetrable shadows defied definition. She picked her way forward by avoiding dark objects until the form lay before her. A new shock wave crushed her chest. It was a man. Probably Mac. But his face was hidden in the black shadow.

Suppressing an inclination to scream in anguish, she raced back to her Jeep. Somehow, she avoided the cactus and yucca which could end her mission of mercy on a single misstep. The flood lights blinded her, and she tripped twice on rocks and bushes invisible in the shadows. She cursed her own clumsiness and ignored the scrapes on her hands.

Rover roared into action as she slammed it into gear. Like a wild woman she slewed the Jeep around the Ranger's rear to illuminate the crushed mesquite and scattered debris in brilliant light. The scene was gruesome.

She vaulted out of the Jeep and fell, sprawling at Mac's side. In the directional light he looked ghastly. There wasn't much blood, but those horrible dung beetles were already crawling on his grotesquely sprawled form. His body seemed strangely swollen and his head misshapen. One arm was possibly broken, and he was deathly still. A drop of sweat fell from her nose as she felt Mac's neck for a pulse. She gasped for breath.

He was still alive!

Chapter 9

There wasn't any time to waste. Mary Lou knew a badly injured individual shouldn't be moved except by trained medical personnel. Forget that! It would be at least an hour and a half before she could return with an ambulance. Without hesitation, Mary Lou seized the dead weight of Mac's body by his armpits and dragged him to her Jeep. Somehow she found the strength to manhandle him into the front seat, positioning him upright and strapping him in with his seatbelt.

She backed Rover onto the trail as Mac flopped wildly in his seat. His head started bleeding from his left ear, and she pressed it against her right breast to stem the flow. The Jeep started up the track, but the jarring was terrible from the stiff springs as she attempted to hold Mac tightly to avoid further injuries. The land seemed to rise up and contest her passage, throwing rocks and holes in her path. Several times she almost lost control bouncing over *caliche* ledges on the badly rutted track, and she cried out loudly in protest.

She screamed to God for help, and cursed the Jeep for its handling. Her white T-shirt quickly became saturated with Mac's blood. Tears of frustration and fear mingled with sweat to soak what the blood missed. With two free hands it was a difficult drive; with only one, her swift exit from the Bar-D range would take a miracle.

A large mesquite bush slapped at her, raking her face and almost sweeping her from her seat. Her face and chest stung from the blow, and she wailed her distress without shame. Crying helped, and within minutes, she passed under the power lines that signified she had negotiated the roughest terrain. She prayed aloud, reciting the 23rd Psalm for God to hear.

The Jeep emerged onto the county road. The impossible had

occurred, and she shouted her thanks to God. Minutes later she reached Doniphan, and turned toward El Paso with her flashers on. She reached the interstate and swept into the passing lane without a rearward glance. Mac's head lolled out of control as the fear of being too late caused the road to swim before her. The closest hospital was Providence Memorial, across from UTEP and almost fifteen minutes away.

Where were cops when she needed them? There wasn't even the usual Texas state trooper in his black and white Mustang. She floored the Jeep down the interstate into El Paso, barely noticing when the posted limit dropped to fifty-five. The wind whipped her hair as she struggled to maintain control. The Wrangler was not designed for high speeds, and other vehicles gave her a wide berth as she shot past.

Traffic was light, and she ran the lights on Schuster with hardly a glance for oncoming vehicles. She missed a Corvette by inches and ignored the two stop signs on Rim Road and El Paso. Somehow she maintained control as Rover slid around a sandy corner and squealed into emergency receiving at Providence. An ambulance blocked the covered entrance to the ER's double doors, and she stopped the Jeep just inches behind.

In the surprisingly dim light from two yellow bug lamps, Mary Lou honked and screamed for help. She ran through the doors and collided with a nurse answering her cries. Another nurse and attendant in white and blue uniforms materialized from an adjoining room, and Mary Lou ran back out to Mac. He was lifted from her grasp as flood lamps illuminated the surrealistic scene. She shrieked at the attendants to be careful of Mac's injured arm, but they seemed to ignore her in their haste to place him on a stretcher.

The light inside was blindingly bright as Mary Lou steadied Mac's body on the gurney. Blue-coated men rolled him into the emergency room at breakneck speed, forcing her to run alongside to keep up. Hands grabbed at her and a heavy-set nurse seemed hysterically committed to blocking her entrance.

"Get out of my way!" Mary Lou yelled. "He's hurt bad. Don't you understand? Get out of the way!"

She let go of the gurney and tried to shove the nurse aside.

The room burst into bedlam. Two attendants seized her arms as Mary Lou screamed obscenities at the uncomprehending nurse.

Fighting every inch of the way, she was dragged into a side

47

room and pushed onto an examining table by the burly orderlies. She lashed out and kicked one in the groin with all the force she could muster. He doubled up and fell back in pain. Before the other could react, she thrust herself into a sitting position, and knocked the nurse to the floor.

"Goddamnit, leave me alone!"

Everyone was shouting. Need help here! Calm down! Relax! Get a sedative! Grab her arms! Watch her legs! Stop fighting us! We're trying to help!

Mary Lou dimly realized they thought she was injured.

"I'm not hurt!" she screamed.

The nurse in front of her was pointing to Mary Lou's chest and saying something she couldn't understand. She glanced down, suddenly aware her white T-shirt and right arm were painted red with Mac's blood. She yanked up her T-shirt in front of the nurse and orderly, exposing her bra-less torso.

"Look! It's not mine!"

To her amazement her right breast and side were streaked with blood. She wiped at the blood with her hands. Her skin was unbroken underneath.

"See! It's his blood!" She looked up and practically thrust her chest into the orderly in front of her.

The stunned orderly stepped back as if slapped in the face, giving her a few feet of room for the first time. Mary Lou hopped off the examining table before he could object. The nurse became calmer, visibly receding in size and authority. A towel miraculously appeared in Mary Lou's hands from nowhere. Her energy seemed to vanish as if someone had turned off her engine, and she staggered into a chair and collapsed. Her legs were rubbery, and it took a major effort to keep from sliding to the floor.

It was all a terrible nightmare that wasn't getting better. The nurse disappeared, but the male orderly remained. More like a guard than an attendant, he loomed over her, asking if she was all right or needing anything. Of course she wasn't all right!

Words lost their meaning, but so did action. Nothing made any sense, and the room narrowed to the orderly and herself. Her eyes stung from sweat and her jeans were wet and raw. She must have lost control of her bladder in the struggle, and she felt sick to her stomach.

Mary Lou tried to wipe away Mac's blood under her wet and shapeless T-shirt. No doubt the attendant was getting a good look, but she couldn't care less. She wanted to use the ladies' room, but her guard didn't seem interested in providing help or information. Then a female hospital employee began asking stupid questions.

A form appeared on a clipboard, and the woman was asking her to sign something. She scrawled her name, hoping that was all the lady wanted. But it wasn't. The woman continued to ask about personal information and stuff about insurance. Mary Lou couldn't concentrate, and found the simplest questions difficult to answer. She was a far-away observer transmitting words into the mouth of a woman who looked like her but wasn't, providing inane information for robots and automatons about something that didn't make any sense. To several of the questions she told the lady to contact Stuart Prescott.

A man in street clothes came in with her purse and said the Jeep had been moved to the hospital's parking lot. Mary Lou had forgotten her purse, and vaguely wondered if everything was still there. She suppressed the urge to look.

In a stroke of compassion, the attendant she had kicked loaned her a blue orderly's shirt and pointed the way to the ladies' room. Mary Lou headed down the hall to change and wash out her T-shirt with cold water. To her relief, she hadn't wet herself earlier. It was all sweat and blood, and she did her best to make herself presentable. They were waiting for her when she emerged, and escorted her to a waiting room near the entrance.

Somebody brought her a Styrofoam cup of coffee that tasted like water flavored with a rusty nail and an old boot. When she looked up, the room was empty except for a nurse stationed where the hallway began. A subdued television set in the corner bid for her attention with a re-run of *Jaws*, but she ignored the screen and the magazines on cheap plastic tables.

Mac was gone, she was sure of that, and a crushing loneliness pressed in upon her. She had nothing without Mac. For five years he had been the epicenter of her existence, and she had neglected to build new friendships as old ones fell away. It was too late now. Her life had been turned upside-down with the Ranger.

She thought about her dreams of an idyllic life with Mac on the ranch. All the good times, Mac's strength, his beautiful body and inexhaustible energy, were gone forever. She'd never find another Mac. Her life was ruined, destroyed at an early age by an act of God. Why her? What had she done that was so bad?

Exhaustion crept over her like a thousand red ants, sensitizing her skin but dulling her mind with images of funerals and bank foreclosures. There was no escaping reality, even in her imagination. Time passed, but without awareness or relief.

Almost forty-five minutes elapsed before a young doctor materialized in front of her. Mary Lou expected the worst, and his news was only slightly better. Mac was in critical condition from a fractured skull and internal chest injuries. Mary Lou felt her stomach tighten as if Twister had kicked her, and doubled over in a wave of nausea.

"Will he make it?" she whispered.

"We don't know yet," the doctor said. "There are multiple skull fractures and massive cranial hematomas."

"So you don't give him much chance?"

Mary Lou eyes were filling with tears. The room blurred, and the doctor's voice became practically inaudible. She hadn't wished this on Mac, and felt terrible about letting so much distance build up between them. He was a good man, and she had denied him what he wanted most. Then he'd lost his dog, and now stood to lose his life. It was her fault; she should have done something to make him stay home.

"There's always a chance. You need to remain optimistic."

"Doctor, I saw him." The tears started falling from her cheeks. "Tell me the truth."

The doctor said something, but that wasn't what she heard. Across the room an attendant asked the desk nurse if the train wreck had flat-lined yet. The doctor spun around and barked at the attendant to shut up. Hospital slang was not difficult to figure out. Mary Lou gazed through her tears at the dark-haired Anglo doctor, seeing him for the first time. He was thin and nervous, about Stuart's height and not much older than Mac.

He took a deep breath to compose himself and started again. "Frankly, we're surprised he's lasted this long. That's a positive sign in itself, but his chances aren't good. If he does pull through, there may be permanent brain damage."

Mary Lou broke down sobbing. Either way, Mac was gone—dead or a vegetable. God was punishing her for her evil thoughts and bad intentions. It was all her fault.

Her head spun. Hands lifted her up and someone guided her down the hallway. She offered no resistance. People stood around her, talking softly. Mary Lou allowed herself to be given an injection and laid back on a bed without an argument. Her body was limp and useless. Someone removed her boots and jeans, and covered her gently with a sheet.

The universe imploded inside her consciousness. Steel balls rolled down an incline to clash with others coming up. Then the stand was flipped over and the balls fell down. They were glass marbles which shattered on the brown floor, spreading red fluid in all directions. Sleep mercifully arrived not a moment too soon.

Chapter 10

Deputy Juan Beltran had drawn the assignment to investigate the Frazier accident, and he carefully studied the Anglo woman sitting cross-legged on the bed in front of him. Obviously still distraught from last night's events, she was wearing a hospital gown over a pair of jeans. Her tousled brown hair was straggly and matted, and without makeup, she looked pale and drawn. Like many Anglo girls, her mouth was large but little more than a thin line across her face. There was something unmistakably carnal about that mouth, but her vacant eyes altered his description of her from sexy to haunting. For some reason her jeans were partially damp, particularly the right leg. Her tan boots were on the floor, and they too, were spotted with water. The leather looked soft, probably kangaroo, and well-worn from frequent use. In spite of the girl's shapeless gown, his practiced eye discerned a stunning figure under those jeans with an upper unit to match.

Trying to conduct an investigation in a hospital room with a disoriented relative was probably a bad idea, but Juan had been in Anapra early this morning and it was logical to stop by Providence before returning to Cruces. Still, such an interview was unusual. A single vehicle accident on private land normally didn't warrant a quick response, but evidently someone high up knew the victim and wanted prompt action.

The drabness of hospitals and their rooms sometimes made interviews easier by eliminating distractions, but the wife's emotional state neutralized the room's effect. She seemed oblivious to her appearance or the sunlight streaming in from a gloriously bright day. She was in one of Providence's rooms, and it reminded him of a cheap motel with linoleum instead of carpeting. Juan seated himself in one of two vinyl armchairs to keep from towering over his subject.

He tried to pinpoint the accident's location, but the woman's directions seemed almost hopeless. Juan spent most of his time in Las Cruces or working at Sunland Park Racetrack, and isolated ranches were off his usual beat. He was a city boy who grew up in El Paso, moving to Las Cruces after high school. He decided to move on to other questions, figuring her ranch hands could help him locate the accident scene. "Is there any reason you think this wasn't an accident?" he said.

The girl nodded. "Yeah, but I don't know who."

Deputy Beltran's head snapped up. He hadn't expected an affirmative answer, and his interviewee wasn't making much sense. Her state of mind was worse than it appeared.

"Really? Not an accident?"

"Maybe. I don't know."

"What else could have happened?"

"I don't know. It's just hard to believe Mac would lose control. He'd been checking into illegals crossing our ranch, and it might have been them."

Juan watched as the first tear coursed down the girl's cheek, then drew back as a flood followed. She wept uncontrollably, covering her face with both hands. Juan waited patiently for her to regain her composure. Experience had taught him to stay away from emotional women, particularly Anglo women. They were unpredictable. He held out a tissue when she finally looked up.

"Thank you," she wiped her eyes, then took another tissue and blew her nose.

Would you like to call someone to be with you? Maybe a best friend or family member I can call?"

"No, there's no one. Let's just get this over."

"I'm sorry I have to ask all these questions," Juan said. "Perhaps another time would be better."

"No. It's not going to get better."

Juan wanted her to expand on their illegal alien problem. Illegals crossed all the ranches near the Mexican border sooner or later. That wasn't news, and usually the ranchers ignored trespassers unless they killed stock or stole from ranch houses or buildings. "Why was your husband worried about illegals? How would they be involved?"

"Someone shot his dog four nights ago, and he thought

something funny was going on at the fenced-in property on our northeast corner."

"Funny? Like what? Why?"

"The acreage is small, and the fence is worth more than the land. I haven't seen it myself, but it's only a mile from where I found Mac."

The deputy scribble notes while she spoke. He was a big man, with hands that were like paws. The knuckles were almost hidden under smooth brown flesh, not at all like her thin, protruding ones. He printed in disjointed jerks as he continued the questions. Most were routine, but some required her to focus on the events as she knew them, and he wasn't always sure her responses were accurate. Finally he decided to end the interview.

"I'm very sorry about your husband," he said. "I hope he pulls through and you'll be able to put this behind you."

She blinked and looked up. "Thank you, but you needn't be concerned. I was going to leave him before this happened."

Juan was accustomed to people sharing their deepest secrets with him in such situations, but this one shook him. This woman had made Herculean efforts a just few hours earlier to save her husband. No, it was her eyes. In normal times they undoubtedly sparkled a bright blue, but now they were empty. She was empty, without purpose or emotion. She was looking at him like his dog did before he'd put her to sleep. This woman was a lost puppy, alone with her thoughts and facing a hostile world. It was time to leave.

On the drive north to Canutillo, he reconsidered his hasty departure. In his twelve years with the Doña Ana County Sheriff's Department, this was the first time a victim's wife had reached in and tugged at his heartstrings. Not only that, she was an Anglo.

Large for a Hispanic, Juan was relatively dark and not considered particularly good-looking by girls. His ex-wife had left him for an insurance salesman, and his current girlfriend spent more time in church than with him.

Yet apparently, this woman had announced she was available, and his response had been to run like a scared rabbit. No doubt she regretted her openness. Maybe he could repair his negative impression when he saw her again. He'd automatically get a second chance when he reported his findings. But first he had to investigate the accident so he'd have something to report.

Her directions turned out to be better than expected, and he found the over-turned Ranger without difficulty. In fact, it was easy in daylight, and he spotted the wreck from almost a mile away. He drove down the ranch road Mac Frazier had apparently followed, and Juan saw the Ranger had entered the scrub where another track joined the main trail from the left. Frazier evidently lost control and hit deep sand on the right, throwing his pickup into a roll. Juan left his cruiser to examine the truck and its tracks.

There were other recent tracks, some probably made by the Jeep when Frazier's wife found him. The ubiquitous breeze made time estimates impossible, and even the Ranger's tracks had already lost their clarity. Depressions in the sand were probably the remains of footprints, and both tire and shoe impressions were completely out of the question.

The truck itself was a mess. All its glass was broken out although both door windows had been down when it rolled over. There were marks on rocks near where Frazier's body had apparently lain, and he figured the pickup's cab had rolled over the victim. Somehow Frazier must have been thrown out first.

Juan checked the cab again. Yup, the seatbelt was still in place and unused. He searched for beer bottles or a flask, but all he found were normal truck tools, emergency equipment, maps, and a rope. Nor was there any odor of alcohol. Providence had reported an insignificant blood alcohol level, but six or seven hours had elapsed between the accident and when the sample was taken. Still, he decided to report the accident as not being alcohol-related.

All four tires were still inflated so a blowout was not indicated. He checked the severely damaged bumpers, but couldn't identify any marks that would point to a second vehicle being involved. Bumpers on range vehicles took a heavy pounding, and the damage he saw could have been accumulated over a number of incidents. There were no paint scrapes of another color, or impact damage like he was accustomed to see in multiple-vehicle accidents. As far as he could tell, all the major damage could have occurred in the rollover.

Juan walked back along the trail, searching for broken glass or other pieces which didn't belong to the wreck. He couldn't find anything like that either. There simply wasn't any evidence of a second vehicle, and the only plausible explanation was that the victim had become distracted, maybe by some animal, or fallen asleep. In any case, he'd lost control and driven into the sand, which had caused the front wheels to bury themselves in the sand and the truck to flip over.

To satisfy Frazier's wife, he decided to check out the property she had mentioned. The shortest route to Cruces followed Frazier's northern fence line, and he would pass by it anyway. Less than a mile later the enclosure became visible, and Juan immediately noted what had caught Frazier's interest. There was no reason for such an expensive fence in this area, and the few cows inside hardly seemed worth the property's development. He made a mental note to check the ownership and see if the department had any record concerning the site. He didn't know anything about cattle, and maybe this was some transshipment point or a stud ranch. He didn't see any large bull, but it could be in one of the sheds. There certainly wasn't any overt indication of illegal activity, so it probably wasn't worth his effort to make inquiries.

He drove across the flood control dam, stopping for a moment to view the unusual fenced-in area and consider his options. The doctor had said Frazier's chances were slim to none, and even if he survived, he'd probably suffer brain damage. The wife wouldn't complain if he recorded the whole thing as an accident, and might even prefer that foul play be eliminated from consideration. His report could make a difference with Frazier's insurance coverage if he came out a vegetable. An accident was always preferable to a homicide for insurance purposes, and there was no physical evidence indicating anything other than driver error. It was time to return to Las Cruces and file his report.

In the afternoon Juan found himself thinking more and more about Frazier's wife. He noted her name was Mary Lou, one of those typical double names redneck Anglos liked to hang on their kids. He recalled a country-western song where the wife was named Betty Lou... Thelma Liz... something. Redneck girls were supposed to be wild, and in spite of her disorientation during his initial interview, she had impressed him with an inner resolve and strength most women didn't have. His experience so far was only with Hispanic girls, and few of them would have been able to give him such explicit directions under the circumstances.

She had broken down only once, and her ability to regain control of her emotions was impressive. That she cared deeply for her husband was evident, but apparently was about to divorce him over some issue. But the Frazier woman hadn't given him the least indication of involvement in an extra-marital affair. Men leave women to get away from them, women leave men to go to other men. Maybe that was why she hadn't filed yet. She didn't have another man.

He telephoned the Frazier ranch, but there was no answer. Evidently the wife was still at Providence. That made things easier. He needed to call the hospital anyway for an update on her husband's condition.

After an abnormal level of effort to convince the switchboard operator his inquiry was official business, he was put through to the intensive care unit's nurses' station. All his powers of persuasion were required again before he learned that Mac was still on the critical list. Talking with the nurse on duty, Juan asked to speak with Mary Lou Frazier. He wondered what he was going to say.

The wait was interminable, but a series of clicks told him somebody was finally coming on the line.

"Yes, this is Mary Lou Frazier," a soft voice said.

"This is Deputy Beltran."

Mary Lou sounded as if she had been sleeping, and Juan feared he was intruding at a bad time. In contrast, his voice was overly friendly. He toned it down immediately to sound more concerned.

"I was coming down to Providence, and wondered if you would like me to stop by your ranch and pick up anything. That is, if you're going to be staying at the hospital."

His smooth approach under pressure astounded him. The offer had rolled off his tongue all by itself.

There was no response. He quickly spoke again to keep the conversation going. "I called your ranch earlier, but no one answered."

Mary Lou finally replied, and her voice sounded brighter.

"That would be very nice, I haven't been home and do need some things. And the hands are still in the dark about what's happened."

"Why don't I call you from the ranch, and you can tell me what to do and bring?" Juan said. He felt like a knight in shining armor rescuing a lady in distress.

She protested only mildly about making him go out of his way, and was clearly relieved when he repeated his offer of assistance. She gave him the number she'd be at when he called, and told him where to find the house key.

This was not something he ordinarily did, and he hoped she would recognize his help went beyond normal duty. The lady was ripe for a friend to step in and provide support while her husband died or became institutionalized. Juan was already thirty-five, and one needed to take advantage of opportunities as they presented themselves. Women often appreciated kindness, and with appreciation, came friendship. Moving into the bedroom would be the hard part.

It was late in the afternoon before Juan arrived at the Frazier ranch. He was greeted by two vaqueros who arose lazily from a shaded bench alongside the garage and stamped out their cigarettes in the dirt. They shuffled over to the yellow and white cruiser as it rolled to a stop and asked him what he wanted. Their bold approach tossed any thought of checking their green cards out the window immediately.

One was a grizzled character of indeterminate age, and the other a young lad about twenty. Together, they outweighed Juan, but not by much. There must be something about ranch life that kept people thin, he decided. Neither of the Fraziers carried excess baggage, and even the two cats eyeing him from the open garage looked scrawny.

"You fellows hungry?" Juan asked in Spanish. "Mrs. Frazier probably won't be back for a while."

"Nope," the older one said. "We cook for ourselves. So what's happenin?"

There was no reason to withhold his information any longer, and Juan related the events of the previous evening. The hands did not seem unduly disturbed or inclined to action. Waiting appeared to be their natural pastime. Juan ordered them to remain around the ranch until he returned with assignments from Mary Lou. Neither spoke much English, and weren't particularly talkative in Spanish. They'd need groceries in a few days, but otherwise could take care of themselves. They resumed their shady seats when he went into the equipment shed.

58

Once again, Mary Lou's directions were perfect, and Juan easily found the house key wedged behind the spare screen door. He soon found out why the door wasn't in use. The house itself was completely barred with decorative steel grills, a standard security precaution in a land where windows were left open as exhausts for evaporative air-conditioning. Fancy steel screen gates protected both the front and patio doors, although each door was formidable by itself. The key fit the steel gate, and the antique oak door behind it was unlocked. He located a phone in Mary Lou's kitchen near the patio entrance and dialed Providence.

Mary Lou had made up a list of items she wanted since his initial call, and also read off a series of instructions for the hands. She stressed which chores had to be accomplished first. The lady apparently knew how to run a ranch, but couldn't do it all by herself.

The personal items she wanted him to bring were another matter and somewhat embarrassing for both of them. Juan went through Mary Lou's bedroom drawers, selecting panties, stockings, blouses, and jeans for a three-day stay at the hospital. He retrieved an already packed overnight bag of toiletries and cosmetics from underneath her bathroom wash basin, and included several tampons as an afterthought.

He had searched bedrooms before as part of his job, but this time, he went through some of Mary Lou's belongings out of sheer curiosity. Restraining a sense of voyeuristic guilt, Juan examined a drawer of sexy undergarments and discovered items guaranteed to bring the deadest man to life.

The biggest surprise was in the husband's drawer of accessories. In a box of boas, pins, and miscellaneous junk, he found a series of photos featuring Mary Lou in nude poses and various stages of undress. He whistled involuntarily. Her body was spectacular! He had never seen maracas like hers, and her posterior was outstanding.

Unable to control his baser instincts, Juan slipped one Playboy-quality nudie into his breast pocket. Her husband would never miss it, and Mary Lou had probably forgotten the photos existed.

At the bottom of the drawer was an envelope that contained photos of the Fraziers making love. He noted Frazier's unusual endowment, every inch of which was handled by his wife in various poses. Juan was overwhelmed. It took only a few minutes to relieve

59

himself of the resulting sexual tension, marking the nightstand as his territory. He scooped up all the photos, and quickly pocketed them before his conscience made him change his mind.

He stood in their living room and looked around. The house was an excellent combination of elegance and gracious functionality, far better than any place he had lived. The large living room took up the house's entire south end and was dominated with a huge fireplace like he had seen in John Wayne westerns. The floor was hardwood with woven Indian rugs, and the furniture was wood and leather in some massive style Juan couldn't name. A hallway separated a front formal dining room on the eastern side from a large modern kitchen on the west. This was really living in the hacienda style he imagined his Spanish forefathers enjoyed. His imagination began to run amuck, then he remembered his duty as a low-paid deputy. Well, he didn't have to remain one forever. Maybe with some effort he could snare the widow when her husband died. Opportunities like this didn't grow on trees, and he needed to take advantage of this one.

Chapter 11

For five long days Mac hovered in critical condition before he took a dramatic turn for the better. Stuart visited in the mornings and evenings, but Mary Lou remained with Mac the entire time. Stuart also purchased every romance novel in the hospital's gift shop to help Mary Lou pass the time.

"You don't have to stay here like this," Stuart told her.

"Yes, I do. What if he wakes up and I'm not here? It would kill him."

Stuart brought Mary Lou breakfast and supper when he came, and they ate together in a friendlier atmosphere than Stuart expected. There had always been an element of competition between them for Mac's attention, but now they were on the same side. Stuart saw a new, nurturing side of Mary Lou and he approved. She still looked like a ravishing sex machine, but underneath that body beat a woman's heart. His attraction for her forced him to maintain some distance, and be careful of what he said. He didn't want her to think he was taking advantage of her vulnerable state, and anyway, he couldn't do that to Mac.

Mary Lou's devotion paid off when Mac was removed from the critical list. She had done the right thing for Mac and herself. Even the doctors said he couldn't have pulled through without her. She had made amends for all her past mistakes and atoned for her earlier lack of sensitivity.

The doctors said Mac's constitution was unbelievable. Not one in a hundred would have survived his injuries, and not one in a thousand would be able to recover and pursue anything like normal activities. In Mac's case, the prognosis was excellent, although they wouldn't learn the full extent of his brain damage for another week. His speech was partially impaired, but it was difficult to tell how much of that

61

was due to his heavy sedation. Massive doses of pain killers were required to keep him reasonably comfortable.

Even if he regained his faculties, the change in Mac's physical appearance was going to be frightful. His left temple was horribly misshapen and his face was an evil mask like a monster in some Hollywood horror movie. The left side was lower than the right, and the swelling in his forehead forced his left eye into a permanent, evil squint. His skull looked excessively large, and his ears abnormally indented. The doctors said some of the swelling would eventually recede, but there was no way Mac would ever recover his good looks.

*****

Mary Lou tried to remember Mac as he'd looked before the accident, but his deformity overshadowed her attempts. He was a different person now, and not one who would attract her physically. She told herself his appearance shouldn't make any difference, but it did. Meanwhile, she took one day at a time, being as supportive as possible and playing the dutiful wife. After all, he would have done the same for her.

Thinking about Mac was torturous. In a sense her situation was worse than ever. Earlier, she'd felt guilty and responsible, praying he would live, but sometimes hoping he would die. When the coma threatened to continue indefinitely, she'd imagined spending the rest of her life caring for an invalid. There was no way she could do it. At only twenty-six she had her entire life ahead.

Now he would live, but everything had changed for the worse. She was still faced with her dilemma, with grimmer decisions and more terrifying consequences. If she remained with Mac her life was over; if she left, it would end his and probably hers in the bargain.

During the second week, Mary Lou began to taste the bitter reality of Mac's injuries. He was awake much of the time and in constant pain. His emotional state alternated between anger and helplessness, and he was uncompromisingly nasty to those around him. The doctors said it was a combination of his headaches and the shock of being disfigured. Each day became increasingly difficult rather than easier, but the doctors told her not to give up hope. The question was… hope for what?

From the moment he regained consciousness, Mac talked mainly about how three Mexicans tried to kill him. In the first few hours he was barely coherent, repeating over and over the same description of their truck and how they flipped his Ranger. The babbling was soon replaced with virulent verbal attacks on Mexicans and violent reactions to the slightest perceived disagreement from his visitors.

The doctors counseled rest and quiet, and only Mac's tenuous hold on life abated his anger and scathing denunciations. Deputy Beltran came in for particularly heavy criticism although Mac refrained from ethnic insults while the big deputy was at the hospital. That he had not discovered any evidence of a second vehicle convinced Mac that the Mexican had been bought off or was part of the conspiracy against him. When he mentioned his suspicions to Mary Lou, her response set him off again.

"I don't think he's part of any conspiracy, hon," she said. "His assignment was happenstance. Stuart got the investigation started after I called him. Deputy Beltran was in Anapra at the time. Stuart wanted immediate action and he was the nearest available officer."

Mac refused to be mollified and launched into a tirade about how no Mexican could be trusted. They were all stupid, dirty, and bred like bunnies. "Stuart should have demanded an Anglo heading the investigation. He should have used his political pull and gotten the job done right. What the hell is friendship worth?"

"Honey, seventy percent of the population is Mexican," Mary Lou said.

"I know that!" he yelled. "Don't you think I know that? Stupid bitch!"

He yelled for Stuart—who didn't happen to be there at the time. The brunt of his anger fell fully on Mary Lou. She should have refused to cooperate with the Mexican. Demanded an Anglo. Taken Stuart out to the ranch and showed him the wreck that very day. She was stupid. Like all women. Just a life support system for a pussy.

Exhaustion finally ended Mac's outburst, and he lapsed into unconsciousness. That was fortunate for everyone in Mac's wing, especially Mary Lou. In spite of understanding the cause of his vile temper, she was reduced to tears.

Stuart fared little better when he arrived. Mac awoke soon afterward and reviled him for allowing a Mexican to be put on the case. He repeated his earlier diatribe on the perfidy of Mexicans and their worthlessness as human beings. Mary Lou fled the room before Mac started in again on her.

Showing more patience than he thought he possessed, Stuart allowed Mac's acrimonious monologue to run its course. He promised to make his own investigation, both into Mac's accident and Beltran's findings, and then have the Ranger towed back to the ranch. The word "accident" triggered another torrent of illogical accusations, and Stuart promised to avoid that word in the future.

Over the next several days Stuart learned it was best to take Mac in little doses. Dealing with him was a trial which required a thick skin. Mac tended to fill any awkward conversational pauses with negative comments on Mexicans, and it was hard work to keep him focused on other issues.

Mary Lou usually attempted to maintain a cheerful disposition to improve Mac's mood. It was a doomed project from the outset. Mac associated her with his injuries, and more often than not, she received unbridled abuse. To her intense frustration, his malevolent nature grew more pronounced as he became ambulatory and stronger.

"Woman!" he yelled.

Mac seemed to take special delight in yelling that word at Mary Lou. When she related happenings that didn't interest him, he would interrupt and order her about.

"Shut up when I'm talking to you. Get my slippers and help me out of bed."

She hated being called "woman," but when she was slow in responding to his demands, Mac's behavior degenerated into that of a psychotic child. Mary Lou endured his ill treatment in silence. His doctors believed Mac's extreme reactions were physically induced and temporary, but that didn't make them easier to withstand.

Mac constantly questioned her about ranch affairs, and nothing she did met with his approval. When she told him that Stuart had towed the Ranger in for salvaging, he became unhinged.

"Fucking Mexicans try to kill me, and Stuart destroys the evidence!"

"The police had completed their investigation. There wasn't any reason to leave it out there."

"If he wanted to get those greasers, there was!"

"The sheriff closed your case. There was nothing more they would do."

Mac calmed down. "That dumb Mexican deputy. He couldn't tell a bullet hole from his navel—if he could find it in all that fat."

"He wasn't so fat," Mary Lou said. Juan deserved at least a little defense.

"Probably has five fat Mexican kids and a two-ton greasy sow for a wife," Mac said. "Probably collects welfare and buys food stamps."

Mary Lou let the conversation drift. She already knew Deputy Beltran was divorced without children, but refuting Mac's allegations would serve no useful purpose. By now, Mac simply hated all Mexicans and made derogatory comments about them at every opportunity.

A nurse popped into Mac's room and reminded him it was time to exercise. Mary Lou helped Mac out of bed and to stand up.

"Watch it!" he bellowed. Mac knocked her hand away from his chest where she had placed it to provide support.

Multiple ribs were broken on the right side, and she had momentarily forgotten.

"Stupid bitch! Just take my arm."

He placed his good arm over her shoulders and leaned on her, allowing her to carry most of his weight. Mary Lou staggered, and a stream of invectives issued forth from Mac's lips.

"If you're going to talk like that, the nurse can walk you," Mary Lou said.

"Bullshit. You're my wife, and I have to piss. It's your job to shake my cock, not hers."

That was the one thing which gave Mac pleasure; seeing her clean him after urinating. Every day, Mary Lou half-expected Mac to demand she perform oral sex afterward. There was no way that was going to happen, regardless of the circumstances or consequences. She steered Mac into the small bathroom off his private room, and this time turned him to sit on the toilet.

"No! A man stands up to piss!" he shouted.

As always, Mac's voice carried down the hall. His obnoxious behavior had caused the hospital to give him a private room off a small hallway, but their minor attempt at isolation wasn't sufficient to bring peace to his wing.

"Setters sit, pointers stand!"

"Okay, then stand," she said. Mary Lou turned him around and lifted up the seat.

"Ha, didn't expect a split-tail to remember that!"

"Our tails are just split a little more than yours," Mary Lou said. She hated that term with a passion. "Besides, I've lived with you long enough to know you need the seat up."

It was the wrong thing to say. Mac launched into a loud discourse about how he had never pissed on the seat, either up or down, and how he had found her bloody pads stopping up the toilet. It took Mary Lou ten minutes to shut him up and get him back to bed. She decided to let the floor nurse take him for his exercise walk.

*****

Hardly less rational was Mac's behavior when Stuart arrived to report on his own investigation. He had examined the wrecked Ranger and also gone over Beltran's report. Stuart first showed him the deputy's report, and Mac flew apart as he read it.

"This is bullshit! Sheer bullshit!"

He threw Beltran's report at Stuart with his good hand and began swearing about the deputy. Several minutes passed before he calmed down sufficiently for Stuart to continue.

"Mac, there isn't any evidence of another vehicle. I looked all over. It's not there."

"It's not there now! You had the truck towed in."

"I spent an hour out there. There was no evidence of another vehicle."

"So you don't believe me either. Just like all the rest."

"No, I believe you. I'm just saying there's no physical evidence to support your story."

"Then you don't believe me."

"Dammit! I believe you! Evidence or not, I believe you."

"I'm not so stupid as to flip over my truck for no reason."

"Okay. Let's start from there. Although there's no physical evidence of another vehicle, I found evidence that another person was there."

Mac sat up. "See, I told you! What was it?"

"Well, I assume you were driving with your lights on."

"Of course they were on. How else would I drive?"

"Right. But one headlight was still intact, and when I switched the lights on, it worked. So who turned off the lights?"

"See! See! I told you! That proves I'm not lying."

"So I believe you."

"How about Mary Lou?"

"She believes you, too. I've talked to her. We're both on your side."

Stuart wished his last statement was true. Mary Lou might believe Mac's story, but her commitment to him appeared to be wavering. Mac's abuse was having an effect. Stuart had countered by trying to get her to see the situation from Mac's point of view and have more sympathy. He was in the unenviable position of knowing something that nobody else believed and was not able to prove he was right. Just that alone would make lots of people irritable.

*****

Mary Lou knew it wasn't all Mac's fault, but the situation was fast becoming unendurable. Icepacks helped reduce the swelling and lowered the intensity of his headaches, but Mac hated lying there for hours with an icepack on his head.

One day she touched his temple where a drain had been placed to relieve pressure from internal bleeding. Mac suddenly lashed out and blindly struck her as hard as he could. He hadn't aimed for anything in particular, but squarely hit her left breast. The blow took Mary Lou's breath away, and stunned her into sitting down until the wave of pain receded.

She expected him to apologize, but he didn't. Quite the contrary, he berated her instead.

"The next time you do that, I'll knock you through the fucking window."

He glared at her as she sat coughing in the plastic chair, then turned away as if her problem didn't concern him.

Mary Lou cupped her breast and fought back tears of pain. She hadn't meant any harm, and the blow caught her by surprise. She coughed to control the pain and keep from crying. Her breast was probably bruised, and she wondered if Mac had caused permanent damage.

"You hurt me."

"You don't know what hurt is," Mac said. "When I walk across this room my head feels like somebody is jabbing it with a cattle prod."

"I'm sorry you have so much pain, but there's nothing I can do about it."

"You make it worse. Try making an icepack instead."

Mary Lou rose and stuffed a number of small cubes from Mac's ice bucket into the light rubber bag. She started to place it on Mac's forehead, but he grabbed her wrist and pulled it away.

"I'll put it on! You don't know where the pain is!"

"Well, excuse me! I was just trying to be helpful."

"Stupid bitch. I'd already be home if you had come looking for me as soon as you realized something had happened."

"How was I to know that?"

"Being gone for more than an hour on a half-hour drive. You tell me."

There it was again. Everything was Mary Lou's fault. She tried to change the subject, but there was little to talk about that didn't bring them back to Mac's accident. Key words would catalyze tirades from Mac, and Mary Lou hardly knew what to say.

The doctors were thrilled with Mac's physical progress, but his mental condition had become increasingly psychotic. Yesterday he'd wanted Mary Lou to bring his rifle to shoot an incompetent asshole doctor, and another time, he'd been certain some Mexicans were planning to kill him there in his hospital bed. Mary Lou initially assumed these aberrations were temporary, but his behavior patterns were becoming repetitive.

She sat in the chair next to his bed, surveying the cold but functional hospital room. The temperature outside was supposed to hit a hundred that afternoon, and humidity was less than fifteen percent. It was a glorious day, but she couldn't see the cloudless blue sky through the drawn shades. The room was being kept in semi-darkness to help reduce Mac's headaches, and the effect on her was depressing. It accentuated the tragic state she was in, denying her access to El Paso's best feature. In darkness or light, she was intimately acquainted with every item in the room. Each one had been the object of extensive study at some time to divert her thoughts from Mac and the hopelessness which weighed so heavily on her psyche.

It wasn't her fault she needed brightness and laughter in her life. Every woman deserved that, no matter what. Mac took those things away, and didn't have a clue to her desire for happiness. Nor did he realize they were facing financial ruin. His insurance was woefully inadequate, and medical bills were mounting higher than the national debt. She couldn't see any possibility to pay off the hospital without selling the Bar-D, and that meant the end of everything good in her life.

There was also the danger of losing her life completely. The doctors weren't certain Mac could return to working outdoors, and certainly not for a long while. Considering his mental state, she doubted he'd ever be able to find and hold a reasonable job. Losing the ranch would probably send him over the edge, and she'd have to bear the brunt of his anger and frustration. He might commit suicide, but would probably shoot her first. Men did things like that—they took their family with them. She needed to protect herself from Mac. There were guns all over the house, but they had never killed anything more than a snake or jackrabbit. Well, she'd unload them all, except for her own hunting rifle and 380. Then she'd hide the ammo. If Mac tried anything, she'd be prepared.

Chapter 12

On her first evening back home, Mary Lou helped the two ranch hands start the diesel pump on her orchard irrigation well. The gushing water meant a renewal of life, and she turned her thoughts to the deputy and Mac. The doctors anticipated Mac wouldn't be released for three more weeks, and she'd have to fend for herself until then. That was okay, but after coming home, he'd probably make her life unbearable.

They had warned her of distinct personality shifts which could be expected due to pressure from his shattered skull and bleeding on certain parts of his brain. The next few weeks would determine what those shifts would be.

At the very least, Mac would be subject to frequent and violent headaches which would severely impact his behavior. If she hadn't trusted his mean streak before, she could expect it to become ungovernable in the future. There was no question in her mind that she'd need help from somewhere.

It was possible that help might come from the deputy. He had been sensitive to her needs, even overly solicitous and caring. She wondered if those characteristics extended to making love, but Mary Lou was wary of super-macho Mexicans. Some of her friends had dated Mexicans during high school and college, and had said they weren't particularly good in bed or worth the effort to train. Sooner or later, they treated women as baby-making possessions, and that wasn't her thing. Nor did she want to put up with mistresses or worrying about who her man was visiting when out of sight.

This afternoon the deputy had arranged for the Ranger to be checked out by a mechanic at the ranch. The outcome was discouraging, and the most she could expect to salvage was the

70

engine and a few other parts. Juan hadn't stayed for supper, but she'd noticed he was overly attentive around her in that funny and polite Mexican fashion she found so quaint.

His reward was a good-bye hug, and she felt his breath quicken as she pressed herself into him. He was surprisingly soft and fleshy, not hard and lean like Mac. She wondered about him, and couldn't imagine a man more unlike Mac.

If she were honest with herself, she'd have to admit Juan was fat. His rear end was broad and bulbous, his waist made even thicker by that belt cops wore with their pistol and all those other things. A man that broad could crush a slender girl like herself in certain positions, but a lot of women preferred large men. Idly, she wondered why.

Juan exhibited greater sensitivity toward her than Mac, but it was difficult to believe a cop wasn't macho. She wished she hadn't restricted her relationships to Anglos in the past, but trying out other races had seemed like a really bad idea.

Mary Lou lived in El Paso's heavily military northeast during high school, and the prevailing belief at Andress High was that smoking Marlboro cigarettes would prevent pregnancies. She was hardly dumb enough to believe something so obviously absurd, but the Mexican boys refused to use condoms. She had avoided them, and now there was little to do except trust her instincts and take her chances.

There was one aspect in particular concerning Juan which heightened her interest—he might be controllable through sex. She wasn't proud of her attitude, but all relationships ultimately developed into struggles for control. Mary Lou guessed that control alternated in a healthy relationship, and given the male's physical strength and economic muscle, a girl had to develop a counter-balancing force. She hadn't been able to do that with Mac, although for a long time, it hadn't made any difference.

All in all, the single bright spot in Mary Lou's pathos was Deputy Beltran. She had taken advantage of his offer to run interference at the Bar-D during her hospital sojourn, and the big deputy had proven a godsend. He was her main support throughout her ordeal, constantly phoning and assuring her the ranch was in good hands. Stuart spent an enormous amount of time with Mac and her, but his attention was directed more toward Mac than her. Mac's chilihead friends came by occasionally, but they didn't give material or emotional assistance directly to her. Only the deputy did that.

The next day Mac was quiet under his icepack, and Mary Lou decided to leave for a few hours. She had a lot to think about. Mac hardly acknowledged her departure, merely giving her a half-hearted wave to send her on her way.

Instead of turning off at Canutillo for La Union, she continued on Interstate 10 to Las Cruces. Mary Lou drove north on I-25 along the east side of town, turning toward Alamogordo after passing the huge earthen flood control dam that protected the city from runoff on the East Mesa. It was time to commune with God, and the best place she knew for that was White Sands. She hadn't been inside a church for years, and wasn't about to look for one now. In the desert, God was nature. At night the stars descended to fill the sky and comfort her with their presence. Sometimes the effect was overwhelming, and she felt like crying out for joy and announcing her existence to the world. That was when God was most real, touching her with his magic wand, and making it all worthwhile.

Traffic was light as Mary Lou threaded through the Organ Mountains and descended from St. Augustin Pass on US 70. The absence of a roadblock told her the missile range was inactive. She crossed the test facility's firing zone without being halted, and the National Monument's gypsum dunes soon appeared on the left. The entrance facility was almost deserted, looking sleepy and hot under its fluttering American flag. The visitor center contained various exhibits explaining the dunes that were interesting, but she had seen them already.

A female ranger took her money at the entrance booth, handing her the standard brochure about the park. Mary Lou ignored the brochure as well as the points of interest noted alongside the road. She drove to where the access road looped back upon itself, glad that the weekday was limiting visitors to a smattering of non-local vacationers.

She left her red Prelude between two large dunes that were almost devoid of vegetation. Her mechanical link to the outer world disappeared as she broke a fresh trail in her bare feet. She wound around and over the dunes, trusting that her trail would remain distinctive enough to follow on her return. There was almost no breeze, and the sand had a light crust from rain which must have fallen during the night.

Soon she was alone in the expanse of white gypsum, isolated from sounds of civilization. A few scraggly bushes maintained their tenuous hold among the dunes where nature was burying the flora, but otherwise it was just the sand and her. Above was the sky and God. The sand was already warm, but scooping out a small pit she found it cool to her touch only inches below.

Mary Lou stripped off her blouse and lay back on the gently sloping side of the dune. The sun was warm, and she watched a few fluffy clouds make their way northeastwards above her. She ignored the sand which found its way into her jeans, and scraped out an angel with her arms like she remembered doing as a little girl in the snow.

White Sands was wonderful—a paradise without the fishy smells and sharp shells and rocks of ocean beaches. The flies and insects which normally abounded in the desert were totally absent, and the universe consisted of only sun, sand, wind, and sky. A person could be alone in its beauty like nowhere else, but it was also the best place in the world to make love.

She turned her thoughts to the former UTEP professor who'd introduced her to making love among the dunes a lifetime ago. He had challenged her, stripping off his clothes and daring her to do the same. It was scary initially, and she feared discovery by other visitors or arrest by park rangers. Then they were together, and she had lost herself in the happening. The thrill of being outdoors and element of risk had elevated her sensitivity to unbelievable heights, and she still rated that first time at White Sands as one of her best love-making times ever.

Thinking about those days made her want to run naked through the dunes, but she was an old married lady now of twenty-six. Life had become more serious, and she was no longer impulsive and carefree. She compromised by removing her bra. That felt better. It restored some of her youthful spirit of adventure. Her partial nudity seemed to bare her heart as well as her breasts. She lay exposed in the sand, sharing her body with the elements around her, knowing she belonged, and receiving nature's blessing as her right for belonging.

An intermittent and gentle breeze picked up, softly stroking her bare torso. She tossed handfuls of sand into the air, and the light currents seemed to lift her burdens and carry them away. Even Mac's abuse faded into the next dune and was erased by the all-powerful sands of time. How could anyone be depressed while surrounded by such untainted beauty?

She imagined herself soaring above the dunes, silently, effortlessly, gliding to land in the sand where she currently lay. Then she was a coyote, loping across the dunes, searching and calling for her mate. But who was that?

Not Mac. He could never understand her feelings, how she needed the open space, its life-giving freedom, or how nature and God were one. He was too conventional to make love in public, regardless of how heavenly the setting. She wondered idly if Juan had experienced love in White Sands. Probably not. She'd have to show him what it was all about.

That was a surprising thought. In her mind she was actively considering Juan. She hadn't thought her interest in him was that advanced. Apparently, she had accepted sex with Juan as happening; she just hadn't decided when it would be appropriate. But she was a married woman whose husband was faithful. Breaking his trust would be an irrevocable step, ultimately leading to divorce and a radically altered life. What if that wasn't what she wanted? Once the die was cast, there would be no going back.

The sun warmed her body, sending a subtle reminder of the beauty she possessed and her ability to provide limitless pleasures to her chosen partner and herself. Mary Lou made sand designs on her chest while pondering her feelings, alternating between covering and uncovering her breasts. She was a child of nature, a woman with desires and needs, and it was time to be true to herself.

She had her answer. It had come to her among the dunes. Life had to go on. She had to protect herself and not allow Mac to drag her down into emotional and financial ruin.

Chapter 13

It had been a long week of spending every spare minute on Mary Lou's behalf, but Juan felt intensely satisfied. The poor woman had been a basket case when he first met her, but at her ranch today she was a beautiful, self-assured, and dynamic lady. To a great extent, that was his doing, and he was proud of himself. Although he hadn't seen her in the buff yet, the sexy woman in his purloined photos had re-emerged before his very eyes.

She was drifting his direction, and his best course lay in maintaining his ready availability. Sooner or later, she'd come across. He could afford to wait.

On the afternoon when the mechanic checked out the Ranger, she had taken the first step and given him a hug. The chemistry was there; he had felt it. She'd already accepted him as a friend, and hadn't ruled him out as a lover. A kiss would be next, and its timing would be all-important. Married women always blamed their lovers for leading them astray, but it was the women who actually chose when and where. Mary Lou needed space to select the appropriate time for jumping ship, but he had to be there at the right time to throw her a rope.

The only complication was his current girlfriend.

He was already late for their date that evening. He had promised to take Maria to dinner at the Desert Rose tonight, but time had become his enemy. Maria would think he forgot, but he hadn't. Frankly, he wasn't interested in seeing her. If Mary Lou phoned, he'd head south without hesitation.

Maria was waiting at his apartment when he arrived, obviously piqued over his tardiness.

"Thanks for remembering," Maria said in Spanish.

She stood in the living room and picked up her purse next to the door. Neither made a move to kiss the other. She couldn't make the first gesture without losing her pride, and he wasn't particularly interested in playing kissy-face.

Juan sighed and considered offering some excuse, then realized he didn't care enough to make one up.

"It was a long day," he said.

The woman in front of him was pudgy like himself, with short, fat legs, a dress at least two sizes too small, and heavily made up. For the first time in his life, Juan noticed her over-use of cosmetics, but only because he was comparing her to Mary Lou. Maria was round and jiggly, with heavy breasts he formerly found exciting. Now she looked cheap and vulgar, not at all like someone with whom he wanted to be seen in public. He decided not to bother cleaning up.

She hadn't moved and was waiting for him to say or do something.

"Come on," he ordered. He almost added, "Let's get this over with," as he pushed her out the door.

The dinner did not improve Juan's mood, and he found himself comparing Maria to Mary Lou with every sentence and gesture. She chatted about church in the morning, how she had worked with the priest in arranging a social, why her latest diet wasn't working, and which of her girlfriends was dumping her no-good boyfriend. It was all the inane prattle of a dumb girl who couldn't do anything in her life other than gossip and have kids. She was a totally boring space cadet without even the redeeming characteristic of being pleasant to his eyes.

He looked around at the other Hispanic girls, and discovered they exhibited the same features as Maria. All were wearing too much makeup; their eye shadow and liner gave them garish, vampire-like appearances, their lips were bright red like Marilyn Monroe, and their use of blusher was almost clownish. Most were overweight, with comically short legs and dumpy bodies.

He wondered if he wasn't a stereotype. With dark, wavy hair, the obligatory mustache, and a growing paunch, Juan suddenly realized he looked like any one of a thousand Hispanic policemen sitting there, speaking Spanish with his fat, sleazy girlfriend. Men were judged by the women they kept, and Maria hardly made him look important. He rapidly finished his dinner and hustled her back to his apartment.

Making love promised to be even less exciting than dinner, and he watched Maria disrobe without enthusiasm. She climbed into bed and waited for something to happen, so Juan decided to see if he could maneuver her into performing oral sex. He reversed his position on the bed, but she didn't take the hint. He pushed her head down on his stomach, but that didn't work either. She was hopeless, and he gave up in exasperation.

Anglo girls were supposed to be experts in giving head, going crazy over brown joy sticks. He thought of Mary Lou in Maria's place and felt himself becoming hard. Anglos also liked it from behind according to one of his fellow deputies. That was an idea. He rolled Maria over and assaulted her, keeping his eyes tightly closed and picturing Mary Lou in front of him. He exploded almost immediately.

"Pretty excited, weren't we?" Maria said. She turned to look back at him, and smiled broadly. Evidently, she was proud of her achievement in getting him to finish so quickly.

His image of Mary Lou disappeared, and Maria's loose flesh became almost revolting. He disengaged himself and rolled onto his back. Her attitude disgusted him. She laid her head on his chest while he purposely ignored her.

"I was ready for a piece of ass," he said.

"A piece of ass!" She bolted upright as if stung by a wasp. "Is that what I am? A piece of ass?"

"All women are a piece of ass. Don't take it personal." He dimly realized he was making the situation worse, but really didn't care.

"All women? I'm just like all women? Was that why you were late? All you wanted was a piece of ass from some woman?"

"Don't get your titties in an uproar." Juan made a feeble attempt to talk his way out of trouble. "I didn't mean nothing. It was just an expression."

He reached for her, but Maria batted his arm away and moved to the edge of his bed.

"You make it sound like I'm just good for sex," she said.

"You're more than just sex." Juan wished she'd calm down and either go to sleep or leave. He wondered if she was leaking onto his sheets. He hated scenes like this.

"You know I appreciate you," he said.

"Do you love me?"

God, how had this gotten so far out of hand? Juan thought over his options. He didn't love her, and wasn't going to say so just because she wanted him to say it.

"Let's not ruin a good relationship. If I didn't care about you, you wouldn't be here."

Maria bounded up, quickly strapping on her bra without another glance at the bed. Wordlessly, she gathered her clothes and disappeared into the bathroom. Juan let her go and rolled over to sleep. All too soon she returned fully dressed, and stood beside his bed. He felt the heat of her glare for a long minute and feigned being asleep to avoid further confrontation. Mercifully, Maria left without comment. The slammed door said it all.

He told himself she'd be back. She hadn't left her key, and was probably just throwing one of those manipulating snits girls utilize to get their way. In this case it wouldn't work because he didn't care.

Nothing ventured, nothing gained, and he had no doubt Mary Lou would be a hell of a gain. Her pictures were in his nightstand, and he studied them once again to reassure himself. There was no doubt. She was awesome beyond compare. He fell asleep thinking about that matchless body abusing his.

*****

Almost every day during August, Mary Lou received a visit at the ranch from Deputy Beltran. His attention helped counter Mac's abuse, and his politeness rekindled feelings of self-worth that were destroyed during her hospital visits. He frequently brought something for them to eat, and constantly reminded her that she needed to maintain her health to face the trials and tribulations of coping with her husband. Mary Lou was impressed, particularly since Juan was losing weight. His paunch was visibly smaller, and Mac's nasty comments about "her fat deputy" might not need defending in a month or two.

Juan was obviously smitten by her, and she gradually raised the ante with little familiarities. Touching became commonplace, and he never went away without a hug. Each touch and hug was more significant than the last, and she was sure they both understood a social outing was inevitable and necessary.

When Juan finally broke the ice, she experienced a sense of relief. Since her afternoon at White Sands, Mary Lou knew she wouldn't turn down any reasonable proposal. She had begun to wonder why it was taking so long. After all, he wasn't married.

The invitation was to accompany him to Las Cruces's annual "The Whole Enchilada Festival." It was a weekend event over Labor Day, complete with a cook-off featuring green chili instead of Texas red. This would be the first time together, and it was time for a little fun. She felt no guilt in accepting his invitation. Besides, she could hardly refuse. He had devoted most of the month to her without asking for anything in return.

She suspected a girlfriend was the reason he hadn't made an earlier move. Supposedly, a Mexican male was never without a woman, if not for sex, then to cook and clean. Males stayed home with Mother until time to acquire a wife, then added other women to perform various duties as their financial status permitted. She knew that wasn't totally true because of Mac's two vaqueros, but it did seem fairly common.

Being invited to the festival pretty well ruled out competition from a girlfriend. Now her problem was deciding whether to wear jeans or shorts for the hot Labor Day weekend. Shorts would be more comfortable, but wearing boots made her legs look longer. Not to be forgotten was that the jeans hid her heavy calves. She opted for jeans as the sexier attire, but chose to take a pair of shorts along in case the day became too hot.

She had barely finished exercising the horses when Juan appeared almost twenty minutes early. Mary Lou grinned watching him drive up the road; Mexican males reputedly ran late, but apparently hers was an eager beaver. This time he'd be disappointed. She smelled like a horse and his early arrival would not affect their time of departure.

He waited in the living room while she showered and dressed, and as expected, was a perfect gentleman. He didn't try to take advantage of any stage of undress, and sat patiently on the couch while she blew-dry and combed her shag.

As a reward for Juan's good behavior Mary Lou resolved to be extra sexy. The bra she selected earlier went back into her dresser, and she donned a western-style blouse. It fit loosely and didn't advertise her new bra-less condition, but the three open snaps begged for attention.

She examined herself in the full-length mirror on her bedroom door. Nope, she could do better than that. She pulled the blouse up, then folded and tied it in front like a halter. That left her midsection open, and with her well-shaped torso, made her look positively ravishing. The jeans hung on her hips without showing an ounce of fat, and her belt buckle beckoned like a bull's-eye. There was no way Juan could look at her flat stomach and not be turned on.

She made a grand entrance from the hallway and watched Juan's expression turn instantly from boredom to lust. He licked his lips and bolted to his feet.

"My God, you're a stunning creature!" he blurted.

"Glad you think so," Mary Lou said. She smiled at him but kept her distance. She retrieved her handbag from the kitchen counter to signal her readiness to depart.

Juan moved forward with glazed-over eyes, and Mary Lou imagined the floor shaking from his pounding heart. For a moment, she wondered if she had over-played her hand. He was going to take her to the festival, not get romantic in her own house. She rotated her wedding band several times to draw his attention to its presence. That seemed to work, and Juan stepped backward to open the kitchen door.

She brushed by him lightly going through the door, adding to his discomfort and giving herself a perverse sense of power. Juan reminded her of Tommy in high school. A touch here and there would be all it took.

She waited for him to step outside before turning to close the steel screen gate. "What happened to your mustache?"

Mary Lou had noted its absence immediately, but waited until they were on the patio to comment. She wasn't wild about mustaches when it came to kissing, but beards and mustaches were valuable assets for other activities.

"Shaved it off," Juan said. "Didn't think you liked it. Besides, I wanted to change my image."

"Maybe I should have become a blonde. We could have gone incognito."

Juan looped a hand around her tiny waist and pulled her hip to his. "I like you the way you are." He turned away, but not before she noticed an embarrassing enlargement.

Mary Lou bounced into Juan's car and stretched over to the driver's side to open his door. Somehow everything stayed in place, but she treated him to a show that would raise the dead. Everything was firm and shapely, and the jeans molded her like cling wrap.

Mary Lou didn't look back, but maintained her extended posture while he came around to his side. This was first time they'd be out together, and she wanted to create the impression that she would do for him what he did for her. No Mexican girl would act that way, and it gave her a decided advantage.

On the drive to Cruces she couldn't help becoming animated, keeping up a constant stream of chatter about how happy she was to have a holiday from the hospital and ranch. She was careful to avoid mentioning Mac by name, and tried to keep the conversation on subjects Juan could discuss as well. It was exciting being on a date with someone other than her husband, and Juan wasn't the only one experiencing some nervousness.

She speculated on what she had put in motion. White Sands suddenly seemed light years away. Everything then was academic, but this was reality. Juan probably expected her to put out after the festival, and within a few hours would ask her to be unfaithful to her husband. A response would be required, and it couldn't be a halfway measure like in high school.

Chapter 14

The festival was exciting, and they were like two kids in a candy store. They wandered the open downtown mall and stopped at almost every booth. Mary Lou's bare midriff became a resting place for Juan's hands, and a few minutes later, she slid her hand into one of his hip pockets. She could feel his large gluteus maximus rise and fall as he walked, and it created a sensation of power she found strangely compelling. Mac's rear was small and bony, but as she thought about Juan, she stopped comparing him to Mac. The Mac she knew was gone and would never return.

There was competition in abundance as they saw other women more scantily clad than Mary Lou. In front of the Pic-Quik booth, Juan's attention was diverted by several cute high school girls who practically jiggled out of their halters. Mary Lou gave in to an irrepressible urge and squeezed his buttocks as hard as she could. Juan turned quickly and grinned.

He curled his fingers under her rear and lifted her bodily off the ground. Her blouse came loose as it rubbed against his chest, and she squealed for him to put her down. Plastered on his side, Mary Lou slowly slid earthward while Juan demonstrated his strength almost casually. Her breath quickened as she re-tied her blouse, and she felt a warm sensation below her belly button, thickening and flowing downward. He hadn't even kissed her, and Mary Lou's face flushed from the realization that her body was reacting to his with unmistakable signals. She kept her hand out of his pocket while she regained her composure.

They continued down the mall, but Mary Lou's mind was no longer focused on the booths, games or food. She wanted Juan to take possession of what could be his, and the sooner he claimed it the better.

Nature came to her aid with an unrelenting New Mexico sun. Juan suggested they relax in his air-conditioned apartment until the nighttime festivities and dancing began. She squeezed his waist in agreement, and Juan needed no further encouragement to steer her to his car. His proposal had come not a moment too soon. Her skin was beginning to toast in its own dried perspiration, and her arms were gritty from a light layer of salt.

His apartment was near New Mexico State, a five-minute drive from the festival. Mary Lou was relieved to discover he lived in a modern complex with full facilities. She had feared he lived in a traditional Mexican strip-type apartment building, one that looked like a motel with double rooms. These digs were vastly superior.

Even more comforting was the apartment's sheltered access. Located on the second floor of a two-story stucco structure, its entrance was surprisingly private in a covered, four-unit staircase. The doorway was not visible from the street, and Mary Lou was thankful her presence could be well-hidden from prying eyes. Regardless of her actions in private, she was not prepared to make a public statement.

The quick tour he gave her was patently superfluous. She could stand in the middle of Juan's living room and see into the other rooms without difficulty. The combination living and dining room was larger than expected, and Juan's small balcony looked out over the complex's inner courtyard. She half-expected to find a water bed in the large bedroom, but Juan explained they weren't allowed in second-floor apartments.

His double-sized platform bed looked small in comparison to Juan's bulk. Mary Lou gazed at the black and white checkered bedspread, and wondered if he used it to play chess. The bed was solidly constructed and firm, and she imagined it as a throne or sacrificial altar. Paying obeisance on a throne wasn't her thing, but being sacrificed might be fun. She shook her head at entertaining such weird thoughts, and excused herself to freshen up in Juan's bathroom while he prepared iced tea.

She quickly rinsed the salt off her arms, and shedding her jeans, carefully washed those parts she wanted squeaky clean. She laid her nylon socks over a towel rack and stood on Juan's bathroom tile wearing only her blouse. It felt wonderfully cool and sexy, and with her panties damp from the hot day, Mary Lou decided shorts alone would be sufficient. Rubbing her legs to eliminate stocking marks, she became acutely cognizant of wearing only two light garments. Unencumbered but properly attired, Mary Lou was well satisfied with her appearance. She returned to Juan's living room and stretched out on his sofa.

She ruffled the sofa's peach-colored fabric with her hand. It was unusual for a man to buy anything peach. It was a woman's color, and Mary Lou assumed Juan had inherited the furniture from his ex-wife. The rest of his apartment was early harassed bachelor, strictly utilitarian for someone who spent little time at home.

Suddenly she remembered another female might have a prior claim on Juan and this space. She hadn't noticed feminine items in his bathroom, but she hadn't looked for them either. Piqued at her failure to be observant for things which indicated relationships or personality quirks, she jumped up to go back and check out his bathroom.

Juan stopped her as he entered with the iced tea.

"You look cool." He handed her a tall glass and smiled as if seeing her for the first time.

Mary Lou suppressed her suspicions and sat down. Only three cubes of ice were in the large glass, and she presumed Juan had forgotten to keep his freezer stocked. She took a quick drink of her tea, then set it on the heavy coffee table. She patted the sofa and wondered what it would take before he would kiss her.

He didn't take her hint, and remained in front of her like a statue, staring at her shorts. With a glance, she realized they were sufficiently loose to be playing peek-a-boo in his line of sight. Enough was enough. Looking was fine, but she had other needs. She stood up and pulled him down onto the couch.

"Time for us both to get cool," she said. Her voice was husky as she leaned over and tugged at his belt buckle.

Juan grabbed her face in his meaty paws and smothered it with kisses. Mary Lou lost her grip on his buckle and fell forward. He wrapped his arms around her and pressed her into his chest as he leaned backward on the couch. His mountainous bulk took her breath away.

Struggling to maintain her balance, she pushed herself up and began unbuttoning his shirt. Her blouse unraveled of its own accord, and Juan sat up to reach her boobs. He fastened onto her like a remora, and she twisted sideways to push him back onto the cushions. Mary Lou yanked his belt apart in an unseemly frenzy and tore at his fly. Within seconds everything was exposed and she bent down to take control of his body.

The aroma that greeted her was distinctly non-hygienic, and Mary Lou recoiled at the repugnant odor. She had forgotten to allow him time to wash up. The day had been hot, and Juan's beer drinking had caused him to make several pit stops on the mall. She jumped up and suggested they take a shower together.

He peeled off his clothes, and chased her into the bathroom in his birthday suit. Within moments, he was nailing her against the tiled wall, with lukewarm water going everywhere. It was incredibly sexy.

All too soon it was over. He would need more training than anticipated, but she wasn't disappointed. She had done it. The ice had been broken. She was once again a woman controlling her own destiny, able to command men if she desired.

She led Juan into his bedroom.

By nine he was worn out, and Mary Lou knew it was time to leave. Mac might call home, and she needed to be there. She turned to the dozing form beside her. His skin was extremely dark in contrast to hers, and in the dim light, it was difficult to see his features. Her other men had been light-skinned like Mac, and somehow this seemed unnatural. Juan was darker than some blacks in El Paso, and she could well imagine Mac's reaction to her affair. He'd surely kill them both if he saw them together like this.

Her agreeing to accompany Juan to the festival was risky in itself, and the probability she'd encounter some friends in the crowd had been high. But she had run into nobody she recognized. The weirdest thing about her day was that she felt both relieved and guilty. She didn't want to dwell on it, but her guilt undoubtedly came from cheating on Mac and the relief from not getting caught.

It had been an important day, but not quite the momentous event she expected. For Juan, her presence had greatly increased his stature, and he obviously reveled in having her by his side. Of course, the sex was undoubtedly the best he'd ever experienced. Mexican girls couldn't compete with her. After tonight, he'd never be satisfied with a brown chick again.

For herself, she wasn't sure an encore was necessary or desirable. Her curiosity concerning Mexicans had been satisfied, and she felt no need to pursue that issue further. There were cultural differences which could not be overlooked, and training a lover didn't interest her. She had done what she needed to do, and nothing could be undone. On that score Mary Lou had no regrets, but it didn't have to be done again.

Juan's bulk—actually fat—was a problem. He was seventy to a hundred pounds overweight, mostly concentrated in his broad rear end and spare tire. Several times he had let his full weight rest on her, and she was forced to push him off to breathe.

She shook his member to awaken him. "Time for me to head home," she said.

Juan opened his eyes and groaned. He reached for her, but she resisted.

"It's too late, and I'm too tired," he said.

Mary Lou was taken aback by his cavalier attitude. She couldn't imagine a man refusing to take his date home, especially when he had just enjoyed her in bed.

"You want to see me again, don't you?" she said.

Juan nodded.

"Then take me home. We don't want my husband to shoot me on our first outing."

She looked down at the wedding band she hadn't taken off. The ring signified her marital status. With effort, she pulled Juan into a sitting position and pointed at her ring.

"Remember, this is still here."

"Yeah," he said. "I noticed it watching. It really enjoyed seeing me inside you."

His words touched a nerve, but it was time to act instead of argue. She jumped off the bed and stepped into her shorts without further comment. In less than a minute, she was ready to leave and stood by the door to pressure Juan into action. He didn't move, and she stamped her foot for emphasis.

That did it. He reached for his pants and began making progress. He used the bathroom, but did not keep her waiting.

The trip back was spanned with desultory conversation, mostly about the festival and booths of artwork and gifts. During the quiet times, Mary Lou decided this might be a one-night stand. If he didn't contact her again, she wouldn't consider it a tragic loss. Their differences were simply too many.

He stopped in front of her kitchen door, and leaned over with a kiss. It was not the most passionate of kisses. She got out of the car, unlocked the gate, then returned and leaned through her window.

"Thank you for a lovely day and an even better evening," she said. "I enjoyed absolutely everything."

Before he could reply she turned and vanished into her house. What she hadn't said was that they should do it again.

Chapter 15

The mystery of the fenced-in property baffled Stuart and his usual sources of information in the sheriff's office and among county developers. Castillo wasn't a household name, and he wasn't involved with any of Stuart's friends in real estate. He was a "Mexican only" attorney, and not native to the area. Feelers were out, but Stuart doubted he'd gain much information without a direct approach.

With respect to Mac's incident, the trail was ice cold. It wasn't until six days after the accident that Stuart had checked the crash site, and by then, whatever critical evidence had been present was lost in the wind and sand. To a large degree Stuart felt he had let Mac down. He should have talked to Beltran and obtained the police report as soon as it was filed, then checked the site himself the first day. Such swift action was hardly indicated in the absence of suspected foul play, but in hindsight he should have done it anyway.

He had examined the Ranger and surrounding area, partly to placate Mac, but also to satisfy his own curiosity. He still hadn't interviewed Beltran, but the deputy's accident report appeared professional, complete and thorough. It left little room for disagreement, particularly with respect to Mac's charge of attempted murder. The only thing supporting Mac's account was that someone had turned off the Ranger's lights before Mary Lou arrived.

At first Stuart had assumed Mac was drunk when the accident occurred, but hearing Mac's story changed his mind. He had seen for himself that Mac left the chili cook-off relatively sober—at least in comparison to him. Then Mary Lou had said Mac didn't drink on the way home. If he wasn't drunk, it must have been something else. Mac knew the roads on his ranch and wouldn't be likely to flip his pickup for no reason. Then someone had turned off the lights. So Mac was right, but what did Mac know or possess that marked him for extinction?

The only thing Mac said was that Mexicans were using Bar-D range as a highway for bringing wetbacks into the US. This wasn't extraordinary or even news—crossings occurred almost daily on well-situated ranches, and Mac's extended from a stretch along the border to the Rio Grande valley. Wetbacks could turn west toward the Columbus-Deming highway or east toward the valley, and Mac's ranch was one of a half-dozen that afforded ready access eastwards. The valley was a natural route northward to Las Cruces, and from there, illegals could go north to Albuquerque, east to Alamogordo, or west to Tucson. Most importantly, Highway 70 heading east was uncontrolled. It was a hole in the border patrol's defenses. All the other high-speed routes from El Paso and Las Cruces featured border control checkpoints.

At The Whole Enchilada Festival Stuart sat with Mac's chili partner, Norm, in the Budweiser booth with Norm's current girlfriend, Mona, and ex-girlfriend, Gloria. Gloria was responsible for introducing Mona to Norm, apparently with a replacement waiting. In no time at all, the two girls teamed up to give Norm a hard time about mistreating women. They contended he never did anything for a woman without expecting something in return.

"That's pretty good talk from a couple of split-tails," Norm said. "All you do is move money from one man to another."

Stuart was surprised. Norm was normally so laid-back that his usual posture was supine.

"What is this? Are you better than us because you dangle instead of wiggle?" Mona asked. The band's music was catching, and she was keeping time with her head. Both girls seemed more amused than affronted by Norm's comment.

"No offense, but women are nothing but transfer mechanisms," Norm said. "They transfer funds from one male to another, or from males to their kids. The traditional wife manipulates her husband into being a good provider, then transfers his earnings into benefits for her children. A hooker takes money from a john and gives it to her pimp. Whether or not he rebates enough to meet her needs is totally irrelevant."

Norm directed his last remarks at Gloria, and Stuart found himself wondering about Gloria's history. She looked a little shopworn for her age, but redheads normally got leathery skin in their twenties. Thereafter, they looked ten years older than their actual age, and got ridden hard and put away wet. He guessed she was nearing thirty, but knew only that she was a single parent without benefit of clergy.

"I think you've smoked too much grass," Gloria said.

No one was taking Norm seriously. Stuart wondered if that was because of what Norm was saying or because of Norm himself. The message was often only as important as the messenger.

"No, really," Norm said. "I've had a woman put the bite on me even though a man was home supposedly taking care of her. She was transferring my funds into her household for the benefit of her kids and male partner. For all women, men are either givers or receivers of resource transfers. There's no middle ground."

"So we're evil," Gloria said. "Yet you sleep with us."

"Don't get me wrong, I'm not saying that's bad. Food's got to be transferred to children to ensure the survival of our species. It's only when women confuse men with children that it gets out of hand. You know, like in maternalistic societies. Mexicans and blacks, for instance."

Mona unwound herself from her chair and sauntered away to the bar. Stuart waited for a riposte, but even Gloria seemed startled and reflective. Mona came back holding two bottles of Bud. She went into an exaggerated Playboy bunny pose and slammed a beer down in front of Norm.

"Here! From old split-tail Mona, not from any man. Drink up so you can transfer whatever little you've got."

Thinking about what he had seen a few minutes earlier reminded Stuart that Norm's theory wasn't all wrong. Mary Lou wasn't transferring assets to her children, but switching Mac's property to another man. He had seen her hanging on some big Mexican's arm. She was showing off her possession of the macho mother like a five-dollar whore.

Mary Lou and her lover had frolicked openly with each other's bodies like dogs in heat. She didn't see Stuart sitting in the large Coors' tent with several acquaintances, but her behavior dominated his table's topic of conversation while she was in sight. Stuart's companions weren't acquainted with either Mac or his errant spouse, and their ribald condemnation of the stunning Anglo chick servicing the ugly Mexican ruined his afternoon. Then Mary Lou and her cuckolding fat farm reject weren't at the evening events, and that made things even worse. No doubt the brown banger was playing three-hole golf on Mary Lou's private course.

Damaging as her actions were to Mac, she had put Stuart in an embarrassing and untenable position. One could hardly be expected to condone such a public display of affection by his best friend's wife for another man. Especially not when that best friend was in a hospital fighting for his life. In olden days, Stuart would have been expected to wreak vengeance on the miscreants and defend his friend's honor. Supposedly times had changed, but not all that much. If Stuart didn't defend Mac's honor, then his own honor and reputation would be stained.

In the area's culture, a wife's duty was to bear children for her husband and be their mother. Husbands could have whores and mistresses, but not the other way around. A single woman was a failure in life for not having found a man, but much worse was a married woman trafficking with other men. She was a whore, pure and simple.

Stuart needed to determine the Mexican's identity and the extent of the relationship. If her affair was of long standing, she might have paid someone to kill Mac. Mary Lou might be thinking she could run the ranch better than Mac, or maybe she had a buyer. All things were possible. And he couldn't tell Mac.

*****

Although the vast majority of Stuart's property was located in the Rio Grande valley between El Paso and Las Cruces, he had engaged in desert speculation beyond the western boundaries of the Bar-D. The two properties included small wells for non-agricultural uses, and like Mac, he was betting on obtaining permits to sink wells for irrigation. It was a crap shoot given the El Paso suit over water rights, but wineries and jojoba producers were interested in moving down the Columbus highway if good Deming water could be made available.

The most direct route to his parcels led through Mac's ranch, and Stuart used the excuse of visiting his properties to start driving the county road each evening after supper. There was only an off-hand chance he might see something out of the ordinary, but the road passed close to the ranch house, and unusual activities would be readily visible.

On his third trip Stuart got lucky. Mary Lou's festival escort passed him driving a Doña Ana County sheriff's cruiser, and there was no mistaking his identification. The cruiser turned into the Bar-D's access road, and was still parked behind the house when Stuart sped by on his return trip.

Already suspecting the answer, Stuart phoned his contact Jed Akers in the sheriff's office. Confirmation was immediate. Jed said Deputy Beltran was a sloppy six feet one and well over two hundred and sixty pounds.

Mac was in trouble. The deputy was drilling his wife, and the only question was the fat Mexican's depth of involvement in Mac's accident. Beltran easily could have erased evidence of another vehicle's involvement during his investigation. Stuart's own puny inquiry was doomed from the outset. It looked to Stuart like Mary Lou and her lover were making fools out of both Mac and himself, and he didn't like it. Well, if Stuart couldn't touch Mary Lou without hurting Mac, Deputy Beltran presented him with no such problem.

The following day, he met Jed for lunch at Tegemeyer's Salad Bar. Located on Lohman Avenue and arguably the best luncheon restaurant in Las Cruces, Tegemeyer's was normally crowded at noontime. Stuart arrived before eleven thirty to obtain a good table.

He was in luck. On the right side, a table beckoned with a modicum of privacy. The owner guided Stuart to his seat, and he'd just re-arranged the table when Deputy Akers walked through the front door. Like most of Stuart's friends, he was an Anglo and had known Stuart since childhood.

They quickly filled their plates at the extensive buffet, both men stocking up on the blueberry rolls and soup. Two large glasses of unsweetened iced tea were waiting when they returned, and Stuart allowed the conversation to drift while they ate.

Jed was about Mac's height, but filled out with a typically western paunch. He walked a little bow-legged and talked like a cowboy, but Stuart had never seen him ride a horse. Actually, no one would guess Jed as anything but a law enforcement officer. He was the quintessential cop, with wavy dark hair, brown eyes, and scars from a severe case of adolescent acne.

Stuart ended the local gossip and small talk in his usual oblique fashion. "You really ought to move south of Route 10," he said.

Deputy Akers blinked. "Why's that?"

"There's good land available. With the construction slump, you should be able to build something pretty nice for reasonable bucks."

"You got a line on a good lot?"

"More than that." Stuart lowered his voice. "I'm negotiating for a forty-five acre parcel, about half of which is in pecan trees. If you'd like a lot—say an acre or two—that could certainly be arranged."

"Not sure I could afford it on a deputy's salary. You're a heavy hitter; I'm not."

Stuart let the conversation lapse for a moment to let the possibilities sink in. Like Stuart, Jed had grown up in Anthony, but unlike Stuart, Jed was born into a poor family. He tried attending UTEP, then known as Texas Western, but college hadn't suited him. Two enlistments in the MPs had convinced him that law enforcement suited him better. He returned to find a home in the Doña Ana County sheriff's department, a relatively low-key organization only recently becoming modernized and facing current law-enforcement issues.

Then Jed found himself a pretty little Anglo girl from White Oaks. She was a dyed-in-the-wool New Mexican, at home in the mountains as well as the desert. Her dad had been a miner, scraping by on prodigious effort and futile hopes. Growing up without amenities like food and indoor plumbing had hardened her, and the two deserved a little sunshine in their lives.

"No problem. I happen to need some security help, and would be willing to trade the land for some of your time."

Jed's interest picked up immediately. "Sounds good, but I'm still not sure I could swing a house."

"I'd be willing to help. After all, what are friends for?" Stuart smiled discretely, hoping he wasn't coming on too strong.

"Now I'm worried. Sounds like you need something from the sheriff's department. Something pretty bad."

"Nothing that wouldn't occur anyway. I'd just like to speed it up."

Jed chuckled. "Like getting a new sheriff elected?"

Stuart shook his head. "No. I don't want to see someone get in; I want to see someone get out. What do you think of Juan Beltran?"

"Juan? Just a run-of-the-mill Mexican. No great shakes, but seems to do his job. Maybe a little slower than most, but that's the way those guys are."

"Ever been in trouble? Drugs, girls, on the take?"

"Not that I know of. He's not that bright, and not the type to get it up more than once a week. Might have gotten a little *mordida* from the Anapra crowd to look the other way, but it would've been small potatoes. I think he moonlights at the track in Sunland Park, but that doesn't mean anything. Hell, everybody likes horse racing."

"I think he's dirty. How difficult is it to get somebody like that bounced out on his ass?"

"It'd be easier if he wasn't Mexican. They're in court the minute after being fired yelling discrimination. If you have some irrefutable evidence, though, it might be a tube shot."

"Unfortunately, I don't. But I want him out. And without a pension or bullshit recommendation so he can get another job in law enforcement." Stuart leaned forward for emphasis. "Can you do it?"

Jed bowed his head. A minute passed. "Probably. He could be set up with drugs or caught falsifying his expenses. Everyone does that to some extent, but Mexican deputies are the worst abusers. Particularly with overtime. They put in for it, but dog the time to bang their girlfriends. An investigation of his on-duty activities might be all that's needed."

"Well, let's put it this way—the day he's fired is when your lot is totally paid off. And I'll still help with your home mortgage."

Jed extended his hand and grinned. "Better start drawing up the papers."

Chapter 16

The Whole Enchilada Festival put events into motion like a winter avalanche, claiming all those in its path, and altering the landscape forever. On Sunday, Mary Lou was particularly solicitous during her two hospital visits with Mac, staying extra to make up for the time she missed the previous day. Mac didn't ask what she did during Saturday afternoon or evening, and she didn't have to make up a story. Oddly enough, Juan didn't call while she was home, and Mary Lou began to wonder if he was no longer interested. She told herself he might have only wanted to score, and she had made it too easy.

On Monday, her life went to hell in a hand basket. The day was a scorcher, and she wore shorts to the hospital. Mac became a raving maniac, swearing at her for wearing shorts and giving the Mexican rabble a show. Mary Lou endured his outburst in silence, initially thinking he knew about Juan and the festival. When he began repeating himself, she realized his rants were normal fare. She bit her lip to avoid saying one particular Mexican got a lot more than a show on Saturday. He got the whole enchilada, but she kept those words to herself.

Stuart arrived in late afternoon, and his demeanor wasn't much better than Mac's. For some reason he treated her like a dead plant, never once offering a kind word or including her in his conversation. Mac became doubly malicious in front of an active accomplice, and the two ganged up on her until she left. Stuart was probably having problems again with Ermie, but that didn't mean he had to take it out on her.

At suppertime, the pump broke down on her deep well. She worked two hours with Jose, the older of her vaqueros, in a futile attempt at repair. Mechanical equipment was not her forte, and this was something Mac handled earlier. In total frustration and desiring a shower above all else, she paid a mechanic one hundred and forty-two dollars to come from El Paso and fix the damn pump. It was money she couldn't afford, but she got her shower before going to bed. And Juan didn't phone that day either.

It didn't seem possible things could get worse on Tuesday, but they did. Both Mac and Stuart continued their rancor at Providence during the morning, and Mary Lou almost didn't return in the afternoon. This time Mac berated her about the pump and how worthless she was without him. As his headache increased in intensity Mac brought up "her" deputy, attacking him for his incompetence. Mac's assault was devastating, especially considering her dejection over Juan's lack of communication.

When Mac ranted about Juan probably spending all his time getting his ashes hauled by diseased Mexican whores, she began to feel ill. She tried to change the subject, but Mac was on a roll and taking feral delight in her discomfort. The crowning blow came when Mac's headache triggered his own nausea. Mary Lou struggled to help him reach a basin, but he lost control and heaved unexpectedly on her shoulder. With unerring accuracy the vile-smelling vomit coated her hair and plunged inside her blouse, pooling at her waist. Her attempt to clean herself in Mac's bathroom fell far short of satisfactory, and she fled for the sanctuary of her home.

She yelled and screamed at Mac in the confines of her Honda all the way back to the ranch. For three days she had endured Mac without a word from Juan, and her patience was nearly exhausted. She stripped off her odious clothes in the laundry room and marched straight into the shower.

Twenty minutes of scalding water cleansed her body, but there was no palliative for her soul. She rubbed herself pink, and angrily stomped around the house in her birthday suit. All men were bastards, but Mac most of all.

Her father had never hurt her so badly as Mac. Her emotions raged out of control as she stood in the bedroom, unable to decide what to do next. A man, that's what she wanted. She'd head for a honky-tonk, get drunk, and pick up some guy. She turned toward El Paso and shook her fist in the air.

"Bastard!" she yelled. "You rotten bastard! The first man I see, I'm gonna fuck his brains out!"

As her voice reverberated throughout the house someone knocked on her back door.

Mary Lou would have jumped out of her panties if she were wearing any.

The knocking came again.

Stunned that she wasn't alone, Mary Lou started to retrieve a robe from her closet, then decided against it. Her pulse throbbed like her diesel pump, and her ears reddened from the heat. She crept silently into the kitchen and cautiously peeked out. A bolt of lightning had struck! Juan was standing on her patio, patiently waiting for her to open the door! God was daring her to make good on her statement!

She hid behind the door, opening it slowly as if it was moving by itself. It seemed like an eternity before Juan stepped into the house and peered around to find her. Naked and still pink from her hot shower, Mary Lou grinned evilly while she latched the door behind him. Juan stood motionless as if struck dumb by the sight of her.

Silently, and without so much as a kiss to say hello, she unbuttoned his fly. That brought a reaction, and he started to caress her body. Immediately, she grabbed his cock and pulled him into her bedroom. She allowed him no chance to undress.

A sense of unbelievable relief flooded over her as she shuddered under his vicious hammering. She felt herself about to pass out. She was amazed that she didn't.

It was over too quickly. She wanted to cry in frustration, but that wouldn't do any good. She undressed Juan while he rested, barely able to control her discordant symphony of emotions. Her heart pounded with an unsettling nervousness. There was unfinished business at hand.

She pulled Juan off the bed and made love to him in every room and place she remembered doing it with Mac. Like an animal, she marked her territory. Every trace of Mac's sexual turf was obliterated. The house became her possession, her exclusive realm of control. The power flowed from inside her, relieving her own frustration multiple times, and engulfing poor Juan in its heat and strength. He finally begged her to stop and give him a time out.

Lying on her bed, Mary Lou reflected on the turn of events and her own impulsive actions. The timing was too perfect. It wasn't her, it was God who caused all this to happen.

Her lover snored beside her, sleeping soundly after his exhausting activities. He could probably fall asleep flying an airplane, and she didn't take it personally. He simply had limited energy, whether due to being heavy or Mexican or both.

Mary Lou looked at the portraits of herself and Mac on the dresser, suddenly feeling closed in and oppressed. She remembered the ranch hands, and shook Juan awake to send him home. She was still a married woman, and a certain amount of decorum was necessary. It was hardly appropriate to announce her freedom through vaquero gossip by letting Juan spend the night. She felt a little hypocritical, but Juan had to leave.

He objected, but she insisted in no uncertain terms. She helped him dress, and pushed him out the door when he hesitated at the threshold. Earlier, she had been Mac's woman, but now she belonged to herself.

Without regret she watched him drive away, the dust from his cruiser visible in the bright moonlight. The night was cooling, and she shivered on the terra cotta tiles. Goosebumps appeared on her nude body, but there was no guilt. Not this time. She noticed the pungent odor of sex lingering in her bedroom, and felt intensely satisfied and invigorated. She refrained from washing.

The telephone woke her in the morning quiet. The sun was high in the window, and Mary Lou realized the day was well along. Her caller was Juan. He wanted to tell her how much he enjoyed the previous evening. She invited him down for lunch.

The next two hours were spent in cleaning her house and rendering herself immaculate beyond conception. She applied her best skin freshener and put on a single garment, a modest sundress with nothing underneath. As noon approached, she felt herself dampening in anticipation. Just like in the early days with Mac, only better because it was now.

She greeted Juan with a passionate kiss, and found herself being carried into the bedroom. For the first time, she experienced him being the aggressor. Her dress disappeared over her head, and she lay back to be pleasured.

Within seconds she felt his raw heat slamming into her as he yelled that he was coming. Suddenly, that was met by a convulsion of her own, a spasm as if something had torn away. She had ovulated, but it was more than that. Her eyes opened wide in the certain knowledge that she had just conceived, and a moment later, Juan collapsed on top of her.

She started to push him from her, but her arms and legs refused to move. She lay quietly under his bulk. A feeling of indescribable calm overwhelmed her as his breathing returned to normal.

Juan withdrew and studied her, apparently surprised at seeing her almost catatonic.

She ignored him, staring at the ceiling as if totally indifferent to his presence.

"Was it good?" he asked.

Mary Lou looked at Juan as though he had asked if she were alive. "Better than good."

His face brightened immediately, and he pushed himself up and off her bed. "Well, how about lunch?"

She remained motionless on the bed, spread-eagled, feeling carnal and lewd. She stared at Juan without speaking, wishing he would cover her nakedness with a sheet.

He pushed her legs together, and pulled her into a sitting position. "Come on. How about it?"

Mary Lou nodded and slowly swung her feet onto the floor. She wasn't supposed to be able to get pregnant, but it had happened. There was no doubt in her mind. Most women didn't know they were pregnant for weeks and months, but already she felt different.

Gingerly she stood up, then walked to her dresser as if treading on crushed glass. She selected a pair of beige panties, and carefully stepped into them before retrieving her sundress. By the time she finished dressing, Juan was already in the kitchen rummaging through her refrigerator.

The man had done his damage and was seeking his reward. He knocked her up, and she had to feed him. Preoccupied, she mechanically made sandwiches from the turkey slices he selected. The world had turned upside-down. On the one hand, she wanted to scream and chase Juan from the house, on the other, she wanted him to kiss her, hold her tightly, and whisper that everything would be all right. Neither happened. Instead, Juan left immediately on a call.

Her afternoon visit to the hospital took on an added dimension as she listened to Mac complain about the doctors, the food, and everything else. She noticed the lack of rancor in his tone, a clear sign he was getting better. But her attention was concentrated on the growing life within her and the enormity of the changes her noontime activity had wrought. She listened to Mac, but could still feel Juan pulsing within her. She resisted the constant urge to check her crotch for wetness, not wanting to draw Mac's attention to her body.

Mercifully, the doctors had scheduled tests for late afternoon, and Mary Lou took the first opportunity to escape. Stuart arrived, and started talking about government waste in the county without Mac becoming irrational or abusive. The pressure on Mac's brain was lessening, and one doctor thought he might approach normalcy after several months of concentrated therapy. Mac preferred talking to Stuart, and her departure went almost unnoticed.

For the next two days, Mary Lou avoided Juan, limiting her contact with him to telephone conversations. Time was required to focus on her growing dilemma, and assuming control over her life was paramount.

The growing life within her pressed for a decision. There were only two options as she saw the situation; becoming a single parent, or including Juan in her life. In the latter case, it was important to know Juan's intentions, and she didn't know where he stood. It was probably too early for him to know himself, but at least she could test him for faithfulness. After telling Juan she was tied up for the evening, she waited two hours, then drove to his apartment.

It was a plunge off the deep end, and Mary Lou was half-hoping to catch Juan with another woman. Then her decision would be easy, and she could terminate her affair without being the guilty party. But Juan was at home, watching baseball on TV to pass the time. She stayed the night, and then adopted the habit of driving straight to Juan's apartment after visiting Mac during evening hours.

They had a great deal to discuss, but Mary Lou kept her pregnancy to herself. Juan was fairly traditional, a Catholic who would require her to convert, and a man who expected a woman's career to be strictly secondary. When she mentioned that she was completing her education, he reacted as if threatened by the prospect of her becoming a college graduate. In comparison, Mac had not objected to her taking courses at NMSU.

Sex was pleasant but not compelling, as Juan had little stamina and fell asleep soon after he finished. There was no afterglow to be shared, indeed, there was no sharing at all. She was just a sexual object.

The data indicated the affair to be less than promising, and Mary Lou leased an apartment about a mile from Juan's. She moved her belongings to Cruces without Juan's help, and furnished the one-bedroom flat from floor stock at Las Cruces Furniture. She didn't want Mac to say she took anything from him other than herself. Nor did she want to move directly from one man to another.

Chapter 17

Mac made steady progress during September, and was soon ready to be discharged. Since Labor Day weekend, Stuart had spent almost as many hours visiting at Providence as Mary Lou, and he volunteered to drive Mac back home. Mary Lou wasn't sure why Stuart made the offer, but it didn't fit into her plans.

Stuart's hostility toward her was still evident, and she suspected somebody in Cruces had told him of her involvement with another man. Rumors were probably floating around, but there couldn't be anyone professing firsthand knowledge. Other than at the festival and those two times at the Bar-D, she and Juan had been absolutely discrete. Since their affair started, they had not been out in public together even for lunch, and Mary Lou doubted more than one or two of Juan's apartment neighbors had seen her at his complex.

Pursuing an affair while married was taxing, but Mary Lou was learning the ropes. Having a husband immobilized in a hospital helped a great deal, and one of her former New Mexico State classmates educated her in the finer points of discretion. She had been having a relationship with a man for over a year, and her husband didn't suspect a thing. Mary Lou wasn't particularly devious, but understood why caution was necessary. Stuart, for one, knew just about everyone in the county.

The Providence neurologists counseled Mary Lou that stability for Mac was a long way off, but she listened only out of courtesy. They had done a miraculous job saving Mac's life, and deserved every dollar they billed. She couldn't pay them, of course, but they didn't know that yet. With luck, she might be able to avoid paying them altogether through a divorce settlement, but that would be up to the lawyers. Of more immediate importance was Mac's current condition. He was still subject to episodes of violence and rage, and the doctors warned her to protect Mac from becoming unduly excited. In some respects, they were placing an unexploded bomb back on the streets, and were naturally concerned with their potential liability. Time might defuse it if given a chance, but nothing was certain.

When Mary Lou asked for their best guess when Mac would approach his former rationality, the doctors demurred over giving a specific prediction. One frankly didn't expect Mac to ever heal completely, and the other said it could be months or years. Both were amazed Mac was recovering so rapidly, but relapses and problems with mental instability were likely in future months. Again, they cautioned Mary Lou to make Mac's next few months as free from stress as possible.

The situation would have been laughable if it wasn't so tragic. His doctors counseled freedom from stress, but Mary Lou was leaving Mac's life forever upon his return home. It seemed especially cruel, but there was no assurance Mac would be able to cope better with her departure at a later date. Delaying her action would only put her life on hold and increase her exposure to bankruptcy from Mac's medical expenses.

There wasn't any choice in Mary Lou's mind, but she did owe Mac the courtesy of taking him to his ranch and telling him face-to-face. She thanked Stuart for his offer to drive Mac home, but insisted on doing it herself. Mac was still moving gingerly, so Stuart carried Mac's luggage while Mary Lou helped him into the car.

She closed Mac's door and turned to Stuart.

"Why don't you come over in an hour or so?" Mary Lou said.

Stuart frowned and didn't respond.

"Seriously," she said. "It'll make Mac feel more at ease on his first night back."

Mary Lou pressed Stuart's hand, pleading non-verbally for his understanding and acceptance of her invitation.

Stuart clearly didn't understand why he was being invited, and she couldn't tell him.

"I don't know. You two have a lot to talk about."

"Not tonight. It'll be better if Mac has other people around." Mary Lou looked at Stuart as if wanting to say something but not knowing how. "Please, do me a favor. And for Mac, too. It's important."

Finally he weakened. "Okay," he said.

Mary Lou got in her car and rolled her window down. "In an hour, then."

The drive home promised to be eventful, but Mary Lou concentrated on the rush hour traffic rather than Mac's presence. He talked about hospital costs and the financially strapped times they had ahead of them. Not wanting to jostle Mac more than necessary, she drove carefully and slower than usual. Passing through La Union, he seemed to remember the fire department cook-off and remarked how nice she'd looked in her pink and white dress.

"I'll bet you missed me at home," he said.

"It was quiet there without you." She let her statement stand without enhancement or clarification.

Suddenly Mac ran his hand up under her dress, rubbing the inside of her right thigh with a surprising show of strength and dexterity. Lengthening an upwards stroke, he touched what was no longer his to touch.

Mary Lou squirmed slightly and caught her breath. His touch was like an electric shock, but she maintained her composure. She neither opened nor closed her legs, and purposely allowed him to continue without responding.

"Now's not a good time," she said.

She kept her eyes on the road and ignored his hand. Her usual dampness was absent, a condition that Mac couldn't help but notice. As expected, he withdrew his hand, apparently accepting her implication that it was the wrong time of the month.

"Sorry. I didn't mean for my timing to be so bad," he said. "It's been a long time, and you look ravishing."

"You're supposed to rest and avoid excitement."

"I was supposed to die, too," he said.

And I wasn't supposed to get pregnant. That's how much doctors know.

The conversation returned to ranch business, and Mary Lou was thankful Mac behaved for the remainder of the trip. Her nervousness increased exponentially as they neared the house, and she hoped Mac's concern for his own problems prevented him from noticing. The moment of truth was fast approaching.

She circled in the rear garage area to put Mac's side nearest the kitchen door and face outward down the driveway. Leaving Mac on his own, Mary Lou hurriedly carried his suitcase into their bedroom. She returned to find Mac ensconced in his favorite leather chair, obviously pleased to be home. She popped open a Coors and placed it beside him before he had time to think about being thirsty. He downed his first gulp of cool suds in almost two months while she stood in the open entryway to the kitchen. The rear door was still ajar behind her.

"I've made arrangements for Helene Perrigo, a registered nurse, to look in on you twice a day for the next three weeks," she said. Her heart was pounding, expecting a violent outburst which might end in injury to one or both of them.

"Why? I don't need a nurse. Where will you be?"

His quizzical expression showed he hadn't yet guessed her intentions. The living room looked exactly the same as before his accident, and he had not seen the bedroom and noticed that her belongings were missing.

"I won't be here," she said. She kept her voice even, somewhere between sweet and cold.

"Where will you be?" he asked again. Mac still hadn't grasped the obvious and was apparently expecting her to say her mother was ill or something.

Mary Lou took a deep breath. "I've taken an apartment in Las Cruces. I'm leaving you. It's best this way."

"Best? Best for whom?" Mac was raising his voice, but the expected anger had not yet materialized. "What the hell's going on? I come home from the hospital, and my wife is leaving? Why?"

"Because I want a divorce."

"Why?" he yelled.

He struggled to get out of the deep chair. Mary Lou grabbed her purse and backed toward the door.

"I'll talk to you later when you're better," she said.

With more speed than was warranted in view of Mac's condition, Mary Lou dashed through the door to her Honda. She berated herself for not keeping the car's engine running, but to her relief, it started immediately. She tromped on the accelerator and spun down the driveway without looking back. Mac was left grasping his chest in the driveway dust.

It was over, and Mary Lou had broken free. She had found the strength to do it, and nobody had gotten hurt. She prayed that Mac wouldn't hate her forever or come after her. Hopefully, Stuart would arrive to keep him from doing something stupid in the next few hours. In the meantime, she was going into hiding and look out for herself.

*****

The sudden turn of events simply swamped Mac's capabilities to comprehend what she had said. He stood dazed, thinking this wasn't happening to him. It was a soap opera, something on TV, a story he had read and was now dreaming in his excitement of returning home.

It couldn't be real. Mary Lou had saved his life with her quick action the night he was injured, and had been a loving wife during his stay at Providence. She had never mentioned divorce before, not even said she was unhappy.

Slowly the realization that she was gone began to sink in, and Mac's head started to ache. His chest felt like it was ready to burst, and the ribs which hadn't hurt for a week were collapsing on his lungs in an orgy of agony. He staggered back into the house and collapsed in his chair. God, if the Mexicans couldn't kill him, his wife would.

Mac's face twisted in agony as he faced the fact he was alone. His headache pain jumped two levels of magnitude and moved over his head as if he was being scalped by an Indian. It came to rest in his cerebral cortex where it could inflict maximum damage, hammering him into submission and bringing on successive plagues of prostrating nausea. Mac cursed his head, wishing someone would throw him under a guillotine and remove the worthless appendage. Blinded by pain, he grasped the arms of his chair to steady his world until the thundering waves subsided to simple rollers.

He rose and made his way into the bedroom. It was true. Mary Lou had emptied her closets and dresser. Mac glanced into his top drawer for his checkbook. It was there, but she had withdrawn half of the balance that morning. He examined the passbook; half their savings had gone south, too.

God, even his photos of her were missing. She was attempting to destroy his memories. In a rising panic he ransacked the bedroom looking for their wedding pictures and mementos of their intimate life

106

together. Everything was gone. She had sanitized his life by removing everything that might remind him of her.

Mac howled like a wounded buffalo and smashed the medicine cabinet. His headache shattered his vision with tiny stars and its pain mutated into sheets of sleet, momentarily freezing his brain into steely numbness. Only dimly conscious of his pain's suspension, Mac stormed into the kitchen to get the keys to Rover. He'd bring her back if it killed him.

Chapter 18

Stuart was standing in the doorway like a wooden Indian, blocking Mac's exit.

"What's happenin', podge?" Stuart said.

Mac glanced at his best friend, then put his hand on the counter top and dropped his head in defeat. He stared without focus at the counter.

"Are you in this, too?" he asked.

"In what? What are you talking about? You know as much as I do about the wetbacks."

Mac shook his head, maybe in response to Stuart, but more as a statement about his disbelief of the whole situation. Whatever pain suppression mechanism he'd invoked before had vanished, and his headache returned with a vengeance. "No, I mean Mary Lou's leaving."

"Leaving? Where to?"

Mac recognized immediately that his friend knew more than he was saying. "You tell me, Stuart."

For a moment he had visions of Stuart setting Mary Lou up in some apartment to become his mistress. After all, Stuart's father had done that numerous times, and like father, like son. Then Mac realized Stuart wouldn't have showed up like this if he were part of some conspiracy. Mac looked down at his hands, soft from his time in the hospital.

"Apparently she's decided to divorce me," he said.

Stuart shuffled to the fridge and helped himself to a beer. The can opened with a loud pop and sprayed foam on the tile floor. "Well, that wasn't entirely unexpected, was it?" His tone was sympathetic but firm.

"It was to me," Mac said, still leaning on the counter. "I thought we were getting along better than we had for a long while."

"She must have thought otherwise. Come on, let's go sit down."

Stuart steered Mac into the living room and sat down in the recliner while Mac mumbled his disbelief. He waited patiently until Mac paused after contending that Mary Lou had given him no warning.

"You know there's a rumor she's been seeing someone else?" Stuart said.

Mac snapped his head up in surprise, and his headache got worse immediately. "Hell, no! How would I know that? I've been on my back in a hospital bed, depending on my so-called friends to keep me informed. So who is it? How long has this been going on?"

Stuart winced at Mac's rebuke. He put down his Coors and held up his hands.

"I don't know for certain, but she was seen with her boyfriend at The Whole Enchilada Festival. Apparently it's pretty recent, 'cause he's the deputy who investigated your accident."

Mac leaned back to steady his head and close his eyes. The pain in his head was now matched by one in his chest and stomach.

"That fat Mexican? Mary Lou's fucking a Mexican?"

"That's what I heard," Stuart said.

Blasts of heat seemed to engulf Mac again as the enormity of Mary Lou's crime hit with full force. His arms ached, and his skin prickled with thousands of tiny jabs of pain. His cheeks flushed, and his breath disappeared in the shock. The unthinkable had happened. His wife had cuckolded him with a Mexican! The woman bearing his name had taken a Mexican into her body. He felt sick. "I'll kill them both."

"Mac, she's not worth it."

"Maybe not to you. She's not your wife."

Mac's eyes were still closed, and he could visualize himself pumping bullets into Mary Lou and her lover as they lay in bed. The image of that fat ass on top of Mary Lou was nauseating.

"Get yourself well first, and take care of Castillo's crowd second. They were the ones that tried to kill you, not Mary Lou. She comes third."

"How do you know? Maybe she was in on it."

"Hell, Mac, think about it. She did everything she could to save you. Why would she do that if she wanted you dead?"

109

Even in his fuzzy state, Mac knew Stuart had a point. There wasn't anything he could do tonight anyway. He'd never find her without Stuart's help, and Stuart would probably refuse. After all, Stuart was married to a Mexican and couldn't be expected to understand.

They had to die. He couldn't let such an insult go unavenged. Earlier he had hoped to watch her body bring him back to life tonight, but obviously that was gone forever. There was no way he'd ever touch her again after she'd been polluted by that greaser.

Stuart might have the right idea. He could practice on Castillo and his cohorts while perfecting a plan to take care of Mary Lou and that fat deputy. He wasn't thrilled about going to jail, and killing a cop was dangerous. Even if he found them in bed tonight and claimed temporary insanity, he'd probably be institutionalized for a long time. It could go worse if he got a Mexican jury. They wouldn't understand his feelings and could sentence him to death for killing one of their own. That would be the final insult, dying because he'd killed a Mex.

Besides, there was always the chance Stuart was wrong. Maybe she hadn't gone to bed yet with the Mex. Maybe she just wanted time away from him to get her head straight. Maybe she'd come back if he gave her the time she needed. She loved the ranch, and the fat deputy had nothing to offer.

Mac alternated between hope and anger. It didn't make any sense, and Mary Lou would see that eventually. If she did come back, things would have to be different. But God, he missed her. Why did she have to do this?

There was much to learn and do, and he wanted Stuart's promise to help. This was all-out war, one man against the Mexicans. So far, they had killed his dog, nearly killed him, and captured his wife. Lions three, Christians zero. But now the advantage passed to him. He had nothing further to lose, and they didn't know he was coming.

"Stuart, how about getting me another beer?" he said.

*****

Within a week Stuart had good news to report. Deputy Beltran had been placed on suspension. Several ounces of cocaine had disappeared from the department's evidence locker, and traces of coke

110

were found in Juan's cruiser. In addition, a cash deposit of three thousand dollars had been made into the deputy's bank account the day before the drugs were discovered missing. Stuart chuckled over the timing. The account was seized before Beltran knew the funds were there.

Internal investigators turned up Beltran's involvement with Mary Lou, and determined he had spent an unusual amount of departmental on-duty time and money on the Frazier case. Beltran's expenses were thoroughly examined, and they discovered the meals he brought to Mary Lou had been reimbursed by the county. Worst of all, the other deputies turned their backs on him. He was lower than a gila monster's belly. He had taken advantage of his position with a victim's distraught wife while the man couldn't defend himself. Feelings were running high when the deputy was placed on suspension without pay.

Evidence was mounting, although most of it was withheld from the Las Cruces and El Paso papers in hopes of salvaging the department's reputation. It might not be enough to send Beltran to prison, but would certainly result in his termination.

Two days later, the sheriff issued a press release. Deputy Beltran's financial improprieties were sufficient for dismissal, and the drug theft was still under investigation. Mary Lou's name did not appear in print or on TV, a matter of grave concern to Mac. The sheriff had promised Stuart he'd try to keep Mary Lou's name under wraps, and so far was as good as his word. Election year was approaching, and Stuart's support would be invaluable. It looked like Mac would be saved from public embarrassment.

No sooner did Stuart report the press release than he received word concerning the case's settlement. Beltran had been allowed to resign under the stipulation he make full restitution and never again seek employment in law enforcement. The department kept the three thousand, and Stuart wondered idly how Beltran and Mary Lou would feed themselves in the coming months. But their problems were not his problems, nor would Jed Akers have any such difficulty. He received title to a prime building lot of two acres and actively began looking for a contractor.

Stuart's problem continued to be Mac whose physical health improved daily, but mental state appeared unchanged. He maintained a strict regimen of constant exercise and proper food that was lessening his headaches, but that was just physical. Psychological healing had to come from within, and Mac wasn't sharing his feelings with anyone. Even after Stuart related the final demise of Deputy Beltran, he continued to be concerned. Mac was happy for a day or two over the deputy's comeuppance, then sank back into grim single-mindedness. Obviously, he was preparing for war.

Chapter 19

Summer was ending when Mac showed Stuart his lime pit. A year ago, Mac found a dead Mexican on the western edge of his range. He threw the remains into the pit, and all traces had disappeared when he'd checked a few days later. The Mex had probably been a stray illegal, and judging from his empty water bottle and signs of dehydration, had succumbed to the sun and heat. Mac kept the few dollars he found, and disposed of the desiccating body without mentioning his find to Mary Lou. There was also no reason to inform the authorities and cause excitement.

"Handy disposal unit," Stuart opined. "Planning to use it?"

"One never knows," Mac answered. "I'm ready to take on the Mexican operation on my north fence. Might have some customers."

"You gonna want some help?"

"Maybe backup at times, but otherwise, no. It might get dicey, and someone has to remain on the outside with bail money."

"How're you getting along with your nurse?" Stuart asked.

"She's ancient history. She couldn't do anything I can't do for myself, and the cost was a luxury I couldn't afford. I'm pretty well down to constant headaches except for occasional sharp pain where my skull was pieced together."

It was all up to him, and Mac was determined to prove the skeptics wrong at every turn. The region's dryness helped considerably to reduce water retention, but every time he visited Providence for a progress check, they told him to slow down. It wasn't going to happen—not in his lifetime.

His arms were in better shape now than before the summer. His ribs were still tender, and he tired sooner than before, but he had started running to increase his stamina. There was no more powerful force in the world than vengeance. Love might be as strong, but in his case, it only enhanced his thirst for revenge.

"You know, I couldn't have done this without you," Mac said.

"Glad to help." Stuart had showed Mac how to delay medical payments to the hospital and doctors, then loaned him enough money to stave off the bank holding the Bar-D's paper. To minimize the impact a divorce might have on the Bar-D, Stuart purchased Mac's line of credit. New Mexico was a community property state, but Mary Lou had signed the papers for the line of credit secured in part by a second mortgage on the ranch, and Mac then ran it up to its maximum amount. It would prevent Mary Lou from receiving any part of the ranch. In effect, Stuart and the bank owned the Bar-D.

The Bar-D's second hidden asset, an abandoned tin mine, lay not far from the lime pit. Mac left Rover in an arroyo hidden by thick mesquite bushes below an unusually rocky hill, and they made their way to the mine entrance on foot. During World War I the small mine produced for the war effort, but the deposit was too low-grade to be recovered economically in times of peace. No one remembered this obscure bit of history, and Mac had re-opened the mine as a place to store useful items on the north side of his ranch. As in the case of the lime pit, he and Stuart were the only ones who knew of its existence. The mine was fully provisioned to meet any emergency, and a person could hide there for weeks if necessary.

A steel gate guarded the entrance against humans, and an ancient but heavy door sealed the horizontal shaft from penetration by stray animals and snakes. Stuart placed the batteries he lugged in from Rover alongside the small generator, while Mac turned on an industrial fan to blow out stale air. The ventilation system was old but operative, and the mine's atmosphere quickly became quite pleasant. Stuart used the mine to store gold and silver, and he brought in another box of coins he had obtained over the summer.

They locked the mine and returned to Mac's waiting Jeep. Over the past two weeks Mac had noticed heavy traffic on his northern ranch trails. Apparently the border-crossing operation was running in high gear. His cattle were again on the south side, and coyotes were enjoying complete freedom to move illegals through the northern half of his ranch. It was possible they didn't know he was back running the

Bar-D. Mac had questioned his vaqueros about illegals crossing his property, and they professed to have seen no one for several months.

The fenced-in property hadn't changed from the first time Mac and Stuart had seen it. Mac checked on it every other day, but saw no visible activity during daylight. The only time anyone inhabited the trailer was during the evenings, although one or two individuals infrequently remained overnight. A telephone wire ran to the trailer and the compound was supplied with electricity, but other than the few cows in their pen, the place generally looked deserted.

The property itself was barren of vegetation other than small desert plants and grasses, but relatively isolated and private. There were several low hills on the northern edge of his range which overlooked the compound, and it was partly shielded from the north and west by the earthen flood control dam. Eastward the desert gave way to the fertile valley floor and a number of cottonwoods intermixed with orchards of pecan trees and other fruits.

There were no houses within a mile, and the two they could see were hidden in their surrounding trees. Most importantly, the ground rose rapidly from the valley, then leveled off before reaching the compound and its trailer. A person could stand alongside the pump and not be able to see the nearest houses. It was diabolically clever. One could view the place from afar, but not from close up. It was totally in the open, but well hidden. Except from the Bar-D.

In the afternoon Stuart took off and Mac drove to El Paso to purchase last minute items at Sunland Mall. It was getting dark as he returned up Interstate 10, and he decided to treat himself to a steak at Great American Land & Cattle Company. The restaurant was where he'd met Mary Lou, and it was fitting he should eat there again to kick off this rejuvenating activity.

It was located on the freeway immediately east of the La Tuna federal penitentiary, and the restaurant's owner joked he'd picked that spot to give escaping prisoners their first good meal. The story wasn't true, of course, but in Mac's opinion Great American was the best restaurant in Doña Ana and El Paso counties. It processed its own meat, aging the beef for forty days in its own specially constructed cooler behind the main building. With the exception of the Japanese restaurants that claimed American beef was inferior to Japanese, GALACCO supplied most top restaurants in the area with prime steak. There was still no place like the source for ranchers like Mac, and he pulled in before starting his little operation.

It reminded him of Mary Lou, and that he hadn't heard from her since she drove away from the Bar-D. Stuart saw her only when she'd returned Rover's keys, but had heard she was attending NMSU. Supposedly, she had rented an apartment for herself in Las Cruces, and if she was seeing the Mexican, at least she wasn't living with him. Divorce papers hadn't shown up yet, and Mac told himself there was still hope. Stuart said it was best to get angry at her so he could move on to another woman. Anger was there all right, but mixed with sadness and longing. If she asked to come back, he wasn't sure what he'd do. In any case, no woman would look at him twice with his misshapen head and scary face.

Both GALACCO's dining area and bar were crowded, but Mac saw nobody he knew. Most patrons came from El Paso, and the college-aged waitresses turned over with regularity. He hadn't been there for a long time, but the menu was still the same. Even the prices hadn't increased, and Mac chowed down on a one pound steak.

Great American's owner had designed a unique slanted grill that allowed all cuts and orders to be cooked in the same length of time. Rare steaks were placed low in the front and well-done on the upper rear. His rare sirloin was done to perfection, and he took that as an omen for later success. He left the ranch beans, pineapple coleslaw, baked potato, and hot bread relatively undisturbed, not wanting to eat too heavily. He might have to move fast, and didn't want to feel logy.

It was almost nine when he left the restaurant, and Mac drove directly to the point on his ranch where he would leave Rover. There was a small but steep rocky hill immediately south of Castillo's compound, and Mac could approach from that direction to within two hundred yards without risking detection. He parked the Jeep and skirted the hill's western edge on foot. The moon had already risen, and negotiating the desert was easy in the cloudless night. The sand was white against the darker cactus and scrub bushes, and Mac merely avoided the dark patches before him. His ranch barely supported a steer per fifty acres in this quarter, but tonight he was glad its vegetation was so sparse. Even so, his trail zigzagged like a drunk's.

The day had been unusually hot for late September, and the

ground was giving off its heat. Most people believed the hottest time of day was in early afternoon, but in desert climates it came much later, around five. During evening hours the air was heated from the slowly cooling ground, and official weather bureau temperatures were often quite deceiving.

Mac loosened his jacket in an effort to keep cool. His headaches became worse when he overheated, and he didn't want to risk a debilitating attack if things got sticky. As a result of the excellent steak his head felt light with a dull and harmless fuzziness, but that could change rapidly at any moment. He focused on the trailer in front of him and ignored his head to help maintain control.

Castillo's western gate was closed, and he used the bolt cutters he'd brought to easily snap the cheap padlock. Mac grinned to himself. Security was only as good as the weakest link. He placed his cutters behind a small bush and eased himself through the gate. To his surprise, it was well oiled and didn't squeak.

Mac had saved part of his steak in case a dog was present, but hadn't seen one earlier and didn't see one now. Apparently the people in the trailer wished to avoid whatever attention a barking dog might cause. He carefully crossed the open area by the well and diesel pump, stepping high to avoid making noise or accidentally kicking anything he didn't spot in the moonlight. A soft crunching in the crushed rock was unavoidable, but he reached the trailer without difficulty and flattened himself against its side.

There were several lights on inside, and he could hear Spanish being spoken. Mac counted the voices, and concluded there were three men inside. He expected at least one female to keep the coyotes happy, but if one was present, she wasn't taking part in their conversation. The only visible vehicle was a Chevy S-10, and its cab was empty.

The trailer door was slightly ajar in spite of the air conditioning units going full blast. Mac unholstered one of the two revolvers he was wearing and crept to the door. He paused at the crack to peer inside, but only the back of someone's head behind a dinette bench was visible. A single metal step projected out under the door, a sure-fire obstacle to trip him if Mac ever saw one.

The moonlight played on the desert around him as he steeled himself for his next move. It was now or never, and Mac had come this far undetected and fully prepared. According to his neurologist he wasn't supposed to be alive anyway, so in a sense, he had nothing to lose.

Taking a deep breath, Mac flung open the door and jumped into the middle of the trailer. He imagined himself being an old-time sheriff hurtling through the double doors of a saloon to dispatch the bad guys.

"Hands up!" he yelled. "Hands up!"

Two scruffy Mexicans were sitting at a four-person bench-style dining table with the Mexican he had met on the ATV. Mac backed into the kitchen area at the trailer's front end, holding his gun on the Mexicans. He could see down the length of the trailer into the rear bedroom, but couldn't see into the bathroom on the side. The bedroom looked empty, and the door to the bathroom was open. Mac decided he was in good shape unless someone was in the dark bathroom.

"Get your hands up where I can see them!" he yelled, this time in Spanish.

The Mexicans were slow to respond, but they didn't make any threatening gestures. Multiple bottles of Budweiser attested to a probable state of mild inebriation, and they didn't seem unduly upset by his interruption. Mac's revolver was not having the desired effect. The ATV rider hurriedly told the other two in Spanish that Mac was the rancher south of them.

"Yeah, I'm not the police," Mac said, continuing in Spanish. "I'm worse. If you don't do as I say, you're dead meat."

"Hey, man," the coyote sitting nearest to Mac said in English. "We ain't hurtin' you."

Mac stepped to the Mex who spoke, taking his second revolver out of its holster. He gave the Colt a quick flip, grabbing it by the barrel. The man was slow to react, then it was too late.

Mac clubbed him hard over the head with the heavy butt. The coyote dropped like a stone onto the table, then slid to the floor. He lay still, not making a sound. The unconscious man's head starting bleeding where the Colt creased his skull, capturing the attention of the other two Mexicans who seemed stupefied by the violence. Mac placed his foot in the guy's crotch and pushed the body out of his way.

"Anybody else want to say anything?" Mac asked.

Both remaining Mexicans glared fiercely but said nothing.

Mac replaced his second revolver in its holster, then reached into his black leather jacket. Mac was sweating in the trailer's warmth, but wore the jacket because of its convenient pockets. His headache had mutated into an icy wind. The pain was gone and his forehead sent dulling shivers back along his temples. He slid two sets of handcuffs over to the ATV rider.

"Good. Now that we understand each other, handcuff those two." He nodded at the coyotes and motioned with his hand. "Behind their backs."

The ATV rider glowered, but did as directed. Mac noticed he knew how to work the cuffs in spite of his unwilling attitude. The man moved slowly as if looking for the right instant to throw himself at Mac. Apparently the desired opportunity didn't occur, and in a moment, the other two were securely cuffed. He turned and faced Mac, a little too close for good security. Mac took a half step back.

"Now you two get face down on the floor," Mac said. His gun never moved from pointing directly at the ATV rider's stomach.

Several seconds passed, then the ATV rider knelt down and stretched himself out on the floor. Resistance seemed broken for the moment, and the other Mexican reluctantly followed suit. Mac stepped over them, quickly handcuffed the ATV rider, and pulled the unconscious coyote alongside. He was bleeding profusely from where Mac cracked his head, but the other two remained silent.

"Keep your heads down," Mac said.

Taking advantage of his temporary superiority, Mac quickly checked the bathroom and bedroom. Both were clear, and he returned to search the prone figures. All carried knives, and the ATV rider had a .22 automatic in the top of one boot. He also wore a money belt, and Mac guessed it contained upward of twenty thousand dollars.

He pulled off their boots and socks before proceeding further. A fetid stench of smelly feet assailed him, but it was a necessary precaution. The desert was not a place to be barefoot, and if they rabbited on him, they'd pay a fearful price.

There was nothing in the trailer to which he could handcuff his prisoners, so Mac embarked on another course of action. Starting with the ATV rider, he removed their pants and shorts.

"You queer or something?" the ATV rider said as Mac pulled off his briefs.

Mac kicked him hard between his legs. "Speak when you're spoken to!"

The ATV rider coughed in pain, then lay groaning with short breaths. Clearly the most dangerous of the three Mexicans, he was in need of an attitude adjustment.

Leaving the handcuffs in place, Mac cut off their shirts with his hunting knife, then wired their feet together. Rolling them over, he inspected his naked prisoners. The coyotes were scrawny and unimpressive, but the ATV rider looked like a daily visitor to a fitness center. About five-feet-eleven, he was a well-muscled athlete who probably played handball or some other strenuous sport to keep in shape. Medium brown, with dark hair and well-shaped features, he would turn the head of any Hispanic girl in the valley. She'd probably come back for a second time after she saw his endowment. Mac was impressed, it was at least equal to his.

Without much difficulty he manhandled all three onto the living room's hard orange vinyl sofa. Their legs spread automatically, and Mac wondered if men usually sat that way or only if their feet were together. The bleeding coyote had regained consciousness and began moaning in pain. Mac ignored him.

A pungent smell of fear and rancid body odor assailed Mac's nostrils. The injured coyote's head fell backwards, and he rolled his eyes uncomprehendingly around the ceiling. Several inches shorter than the ATV rider, he probably didn't weigh over a hundred and thirty pounds. Both coyotes were swarthy, with narrow, pock-marked faces and broad Indian noses. They hadn't shaved for several days, and from the stink, apparently hadn't showered either.

Mac retrieved a metal chair from near the kitchen table, turned it to face his captives, and sat down. "So tell me. What are we running here?"

Nobody spoke.

"I said, what are we running here?"

The ATV rider and uninjured coyote glanced at each other as if seeking solidarity, then turned back to Mac in silence. He waited a moment longer, but there wasn't a peep from his adversaries.

With an exaggerated sigh Mac went into the kitchen area and

searched through several cluttered drawers. He returned with a large three-pronged utility fork and wrestled the moaning coyote into straddling an arm of the sofa. About four inches thick, the arms were sturdy and topped with wood for added durability. The two Mexicans sitting on the sofa's hard cushions watched suspiciously while trying to project an attitude of disinterest.

Mac gave them an insincere, angelic smile.

"Gee, sorry you don't know what's going on," he said.

Hesitating only a second to secure his spectators' undivided attention, he plunged the fork into the injured coyote's genitals. The sharp fork pinned them to the sofa arm, and the stuck coyote let out a horrible scream of pain. A stream of urine shot out and narrowly missed Mac's arm as the coyote lost control.

"Jesus Christ!" yelled the second coyote. "We're just running illegals!"

The howling continued, making it difficult for Mac to hear what the second coyote was saying.

"What was that?" he shouted.

A torrent of Spanish issued from the uninjured coyote, but most of it was drowned out by the other's screams. The room began to smell like an outhouse, and it was evident someone had shit himself.

Mac held up his hand. "Wait."

He stood up and yanked the screaming Mexican off the sofa arm. Showing a perverse sense of professional interest, Mac checked to see which had ripped out, the fork or the coyote's family jewels. The fork had lost.

He grunted his approval of the "tough little buggers" and pulled the shrieking coyote to the trailer door. As Mac's knife slit the man's throat, the high-pitched yowls were replaced by gurgling, then a dull thump as the quivering body fell outside on the sand. All was quiet as Mac turned to face the remaining two.

"Sorry about the noise. Now, what are we running here?" he said.

This time it was the ATV rider who spoke, and he rapidly developed diarrhea of the mouth in his eagerness to provide information.

They were indeed running illegals up from Mexico every night, although most of the people were coming from Central and South

America. It was a well-organized operation, and this station was merely a transfer point for traveling further north. Illegals were picked up here in specially built water tankers that could hold fifty people. Travelers climbed into their bottom compartment, the hatch was sealed, and water poured on top. Passing through Border Patrol checkpoints was no longer a problem, and even if the tankers were checked, they appeared to be full of water.

The illegals were taken to Albuquerque, and from there they usually went to Denver or Chicago. The dead coyote had brought a group that evening, as had the other sitting on the sofa. The ATV rider, whose name was Garcia, worked for a man named Ramirez, Castillo's hidden and well-connected partner. Immigrants were charged from five hundred to two thousand dollars apiece depending on where they originated and their final destinations. Garcia was responsible for collecting the final payment—half of the fee—upon their entry into the United States.

"You're a dead man," Garcia said at the end of his discourse. "Ramirez will see to that."

"Maybe," Mac said. "But for now, I'm taking over this segment of his operation."

"You're crazy!"

Mac smiled, realizing his headache had dissipated into gentle flickers of chilling pulses. His forehead felt cold to his touch. He had never been saner, and maybe killing Mexicans was just the thing to keep headaches away. He raised his eyebrows in mock disappointment. "Are you saying you won't work for me?"

"You bet your life," Garcia said.

"Well, you just bet, and lost."

Chapter 20

The morning sun was warm and refreshing, reminding him of nature's daily rebirth. Mac sat on the rocky hillside to enjoy the desert's tranquility before returning to the trailer. He was twenty-three thousand dollars richer, but didn't have much of a life expectancy. The lime pit was doing its duty gobbling up the bodies of Garcia and his coyotes, and as of the moment, nobody knew Mac was involved. But it wouldn't stay that way. Sooner or later the guys in the speeding truck would come after him.

It was funny about his head. It had behaved itself while he snuffed the Mexicans, but afterward at the ranch house, his headache returned with great intensity. Evidently he could suppress the pain during certain emotional activities, but paid for it later.

Garcia had talked fast and long trying to convince Mac to spare him, but that wasn't an option. Killing the Mexicans wasn't satisfying, but it wasn't unpleasant either. They were simply vermin to be exterminated, blood-suckers on society who didn't deserve to live. Mac had taken six sets of handcuffs with him to the trailer, and if there had been six Mexicans present, six would have died.

He left Garcia to last, and the coward pled for his life on his knees. Garcia swore he would leave the area and never come back, never tell anyone about that night, and do anything Mac asked. Mac heard all about the Virgin Mary, Christ, how Garcia had never done anything wrong, and how he was too young to die. Invoking religion was an error. Good Catholic Garcia didn't realize Mac was an anti-Papist Amulot.

The second coyote at least died like a man, taking his medicine with dignity and in silence. Garcia's blubbering made Mac angry. He did things to Garcia that he otherwise wouldn't have done. Mac told himself it was Garcia's fault, and the scoundrel got what he deserved.

In the morning he discussed the evening's events with Stuart. At first Stuart played Sergeant Schultz, knowing nothing about nothing, but then, in for a penny, in for a pound. Stuart wasn't a lawyer so the conversation wasn't privileged, but between the friends, it was more than that. Mostly Stuart listened, and that was what Mac needed.

Mac had struck at expendable elements in the wetback operation, making only a small dent in the organization. But he hadn't found the men who tried to kill him. Tonight promised to be different. Ramirez would probably show up looking for Garcia, and Mac might have the opportunity to do him in and take over the operation.

Garcia had said the tankers were owned by a small company in Deming originally incorporated to market water extracted from the area's underlying bolson. Both Mac and Stuart knew the owner from New Mexico's interminable water hearings, and he was an Anglo who had fallen on hard times. Tankers weren't needed if the water couldn't be pumped out. He would probably agree to work with a new partner if there weren't people behind Ramirez with too much muscle.

The Denver and Chicago connections were most likely low-level drop-off points, but the organization in Mexico was crucial to maintaining a strong supply of paying customers. Ramirez was undoubtedly important to them as a known contact, but since they were in Mexico, they might be amenable to a replacement if their operation didn't suffer. The key was Ramirez, and to a lesser extent, his legal mouthpiece, Castillo.

Attempting to take over the pipeline was an interesting proposition with possibly great rewards. Mac had nothing to lose except his life which was barely worth the suffering anyway. He decided to play out his hand and see what developed. After all, the game was the only one in town. Stuart reluctantly approved, deciding to support his friend against this bunch of human trafficking criminals. He called them slave merchants, a term the progressive politicians declined to use. Mac hitched a ride from Stuart back to the trailer.

There was clean-up to perform. Mac picked up Garcia's S-10 at the trailer and drove it to Juarez. He parked on a side street only three blocks from the international bookie joint favored by Americans. The usual little man in a pseudo-official green uniform materialized immediately. He asked for money to watch the truck, and Mac sent him packing with a short burst of abuse. Between its New Mexico plates and the sidewalk stalker's enmity, Garcia's pickup would be stolen before noon. Either that or some Mexican police official would claim it.

He placed a fifty dollar bet on a trifecta at Santa Anita, and sauntered back over the Paso Del Norte bridge to meet Stuart for a late lunch. Soon would come the evening and its nightly shipment. One way or another, the next few hours would determine his longevity and economic status.

Stuart dropped him off at the trailer to prepare for the evening. The inside was barely habitable, and Mac found a bottle of Lysol and some rags for cleaning. It took some effort to wash away all traces of his interrogation. His headache flared up, and he decided the remainder of the trailer could wait for another day. He rested with an ice pack to suppress his headache pain and mentally prepare himself for what had to come.

About an hour after dark he spotted lights bobbing at a distance on his range. Mac's headache had subsided, and he felt only mildly excited watching the caravan approach in three battered vans. He wondered what had happened to the vehicles used the previous night. Coyotes sometimes used stolen American vehicles that they ditched if detected by border patrol units. These looked like vintage Mexican crates of minimum value.

The lead van pulled up to the trailer, and a stocky Mexican in baggy pants stepped out.

"Where's Ricardo?" the driver asked in Spanish.

"You mean Garcia? He's gone to do his own thing." Mac studied the Mexican for a reaction, but since Mac had answered in Spanish, the coyote didn't seem perturbed in the least.

"I've taken over reception, and you'll deal with me in the future. How many we got?"

The coyote took a paper out of his shirt pocket and handed it to Mac.

"Good group," the man said. "Mostly from El Salvador."

Mac unfolded the paper and smoothed it out against his leg. It was a manifest giving names, destinations, and amounts owed. He glanced at the illegals being herded into the trailer. They were a mixture of families and singles, from babies to grandparents, and gave a decidedly human quality to the sterile document in his hand.

"Everybody back outside!" he yelled in Spanish.

He pushed his way into the trailer and cleared it of the half-panicked people. Loudly speaking with as much authority as he could muster, he announced they would not be allowed inside until they paid in full for their trip. The travelers clustered outside around the coyotes.

He handed the manifest back to the first coyote and ordered him to line up everyone in the order they appeared on the sheet. The coyotes shouted and shoved the unresisting bodies into a ragged line. Order was restored in a twinkling, and all eyes were fastened on Mac to begin. He gruffly checked off each name and accepted payments at the door. The illegals were humble and polite, disappearing immediately into the trailer.

One individual remained outside the trailer for processing when Mac reached the end of the manifest. A relatively pretty girl about fifteen years old, she was attempting to make herself inconspicuous behind the youngest of the three coyotes. The girl was dressed shabbily, in nondescript old jeans and a rough sweater several sizes too large. Instead of boots, she wore a pair of well-worn tennis shoes, and appeared to have no luggage.

Mac beckoned to the boy she was hiding behind, a thin kid not over twenty-one. "What about her?"

"Ah, ah, she's extra," the lean, pimply-faced Mexican said. He shrugged his shoulders and gestured with his hands to indicate the situation was of no importance. "She don't got no money. She work her way."

"Not interested," Mac said. "No money, no tickee. You can take her back."

"Ah, ah, can't do that," the coyote said. "It'd be trouble. You keep her. She be very good to you."

With bigger fish to fry, Mac decided to let this one pass. He could deal with the girl tomorrow if he was still alive.

"Just this once," he said. "Don't ever bring me another. They all have to pay their way."

The coyote offered no excuse for bringing the girl and accepted Mac's rebuke in silence. She might have been brought for Garcia, but Mac was not interested in picking up AIDS from some teenage puta. Probably been screwed by everyone on her trek north from wherever, including these three coyotes. He couldn't guess what they told her, and if she wasn't for Garcia, they probably expected to lose her in the crowd when he processed the wetbacks. Mac foiled that with his insistence on organization.

He dismissed the kid and motioned for the girl. The coyote spoke quickly to her and pointed in Mac's direction. When she hesitated, he pushed her forward without a trace of gentleness.

She approached slowly and stood before him as if awaiting words from a priest. Mac assumed his face was scaring her to death, but she didn't act afraid. He noticed all three coyotes watching with interest and spoke as if disgusted with her presence.

"You will stay here until you earn enough money to pay for your trip," Mac said.

The girl shrugged her shoulders, and waited silently for instructions. He led her to the larger of the two storage sheds, the one that was not being used. She entered without protest, and he ordered her to remain there until the other illegals were shipped out. Mac closed the poorly fitting door and dropped the pin in its latch. For all intents and purposes, the girl was locked inside. A good kick at the flimsy cross-nailed boards would enable her to escape, and Mac didn't care if she fled or not. His was creating a tough image to impress his new business associates.

On his way back to the trailer he thought about her needing the bathroom. It was too late, and he didn't want to show weakness. Well, she'd have to use a corner of the shed. Indoor plumbing was probably a luxury to her anyway.

He paid each coyote his cut according to Garcia's established rate. There were no objections. Mac pulled their apparent leader, the one who had given him the manifest, aside for a discussion before they departed.

"This operation's being expanded," Mac said. "We're looking for connections in Mexico for more than just transporting people."

The coyote nodded. "I wondered when your side would get smart. That's where the real money is."

"We're considering everything. See what you can arrange."

The coyote's name was Villareal, and Mac decided he was relatively smart for a Mexican. He mentioned several possibilities for Mexican brown, and Mac promised to consider all options. All such contacts were shots in the dark, but nothing would happen if Mac didn't put things in motion.

Villareal made no attempt to communicate Mac's interest to the other two coyotes and drove off toward Interstate 10 by himself. Mac watched him leave with satisfaction. Maybe Villareal had potential. He had accepted Mac's explanation of Garcia's departure at face value and hadn't asked about the others. In an occupation funneling people into a land of unknowns, disappearances were evidently standard fare.

Mac was not alone with his charges for long. Within a half hour, he spotted two vehicles approaching from the valley. One was a tanker, but the other looked like the truck that had hit the Ranger. He told the illegals to remain inside the trailer until called and closed the door. His adrenaline began to flow. He had waited almost three months for this moment, and it was coming with the speed of those two trucks.

It was a good thing they were arriving so soon. His headache was starting up again. He talked to himself, telling the pain to go away for a few more minutes, but it didn't listen. He would have to work fast while he still could.

The tanker drove to the well's hanging canvas water hoses while the queen-cabbed Explorer stopped across from the trailer. Mac dimly remembered the truck in summer as being bigger, but recognized its features. Evidently the queen-cab had looked larger while bearing down on him in the gathering darkness.

Three Mexican men got out from the Explorer, none of whom looked familiar. Mac tried to think back to August, but couldn't remember any faces from that night. The driver was a fat, brain-dead heavyweight, and Mac assumed he was looking at the man who tried to kill him.

The first man climbing out of the passenger side was about the same age as Mac, medium height, and expensively dressed in casual clothes. He wore several gold chains around his neck in current drug-lord fashion, and his hands sparkled with rings. The third man was dressed in a business suit, totally out of place for the desert night. Mac surmised the gold-wearer was Ramirez, and the power-suited individual none other than Castillo. They probably came out together because they hadn't heard from Garcia. At this point, Mac was an unknown interloper.

"Where's Ricardo?" The one wearing the gold spoke first. Had to be Ramirez.

"Gone." Mac moved forward. "I've taken over the management."

In four strides Mac passed the heavyweight to approach Ramirez. The fat driver stepped to position himself behind Mac, a little too close for comfort.

Mac whirled, drawing his large hunting knife from his armpit and slashing the bull-like Mexican across the throat. The knife cut deeply into vertebrae, severing the Mexican's windpipe, gullet, and arteries. The thin line widened into a slobbering smile, then gushed black in the dark. The Mexican gargled once in a dying reflex, then crumpled in his tracks.

It had been a perfect swing, and Mac knew the guy's death was imminent. There was no time to check the sprawled form, and Mac knew he couldn't afford any sign of weakness. He turned back to Ramirez as if he had swatted a fly, keenly aware that the pain in his head had momentarily ceased. If anything, he felt lightheaded. "Like I said, there's new management."

He expertly flipped his hunting knife into the ground next to Ramirez's foot. Mac watched his adversary closely for any motion toward drawing a gun. He would have to be faster.

"Pretty sure of yourself," Ramirez said. "Who's the new management?"

"Nobody you know. You Ramirez?"

"Yep. You?"

Mac ignored the question and spoke to the Mexican wearing the suit, glancing at the probable lawyer with his eyes but without turning his head. His entire attention remained focused squarely on Ramirez.

"You Castillo?"

"Yes, that's Castillo." Ramirez answered. His voice betrayed his rising anger. "Now, who in the hell are you?"

"Mac Arnold," Mac said, using his first and middle names. He doubted either of them would be able to make the connection.

Mac motioned toward Castillo. "Hector, how about moving that mound of garbage where our travelers won't have to step over it? Pull it around the end of the trailer." His tone was firm and authoritative.

Castillo stood rooted in place.

"Go ahead," Ramirez said.

The lawyer began to move, walking cautiously as if he expected Mac to turn on him at any moment.

"Good. Now let's you and I step behind your truck and have us a little chat," Mac said.

A slimy lawyer like Castillo wouldn't have the guts to use the fat Mexican's weapon, but Ramirez was still dangerous. Mac extended his arm to encompass the smaller Ramirez, but the Mexican stepped quickly out of reach. He kept two paces away, and walked in front of Mac behind the Explorer. Mac continued speaking with an overly friendly and conciliatory tone as they stopped and faced each other.

"Now then, shall we agree to work together to continue this operation profitably for all?"

"I don't know you," Ramirez said.

"No, but you've seen me work. And Ricardo and two coyotes are missing."

"That your work, too?"

"Let's just say it's all among friends. You've got the connections south of the border, and I've got the push up here."

"You got nothing," Ramirez said.

"I've got Castillo, and he's got ambition. It's you who's got nothing." Mac was pulling a gigantic bluff, but he stood to gain a significant advantage by implicating Castillo.

Ramirez seemed momentarily taken aback. "Castillo's a lawyer. He works with his mouth. They know they got to have me."

Mac smiled. Ramirez had just given the game away. Castillo knew the Mexican contacts, and that was all he needed. Ramirez was a liability, while Castillo was an asset.

"I'm sorry you feel that way," Mac said.

He had been standing with his arms folded across his chest, but his right hand was gripping a thirty-two caliber Walther PPK under his light jacket. The automatic was already cocked with a round in the chamber.

In a single motion Mac pulled out the gun and fired into the middle of Ramirez's forehead. The Mexican's knees buckled, and he dropped flat on his back.

Mac listened a second as the report echoed in the evening breeze, then was lost forever. He stepped over the body and stomped hard with his heel on Ramirez's neck. The crunching sound told him the slightly protruding Adam's apple was crushed. If the thirty-two slug hadn't already done the trick, his boot provided the coup de grâce. This was not the time to make mistakes or leave a job half done. The little Mexican's legs twitched violently, then fell still.

Thumbing the release, Mac swiftly slid the magazine out and dropped it into his side pocket. He jacked out the chambered round, and hurriedly stepped around the truck to see Castillo staring in his direction, still pulling at the fat Mexican's arms.

"Everything's okay," Mac announced.

None of the illegals were emerging, and the tanker driver was standing by the wellhead, motionless like Castillo. For the moment, Mac was unarmed, but only Castillo remained as a possible threat. And he was a lawyer.

"Let's get everyone out and loaded," Mac called to the tanker driver. "Time is money, and we've got none to waste."

The blond Anglo nodded his acceptance of Mac's authority and headed for the trailer. The driver yanked the door open, yelling at his passengers to hurry out and get loaded. He seemed to have little empathy for his human cargo, and as they emerged, he prodded them to move faster and not be afraid to climb the tanker's side ladder.

Mac walked over to where Castillo had dropped the dead heavyweight.

"Jeeze, that was too bad," Mac said. "Ramirez just wouldn't accept new management. Now you'll have to handle our Mexican connections."

"Me? But Ramirez knows them better than me," Castillo said.

"Ramirez is no longer with us. And you know them and they know you." Mac eyed Castillo evenly. The little lawyer would take some stiffening.

"Yeah, but..."

"No *yeah but*s," Mac said. "That's your job now. Unless you want to join Ramirez."

"But... but I've got a family. A wife and two little girls."

Mac reached into his pocket and pulled out the PPK. He quickly wiped it on his jacket and handed it to Castillo. The lawyer took it with a slight hesitation, turning it over to see the magazine was missing.

"There's no magazine," he said.

"Oh, I'm sorry."

Mac snatched the automatic out of Castillo's hand before he could object. Handling it carefully, Mac placed it in a zippered plastic bag and returned it to his pocket.

"Just insurance. Now it has your fingerprints on it, and I saw you shoot Ramirez."

Castillo looked aghast, and stared at Mac without speaking.

131

"So there's only one way to protect your family. Do a good job."

Mac shook Castillo by the shoulders, but the lawyer was in shock. He stepped backward to avoid Mac's grasp and nearly fell. Mac reached into the dead Mexican's pockets and found the Explorer's keys. He handed them to Castillo.

"Here. Take the truck, talk to nobody, and you'll be contacted tomorrow."

Mac walked away and joined the tanker driver. He purposely paid no further attention to Castillo, and didn't bother to look when the badly shaken shyster sped away.

The chubby young tanker driver started up the pump and rapidly filled the upper compartment with water. Still in his twenties, he impressed Mac with his laid-back attitude. They swapped jokes about wetbacks traveling under water instead of swimming or in boats. After a pause, the driver motioned in the direction of Ramirez's body which lay in the shadows a few feet away.

"Looks like this is becoming more professional," he said.

"Yup. We're all going to be making out better."

"Hope so. Nobody likes the penalties for getting caught moving wetbacks."

"Well, in the future there'll be someone to look out for you in sticky situations. Someone with power on this side of the border. Not like before."

"I can handle that." The driver shut off the pump. "'Course I didn't see anything happen here tonight."

"Naw, musta happened after you left. Your boss'll get the word tomorrow, so don't concern yourself about anything. Good men who can keep their mouths shut are always in high demand."

The driver nodded and kept his lips sealed. "Muuummmm," he said.

They both laughed, and Mac slapped the driver on his shoulder as the man vaulted into his cab. The engine came to life, and the illegals were on their way.

So was Mac, but his headache was returning.

Chapter 21

It had been an eventful night, but Mac's luck was holding. He rifled the pockets of both Ramirez and the Mexican heavy whose New Mexico driver's license gave his name as Jesus De La O. Both were packing, and the gold chains, watches, and rings were liberated to be placed in the mine with articles acquired from his earlier kills. He would dispose of them later.

Mac was amazed at the amount of money Ramirez carried in a belt like Garcia's—almost fifteen thousand dollars. Combined with fees collected from the night's illegals, the money made Mac a walking ATM machine. Something would have to be done about all this cash, and fast.

Fighting his debilitating headache, Mac bundled the two bodies into Rover and sped to his hungry lime pit. His score was now five dead, and if he kept this up he could soon rival Billy The Kid. Mac chuckled over that one; after all, Billy didn't consider Mexicans important enough to include in his count. Indians either, for that matter.

As in the case of Garcia, Mac assumed Ramirez and Gordo were US residents and might be identifiable from their remains. He destroyed any possibility of dental forensic evaluation by thoroughly shattering their teeth with Rover's tire iron. Mac shuddered thinking of himself as a serial killer, but these actions were merely self-preservation. Stripping the foul corpses was nauseating, but that too, was necessary.

Like the previous night, Mac divided the clothes into three trash bags, one for shoes and belts, a second for shirts and pants, and a third for the soiled shorts. Like Garcia and the two coyotes, these corpses weren't circumcised. He thought about that, then understood why. Mexican midwives wouldn't dare mutilate a male child, and their doctors were too lazy.

The two naked bodies soon disappeared in the pit, nature redistributing their DNA as sustenance for lesser species. Mac took a short cut and followed El Paso Electric's high tension wires into the valley. The constant buzzing overhead calmed his headache, but reminded him of the astronomical rates charged locally for electric service. Companies like Phelps Dodge avoided El Paso Electric by installing their own power plants, but individuals enjoyed no such alternatives. Some idiot spokesman said rates were high because people didn't use enough electricity, but only morons with IQs below fifty believed that. The company was simply mismanaged, participating in the ruinous Palo Verde Nuclear Plant to stroke top executive egos.

Mac was partial to Waste Management's dumpsters along Doniphan, and heaved his trash bags into a dumpster that was nearly full. Within two days, some Mexican would retrieve the apparel from the county dump and be happily wearing or selling what he'd found. Of course, this stuff might not even reach the dump. Almost every day the dumpsters were combed for articles of value, and the clothes would be on someone's body before long. It was better than giving them to the Salvation Army.

When he returned, Mac straightened up the trailer. A nagging sense of unfinished business haunted his subconscious as he turned over the blood-soaked sand outside. It was the girl, he suddenly remembered, that teenaged mattress-back locked in his shed. She was probably scared to death in her makeshift prison. He dropped his spade and hurried to release her.

The pin was still in place, and he almost pulled the door apart in his haste. He needn't have rushed, the girl was curled up inside and asleep on the sand. Amazing how anyone could have been so resigned to her fate that she slept while people were dying outside. He woke her gently and escorted her to the trailer.

Her name was Lupe, short for Guadalupe. Mac pursed his lips, thinking how Mexicans gave their female offspring religious names. As if that would make them more virtuous. Boys too, were penalized by their mothers' religious fervor, receiving named like Jesus.

Puta or not, she impressed him with an inner toughness he hadn't expected in such a young girl. He offered her a deal. If she would stay for thirty days and take care of the trailer, he'd provide for her necessities. Then at the end of a month, he'd send her to wherever she wanted to go.

She gazed at him without flinching.

"The nights and other times? I'm to be for your use? Not anyone else?"

"No, no one's use." Mac vigorously shook his head. "That's all over. No one will bother you here. Not me, not anyone."

Her fear that he might pass her around was a damning indictment of a culture in which young girls could be treated as slaves. It was bad enough she assumed he'd take her whenever the mood struck. She was only a little girl, a victim of the Mexicans like himself. Yet from her expression, she didn't believe a word he said.

"Seriously, I swear. I promise not to touch you. This is the U.S., and nobody can use you like that."

Lupe nodded her agreement. "Then I will do it."

Without prompting she took out her rosary, and swore she'd stay. She would work hard and make him happy with her.

There weren't many options available to either of them, and he was glad she accepted his offer. He wasn't eager to kill a young girl under any circumstances. His face might be frightening to her, but as long as she didn't think her life was in danger, he figured she'd hold up her end of the bargain. After all, as a wetback, she wasn't likely to call the police.

His headache subsided to a dull annoyance, and he spent the night at the trailer with Lupe sleeping on a makeshift bed an arm's length away. In spite of the filthy bathroom, Mac took a shower to cleanse his body and soul of the evening's events. It was difficult to maintain a semblance of modesty, and he questioned why he made the effort. He didn't have anything his companion hadn't seen before.

Lupe followed with a shower after Mac vacated the bathroom. He approved. Apparently she felt safe around him and practiced good personal hygiene. On that basis, her presence could be truly helpful. The bedroom was a mess, but no worse than the rest of the trailer. He hoped the girl wouldn't reconsider her decision in the light of day.

In the morning Mac decided to hedge his bet. He skipped breakfast and even refused Lupe's offer of coffee to leave in a hurry for an appointment. But he didn't go farther than behind the nearby hill on his range. He watched and waited, but the compound remained quiet and sleepy. Lupe didn't leave the trailer, and there was no sign of any other activity. Her first chance to escape went unused, and after an hour, Mac drove back around through the front gate.

Lupe was hard at work when he entered. Her cleaning materials were grossly inadequate to turn the trailer into a livable home, but Lupe's industry was commendable. Mac asked her to list the items she needed to fully outfit the trailer for her stay. She rattled off a large number of missing household necessities, and he promised to take her shopping when he returned later in the day.

She placed a cup of coffee on the table in front of him. This time he accepted the drink with a nod of thanks.

"Your eyes show pain," she said. "This is not what you do?"

"No," he said. "I'm a rancher who got involved accidentally."

Mac studied the homeless waif standing beside the table and wondered why he had spoken so openly. It had to be her youth, or those giant, cow-like black eyes she fixed on him like searchlights. She looked more Indian than Mexican, with long dark hair and chiseled features. She was actually very pretty for a Mexican, but her eyes carried sadness instead of joy.

The oversized sweater and loose jeans hid her thin figure, but her hips were clearly narrow and adolescent and her breasts were formless mounds. Her Spanish was from somewhere in the interior of Mexico or Central America, and she must have come a long way already. He thought of the men she had been forced to service on her journey. There must have been many, probably more than his entire count of women. What a life. One dirty Mexican after another polluting her before she had a chance to grow up.

She touched the bulge on his temple that stretched his left eye into an evil slit.

"You got hurt," she said. "Horse kick you?"

Mac quickly removed her hand. Sympathy was not what he wanted. Obedience was.

"No. But I have to go now. You'll be safe here until I return, then we'll go shopping."

The girl smiled. "There'll be a long list of things to buy," she said.

136

Lupe followed him out like a wife seeing her husband off to work. She waved good-bye while holding the front gate, and he headed for Stuart's office in Anthony with a growing headache. It seemed strange to have someone wave good-bye. Mary Lou hadn't done that for years. Mac decided it felt good, even if it was just from a little girl.

He thought of Mary Lou for a moment, then dismissed her. Castillo's activities needed to be cast in concrete, the tanker fleet owner had to be brought on board, and there were enough loose strings in this Ramirez business to weave another Bayeux Tapestry.

Stuart was out, but his office telephone wasn't. Mac set up a meeting with Larkin, the Deming tanker man, then phoned his shifty Mexican ambulance chaser who probably hadn't gotten any sleep since the previous evening.

Castillo was shaky and nervous at first on the phone, but calmed down to say another shipment was expected that evening. He mentioned money was needed to pay certain personnel for the last two shipments, and asked how Mac wished to handle it.

"You'll play paymaster; we'll set that up today," Mac said. "I'll handle collections, you disbursements. Except for the coyotes, of course. I'll pay them on delivery."

"What about Jose's wife? She phoned this morning asking if I had heard from him."

Jose was Ramirez, Mac reminded himself. He cursed his luck. Trust a Mexican crook to have a wife who would worry about him.

"Tell her he's away for a while. That's happened before, hasn't it?"

"Sure, lotsa times. Once for almost a month."

"Then there's no problem."

Mac knew Mexican women frequently allowed their men folk great latitude to disappear for days and weeks without notice or contact. He remembered one woman whose husband disappeared for eighteen months, then walked back in as if nothing had happened. She never even asked where he had been.

"In a few weeks you can tell her he went to L.A., and you haven't heard from him since," he said. "If she takes any action, fine. If not, that's fine, too. After all, you're his lawyer, and everything you know is privileged."

Mac stopped and considered his exposure to a suspicious wife. "Does she have money? Like, would she hire a private dick like J.J. Arms?"

"No way. Jose kept her on a short leash, giving her money for household expenses each week. She'd have to pawn her jewelry to do anything."

Mac heard the obvious. Castillo had access to Ramirez's funds, and undoubtedly would take this opportunity to feather his own nest. Probably cleaned out Ramirez's accounts and safe deposit boxes that morning. Overnight Mac had made him a rich man.

He'd fix that in a heartbeat.

"Good," Mac said. "Now move his former working capital to a new account, this time with my name on a signature card instead of his. You can keep the safe deposit items as a bonus. Except for the business property. That you transfer to me. Just in case his widow decides to claim his assets, of course."

Castillo cleared his throat, apparently taken aback at Mac's assumption of his prerogatives.

"Of course," he said. "But I don't have access to his safe deposit box. Only he and his girlfriend did. You'll have to deal with her."

"Girlfriend? He had some slut involved?" Mac tried to picture what sort of Mexican mistress Ramirez would have. Probably taller than him with long legs and sleek black hair.

"In a manner of speaking," Castillo said.

"Well, no more nooky. She won't be a problem."

"Maybe, but she did more than spread her legs. She was a sort of partner, a go-between, and everything else when they entertained our international connections. Her house was his office." Castillo regained some strength in his voice. "Surprised you didn't know."

"Don't get cocky. Just give me her name and address."

He wrote down the particulars on one of Stuart's note pads, glaring at his writing in disgust while listening to Castillo make her sound like a cross between Lady MacBeth and Cleopatra. The first surprise had been her existence, the second her name. Tippy was a nickname for something, and Gallagher was Anglo. Maybe she picked it up in a marriage. His headache was getting worse, and he decided to visit this Gallagher broad before doing anything else.

"I'll handle her," Mac said. "Stay there and expect to get a call verifying my authority in the new organization. I might keep her around if she can make herself useful, so don't fret."

"I don't fret," Castillo said. "But I'll be twisting in the wind if you screw up."

"Like I said, chill out. I'll call you this afternoon."

Mac hung up without saying good-bye. His simple trick in placing Castillo's fingerprints on the gun that killed Ramirez was paying off in big bucks.

He had talked too much under the circumstances, but didn't want Castillo to warn the lady he was coming. The slippery lawyer seemed content to let him stew in his own dilemma without taking sides, but lawyers could never be trusted.

The Gallagher girl sounded formidable, and she might go galactic when she heard her meal ticket had been punched. If she couldn't be controlled, she'd have to be silenced. Mac took the precaution of sliding his knife into his boot. Dressed in jeans and a cotton shirt, his choices for concealment were limited. He placed his PPK in an attaché case he borrowed from Stuart's bookcase, and headed to Las Cruces for what promised to be another showdown.

Chapter 22

The girl's address turned out to be a Mexican-style hacienda in an upscale section of Mesilla Park. Large for the area, the stucco villa was clearly expensive. Apparently, Ramirez liked to keep his mistress in style. The house appeared to have three or four bedrooms, and with a sizeable lot surrounded by a seven-foot high stone wall on three sides, was more private than usual. A Mazda RX-7 was in the driveway in front of a closed garage.

Mac parked his Jeep in the driveway behind the Mazda and made his way up the walk through the exquisitely desert landscaped front yard. The entry courtyard was faced with adobe-like long brick, and Mac noted the barred windows and metal gate covering the door. He quietly tried the most likely candidate from Ramirez's key ring in the gate lock. It fit as expected.

He rang the door chimes, and watched a female form materialize in the atrium behind the heavy glass trim. The door opened to reveal a stunningly beautiful blonde in her middle twenties. As Anglo as Candace Bergen, she confidently held the door open and scanned him for an indication of his business.

Mac didn't give her the chance to speak first.

"Miss Gallagher?" Mac asked.

"Yes?" Her answer was a question. She waited for him to state why he was there.

The girl's beauty took his breath away. He had not expected to see a woman like this in real life. Definitely movie star quality, she wore a light business dress as if on her way to some important meeting. Her shimmering blonde hair framed a cover-girl face and hung straight down to the middle of her back. Those long tresses were sexy, but didn't detract from her aura of elegance.

140

"My name's Mac Arnold," Mac said. "I'm a business associate of Jose Ramirez and Hector Castillo, and have some things for you." He motioned with his attaché case to indicate it contained items for him to deliver.

The green-eyed beauty unlatched the gate immediately and invited Mac inside. She seemed at ease with Mac's sinister appearance. He figured she probably dealt with ugly characters on a daily basis.

The entryway was terra cotta and impressively styled. Mac stood for a moment to admire the girl's taste. The atrium was flanked by exotic plants, oil paintings, and a small Mexican statue displayed on a marble pedestal, probably an authentic pre-Columbian piece. She escorted him to a large living room whose furnishings included a large bar with cut-glass mirror and shelves. Everything was elegant and expensive.

Tippy was about the same height as the departed Ramirez, with a form that rivaled Mary Lou's. Her face was much prettier, but its classic regularity produced a somewhat cameo and hardening effect. She smiled and offered Mac a glass of iced tea. He positioned himself on her cushioned couch with the attaché case alongside. His headache was abating, and not a moment too soon. For some reason his pain subsided when he was either sexually aroused or in exciting situations. This one contained the potential to be both.

"It's a shame we've never met before," Mac said. "I understand you're very important to our business."

His opening line seemed to have an adverse effect on the beauty and put her on guard.

"What business is that?" she asked. She seated herself in a Chippendale chair opposite the couch, crossing her very shapely legs and smoothing out her dress.

Mac found it difficult to be gruff and intimating in this genteel environment. The living room was well-coordinated with respect to colors and furnishings, and Tippy's dress and accessories matched perfectly, her face a jewel enhanced by its setting.

He extracted Ramirez's keys from his shirt pocket and tossed them across the room. She caught them with both hands, then laid them on the small table alongside her chair. To Mac's amazement, her expression betrayed no emotion or surprise.

"Perhaps you would like to call Castillo to verify my identity," Mac said. "You see, there have been some adjustments in the organization."

Tippy eyed him evenly while waiting for him to elaborate. She reached for the telephone next to Ramirez's keys after Mac motioned twice for her to pick it up. He asked if she needed his number.

"I know the number," she snapped.

The hardness in her face turned it into a mask. She dialed rapidly and flipped her head to place the phone under her hair. It wasn't the number Mac had dialed earlier, and Castillo apparently answered instead of his secretary.

"Hector, this is Tippy. Who's this Arnold character?" Mac could not hear Castillo's reply, but the girl remained silent until she replaced the cordless telephone in its cradle a few moments later.

She took a deep breath and spoke evenly, but with tightly drawn and bloodless lips. "So, where's Jose?"

"Senor Ramirez is no longer with us," Mac said.

His statement must have hit her in the face like a wet towel, but she wasn't giving anything away. For a moment he doubted she was breathing.

"And Ricardo?"

"Also departed, I'm afraid."

The towel hit then, and the girl's chest heaved involuntarily as she gulped a shallow breath. Her face lost color and her knuckles whitened as she gripped the chair in response.

"I doubt you're afraid of much," she said.

The green eyes were boring into him, and Mac could feel the rising tension as he waited for her to continue.

The girl uncrossed and re-crossed her legs. "And me? Am I to depart?"

Tippy was one surprise after another. There was no way he'd let that absolutely gorgeous body cease breathing until it had performed certain functions.

"Not unless that's your choice," Mac said. "In fact, we envision an expanded role for you if you're interested."

She remained silent, affecting an air of superiority by making him speak to keep the discussion going. For the moment, she was giving nothing away.

He sighed audibly as if apologizing for what he was about to do. Slowly he flicked open the attaché case and placed his right hand inside. That pierced her shell. Her chin quivered ever so slightly, and

Mac thought he could smell her menstruating. Or maybe it was sweat. He unfocused his eyes to create a lifeless expression and keep up the pressure.

"It's your choice, but we need an answer now," he said. His hand remained hidden inside the attaché case.

All remaining color vanished from her face, and her eyes widened. Muscle spasms in her cheeks were clearly visible as her jaws clamped tightly together. Without a doubt, she expected to be shot if she answered incorrectly. Mac suddenly realized the ugliness caused by the roll-over was a powerful asset.

"What is it you want me to do?" Tippy cleared her throat, having been barely able to speak above a thick whisper.

"For the moment, you must prove we can trust you. What was Ramirez's is now mine. Garcia's too, for that matter. For openers, I want the contents of Ramirez's safe deposit box."

She shifted in her chair and clenched her hands together. "But—"

"If there's a *but*, we don't need you," Mac said. "It's your decision. One way or another, the box won't be yours."

Tippy squirmed as if experiencing bladder problems. She placed one hand on top of the other and stretched her fingers over her knee. Her eyes dropped to her hands and stayed there.

"All right," she said. "But what's to prevent you from killing me afterward?" She apparently didn't realize she had just used another "but."

"You. By making yourself indispensable."

She didn't look up. "How can I do that?"

"We want to expand this operation by importing goods in addition to people. You know the players. I'm sure you can contribute immeasurably if you don't let your former involvements color your thinking."

She was making a valiant effort to recover her composure and save her life. "If the truth be known, my relationship with Jose was mainly business."

For you, Mac thought to himself. He had already figured Ramirez wasn't her main squeeze.

"And Garcia?"

"Aah..." She swept some hair behind her ear. "He provided some things Jose lacked. It wasn't serious."

143

"Maybe, but it was dangerous," Mac said.

He reflected on Garcia's cat-like grace and other features that would have interested her. She had felt no qualms about being unfaithful to the man paying her tab.

He would do well to remember that.

"From now on you will give me your undivided loyalty. No Garcias, nobody else unless I say. You be good, and you'll be rewarded beyond your wildest dreams."

Mac noticed Tippy quiver slightly and assumed she was visualizing sex with him. His face was something she would have to overcome, but that was her problem, not his. If she could take on Mexicans, she could handle him. There were other parts of his body available for her attention, and she could concentrate on those.

He flashed a wide smile and stood up. "I think it's time we take a trial run," he said.

Tippy proved her worth and then some. She was a natural blonde with alabaster skin, flawless in every particular. Pink where most women were brown, what she provided would make Mexicans go crazy. Mac wasn't entirely unaffected himself, especially when pink turned to flaming red. Her breasts were unbelievable. Perfectly proportioned to her tiny waist and narrow hips, they were exquisitely shaped and firm. Mac guessed her at 36-22-35 or better. Her slender thighs featured muscles that threatened to break his neck, and her legs could make a panty hose commercial. With a face that belonged on Miss Universe, the whole package was absolutely astounding. He could take her to Vegas and easily demand five grand per night. The only question in Mac's mind was why she wasn't there already.

"You reach magnificent highs," Mac rasped in appreciation as they rested.

Tippy propped herself up on one arm and eyed him critically. "That was my mother's doing. She didn't believe looks counted for much. Or at least they don't last."

"What'd she do? Send you to sex school or something?"

"Better than that. She took me to Mexico City for my sixteenth birthday. The seventh son of a seventh son of an Aztec prince took my virginity." Tippy smiled as if granting an audience to a plebeian.

"So what did that mean? You're safe from Montezuma's revenge?"

"Asshole. Of course not. I was a virgin sacrifice to the Aztec gods and became a god's consort. He visits me when I'm asleep, makes love to me, and raises me to his level of prowess. I'm a demi-goddess of love, able to go far beyond a normal woman's capacity. You haven't even scratched the surface of my abilities."

The story sounded hokey to Mac, but who was he to question the power of belief? She certainly looked like a goddess. If she wanted to act the part, that was fine with him, so long as he reaped the benefits.

It was clear why Castillo had spoken so disparaging of the lady. The little lawyer was jealous because she wouldn't give him any. Tippy was close to the power, and Castillo merely a hanger-on with little to offer. Losing out in a competitive struggle to an Anglo bed-warmer must have really damaged his ego.

She would take some managing, and competition from Castillo would help. Above all else, Mac needed to remember that she considered her looks and body as business assets. That could also be extremely useful. A supine belly dance with an infatuated mark could do wonders in cementing a relationship or acquiring valuable information. The trick was in not becoming one of her sexual conquests himself.

In the early afternoon Castillo ponied up the funds he withdrew from Ramirez's business accounts and signed over Tippy's house, the acreage north of the Bar-D, and three other properties. Castillo didn't complain about the turnovers, and Mac decided there were accounts in other cities the little weasel kept for himself. But at this juncture he wasn't willing to go on a search-and-destroy mission. He needed Castillo as a bona fides with the south of the border crowd until he became firmly established, and further boat rocking would probably be counter-productive.

The numbers were amazing, and Mac concluded he had pulled off the caper of his life. Over four hundred thousand dollars were recovered from Ramirez's safe deposit box, and adding that to the hundred and fifty thousand from the dearly departed's business accounts, Mac was a rich man. Without further ado, he could eliminate the Bar-D's debt in one fell swoop.

Everything else was simple. Castillo would handle the Mexican connection until replaced by Tippy and himself, and Larkin agreed to continue providing transportation under the same arrangement as before. Taking over the wetback operation couldn't have gone smoother.

With regard to moving coke and weed in addition to people, Mac needed more help. Both Castillo and Tippy could provide some contacts, but a high-volume operation taking advantage of the tanker fleet required many more. This was where Stuart could come in. He had contacts everywhere, and could walk into any office in El Paso. Everything would take time, but he had plenty. For once, the clock was on his side.

Driving back to the trailer in the late afternoon sun, Mac was well-satisfied with how the day had gone. He was rich, and the recruitment of Tippy was an unexpected perk that promised to spice up his life. And she wouldn't be the only one. Mac reckoned he could get used to this life in the fast lane where beautiful women regularly cleaned his drain.

He wheeled through the compound's main gate, alighting on what was now his property. He had almost forgotten about Lupe, still waiting in the trailer with a shopping list prepared for his approval. The inside was presentable, but months of filth could not be eliminated by water alone. Lupe herself looked neat and clean, but her wardrobe was limited to the clothes on her back. Ten years and thousands of dollars younger than Tippy, she made an interesting contrast. She traded herself for sheer survival, while Tippy used sex to gain money and power.

In the best of all possible moods, Mac drove Lupe to the shopping center behind Coronado Towers in El Paso. Everyone probably thought Lupe was a live-in maid, one of thousands in El Paso. Almost all El Paso houses of three bedrooms or larger featured a maid's room, although the cost of such girls was beginning to lessen their popularity.

Mexican maids had gone up in price recently to fifty dollars per week, and the girls were getting younger. All illegal, they crossed the river every Monday morning in great numbers to be picked up by El Paso's society ladies and driven to their homes-away-from-home. The girls were provided with room and board through the week, and hopefully not all they could steal. In many El Paso families, the maids became adjunct family members, and frequently stayed for years.

Mac soon found himself doing what he least liked—pushing a

shopping cart in a large discount store. Most of its shoppers were Mexican families, and the parking lot was filled with older automobiles sporting Front Chihuahua plates. The dumpsters outside were stuffed full of boxes and wrappings that previously contained new purchases so Mexican customers could claim the items were not bought in the US when returning through Customs. Anglos were few, and Mac felt like a foreigner.

Two shopping carts were soon filled with household items, and Mac instructed Lupe to pick out enough clothes to last her for a week's trip. Unable to read English and not understanding American sizes, she hardly knew how to proceed. Mac was relieved when a teen-aged salesgirl came to their rescue. She quickly found Lupe's sizes, and the two girls tore into the clothes racks, virtually ignoring Mac's suggestions. For the moment, he was a father, paying the bill without an iota of influence.

Lupe's excitement grew as she piled blouses, jeans, and dresses on the cart. The week's trip was stretched into two, but Mac couldn't complain. Not after his coup earlier in the day. His headache was barely a minor irritant, and Lupe's wide-eyed ebullience was infectious. By the time they returned to the enclosure, it was as though she had just experienced the best birthday of her life. She grabbed her new clothes and dashed into the trailer, leaving Mac to unload the household items by himself.

The new clothes she modeled turned Lupe into a typical Hispanic-American teenager. They made her look younger, and she had regained her innocence. The sadness was gone from her eyes and replaced by hope and joy. There was still an exotic, haunting quality to her looks, but now it was softer and livelier.

The duds also loosened her tongue, making her bolder and more self-assured. Instead of shyly waiting for Mac to speak, she overwhelmed him with words as she donned each garment, all indicating her thanks for his generosity and treatment. After showing him an especially pretty dress, Lupe threw herself at Mac and gave him a warm hug. Then she reached up and stroked his still-swollen temple.

"You're a beautiful man and very nice," she said.

Mac didn't know how to respond. Yesterday, she had screwed three coyotes for scraps of food, today she was a schoolgirl arriving home from Coronado High.

He gave her a playful slap on the rear as she dashed back to try another outfit. The couch on which he sat had held three now-dead Mexicans two nights before. He decided to introduce her to Stuart when the month expired and ask him to fold her into his network of Mexican family members. Lupe was a child, and not something for Mac to deal with longer than necessary.

Chapter 23

Within three days, Mac decided his little organization was missing a player. He would not always be available to handle coyotes and their charges, particularly if Tippy continued to monopolize his time. Her practically insatiable sexual demands careened into all-out competitions to establish sexual dominance. Mac held his own, and his endurance increased with every passing night. It took practice— something he'd lacked since being crushed under his Ranger.

The girl was crazy in ways he didn't know women could be. One night, she poked fun at him lying limp after several hours, telling him that little guys were better than big men. Supposedly, they possessed more energy and made up for their lack of endowment with activity. In spite of a throbbing headache Mac became angry, grabbing Tippy and soundly spanking her for needling him. That failed to subdue her. Quite the contrary; she taunted him further until he threw himself upon her and converted his rage into a sexual frenzy.

He attacked with all his strength and masculinity, twisting, squeezing, hammering, pounding her into submission. She countered with the ferocity of a trapped wolverine. The passion she unleashed threatened to consume them both. Like two demons from Hell they had fought, male versus female, making love to the death. Her pearl-white body shimmered with perspiration, then turned scarlet as he ripped her asunder front and back. She thrashed about wildly and suddenly jolted upright. From deep within her the beast escaped. The room swam before his eyes, and he tightened his grip to prevent her from engulfing his consciousness. Ugly bruises sprouted under his hands as she came with the most unearthly screaming orgasms he had ever heard.

He listened and learned. Tippy lived for abuse, handing it out in large doses if not experiencing it herself. His back burned from her slashing fingernails, and tooth marks abounded where they hurt the most. Mac bit the insides of her thighs as her climax subsided, and the exquisite pain sent her off again like a yowling werewolf.

It was warfare. Her man would have to be brutal and unrelenting, living on the edge of ecstasy and pain. Tippy's desires weren't normal, and there was no way she could be trusted. She took everything he gave her and demanded more, but it wasn't in him. Her body was perfect, and he felt bad about marring the landscape. She didn't deserve to own such perfection, certainly not the way she used it. An evil bitch was housed in a pearl enclosure with blonde fringes, a man-eater bent on acquisition and control.

A diversion was needed, an outlet for her energy to level their playing field. She could relieve him of some odious duties by substituting for him at the trailer. It was a solution made in heaven, but Mac realized an increased role for Tippy would necessitate adding checkpoints in accounting to verify counts and amounts. The battle for dominance was not limited to her bedroom, and her feelings for him were known only to herself.

He devised a new system, giving Lupe pre-printed tickets to pass out to each immigrant, and instructions to fax all manifests to his ranch, Tippy's house, and a secured line in Castillo's office. Money collected from wetbacks was balanced by manifest, then each coyote's group was placed in an envelope, annotated with the coyote's code and manifest number, and deposited down a slot into a safe built to Mac's specifications.

Stuart recommended a Mexican contractor from Alamogordo who built a safe room in the ground between the utility sheds. Weighing at least twenty tons and with footers sunk ten feet into the sand, the safe would require a major effort with a large crane to dislodge it from its position. Mac covered it with a pre-fab storage shed, and to a casual observer it looked like some type of pump house associated with the well. The entry to the safe house was inside the shed through a steel door, and both the shed door and the steel door were wired to a hidden alarm system. No one other than the dumbest coyote would even consider attempting a robbery.

The procedure Mac initiated appeared simple to each person involved. Coyotes were no longer paid on delivery at the trailer, but at one of several locations in El Paso where funds were maintained for that purpose. Whoever was controlling the operation for the night, Mac, Tippy, or Castillo, gave the waiting coyotes their reference numbers and location to pick up their money. This added another person into the scheme, but eliminated holding cash at the trailer. With all funds going into the safe upon collection, robbery possibilities were limited to the short time before tickets were issued and collected funds deposited. During that time, everyone was present—coyotes, wetbacks, Lupe, and whoever was working the exchange.

Drivers were Larkin's sole responsibility, and he paid them on whatever basis and timing they negotiated with him. Larkin himself was paid weekly by Tippy or Mac in cash. The safe's contents were retrieved whenever Mac desired. Tippy was responsible for all bookkeeping of collections and disbursements, and a faxed report was required daily by Mac at his ranch.

But the key control mechanism was the accounting of tickets. Unknown to Tippy and Castillo, Lupe issued tickets by number, and the Albuquerque connection was required to report the ticket numbers he received. These were automatically in series, and Lupe recorded the manifest number against each ticket issued in her ticket ledger. It all had to balance: Lupe's tickets, manifests, and money.

During the first week his new procedure went into effect, Mac handled the coyotes himself, and they adapted to receiving their money in El Paso with only minor grumbling. The following few days, Mac allowed Tippy and Castillo to alternate as network manager, and both acquitted themselves admirably and kept accounts in balance. It looked like Mac's system might operate without him on a day-to-day basis. Great. That would get Tippy off his back and other parts of his body, and allow him to concentrate on ideas for expansion.

Lupe seemed to relish her advantageous position as the center of activity. With Mac's blessing, she prepared complimentary travel packages for arrivals to take on their subsequent journey, and refreshed them with food and drink before being subjected to the rigors of riding inside a tanker truck. The coyotes probably assumed she had gained Mac's confidence with bedroom activity, but nevertheless, was an influential person to be cultivated. Even the boy who originally brought her from Mexico showed her respect in Mac's presence.

151

Only when Tippy was around did Lupe tend to snap and get bitchy. This was because Tippy treated her with absolute contempt. She belittled the Mexican girl at every opportunity and spoke to her as if talking to an animal.

In front of coyotes, Tippy played the role of unattainable iceberg, even creating the impression she was in charge. If he didn't know better, Mac would have thought he worked for her. With the tanker drivers, she was businesslike, never wasting time or stopping to chit-chat. Toward Castillo, she acted neutral, as if he knew too much about her to be impressed one way or the other. It would have been amusing if her methods weren't so successful.

She maintained that mien in the bedroom. She professed to be impressed with Mac's sexual prowess, but controlled her sexuality like her checkbook. Orgasms came on demand, when and where she desired. It was only when Mac became brutal and violent that she abandoned control and enjoyed herself without a layer of mercenary management. And that was sick.

Tippy was a sexual machine, able to turn herself on and off like a light bulb. She could roll those startling green eyes up into her head and sustain hours of cataclysmic orgasms. Any man who felt her shudder or heard those toe-curling screams and moans would think she was his forever. But in spite of her sexual talent and great beauty, Mac usually came away with a nagging feeling of dissatisfaction. She rarely kissed him and always washed herself squeaky clean afterward. Like some low-life hireling, he was used and tolerated but not accepted.

But the crucial indication was his own physical reaction. The pain in his head would recede during the act itself, but return immediately thereafter, often even stronger than before. And there was other pain. In certain positions she would flail at his head, squeeze it, or batter it with her legs. The pain became excruciating, but he couldn't allow her to detect his true degree of vulnerability. If she knew his head was his Achilles heel, she'd use that knowledge to her advantage. And he couldn't risk falling asleep in her presence. He'd be dead within seconds.

Chapter 24

Meanwhile, life went on for Mary Lou. Her days were drab, and passed one after another without notice, just like today. Waitressing at Cattleman's was hard work, and Mary Lou was tired from the long evening. Driving home on nights like this, she often looked back at her ranching life with nostalgia. If she could choose between her apartment and the Bar-D for her home, the ranch would win, hands down. She missed the chili cook-offs, morning rides on Twister over the limitless desert, the large ranch house, even Mac. In spite of all her complaints, he had been in her corner, supporting and encouraging her ideas and activities. He was self-centered, but all men were. If anything, Juan was worse than Mac.

And their friends. She missed them. Without Mac, she had no standing, no circle of acquaintances she could visit to pass the time. The men she knew through Mac were out of reach. A few could have become friends, but they didn't know where she was. And regardless of her intentions, she couldn't phone a married man for an invitation. She was isolated, cut off from her previous life.

She could have hedged her bet except for the pregnancy. Mac and she could have remained friends like other separated couples, even dating occasionally to clip each other's horns. But now, it wasn't possible. Mac would never touch her with a Hispanic baby growing where he wanted one of his own. Or even be seen in public together.

Nobody cared whether she lived or died. A couple of girlfriends from NMSU were the extent of her acquaintances—and Juan. The poor boy couldn't find a job and spent most of his time drinking or harassing her. He blamed her for his predicament. According to him, he would never have gotten fired except for her leaving Mac.

And sex, what a joke. He'd come over, climb on top, make a

deposit, and look for something to eat. Or borrow money to go out with his buddies. That was it. He had yet to do anything for her, and hadn't noticed the absence of her periods.

Juan wanted her to quit school. He said college was stupid, and she should spend her time working and making money. Yeah, money for him. He only completed two years himself, and that was why he couldn't write well. What he wanted was a white girl who'd support, feed, and service him. Well, it was time for Juan to pull his weight, get off his fat ass, and earn a living.

Mary Lou pulled her Honda into the parking area beside her apartment building. For once, her parking spot was free, and Juan's pickup was nowhere in sight. He always parked in her spot instead of using the visitor area, so he obviously was out. Thinking about Juan's truck reminded her of Mac and the Ranger. Early in their marriage, they were nude as often as clothed. With Juan, she was rarely nude, even in bed. She didn't feel comfortable around him, and the loss of her freedom was something to mourn.

She studied a bit, then went to bed early. It was nice to have peace and quiet. She decided to sleep in the nude.

A racket in the living room shattered the quiet and interrupted her sleep. In a heartbeat she was fully alert. She snapped on the nightstand light. Her alarm clock showed the time as just after midnight.

"Juan?" She sat up in bed, not bothering to cover her bare chest.

"Fucking chair. What's it doing in the middle of the room?" Juan appeared in the doorway to her bedroom, rubbing his knee, and looking both drunk and angry.

"You've been drinking."

"You should try it, you'll like it." He walked unsteadily to the side of her bed and stood there staring.

She flipped back the covers and swung her legs out to sit on the edge of the bed. She waited for him to move so she could reach her robe. He didn't budge.

"Excuse me," she said. "I'd like to get up."

"Wha for? You're perfect where you are."

Juan unzipped his pants, and thrust himself into Mary Lou's face. "Here. That's what you need." He tried to force himself into her closed mouth. "Open up! Move them lips, girl!"

154

"Stop it!"

"You got to, it's my right!"

"Stop it, you're drunk!"

She pushed him away with both hands. He stepped back to maintain his balance, but his pants dropped around his ankles. Falling in slow motion, he went crashing into the wall behind him. A stunned look crossed his face, then changed to a silly grin as he slithered to the floor.

"Woweee. You mad," he said. He attempted to stand up, but his legs wouldn't work. Groaning loudly, he rolled onto his side to reach her.

Mary Lou knelt before Juan's prostrate form. She hadn't meant to hurt him, just get him out of her face. He had hit his head hard, but was probably more drunk than hurt.

"Here, for God's sake," she said. "Don't move." She pulled off his boots, then his pants. His shorts were already pulled aside, revealing more than they covered. His shirt came off over his head, and Mary Lou wrestled Juan onto her bed. He flopped into the center and rolled onto his back.

She folded Juan's clothes over a chair and returned to find him already asleep. Or passed out, she wasn't sure which.

Then she saw it. There was lipstick on Juan's shorts. She climbed on the bed and examined him closely. It was lipstick all right, supplemented by rouge. And he still smelled of some slut's strong perfume.

Damn! That fat bastard had been out fucking some whore. Then he came home and wanted her to clean him off with her mouth. When pigs fly.

Mary Lou raced to the bathroom to wash her mouth and face. There was no telling what diseases the bitch carried, and Juan had transferred them to her. She scrubbed hard with scalding water, even brushing her teeth again and rinsing with mouthwash. When she returned to her bedroom, she felt cleaner, but her anger had increased.

That bastard! Juan was dead to the world and monopolizing her bed. He was like Gordo, comical with his big belly and little dick. Now he was in her bed like he owned it. Well, this was more than a fight, it was a knockout.

She wanted to cry, but the tears wouldn't come. The Bar-D never looked better. Mac would never have treated her this way. He had class where Juan had none. Juan was just a no-account drunken Mexican out to get as much pussy as possible. What really hurt was that she had donated hers and was carrying his child. It was almost enough to go to a clinic and take care of it.

Mary Lou removed the key to her apartment from Juan's key ring. In the morning, he would go out with the trash. Tonight was the end. Tomorrow she'd set her life on a new course.

Chapter 25

Mac often thought about Mary Lou when he drove back to the ranch. He had money now, and that would eliminate the greatest issue between them. Making love with her was never combative like with Tippy, and they were a much better matched pair. Neither had made a move toward divorce yet, so Mary Lou must be keeping her options open. But she had done him wrong, and she would have to make the first move to come back. That's what Stuart said, and every day he hoped to see her red Honda parked at the Bar-D.

Meanwhile, Stuart had provided a contact in El Paso he knew for certain was involved in drug traffic.

Peter Montana was an Upper Valley lawyer reputed to represent several Vegas mobsters, and Stuart had found out a year ago that one of Pete's clients was a drug lord. Stuart wasn't using Montana for any of his businesses, but they were acquainted socially. The Prescott family's good offices opened Montana's door immediately, and the day after Stuart's call, Mac drove into El Paso for an appointment with the connected attorney.

Montana was a decidedly trendy lawyer, not Mac's type of attorney at all. Instead of a suit, Pete wore an open shirt in the Tex-Mex style adorned with multiple gold chains. He was younger than Mac expected, somewhere around Mac's own age, but moved nervously in short jerks. Displaying an arrogant opulence in his Montana Avenue offices, Pete could almost claim the street was named after himself. His receptionist was nearly in Tippy's league except for her too-heavy makeup that accentuated her large Mexican eyes and high cheekbones. And not surprisingly, her body language told Mac she accorded Pete bedroom privileges.

"Stuart speaks highly of you," Pete said after the obligatory small talk. "I trust your ranch is doing well."

"Before I answer that question, I wish to retain you as an attorney first," Mac said.

"Oh, I see. Yes, of course. This conversation is hereby privileged." Pete moved behind his desk and sat down.

"Ranching is no longer my primary source of income, but Stuart doesn't know that," Mac said. "A better term for my business is international freight forwarding." He studied Pete's face for a reaction, but there wasn't any. "This new venture has been highly profitable, but I wish to change my emphasis from perishable goods to high-density, high-value freight. Not having been involved with such items previously, I need professional consulting from experienced individuals. Possibly you might know of someone."

Pete leaned back in his chair and steepled with his fingers. It was a dominance gesture, but made no impression on Mac.

"Possibly. I have a broad clientele. Transportation is an especially tricky business to develop profitably. They would undoubtedly want to examine your present operation for efficiency before making recommendations."

Mac suppressed the urge to laugh at the double-speak in use. Anything being recorded would be totally unusable in court.

"Absolutely. I wouldn't expect anything else," he said. "I'm very proud of the smooth flow of my system, resulting in minimum warehousing and transit times. Plus, we settle accounts promptly, and although self-financed, I have built our asset position to an enviable point."

"You realize, of course, this cannot be anything illegal," Pete said. He raised his eyebrows and puffed himself up like a pompous judge. "As an officer of the court, I would be required to report any intent to perform criminal acts."

"Oh, absolutely. I'm not proposing anything of the sort," Mac said. "I'm seeking advice and contacts, not criminal representation for any possible wrong-doing."

Pete changed the subject to professional football and the Dallas Cowboys, and Mac realized their business discussion was terminated. He rose to leave, excusing himself for a fictitious bank appointment. At the door Pete indicated he would consider Mac's request for consulting help and check if he knew anyone. It was clear Pete would do his homework on Mac before going further.

Mac returned to Stuart's Anthony office after a quick lunch, and was greeted by Stuart with unbounded enthusiasm. At first, Mac assumed his friend had some hot news concerning El Paso's water suit or something to report about Pete Montana, but quickly discovered he was wrong on both counts. Stuart shook him by the shoulders and slapped him on the back.

"Mac, you're in luck!" Stuart bellowed. "I've got the answer to your love life problem."

Stuart had met Tippy, but didn't know the extent of the relationship.

"How so?" he asked.

"My first wife's youngest sister, Aimee, is coming to El Paso, and I promised she'd meet some interesting men. You're the one for her."

He remembered the strawberry blonde he'd met at Stuart's wedding ten years ago as a quiet but pretty teenager about thirteen years old. She lived in Charlotte, North Carolina, and Mac had accompanied Stuart there for the ceremony. He liked Stuart's first wife, but things didn't work out. She wasn't a westerner, and their marriage failed because of her homesickness for the east. The dearth of trees and green had done her in, although she and Stuart remained good friends. Stuart still helped her financially from time to time, and it was not surprising her sister would visit. How Ermie would take to her was a different matter.

"You want me to play host, huh? Sounds more like you want to keep peace in the family," Mac said.

"Well, if you put it that way... But she's turned into a beautiful young girl, and graduated from some ACC school. It's about time you began hobnobbing with college graduates."

"What's she been doing in the meantime?" The comment about college graduates was rich. Stuart wouldn't touch one with a ten-foot pole.

"I don't know. Finding herself, maybe. Whatever young girls do. How about it?"

"I've got a better idea," Mac said. "Norm still wants to cook at Terlingua, and she can go along. That'll give us a chance to get acquainted."

Actually, Terlingua would be a crash course in survival for the poor girl, and she'd automatically become bed bait. But it was better than simply stashing her at the Bar-D. At least at Terlingua she'd have a fighting chance and the appearance of independent choice.

Stuart saw through Mac's intentions and rolled his eyes.

"Tell you what," Stuart said. "You pick her up at the airport and squire her around for a day, then if she'll go, you're all set. But it's got to be her decision. I can't report back that I sent her to four days of unrestricted debauchery without giving her a choice."

"She'll probably take one look at me anyway and run. My face doesn't exactly cause women to go into estrous."

"Hey, there's a pot for every top. Or is it the other way around? Don't denigrate yourself. You look unusual, but a smile can do wonders."

"Yeah, if I can manage one. You don't know what these headaches are like."

"If you prefer, I'll tell her to forget it."

"Oh, don't do that," Mac said. "I'll be there with bells on." He was glad to have the opportunity to forget about Mary Lou, Tippy, and his modest criminal empire for a while. Terlingua would test his system of checks and balances, and he was eager to see if the operation could truly run without him.

There was still no word from Mary Lou, and Mac had been hoping she'd use the qualifying for Terlingua as an excuse to re-open a dialog. It would be the perfect opportunity for reconciliation. He didn't tell Stuart, but if Mary Lou called, he'd take her instead of Aimee. But for the moment, he didn't know if he'd have one, two, or no girls wanting to go with him.

Three days later, Pete Montana telephoned to indicate that several of his acquaintances were interested in meeting with Mac. It dove-tailed with Terlingua, and in two additional phone calls, everything was set. Mac would meet with Montana's people at Lajitas, directly on the Rio Grande a few miles west of Terlingua. The trip promised to be important even if Aimee turned him down.

Chapter 26

It was Aimee's first time in the old southwest, and her sister had warned her to be prepared for a culture shock. Her home state of North Carolina was called the redneck capital of the world, but supposedly it was light years away from the isolated mix of Anglo Texicans and macho Mexicans.

At least she wouldn't make the mistake of believing New Mexico was part of Mexico. Her sister had told her stories of easterners who expected to cross the Mexican border between El Paso and Las Cruces. She knew better and was set to fit in with boots and jeans. She did hope the roads were paved, however, as she was allergic to dust.

Her flight from Dallas was a six hundred mile hop over practically nothing, and it was like flying to an island somewhere in the Pacific Ocean. Looking at a map of the western United States, Aimee found nothing to the south between Juarez and Chihuahua, and it was three hundred miles to Midland-Odessa, two hundred and fifty miles north to Albuquerque, and three hundred and twenty-five west to Tucson. Other than in Las Cruces, New Mexico, she suspected there weren't thirty thousand people between those spots.

Shortly after hearing the pilot point out Guadalupe Peak on the aircraft's right side, she saw tracts that appeared like ghost towns against the desert floor. Neat city blocks and residential streets had been bulldozed into the desert landscape. She had heard of rampant land speculations promoted during the sixties and seventies in Arizona and Texas. Stupid and destructive, that's what humans were. They were destroying the earth with their greed.

Soon the contiguous cities of El Paso and Juarez came into view ahead. A treeless mountain range cut into the heart of El Paso from the north like a huge gopher run. On the Mexican side the Sangre de Cristo range continued the barrier southwards. Both looked inhospitable and barren. The Rio Grande supposedly flowed between the two mountain ranges in a three thousand-foot-high pass, but Aimee could not locate a river anywhere.

With all the empty space, it seemed strange that the population was crammed into such a small area. There were over two million souls around the pass, known as the Pass Of The North or El Paso Del Norte. Most were on Mexico's side of the border, and, as her plane descended, Aimee located the international boundary. It was nothing more than a chain link fence and a concrete irrigation ditch. She had visions of white people on one side and Mexicans on the other.

North and east of El Paso Airport the land looked bumpy like a polka-dot quilt. Her seatmate, a sergeant at Fort Bliss, told her the shrubs formed sand hills up to five feet high, and the entire area was crisscrossed with dune buggy tracks in the sand. Nothing could live there, he told her, because there wasn't any water. She wondered where El Paso and Juarez got their water if the land was so dry, surely the Rio Grande couldn't be enough.

Then the plane landed without backing its engines, and rolled to the gate as if late for a date. The passengers were out of their seats before it came to a stop, and for the first time, Aimee noticed that many were speaking Spanish. They were dressed casually, mostly in clothes that did not enhance their appearance. The aisle emptied rapidly, and she walked up the ramp, wondering how she'd find Mac Frazier.

That wasn't a problem. He was standing outside the arrival gate holding a hand-printed sign with her name.

"Doctor Frazier, I presume?" she said, mimicking Stanley's famous greeting. She extended her hand and Mac shook it formally instead of giving it a vigorous crush.

"You're Aimee Barnes," Mac said. "I remember you as a shy teenager, not a Miss America contestant. You restore my faith that nature really is God." He winked, and Aimee giggled.

She liked him immediately, with his Tony Lama boots and rough western appearance. His face was disfigured, and she tried to decide how she felt about it. There was something satanic or malevolent about his face, then she realized his eyes were located wrong because his head was lopsided. Girls who liked classically handsome guys probably considered Mac ugly and repellant. Actually, it was more scary than ugly, and not even that when he smiled. She imagined his head hurting, but he seemed strangely strong as a result of his affliction. Tall and graceful, Mac was obviously in good shape.

"I'm glad you decided to make this trip," Mac said. "Stuart has been hiding your assets under a bushel. You're much better looking than he said."

"He hasn't seen me for five years. And then I wasn't having a particularly good time."

"It happens to all of us. But you've certainly blossomed into a beautiful woman."

She thanked him while he took the canvas carry-on bag off her shoulder. He led the way down a long, carpeted concourse to El Paso's main terminal.

"I understand I'll be staying at your ranch," Aimee said. Her words were more as a question than a statement.

"Yeah, Stuart has a pretty full house right now. My place is almost empty. We do this for each other all the time. 'Course you can stay at a motel if you'd prefer."

Aimee scowled at hearing the alternative. "Why would I want to do that?" she said. "If Stuart says you're a gentleman, that's good enough for me."

"Thanks." Mac smiled and squeezed Aimee's hand.

"Do you have horses?" Aimee asked.

"You bet. Best paint horses west of the Pecos. Not many, but the best."

"One I can ride? I love horses, but don't get to ride much back east."

"Twister is there, my ex-wife's palomino mare. She's an excellent horse for occasional riders. She'd probably be overjoyed to acquire a new female rider." Mac winced involuntarily in pain.

Aimee touched his arm. "Are you all right? Do you have a headache?"

Mac took a deep breath. "Just a momentary thing," he said. "A holdover from my accident last summer, but they're beginning to go away."

Mac described his accident and talked about his head injuries which were readily apparent. He changed the subject when they came to the escalator leading to the main terminal and shopping mall.

"Well, here we are," he said, waving his hand at the signs welcoming travelers to El Paso.

At least half of them were in Spanish, and except for the displays of model airplanes in the walkway, Spanish and Hispanic culture appeared dominant.

"Texas isn't bilingual, is it?" Aimee asked. She studied the shop signs in the small shopping mall next to a Spanish-style courtyard.

"Depends on what you mean by bilingual. There's no official language in Texas, so you'll see mostly English with a lot of Spanish. New Mexico has two official languages, English and Spanish. Having only English as the official language is a violation of foreigners' civil rights. Do you speak Spanish?"

Aimee had been listening with one ear to several people talk and turned back to Mac.

"This is not Spanish like I learned in college. It's sort of a Pidgin Spanish. Aren't these people embarrassed?"

"Only when they go south. In Mexico City, they're looked down upon as illiterate peasants. By the way, how much baggage do you have?"

"Two pieces. Will it take long?"

"What's the slowest airport you've been in for baggage?"

"Atlanta. Fifteen to twenty minutes. But I think that's because they search through the luggage for things to steal."

"Prepare yourself then for a shock. The minimum wait here is twenty minutes, and I've waited as long as forty-five."

"But this is a small airport. Why does it take so long? Or do they steal here, too?"

Mac shrugged. "Some say it's inadequate staffing, others say it's cultural. All I'll say is that you need to become acclimated to everything being slower around here."

Thirty-five minutes later, they collected Aimee's bags and climbed into Mac's new Ranger. Aimee couldn't help commenting to Mac on the accuracy of his estimate. The service was risible, but at least nothing was stolen.

They exited the airport parking lot after Mac paid an extra dollar because of the long wait. Aimee could tell Mac was aggravated, but he restrained himself from making nasty comments. He drove south on Airways Boulevard, obviously attempting to put a good foot forward. Suddenly, he wrenched the Ranger violently to the left.

"Wow!" Aimee yelped. The abrupt change of direction jostled her badly, but Mac had deftly avoided an old Chevrolet that bounced into the street from a furniture store's parking lot. As they went by, Aimee noted its driver was a little Hispanic woman who stretched up to see over the dash. Her car was loaded with kids, and she wasn't driving over twenty-five.

"Pretty quick reaction," she said.

"Did'ja see that light blue plate?" Mac said, gesturing toward the Chevy. "That was a Front Chihuahua plate. A Mexican. You've got to avoid them at all costs."

"Why?"

"They don't have any insurance. And if the accident is bad enough, they'll just leave the car and walk back to Mexico. They don't care. Their car's not worth anything. And if it's your fault, every one of those kids will have permanent injuries. As a rich Anglo, you don't want to go up against a Hispanic jury when you've injured some poor Mexican."

"But I'm not rich."

"Makes no difference. You're Anglo. All Anglos are rich compared to Mexicans."

"What if you're in Mexico?"

"It's worse. American insurance policies aren't valid in Mexico, and having an accident is a criminal as well as a civil matter. So even if it's not your fault, you're better off leaving your car and walking back home. Otherwise, it can cost you more than money. There'll be a thousand witnesses taking the side of any local, and buying your way out of jail is no joke. If a cop waves you over to the curb, be prepared with your *mordida*."

"*Mordida*?"

"Payoff money, bribes, greasing their palms. It's their way of life. I'll never understand why Americans persist in going there. They must have a death wish."

Mac glanced at Aimee and tapped her knee. "If you went over there alone in that dress, you'd be molested."

"Why? What's wrong with this dress?"

"Nothing, but it's a dress. And you're a beautiful blonde Anglo girl. You'd find yourself on the street in a press of male bodies, and suddenly hands would be all up and down your dress and your purse is gone. It's a common occurrence."

"You're not painting a very pretty picture of Mexico," Aimee said.

"Well, it's not really Mexico. It's a border town, and like all border towns, it functions above the law a lot of the time. Car thefts and burglaries in El Paso are endemic. Everything goes to Mexico. To own a Ford pickup in El Paso is merely to warehouse it for a short time on its way into Mexico."

"Sounds like a girl needs a protector."

"That's why Stuart sent you to me. Frazer Protection at your service, my lady."

Chapter 27

As Mac drove, he pointed out the various El Paso landmarks and talked about the city and its history. It was unlike anywhere else in the world.

"There's a strong movement in town to declare the two cities an international zone and move the border to Anthony for Customs and Immigration," he said.

"Really? El Paso would become a lawless area like some old pirate island."

Mac nodded. "I wouldn't go anywhere without my thirty-eights."

"Who would want to do that?" Aimee said. "Move the border back, I mean."

"Banks, smugglers, the legal community, industrialists who want to take advantage of cheap Mexican labor. Trilateralists and Council for Foreign Relations guys."

The conversation was becoming depressing, and Aimee concentrated on studying the people and city around her. She noticed most of the people appeared Hispanic.

"What's the percentage of Hispanics in El Paso?" she asked.

"Somewhere over sixty percent and increasing. Maybe even seventy now. For a while El Paso was attracting retirees from the Army and its usual complement of snowbirds, but now Mexican immigration is swamping everything. The other day one El Paso high school girl writing to *The Times* referred to Spanish as being our official language. A radio announcer even mentioned *Cinco de Mayo* as being El Paso's most important holiday."

"Not the Fourth of July?"

"Nope. I guess he didn't believe El Paso was part of the United States. And the fifth of May has nothing to do with Mexican independence. It started in a California mining camp."

"So tell me about UTEP. I understand its campus is one of the most beautiful in the nation."

"It really is. The buildings are unique in the western hemisphere. The wife of an early president saw a picture of a Bhutanese monastery in a *National Geographic Magazine*, and that became UTEP's standard architecture. It's perfect for the hot and dry southwest."

"Is there a lot of hi-tech work? I understand cities in the southwest are the rage for companies fleeing the northern cities for a more pleasant climate."

"I'm afraid not. El Paso is a minimum wage town. A couple of years ago, a UTEP computer science professor attempted to interest the mayor and the El Paso Development Corporation in attracting hi-tech companies to El Paso. The mayor put him down so hard the professor left town. They were only interested in providing employment for unskilled workers. That high-paying jobs would create employment for lower skilled people went over their heads."

Aimee noted the neighborhoods appeared to be a mix of styles, Spanish, traditional, and modern. Some of the houses were painted in pastel colors, and trees were smaller and fewer than in the east. With mostly faded grass or rocky yards, chest-high rock walls, and vehicles scattered at random, the residential areas looked sleepy.

They pulled off the freeway as they neared downtown and turned toward a mountain that reminded Aimee of a razorback hog going the wrong direction. At major intersections, newspapers and flowers were being sold car to car. Then she saw little kids coming to cars and begging.

"Begging? Are these kids American?" she blurted.

"They're Mexican. The vendors pretty much are from this side, but who really knows?"

Mac pointed to several large grates covering the entrance to a huge drainage culvert. "See those grates? They're to keep Mexicans from using the drainage system to sneak into El Paso, burglarize the neighborhoods, and go back under cover. You have to understand, Mexicans don't believe that stealing is a sin. If something is stolen from you, it's your fault. You should have protected it better. That's why the houses in Mexico are surrounded with high stone walls with broken glass embedded on the top."

Aimee felt the need to change the conservation. At one corner, she noticed an old brick mansion with impressive architecture and pointed it out to Mac.

"That was once one of the two top bordellos in town," Mac said. "El Paso used to be wild and woolly."

They pulled off the main drag and parked in front of a row of nondescript stores on a busy side street.

"Where are we going?" she said as Mac turned off the engine.

"Lunch," he replied. "Time to get you immersed in local culture, and this is the best Mexican restaurant in town."

"Where?" Aimee asked. None of the businesses looked like a restaurant.

"That one," Mac said. He pointed to an building with odd-shaped windows jutting out from the strip of businesses. "Casa Jurado. You'll love its *chile rellenos*. They use Hatch chiles rather than the traditional *poblanos*."

Aimee followed Mac into a small, darkened space, crowded with tables and patrons busily eating from plates that left little room on their tables for elbows. A bowl of tostada chips and dish of red sauce were in the center of each table, and customers waiting on their orders were lustily feasting on the chips. The atmosphere was uncommonly friendly, and a young Hispanic guy ushered them to a two-person table. Another waiter appeared like magic, placing tostados and sauce before them and asking if they wanted iced tea. Mac ordered two.

"Try the *pico de gallo*," Mac said, taking a *tostado*. "It's not hot."

Aimee tentatively dipped a large chip in the red sauce as the iced tea arrived. One bite and she was ready to drink the entire glass. She started to cough. "Not hot?"

Her eyes watered, and she sipped the tea to control her throat. The tea tasted terrible, and she realized it wasn't sweetened. She dropped the remainder of her *tostado* and reached for the sugar.

"Oh, I forgot. Tea is automatically unsweetened out here," Mac said. "That's because we drink so much of it. With our low humidity, you have to drink constantly to keep from becoming dehydrated. Most easterners don't realize that, then wonder why they collapse in mid-afternoon."

Mac laughed and waved his hands before continuing. "The opposite occurs when I travel east. The first night I go to the bathroom nine hundred times. Here your skin takes care of excess fluids, there, your kidneys do the work."

Aimee was still attempting to soothe her burning mouth and throat.

"Eat more chips without the sauce," Mac said. "That takes the heat away, not the tea."

She took several *tostados* and woofed them down. Mac was right. Her throat settled down and her mouth stopped burning. Aimee could see that Mac was relaxing. The dimly lit restaurant was apparently helping, and he became less critical. She liked that. There was a lot to learn, and Mac made it fun when he wasn't so negative.

The menus arrived and Aimee was astounded at the low prices. The selections were also different from those in North Carolina's Mexican restaurants.

"They don't have chicken fajitas," she said.

Mac laughed and shook his head. "There is no such thing," he said. "*Fajitas* in Spanish means skirt steak, and chickens don't have skirts."

"I thought it meant strips of meat."

"That's the east coast for you. New York will come out with tuna fajitas next, it's just as logical. Or shrimp fajitas." Mac was shaking with laughter.

Aimee put down the ornate, Mexican-looking menu, assuming Mac would order for her. "I was surprised when Stuart said you would be picking me up," she said. "Was this bad timing for him?"

"Not really. He figured you'd rather see the area with someone who had lots of free time rather than a businessman working seventy hours a week. He also thought you might like to accompany me to the World Championship Chili Cook-off at Terlingua next week."

"A chili cook-off? What's that like?" Aimee's curiosity was aroused. It was difficult to imagine this lean cowboy cooking. Riding in a rodeo would be more his style.

"You need to meet some people," Mac said. "Then you'll understand."

He quickly ordered *rellenos*, and excused himself to use the telephone at the cashier's counter. Aimee was surprised he could use the restaurant's telephone for a private call. That would never be allowed in North Carolina. After a short phone conversation, Mac returned.

"After lunch we'll visit some friends of mine who'll be there, too. They're competitors, but we're all one big happy family who'll be camping together. Elizabeth and Doug Hamm. He's a professor at UTEP."

Aimee blinked at the easy way Mac assumed she'd go along with everything. On the other hand, why not? She had come out west to meet new people and broaden her experience, and Mac was a good place to start. She liked sitting back and letting things flow to her.

The *rellenos* arrived, and they were superb like Mac promised. The hot sauce had prepared her for the chiles, and she downed them with no trouble. Aimee began to study Mac, and wondered about the true extent of his injury. She noticed when he scowled at people, they often recoiled from his scary appearance, but when he smiled at her, all that disappeared. It made her feel special, and it was fun being with someone who scared everyone else. Her male protector was all-powerful, and that made her feel very secure among all these strangers.

She supposed people out west lived more dangerously than those back east. Or maybe differently. Not into drugs and the daily big-city violence. Whatever, it was time for a change, and she decided to accept things at face value and see what developed.

Chapter 28

Lunch seemed to go almost too rapidly, and before Aimee knew it, she was again in the Ranger heading up a quiet residential street.

"How about this?" Mac said. "Kern Place. Laid out during World War I by a drunken surveyor following his drunken donkey."

Aimee doubted the veracity of Mac's statement, but there didn't seem to be any straight streets. It was a beautiful area with trees and lawns, and organized around a pretty little green park. The houses were unique and representing every conceivable style of architecture.

Mac pulled into the driveway of a small Spanish style bungalow. A blousy lady in her middle thirties immediately came out to greet them.

"I'm Liz," she said effusively. "You must be Aimee." Without so much as a *how do you do*, Liz grasped her in a bear hug, kissed her on the cheek, and patted her back. "I understand you're going to Terlingua."

"Ah... I've been invited," Aimee replied. She felt overwhelmed by Liz's ebullience and show of affection.

Liz leaned back. She held Aimee by the shoulders, and looked like she was sizing her up for a fitting.

"Did you bring jeans?" Liz said. "Tight jeans?"

Aimee blinked at Liz's familiarity. "I threw in a pair. Why?"

"Honey, dresses don't cut it around cook-offs. You'll need all the protection you can get. Come on in the bedroom, sweetie, there's someone you have to meet."

Aimee couldn't believe this was happening, but followed Liz into her house and bedroom. She had been surprised to see a housewife as well-endowed as Liz in jeans and a T-shirt, but on Liz they seemed natural. This was a brassy Texas broad, big-chested and able to handle the toughest characters. Aimee felt positively puny by comparison. About the only thing she had more of than Liz was hair.

Hers cascaded in thick strawberry blonde layers below her shoulders, while Liz's brown hair was cut relatively short. There was an undeniable warmth about Liz, and her smile and sparkling blue eyes made her attractive even to Aimee.

Her hostess reached into a specimen case while Aimee couldn't help noticing intimate items strewn around the still-messy bedroom from the previous night. Even invited, she felt like an interloper. A small pile of clothes lay on the king-sized bed, including a pair of panties, man's shorts, and a bra. Much larger than hers, Aimee immediately noted. She turned to Liz.

"Damn!" Aimee shrieked. Liz was holding out the biggest, scariest, nastiest black spider Aimee had ever seen. It completely covered Liz's hand.

"Don't be scared, honey." Liz slowly put one hand in front of the other while the spider walked haltingly forward. "Her name is Satin, and she's a Mexican red-legged tarantula. She's our pet."

"Some pet." Aimee tried to recover from the shock.

At first blush, the huge thing was horrible. Black and orange-red, ugly, and evil. Aimee stood still and brought herself under control.

"She won't hurt you. They're very docile, and they don't have poison, they have venom. Would you like to hold her?"

About as much as a rattlesnake. But she stretched out her hand. Liz placed hers so the next step by Satin would take her onto Aimee's fingers. Satin placed two of her eight feet on Aimee's dampening skin and stopped. Aimee held her breath and concentrated on not fainting. She hadn't expected the west to be anything like this.

"She doesn't know you, and she's sensing whether it's safe," Liz said.

Tentatively, Satin moved forward again onto Aimee's hand. The mammoth spider felt like tiny patches of Velcro being softly applied to Aimee's now extremely sensitive skin.

"Be careful, don't drop her," Liz said. "Tarantulas have no skeleton and will burst when dropped from any height. They also have no muscles, and move by pumping their body fluid through their legs. Building up pressure allows them to spring, but their eyesight is so poor, they can't see more than a few inches."

"How old is she?" Aimee swapped her hands as Satin began to walk more actively.

"About thirteen years old. She's a mature female. One of the largest tarantulas I've seen."

"I can believe that," Aimee said. "Why on God's earth do you have one for a pet?"

"For show. She's part of our act at the cook-offs."

"Wow. I've only seen them trying to cross highways."

"Those are all males. Female tarantulas spend their lives at the front of their burrows, eating passing bugs and awaiting males. The males roam during their mating year, normally their eleventh and last. They approach the female, clamp her fangs with their mating hooks, bend her backwards, and mate twice with both penises. Then they back off, release their mating hooks, and run like hell." Liz laughed.

"Sounds like some guys I've met," Aimee said, "only they didn't have two penises."

"It's not all love; sometimes it's war. The female gets pretty mad about being used and abused, and if she can catch the male within a few feet, she'll try to kill him."

The spider walked back onto Liz's hand, and Aimee was proud of herself for handling it. She had conquered a fear on her first day out west. "It's good to see some males get their just deserts," Aimee said. "So what's this about an act?"

"Oh, we milk her for her venom and put it in the chili. Remember, it's not a poison, it's an enzyme. The tarantula kills its prey by stabbing with her inch-long fangs, then injects her venom into the insect. It turns their insides to mush, and she sucks it out for food. I don't think there's a single recorded instance of a person dying from a tarantula bite."

Aimee listened politely to the short biology lecture, but wasn't sure what to believe.

"You put the venom in your chili?" she said.

"Sure, we milk her like a rattlesnake, but only get a couple of drops. We cut it, and two drops make a quart of venom juice. It adds bite to our chili."

"Blecch," Aimee snorted. It didn't sound particularly tasty. "Hospitals must love you."

"Naw, all they do is deliver Mexican babies," Liz said with a dismissive wave of her hand.

"I beg your pardon? You mean Mexican from Mexico or Hispanics?"

"Mexicans from across the ditch, my dear."

"But why? Aren't there hospitals in Mexico?"

Mac had strolled into the bedroom unnoticed. "Sure," he said. "But pregnant women sneak over here to give birth. Then their kid's an American, qualifying for free education, welfare, medical, and the parents can enter legally to take care of him. They're called anchor babies."

"Don't forget the birthing centers," Liz said. She turned to Aimee. "El Paso has a huge number of midwives, and their birthing centers handle Mexican nationals almost exclusively."

"And if they have problems, Thomason Hospital takes them in. Can't let them go back to Mexico, can we?"

"Let me get this straight," Aimee said. She shook her head as if not believing her own words. "So if they can get born here, the U.S. will take care of them and their families."

"That's right, honey," Liz said. "A quarter-million Mexicans a year cross just to give birth. If we can't keep them out, we have to pay."

Another man entered the bedroom and extended his hand to Aimee. "I see you're scouting the competition," he said. "I'm Doug Hamm, Liz's other half."

Aimee took his hand and shook it. "Mac said you're a professor at UTEP. What do you teach?"

"Sociology. But really I just help warehouse young people and keep them off the unemployment rolls."

Aimee thought Doug looked more like a salesman than a professor. About the same age as Liz, he was almost as tall as Mac but much heavier. Most pronounced of all, there was a cherubic innocence about him that was probably devastating to his female students.

"We're having our last cook-off before Terlingua tomorrow," Liz said. "Since Bar-D Brand isn't cooking, how about joining us?"

Aimee looked at Mac. "You're Bar-D, right?"

Mac nodded. "Yep, so why not? It'll be fun and a good introduction to chilihead society. You'll know better what to expect at Terlingua."

"It'll be fun," Liz added. "By the end of the cook-off, we'll all be related."

175

How could she refuse? Aimee felt like she had sky-dived into a volcano, seething with action and new experiences. She was being treated as a celebrity. None of these people knew or cared about her sordid past. They simply took her at face value. It was wonderful.

"Take me," she said to the Hamms. "I'm yours."

Chapter 29

The following morning, Aimee learned a chili cook-off was quite a production. The Hamms' chili was called "Taranchili," a terrific gimmick name which had become famous throughout the chilihead world. Liz gave her a black T-shirt, with "TARANCHILI" on the back and "HEAD MILKER" on the front. The other sayings were similarly suggestive and Aimee wondered how raucous these cook-offs would get.

Looking at her T-shirt, Aimee realized it was time to fish or cut bait. Her breasts were somewhat large for her slender frame, and tight clothes made them look even larger. She donned the T-shirt. Her nipples became erect immediately, clearly announcing their presence to all who cared to notice.

She sighed her acceptance of reality. Her light bra did little to prevent her nipples from showing, but if she ignored them, they'd be less conspicuous. Liz said cook-offs sometimes held wet T-shirt contests, and Aimee hoped she wouldn't get stoned or talked into entering. The last thing she wanted was to offend her new friends by violating their rules of behavior.

Mac had been a perfect gentleman the previous night. He had given her his guest room, and although the door didn't lock, she'd felt safe. The day had been wonderful, and when Mac left for several hours in the evening to check on his cattle, she made herself at home in his house. They talked more about UTEP and the west after he returned, and when they called it a night, she couldn't decide whether she wanted him to make a show of affection like a hug or good-night kiss. But he hadn't made any such move, and his easy manner suggested it wasn't important.

The smell of bacon and eggs wafted in from the kitchen when she woke. Mac mixed onions and chiles into the scrambled eggs. And they were delicious. Considering that Mac barely knew her, he sure was going out of his way to be a good host.

It was similar with the Hamms. They accepted her as if she was Liz's younger sister and already part of the family. She helped Doug pile gear into his Explorer, and before noon, they were fully set up on the shopping center parking lot in front of Adolph's, the sponsoring business.

The Hamms went first class, with a custom-made booth, eight feet square and seven feet high. The canopy was a heavy red plastic canvas fringed in black, and the booth's front featured an eight-foot table draped with a black cover. "TARANCHILI" was painted on the part hanging off the table in bold white letters. The back panel was red with a huge black tarantula painted in the middle. The entire booth looked sinister.

They were talking with other cooks when Aimee noticed Doug looking at his watch every few minutes.

"What's so important about the time?" she asked.

"See those guys over there?" He pointed to two men standing by some cars parked behind the line of booths.

Aimee shaded her eyes from the bright sun and looked where Doug indicated. The two men wore business suits and were completely out of place on a Sunday morning when everybody else was wearing jeans and T-shirts.

"They're from the Texas Tobacco, Alcohol, and Firearms Commission," Doug said. "It's illegal in Texas to drink alcohol in public before noon on Sundays. So I'm waiting for twelve o'clock."

Aimee couldn't believe it. Her Wild West had turned tame. It had blue laws like the Bible Belt. How could Texas be concerned with beer on Sunday with all the violence around?

She went back to the booth and helped Liz dice the lean sirloin steak into three-eighth inch cubes for the chili. There seemed to be one ingredient missing.

"Where are the beans?" she asked.

"Beans?" Liz roared. "Sweetie, from now on remember one thing: anyone who knows beans about chili, knows there ain't no beans in chili."

They forgave her ignorance because she was from the east, and Aimee recalled her sister's comment about a culture shock. But contrary to her sister's feelings, Aimee felt at home.

Doug popped his beer at high noon and began to prepare the chili. Aimee studiously noted his secrets in making a superior bowl of red. Doug cooked in a cast iron pot rubbed down with bacon grease. He carefully browned the meat by itself, stirring with a wooden spoon and adding just enough water to keep it from sticking.

He sometimes used a bit of venison to add flavor, and said he had experimented with adding onion, but it softened the after-taste, so vinegar had to be added to restore the residual bite rated highly by judges. The spices were sugar, salt, *comino*, red pepper, black pepper, cayenne, garlic, and paprika. Doug and Liz had simmered an unpatented collection of Jalapeno, Sandia, Big Red, and two other chiles grown in the Rio Grande valley in a giant kettle, squeezed out the chile pulp into another kettle, and added the spices. The final mix was blended thoroughly and put into one-cup bags for freezing. Two large oregano leaves were placed in each bag before sealing. One cup would be added to the chili for every eight ounces of three-eighth-inch diced steak cubes. The cooking was timed so the meat would absorb the chile flavor, yet still give up a fresh meat taste and not turn mealy when chewed. Cooked too long and the chili crumbled, not long enough, and the chili separated as it cooled. The last thing Doug did was remove the large oregano leaves.

Aimee worked the crowd handling Satin while Doug cooked. Liz distributed Taranchili buttons and socialized, introducing Aimee to a steady stream of admiring men. The TTAFC killjoys were long gone, but Aimee went light on the beer to keep things under control. No one was smoking pot, and there weren't any other temptations she couldn't handle.

Almost all the cook-off attendees were Anglo, but the few Hispanic guys collected around her as if she was a magnet. Half of the crowd hit on her in addition to the various offers she received thanks to her T-shirt, but nobody was really serious. It was good, clean, dirty fun, even if the men weren't as brave as the women when it came to handling Satin. She collected four pins and a button from other teams, all of which were placed on her T-shirt with some degree of ceremony. One presenter got her laughing so hard he had to hold her boob to keep from sticking it. It was hardly unpleasant, and his ingenuity deserved a reward. And they came in second in the cook-off.

Mac arrived to reclaim her while she relaxed with Doug and Liz in the booth. Without hesitation, she gave Mac the last of her beer. He had told her about UTEP the previous evening, but it was fun hearing it from a professor's viewpoint. She pumped Doug for information on college life and compared it to her own experiences. Especially interesting was that UTEP had a woman president with a Hispanic name.

"Is that because most of the students are female or Hispanic or what?" Aimee asked.

"None of the above," Doug said. "First of all, she's not Hispanic. She's an Anglo who was once married to a Hispanic. Although you're right—most of the students are female, and most are Mexican. The Board of Regents had ulterior motives for appointing her. They look great for affirmative action, while eliminating UTEP as a contender for state and U.T. system funding. That's because she has no stroke at all in the Texas good-ol'-boy system."

Aimee wasn't sure how that all affected UTEP, but evidently Doug felt strongly about the issue. The student body was more interesting to her.

"It's unusual for most students to be female," Aimee said.

"No foolin'," Doug said. "UTEP's the best kept secret in academia. The better families in town send their sons to UT Austin, A&M, the Ivy League, or somewhere else away from home. Their daughters stay here where daddy can watch over things. So UTEP boasts an enormous number of beautiful co-eds, going without boyfriends because local pickings are so slim. Have you seen any good-looking guys here at the cook-off?"

"No, but I've seen lots of beautiful women. The competition's awesome."

"That's it. Courtesy of the Old West attitude of protecting women."

"Must be a tough place to be a young, handsome faculty member." Aimee said. She wondered how Doug would answer.

"For some, sure. We've lost a couple of professors already this year to the temptations. A couple of years ago, even the Vice President for Academic Affairs succumbed. But none of them had a Liz at home." Doug smiled broadly, and Liz plastered a big kiss on him.

Everybody clapped, including Aimee. This party had to go on the road to Terlingua.

Chapter 30

It was time. Aimee had decided to accompany Mac after cooking with the Hamms, but let matters drift for another day to see if Mac would pressure her. She didn't like being pushed into things, and in a way, she was testing him. He passed with flying colors, and she was looking forward to the trip with greater anticipation than her college graduation.

Aimee met Norm and Mona for the first time when they loaded their gear into Norm's Winnebago at the ranch. Mac had told her what to expect, but his was a man's view, and she reserved her opinions for herself. She felt a kinship for Mona immediately, and Norm was a character who would add color and amusement. Both Mona and Norm greeted her with open arms like the Hamms. For an early Wednesday morning and facing a long drive, the group's spirit of adventure was invigorating.

The RV had room for four, and she wondered how their sleeping accommodations would be worked out. Mac was still being a gentleman. They had progressed to hugs after the Adolf's cook-off, and last night he kissed her lightly before they went to bed. That was all. He hadn't pushed the issue. Of course, she had come out to get away from the east and her past, not find a new boyfriend. So far, everything was working out perfectly, and if a little romance was in the air, why not? It would be a fresh start.

It was possible they were trying to do too many things at once. Mac cut a wonderfully romantic figure on horseback, but riding over his range during daytime left her tired and sore for evenings. Somehow, they weren't on the same timetable yet and needed to get synchronized. If that was the problem, this trip was the solution.

There was also another fly in the ointment that Aimee couldn't figure out. Each evening, Mac ran off for several hours and returned dog-tired. Mac said he filled his watering tanks and did other work, but nothing sounded particularly taxing. Nonetheless, he usually arrived with a worse headache than when he'd left. Whatever he was doing, it wasn't helping his physical state.

This trip would change that pattern by throwing them together away from his ranch for several days. They'd have nothing to do, and she'd find out what made him tick one way or another. There would be no evening disappearances, and no invisible competition, if that was it. He'd have to share with her, and the trip promised to be exciting.

If he opened up about his accident and divorce, it'd be a giant step forward. Stuart had filled her in with details Mac omitted at the airport, so Aimee knew what to expect. She couldn't imagine a more tragic story, and hoped he'd give her the chance to show her support. Shoot, how could any woman not be sympathetic if they knew the facts?

It must have been horrible for a vigorous man like Mac to be laid up for almost two months. Then to lose his wife on the night of his homecoming. It was a miracle he could function at all. Every time she thought about his ex-wife, she wanted to scream. Women like that took the good men away and ruined them for normal girls like herself.

The actual chili cook-off was not until Saturday, and they would have plenty of time to themselves. According to Mac, the majority of attendees paid little attention to the cook-off competition. Mostly the event was just a large scale excuse to get drunk, molest girls, and enjoy western music and fellowship around a campfire.

As if to prove Mac's point, Norm and he followed three rules: (1) no drinking until the Fabens exit ten miles east of El Paso, (2) at least one good meal per day must be eaten, and (3) there would be no further rules. The first rule stumped her until Mac said it was a health rule—it took that long for the beer to cool down. It was difficult to argue against them if one's goal was rest and relaxation. Norm, however, maintained his objective was I&I instead of R&R, or as he defined it, intercourse and intoxication. Aimee wasn't sure he was kidding.

They turned off Interstate 10 at Van Horn, and headed south through Valentine to Marfa and Alpine. The road was clear and a Vette flashed by at well over a hundred miles per hour. Mac explained that was normal on state and farm-to-market roads in West Texas. In New Mexico he drove at least eighty-five, and with visibility measured in tens of miles, there was little risk. The only danger came from animals, and then mostly at night. Groups of wild antelope grazed in the scrubby pasture south of Valentine, and they outnumbered vehicles on the road. In a twenty-mile stretch, Aimee saw only three cars.

Mac filled the time with stories of the Old West, relating the sagas of Billy the Kid, Pat Garrett, Dallas Stoudenmire, John Wesley Hardin, Pancho Villa, and the Salt Flats War. He pointed out sights along the way, and told what he knew of the area. It seemed to Aimee that every town in Texas had a story, some better than others, but all begging for an author.

Valentine originated as a crew-change point on the Southern Pacific which ran along the highway, but built its claim to immortality by having a post office favored by romantics on February 14. Almost a ghost town now, its facilities were limited to a gas station and a small cafe that looked closed.

Marfa was famous for its mysterious "lights," said by locals to be extraterrestrials in the hills southeast of town. Mac explained that lights could be seen occasionally moving in the uninhabited hills late at night, and all efforts by authorities and interested individuals to locate their source or explain the phenomena had so far come to naught. Most debunkers dismissed the lights as being drug smugglers or cowboys, but trails were few and the area was remote and wild.

Aimee thought Alpine was just about the prettiest little town she had ever seen. It lay in a beautiful valley, clean and lush, dominated by an exquisitely architected college on a well-landscaped hill to the east. Sul Ross University added a sense of gentility and culture to the western town below, and Aimee surmised that only Alpine's isolation kept it from becoming a retirement community of great popularity.

The two-lane road south of Alpine meandered through a moon-like landscape as it descended into Study Butte. Ancient volcanoes and stark outcrops of multi-colored rocks glowered at Aimee from all sides, daring her to leave the safety of her macadam ribbon and venture into the unknown. A person suffering from depression might well have thought he was descending into Hell, but Aimee felt a surge of excitement from the raw power and majesty of nature's creation.

They arrived at the Terlingua store in early afternoon, and she noted the encampment already featured over sixty campers and RVs strewn across an undeveloped desert area. The only amenities were a few wooden outhouses randomly scattered about, and a large, covered stage backed by hay bales that suggested a Woodstock-type entertainment facility. Trees, of course, were totally absent. So was civilization in the form of water and electricity.

Norm drove up a low hill overlooking the eastern end of the site and parked his Winnebago near a circle of stones containing the ashes of former campfires. Aimee jumped from the RV to stretch her legs after the long drive. The adventure was about to begin.

Visibility was unlimited in the warm November afternoon. The sky was cloudless, and from her hill, Aimee could see for miles in all directions. The Chisos Mountains in Big Bend National Park bordered her view to the south, and various mesas and barren mountains in other directions created a sense of being on some alien planet.

This was indubitably one of the few remaining outposts in the Wild West, and modern civilization represented by the chiliheads and their high-tech vehicles was strictly temporary. Aimee was committed to enjoying herself. Whatever the land lacked in providing food for one's tummy, it more than made up for it with nourishment for the soul.

Norm had done the driving, and it was Mac's job to set up camp. Aimee changed into shorts and a "Virginia Is For Lovers" T-shirt to help out. Norm and Mona headed off to visit other chiliheads while she and Mac set up a folding table outside the RV. No blue laws here. It was to be their bar for the duration, open at all times to all campers.

Soon an array of bottles was displayed: bourbon, scotch, vodka, gin, tequila, and Wild Turkey. The mammoth ice chest went under the table, and she stacked cups and mixes next to the booze. An orange juice carton proved stubborn, and folding the spout as directed failed to produce an opening.

"Here, let me," Mac said, taking the half-gallon carton from Aimee's grasp. He wrenched the spout which resisted even his large hands.

Suddenly the carton flew open, and orange juice splashed out onto the front of Aimee's T-shirt like it had eyes. She squealed and jumped backwards, but only succeeded in saving her jeans from a similar fate.

The icy liquid quickly affected her breasts, and without a bra, Aimee noticed she had unexpectedly entered a wet T-shirt contest. She looked up at Mac to see if she would win. His eyes were glazing over. He reached out and wiped some of the orange particles from her chest, shyly at first, then more vigorously. She held her breath but her chest was heaving. Their eyes met and they knew.

"Let's go inside," Mac said. His voice rumbled and was barely audible. It was only a few steps to the door.

She entered first and walked directly to the Winnebago's rear bedroom. With a single motion, Aimee pulled the T-shirt over her head and turned to meet Mac. He swept her into his arms for the kiss she had been expecting.

Aimee felt the tremor go through her body as Mac unleashed a passion she had only guessed at earlier. The kiss was long and deep, ending only as Mac lowered her onto the bed. She rolled him over on his back, finding him easy to maneuver. He lay still for a second, and she momentarily feared he was having another of his headaches.

"You relax. Let Aimee do her thing," she said.

Aimee quickly pulled off Mac's boots and pants while he shed his shirt. She was impressed by what she found, and prayed Mac's head would not distract him from enjoying what she was about to do.

Mac lay back as ordered and waited for her to begin. She wondered what he thought would happen, but knew he would never guess.

Aimee started just above his ankles, massaging his legs with her hands and tongue, and moving slowly upwards. She spent an eon on Mac's thighs, then finally rose up and scooted forward. She skipped over his groin, brushing him lightly with her hair. She worked his tummy, moving the thin covering of fat slowly toward her goal, pulling and caressing, licking and kissing. Slowly, slowly. Exquisitely slowly. Minutes passed, and she had yet to touch what was standing tall and demanding attention. All the while, she kept up a constant barrage of sexy talk.

"I'm building up your cock. Moving all your life forces from your body into your cock. Bigger and bigger, all you can feel and think about is your cock. Your entire body is becoming a cock and only a cock."

She was getting closer and closer. Her hands finally began

touching his groin. Pressing down hard, she ground Mac's pubic hair into his body, heightening the ache inside, but pulling and pushing it toward the one object in mind. By now all other feeling would have left him, his hands and feet, his arms, his head, nothing else would matter as he knew only her and her touch.

Covering him with her thick reddish-blond hair, she disappeared between his legs, forcing them apart. Slowly she nibbled her way up toward her goal, devouring everything in her path. The nether regions of Mac's body became her private playground. She massaged the area with her perpetually moving tongue like a rotary lawnmower, no part going untouched and unappreciated. By the time she reached the base of Mac's penis, he was fighting to maintain control. His groin throbbed and he groaned from the ache. He pleaded for her to release the mounting pressure.

Alas, she granted no such boon. Up she went on the underside, suddenly cupping the tip. She hummed loudly while moving up and down. Smoothly and rhythmically she drew up, pulling his tummy to her with her hands, and dragging on his legs with her chest. Her hair covered him like a tent, and she drew Mac's entire body toward his now enormous member. It had to be at least triple the size it normally was. Mac's flesh was crawling or running to that single point as she scratched and massaged it, crowding forward as if attempting to reach a rock star on a stage, that being her lips on his cock. She stretched his restraining skin to the bursting point. She did not remove her mouth, but in one long motion dropped as far down as possible and pulled up hard while humming. That did it. Mac came with an explosion that threatened to burst his pipes and blow Aimee's head through the roof of the Winnebago.

He groaned loudly in total relief, thrusting upward with each violent eruption. Hot, molten lava shot out to be captured and consumed immediately as if there was no more precious substance on earth. Mac's body was no longer his. It was answering to a higher power. And she didn't stop. Again and again and again. Mac screamed for her to stop. His throat went hoarse, and he tried to pull her head away. She swept away his hands and continued as he flopped and spasmed on his back. There was no chance for subsidence. He went off again and again, finally collapsing in a pool of perspiration and cackling with joy like one possessed.

Aimee finally released him and beamed. Mac was yet to touch her below the waist.

She scooted up and lay flat on top of him, seizing his member between her legs and nibbling at his chin. Her look told him she desperately wanted to be kissed. He lifted her to his lips, silencing her sigh of joy with a long kiss. Her heart fluttered against his chest as he turned aside for air.

"Where did you learn all that?" he asked.

Mac's throat was raw and raspy. The whole camp must have heard him, and Aimee was almost surprised there was no applause.

Aimee smiled broadly. "It comes from massage and yoga," she said. "Good, huh?"

"The best. How can anyone resist you?"

"They never know. Most guys insist on doing what they want instead of what I want."

"Then they're fools."

"It's the combination of my hands, steady contact, and motions that do it. And I focus on only the top two or three inches. The concentrating of life forces comes from yoga, and I combine it with hypnotic rhythm and suggestion by talking. Humming in order to set up background vibrations is the icing on the cake."

"Some cake. Strictly Angel Food."

Aimee tittered in appreciation and snuggled down on his chest. The warmth of her body would keep his wet skin from becoming cold.

"I've never met a woman who purposely studied how to make love to a man in order to increase his enjoyment," Mac said. "But what about you? What about your orgasm?"

"I had one, actually two," Aimee said. She grinned and looked up. "Not surprised you didn't notice while flopping around like a mackerel."

She produced a towel from a cabinet. She carefully patted and rubbed him dry, taking him once more as if to obtain the last drop. Mac gaped at her in amazement.

"You're beautiful, you know," Aimee said, examining him down below. She didn't look up, but rolled him around in her hands.

"He's perfect, absolutely perfect. I can't imagine one better than him." She covered Mac's groin with her towel and scooted up for another kiss. "Nor a better man for his master."

"It's all you," he said. "You bring out the best in him."

They both laughed at Mac's unintended double-entendre. Aimee rolled off, and they languorously retrieved their clothes. Together they stepped outside to find a grinning Norm and Mona already preparing supper. The afternoon had telescoped into seconds.

"Good thing the springs are new," Norm said. Both he and Mona started laughing. "But the 'Bago's soundproofing needs improvement."

Aimee looked embarrassed and turned away to busy herself at the bar. Mac grinned and threw up his hands.

"Somebody had to test it out," Mac said. He remembered the old Kennedy line and applied it here. "If not us, then who? If not now, then when? And I can't remember ever feeling better. I have no headache at all."

Chapter 31

By noon on Friday, the group of people with whom Mac and Norm shared their campfire had assembled. They came from all parts of Texas, including a sizable contingent from the Dallas Lover's Lane Methodist Church Singles Group. For the past several years they had rented a bus and brought it packed with foxy ladies to camp with their little band. They all wore yellow T-shirts saying, *North Dallas Forty,* but he wasn't sure what that meant.

Over the years the band of friends had grown to almost sixty, and for many it was the only time they saw each other. Two tents, a camper, two pickups with shells, a bus, and six RVs were packed tightly on the hilltop around the campfire and its lounge chairs.

Almost everyone expressed amazement at the change in Mac's appearance, and commended him for his miraculous recovery. But there was a change they didn't notice, and Mac wasn't about to bring it to anyone's attention.

In years past, no one talked about their work or profession, taking each other on faith and face value and simply having a good time. The camp was an absolute leveler of society. Everyone was equal. There were no airs being put on, no wealth or position to be respected, no organizational hierarchy. Everyone knew Mac was a rancher, but nothing more than that. Now he had something to hide. He was something other than he appeared, and wasn't being true to the spirit of the gathering.

This was also the first time he'd brought a girlfriend with him. He had always left Mary Lou at home and had fun with other women around the encampment. By itself, that wasn't important, but it was a change. For the better, Mac thought.

Norm always managed to leave his wife at home in favor of his current squeeze, and Mona was hanging on for her third trip. Such arrangements were not unusual, and the wives in camp accepted girlfriends and mistresses without reservation. Mac had yet to hear of a situation where word of a girlfriend's presence got back to an absent wife, and the unwritten rule of silence concerning Terlingua activities was strictly observed. No one presumed to know better than anyone else, and who was to say what could or couldn't be done in another's marriage? This year, two lawyers from Dallas were accompanied by women other than their wives, as were two oilmen from Pasadena, Texas, a judge from Pecos County, and several others.

The only time Mac had been unfaithful was on one of these outings. He had been in an advanced state of inebriation, and the girl was coyote ugly. When he awoke to find her asleep on his arm, he'd wanted to chew it off to avoid waking her. He regretted it, as Mary Lou was his mate for life, at least before she left him.

There had been other women he could have enjoyed in bed. Lots of them. Now, with his face gone, the other women were gone.

Except for Aimee. She was good to him and didn't object to his face. He hoped it wasn't just a wild fling for her, ending in a week or two when she came to her senses. Aimee drew hits at other campfires like honey drew bees, and her natural exuberance and youthful friendliness appealed to everyone. But Mary Lou had left, Aimee could, too.

Norm and Mona were well-matched, and Mac often wondered why Norm bothered to keep up the shell of his marriage. His wife surely knew Mona existed. He often took Mona out to nightspots in Juarez and Las Cruces, vanishing for evenings, nights, and weekends on the flimsiest of excuses. Only slightly taller than Aimee, Norm was heavy and muscular, and possessed a gift of gab that could charm the pants off a lesbian. Mona was a tiny girl, not over a hundred pounds. Dark-haired and with eyes too large for her thin face, Mona waited on Norm hand and foot, doing everything he wanted and more.

Yep, times had changed, Mac told himself. He had always been the handsome one of their group, but now he'd fallen below average. Way below average—maybe on the bottom. Aimee was the most attractive female around, and several men in the church group could easily turn any female head. The rest came in all sizes, shapes, and ages, some men with beer-bellies, women with fat asses or saddlebags, but everyone intent on swapping stories, dancing, drinking, singing, and having a good time. He needed to get himself into the mood and stop lamenting his conversion from handsome prince to ugly frog. Aimee was with him, not anyone else.

The Lajitas meeting concerned him. There was no way to predict its outcome, and he didn't know the men who were coming. Montana had been cryptic and circumspect in his comments, and demanded a five grand retainer to be paid before the meeting was finalized. Damn lawyers. They took no risks at all, but collected megasums of bucks.

All this thinking was counter-productive, so Mac moved to a lawn chair on the RV's shady side to mellow out. He was joined by Tom Eaton and Dave Hightower almost immediately. Tom was a judge in Pecos County, and Dave a lawyer in the Dallas contingent. Their girlfriends were off with Aimee visiting other campsites, and it was time for a drink. They raided Mac's blue margarita pitcher, handing him a fresh cup as compensation. Mac decided to start a friendly argument.

"Tell me, Dave," Mac said. "In an average court case, what percent of the case's applicable law is known by the arguing attorneys?"

Dave furrowed his brow. "Maybe forty percent. Naw, that's too high. Probably thirty."

Tom nodded his agreement. "Sounds about right to me, but you have to understand that's a lot higher than it is for judges."

"Really?" Mac raised his eyebrows. Suddenly his activities didn't seem so risky so far as the law was concerned. "So what's it for judges?"

"More like twenty. At best twenty-five," Tom said. "We don't have time to become experts in all aspects of the law. We rely on counsel to point out relevant cases and points."

Dave scoffed and kicked a small jagged rock away in front of his chair. "I'd guess ten. No offense Tom, but it's been my experience that lawyers who can't make it as attorneys become judges. Either that or because they have political ambitions. That means the least capable attorneys become arbitrators of the law."

Tom smiled and shrugged. "You'll get no argument from me. I was more or less forced into it by my father-in-law who wanted a judge in the family. I had all the money I wanted, so why not? It's an easy life, and everyone respects you."

Dave grinned and tossed his head in the direction of the ladies walking up the hill. "Yeah, and the fringe benefits aren't bad either."

Mac glanced in the direction Dave indicated. Aimee was there with Eaton's redheaded girlfriend, Amanda. The big-busted girl in her mid-thirties looked like she could eat the lean judge for breakfast. Probably had, Mac thought to himself.

"That's what respect will getcha, all right," Tom said.

"Ain't Texas wonderful?" Dave said, eyeing the girls. "Makes you sorta glad it's not part of the United States."

"Yeah, Norm mentioned when he gets tickets in New Mexico they don't show up on his Texas insurance," Mac said. Dave obviously thought Aimee hailed from Texas.

"Nope. Wouldn't want to give up sovereignty," Tom said. "Got too good a deal going."

Mac stared at his margarita and thought about his budding operation. The tequila was making its presence felt. Speaking without thinking, Mac looked at the judge. "Is it true all Texas judges can be bought?" he asked Tom. "Present company excluded, of course."

"Why exclude present company?" Tom said. "But I think I need more of this brain cell killer for that question." He downed the remainder of his cup and held it out for Dave to refill. The lanky, balding lawyer poured a full cup without spilling a drop.

The judge continued. "We're all bought one way or the other. We're elected, and almost all of our campaign money comes from attorneys who practice in our courtrooms. There's no way we can't be biased."

"At least in the right direction," Dave said.

"Right is relative," Tom said. "Some of our most celebrated cases have been decided on the basis of contributions. Like the oil suit when that high-powered battery of lawyers from New York descended on Houston a couple of years ago and presented a winning case only to hear the judge rule against them. The local counsel had donated hundreds of thousands of dollars to the judge's re-election campaign, whereas the Yankees hadn't contributed a dime."

"But that's not true in criminal cases, it is?" Mac asked, sitting up.

"Not quite so blatantly, but the lean is there. There are lots of rulings on which a judge has wide discretion that can help one side or the other. Defense attorneys contribute heavily, and prosecutors sometimes use tactics which are little better than out-and-out blackmail."

"Like what?"

"Well, you had an alcoholic judge in El Paso until last year who was protected both by the police and DA. He was picked up a number of times for DWI, but always driven home and the incidents quashed. For some strange reason he usually ruled in favor of the prosecution."

"But the money—"

"Prosecuting attorneys collect money, too. It's a system of favors and monetary exchange. That's why my father-in-law wanted a judge. I'm not about to change the system."

"What about you, Dave? Are all lawyers crooked?"

"What the hell's in here? Sodium pentothal? Of course we're crooked. We're part of the system, too. If a judge is compromised for giving the nod to heavy contributors, we're guilty for making the contributions. The whorehouse madam isn't more virtuous than her girls, and the girls aren't better than the madam. Forget what your case is, just get the right attorney and right judge."

"Too bad you guys aren't in Doña Ana County," Mac said.

"I wouldn't have answered your question if we were," Tom said. "This is Terlingua. Olly, olly oxen in free."

"Besides," Dave said, "Decisions have to be made on the importance of each case to an attorney. You sacrifice little guys of no importance to accrue chits for big ones. Like that personal injury lawyer in El Paso who killed two people while driving under the influence. He's still practicing and racking up huge fees. Gives new meaning to the term, 'officer of the court.'"

"How about that probate judge in El Paso giving cases to his pet attorneys and letting them eat up estates in bogus fees?" Tom said. "If it hadn't been for other lawyers complaining about not getting their share, that would have gone on forever."

"So the control comes from pigs pushed out of the trough," Mac said. "As long as all the swine get fed, the system works."

"For us," Dave said, "Not for you."

Tom Eaton looked Mac in the eye. "Damn good margarita you

make. Call me next week, and maybe I can put you on the yellow brick road in your hometown."

Their discussion came to an abrupt halt when Aimee joined them. She chatted excitedly with her usual unrestrained enthusiasm.

"Mac, I heard there's another cook-off down the road. Can we go and check it out?"

"That's the CASI cook-off at Arriba Terlingua."

"CASI?"

"Chili Appreciation Society International. Bikers and tourists— they cater to the great unwashed. There are two Terlinguas in the chili world. Ours is the Francis X. Tolbert - Wick Fowler Memorial Cook-off. The real Terlingua."

"And the other one?"

"It's complicated. Sit down & hear the word."

Chapter 32

Dave freshened Mac's margarita while Aimee pulled up a chair. The whole group listened while Mac recited some Terlingua history. For Aimee, it was a glimpse into a culture unknown to her a few days earlier.

Mac explained that the cook-offs started in 1967 as an outgrowth of a promotional scheme by C.V. Wood, Carroll Shelby of Shelby-Ford fame, and others. Wood and Shelby purchased a ranch between Alpine and Terlingua, and sold hunting rights on their ranch in the guise of land parcels.

About the same time, writer H. Allen Smith became embroiled in a war of words with Wick Fowler over what constituted good chili. Smith, in that queer tradition of New Yorkers who believe their decaying city is the world's apple, claimed his New York recipe for chili was the standard against which all other chili should be measured. Fowler, supported by Francis X. Tolbert, took exception to this, particularly since chili was a traditional Texas concoction.

Smith was right, but not in the way he imagined. New York provided a baseline of zero against which all other cities and things scored positive numbers.

Smith's chili contained all sorts of garbage like beans, tomatoes, tomato sauce, celery, filler, and other obscenities. Texas Red was traditionally comprised of beef, chili sauce made from a blend of chiles, many other spices, and sometimes a small amount of onion. After all, chili originally developed from frontier cooks cloaking unpalatable meat with spices to make it edible. From the beginning, it was East versus West, or ignorance versus truth.

The two arch-promoters, Shelby and Wood, offered their ranch as a site to resolve this chili argument under conditions of Hollywood hype, rustic Texas fun, and true western hoopla. The parties readily accepted, Smith being actively supported by *Holiday Magazine* which expected to obtain an exclusive on this great western event. Without a doubt, the easterners did not understand the true issues involved and the depth of Texas pride.

The first cook-off saw bribery, drunken judges, stolen chili and all kinds of skullduggery. A "world championship" was promoted by Wood and Shelby, and attracted the best—or the worst, depending on one's point of view—of the chili world which did not exist as a cohesive body at the time. Coming out from behind their chili pots were Hal John Wimberly, editor of the *Goat Gap Gazette*, John Raven, alias Bad McFad, Jo Ann Horton, Sam Lewis and his armadillo races, Gary P. Nunn and his band, the artist Tony Shemroske, Troy King, and other assorted laid-back western outlaw types.

One judge voted for Smith, the second declared for Fowler, and the third maintained Smith's chili had so burned his palate he was unable to judge Wick's entry fairly. The contest was officially—an interesting concept which ignored the total absence of officials—declared a tie.

Smith went back to New York in a funk, declaring he would never again set foot in Texas, but the following year, Carroll Shelby took up the challenge from California. The next several years were characterized by his Hollywood showmanship, aided immeasurably by bevies of starlets flown in to support his cause. Gradually the event took on the trappings of organization. The Chili Appreciation Society International was incorporated, and the cook-off changed irrevocably with the times.

Terlingua winners, regardless of the friendly fraud which prevailed, were nonetheless an honor roll of recalcitrant chiliheads. Mac spun off an accurate list from before the split in 1983 that included "Wino" Woody DeSilva, C.V. Wood, Wick Fowler, Allegani Jani Schofield of Houston, and Tom Skipper of Pasadena, Texas.

The cook-off swamped the area each year. The ghost town of Terlingua boasted maybe eight permanent residents. The town itself was primarily adobe ruins, dry as a bone, and honeycombed with played-out quicksilver mines. During Terlingua's heyday in the late

1970s, some 15,000 to 18,000 chiliheads packed themselves into the old adobe ruins, but drop-offs and abandoned mineshafts caused frequent accidents. Hondo Crouch would take over one of the better preserved one-room adobes, spread a canvas for a roof, christen it the "Hondo Hilton," and hold a western style, guitar-oriented court. The "Grand Imagineer" passed away in 1978, leaving a legacy of western songs and yarns about Luckenbach and an unfillable void in the heart of every chilihead.

After Fowler's death, CASI decided to eliminate the free-for-all and regulate cook-offs and chiliheads—the ungovernable, mostly Scotch-Irish hardheads cooking chili—precisely because it was impossible to judge on any basis whatsoever. But the commercial opportunities were too immense. Lawlessness was replaced with regulations, eligibility requirements were established, and the cook-off threatened to become indistinguishable from the thousands of money-oriented contests taking place annually across America.

The cook-off was moved from town to Glen Pepper's Villa Del Las Minas for better management and control. Pursuing a course of folly, CASI became more tyrannical each year. Participation began to decline, and in 1983, the cook-off split apart into two rival and seemingly irreconcilable groups. Traditional chiliheads blew off CASI and attended a new Terlingua championship run by Francis X. Tolbert, camping behind the Terlingua store. That was Mac's and Norm's bunch.

Shelby and Wood went a third direction, forming a group in California in 1975 called the International Chili Society. They offered large cash prizes for both chili and showmanship. When the dust settled, the chili world was split into three factions, CASI, ICS, and "Behind The Store," thereby causing rivalries, bad feelings, and generally divided loyalties.

Mac had barely finished his recounting of Terlingua history when his little group of margarita drinkers was invaded by a highly inebriated lady of doubtful reputation named Jeannie. She had arrived late the day before with her girlfriend, mooned the encampment from her RV, and ended up crashing with one of the Fredericksburg contingent in their camp.

Her story was already well known. Phil the Pill had lured her into his pickup shell when the campfire thinned out under the pretext of needing help getting his boots off. Of course, it wasn't exactly his boots he wanted to get off. Mac never understood how such lines could actually work, but the sleazebag was still there with Phil in the morning.

Now she returned to pick on Mac, singling him out for special attention.

"Hey, cowboy," she said. "You got a little time for a girl down on her luck? I need a pick-me-up."

She plopped her ample rear down on Mac's knee, and threw her arms around his neck. The group sat stunned, and Mac noticed Aimee staring with her mouth open. Jeannie began shaking her equally ample boobs.

Mac slapped her hard on the ass, and pushed her off his knee. "Hell, lady, I wouldn't fuck you with my friend's dick." he said.

She pouted, and for a moment, Mac thought the scene might get ugly. The girl was only in her early twenties, and not half bad.

"Oh," she said, looking around. "Where's he then?"

Mac laughed and pointed down the hill. She had misunderstood his statement.

"Down there. In that big white RV with the awning. Go say hello."

"Thanks." The girl blew him a kiss and headed down the hill to the RV about seventy yards away.

As she staggered out of earshot, the group buzzed with speculation. The question everyone was thinking was put to Mac by Aimee.

"Whose camp is that?" she asked.

"Damned if I know," he said.

The circle broke up in laughter. Hopefully, there wasn't some guy asleep in that RV, or he was in for a big surprise.

The Hamms cooked *giso* for supper while Mac simmered a large pot of ranch beans. Norm and Mona fried biscuits in lard for two solid hours, and the surfeit of food dampened the margaritas' effect. People from other camps materialized by magic to queue up for biscuits and beans, and is seemed like Mac's group was feeding the whole encampment.

One of the visitors was a Mexican named Gonzalez who knew the Hamms and talked a mile a minute. Aimee couldn't understand a word.

She approached Doug and asked him if Gonzalez was speaking Spanish or English.

"It's English," Doug said. "But liberally interspersed with Tex-Mex. About what you'd expect from our bilingual educational programs."

"Bilingual programs?" Aimee said.

"They learn in Spanish for the first four years, then English and Spanish for two, then English after that. It doesn't work. They usually end up speaking border Tex-Mex as their main language with fifty to seventy percent competency in English. And that's *if* they complete high school. Anything less and their English becomes practically useless."

"Why would anyone put their kids in such a program?"

"They believe it's important to learn Spanish first to maintain Hispanic culture."

"But you said it doesn't work. And how do they get jobs if they can't speak English?

"It doesn't. The kids are doomed to subsistence jobs because of their limited English. They're the first group of immigrants to insist on maintaining their language and perpetuating themselves as an underclass."

Liz joined the conversation to put in her two cents' worth.

"Doug misses the obvious," she said. "Political pressure groups want all Hispanics speaking Spanish so they'll feel closer to Mexico than the U.S. Then, when push comes to shove, they appeal to the United Nations, say the Treaty of Guadalupe Hidalgo was a fraud, and that the American southwest should return to Mexico."

"The southwest? You mean Texas?"

"Texas, New Mexico, Arizona, California, Nevada, Utah, and much of Colorado. They'll be the majority in those states, speak Spanish, and might be able to gain control of Mexico because of their greater natural resources."

"Wow, I never thought of that," Aimee said.

"It's the only thing that makes sense, honey," Liz said. "Otherwise, their insistence on Spanish over English is self-defeating."

The Hamms depressed her with their gloomy forecasts. Aimee had come to the west to escape problems and racial conflicts, now she was learning this region simply had a different set of players.

She hoped the campfire would lighten her mood like the last two nights. Coming west was her chance to start a new life. And it seemed to be working, at least in part. But she had to do something about her secret. She wasn't as advertised.

Chapter 33

Aimee wanted to shout the truth from the highest mountain and drop all pretext of being what she wasn't. These people were sweet and kind, accepting her into their lives without reservations, trusting her implicitly. They deserved to know, but she didn't have the courage to tell them.

Last night Mac inquired about her childhood, and she told him how her father had committed suicide in the garage, and she was the one to find him. It had been terrible. She was her father's special pet and loved him as her knight in shining armor. But he hadn't loved her, and deserted her when she needed him most.

In high school, she'd survived her senior year by being stoned every day. Times were tough with her father gone. He had been a lawyer, gotten in over his head with real estate speculation and couldn't face his debts and probable disbarment. The family barely got by. Stuart saved them from losing their house, and without his help, she could never have gone to college.

The campfire developed slowly this evening. Aimee sat in a folding chair next to Mac and studied the fire. It mesmerized her as it danced a thousand leaps of death. Peaceful and fascinating, tiny lives in miniature, the flames were like human emotions, rising, falling, and ultimately being reduced to ashes by their own heat. Most of their group visited other camps in the early hours, and Norm monopolized the conversation.

He was fun, but Aimee couldn't imagine a woman being married to him. He was too small. Sooner or later, a woman wanted a man she could look up to both physically and emotionally. Besides, Norm was a cheat, and every woman wanted a faithful husband.

Norm produced a sack of grass, and passed his pipe to her after each drag. She could fight it, but it would happen anyway. Pot released her inhibitions, and she was stoned before most of their acquaintances drifted back into camp. The loosening of her muscles extended to her tongue. The east coast had arrived.

Innocently enough, Mac brought matters to a head. He began to ask her about college and the great football team her university fielded the past several years.

"Yeah, well, they weren't so great," she said.

Her new cowboy boots were beginning to roast in the fire, but that didn't matter. Norm kept handing her the pipe, and her head floated over the campsite. Several men were complaining about UTEP's football team, and she felt like putting everything in perspective.

"UTEP could be a football powerhouse if you guys would sacrifice," she said.

Doug Hamm took up the challenge. "How so? UTEP's a poor, non-residential school. There's nothing to attract top high school athletes."

"You told me UTEP enjoyed a surplus of beautiful women."

"So what? Having a few good looking co-eds isn't going to make a football team."

"That's exactly what makes a football team." Aimee winced at her words and their unexpected double meaning. "My school had a terrific athletic program with excellent facilities, but that didn't make any difference. You know what did?"

She didn't wait for a response.

"Girls. The ones provided by the athletic department. Girls were placed on alternating floors of the athletic dorm and subsidized with room and board to quote, *date*, unquote, athletes."

"That would never work at UTEP," Doug said. "Most players here are black, and there aren't many black girls around."

"There weren't many black girls in college back east either," Aimee said. "Almost all the dorm girls were white and some made Miss Universe contestants look homely."

"How'd they get the girls?" Doug asked. It was clear he didn't believe Aimee's story.

"Recruited them. The girls were told they were going to meet top athletes. Guys who would be rich and famous some day. They might marry one if they got lucky. Guys like John Elway or O.J. Simpson. It sounded terrific, particularly if you didn't have money."

"It doesn't sound so bad even with money," Doug said. "After all, nobody's going to force the girls to sleep with guys they don't want."

"Exactly wrong. That's not the way it works. The guys pick, not the girls. Black linemen weighing three hundred pounds pick hundred-pound blonde girls."

"They still don't have to sleep with them."

"Yeah, right. Be labeled a racist, get beat up, get kicked out of the dorm. Back east, you can't turn a guy down because he's black. If a girl does, they gang up on her." Aimee's voice was angry in spite of the weed. "What's a girl to do against five or six football players? After going through the team playing jive games of Oreo cookie with bragging black slobs, the girls freak out on drugs. But who cares? Not the athletic department. They get fresh pickings every year."

Doug shook his head. "Never happen in El Paso. Hispanics hate blacks, and interracial dating is taboo."

Aimee grabbed Norm's pipe. "Dating? Dating? That's not what those guys do. Rape and pillage is more like it. Wake up and smell the burning beds. If you want a winning football team, get your most beautiful blondes together and whore them out to black athletes so they'll come to UTEP."

Doug was unmoved by her argument. "Wouldn't work out here. Our girls would vote with their feet after their first black."

"Haven't you heard? Once you've gone black, you can't go back. The white guys on campus won't touch her. And black guys beat up and sometimes kill white girls who try to go back. Not that anybody cares, she's just another whore who fucked blacks."

The conversation turned to dune buggies, and when Doug wandered off for another beer, Mac leaned over and took Aimee's hand.

"How do you know all that about your football team?" Mac asked.

Aimee stared straight ahead into the fire. For a long time, she didn't answer. This was the moment. Either Mac would forgive her or he wouldn't. She took a series of abnormally deep breaths.

"I was one of those girls," she said. "How's that? Put that in your pipe and smoke it."

"It's okay, honey. Everybody make mistakes. Yours doesn't sound so bad."

"It was terrible. Within a month, I was a basket case. If I had as many black pricks sticking out of me as were stuck in me, I'd look like a porcupine."

She turned and glared fiercely at Mac. "You know how I got through the day? Drugs. I did everything. LSD, KW, Quaaludes, grass, hash, meth, and anything that came in pills. Have you ever had fruit salad? That's where there's a bowl of all types of pills, and you just reach in and take a handful. You don't know what they are and you don't care. They get you through another hour and another black guy who expects you to go crazy when he exposes himself. Did you know I can't hold a job? Sometimes it's like waking up from a dream and not knowing where you are. Or what you're doing."

Aimee began to cry, and Mac leaned forward to take her in his arms.

"Don't touch me!" she yelled. She twisted violently in her lawn chair and batted at Mac's arms with her hands. The other campers watched in shock but didn't intervene.

Fending off her resistance, Mac lifted her from the chair and carried her into the RV. She threw her arms around his neck and sobbed into his chest. He tried to lay her down on the bed, but she clung to his neck and wouldn't let go. He lay down with her.

"Now you'll never want to touch me again," she bawled, her head still buried in his chest.

"Yes, I will," Mac said. Actually, he hadn't yet touched her. So far, she had only gone down on him.

"No, you won't," she wailed. "Nobody wants a whore who's been fucked by every black guy on the team. They spread me out so far, I can't close my legs. The white boys in the dorm wouldn't touch me."

"You weren't a whore." Mac stroked Aimee's hair and wrapped a leg around her to draw her closer. "You were just young and impressionable and got into something beyond your control. How old were you? Seventeen or eighteen?"

Aimee nodded and sniffled. "But I'm a wreck. My mind got fried on drugs, and my body's ruined. The only thing I can do is give head." She looked up and sought assurance through her wet and disheveled hair. "That was okay, wasn't it?"

"Best ever."

She buried her face in his chest again. "You'll never want me now, I know."

"There's nothing I'd rather do right at this moment than go inside you and love you."

Aimee lifted her head again. "Really?" Like a little girl she wiped her eyes with the back of her fist and gazed beseechingly at Mac. "But I have a problem with dryness. You might not like it."

Mac unbuckled her belt. "Let's find out. I'm betting I'll never want out again."

Aimee forced a smile through her tears. He was giving her a chance, maybe the only one she'd ever get. She drew up her legs and pushed off her jeans. Mac struggled with his while she lay on her back and prayed. God, she wanted this to work.

Without warning, he touched the inside of her leg, and she was struck by an overwhelming sense of panic. She jerked away and rolled into a fetal ball.

Perspiration broke out on her forehead, and the fear was real. It was the pot. It was making her paranoid. She struggled with her demons, telling herself to stop behaving like a frightened virgin.

Mac was lightly stroking her back and side, letting her know he was there. She reached behind her and found him. He was aroused and ready in spite of her terrified reaction. Maintaining her hold, she slowly backed into him. His body pulsed against hers like gentle waves lapping on the shore, carefully shifting the sand as he worked his way inland with the tide. Then they were together, their forms locked securely, the latch pin fully in place. It felt wonderful, and Aimee wanted to cry from relief.

Like two spoons they lay together, and all movement ceased. Aimee felt a warmth come over her, then an indescribable drowsiness as Mac encircled her with his arms. There was safety in his embrace, caring, forgiveness, and togetherness. This was not sex, this was love. Aimee's head swam in giddiness. She fought the calm to savor the moment, but it was no use. Norm's pot was having its effect. She covered Mac's arms with her own and fell asleep.

*****

205

The grey light of morning and the November chill roused Aimee from dreams of love and happiness. She wanted to continue her dreams at all costs, but discovered they weren't dreams. Mac was entwined around her, and as she attempted to straighten her legs, discovered he was inside her as well. She tried to remember the night, but her mind refused to cooperate.

She hated to break the connection, but her full bladder was making other demands. Slowly easing Mac out without causing him to wake up, she noted everything below was wet and sticky. Evidently he had made love to her during the night, maybe more than once. For the first time in her life, she hoped a man had taken advantage of her. Even more, she hoped he had thoroughly enjoyed himself.

Chapter 34

The morning of the cook-off had arrived. The sky was clear as the sun poked its way over the mountains, and Aimee could see to the Chisos and beyond. She left Mac under their blankets, used the bathroom, and crept out to make herself a bullshot on the outdoor bar. It was a wreck from the previous evening's activities, and two more half-gallons of booze were empty. Various mixes and half-filled cups were strewn about in complete disorder, and the morning dew covered everything with a film of moisture. Aimee ignored the debris and opened a can of bullshot mix. She poured it into a large plastic beer cup, and added somewhat more than two ounces of vodka. One gulp, and her eyes popped open with a vengeance.

It was a rite of passage, and the bullshot initiated her into the spirit of the camp. Aimee had watched others start their days this way and go downhill from there. Well, that wouldn't happen to her. Today was her day. She saw things clearer, as if reborn in the majestic beauty of the west.

No one else was up and about in their camp, and Aimee sat on the RV's doorstep in contemplation. This was a world she hadn't known existed, a world of unrestrained friendship where people banded together and negotiated a peace with nature. She could handle this. Particularly with a good man like Mac at her side. There was no longer any need for drugs to help her face the long nights.

Terlingua itself was the ultimate high. She understood that now. There were no telephones, no rules, no cares, no nothing—just good music, good food, and good friendships. It was the premier hippy escape. She had learned that old-time westerners were alive and well, in smaller numbers perhaps than one hoped, but still resisting organization and regimentation. She knew at least one place they could be found.

It was a redneck Scotch-Irish campout with true country-western singing and picking. It was easy to see what Bob Wills meant to Texas, and why a fiddle was required in a Texas band. Terlingua was a happening, a time when brain surgeons and nuclear scientists could let it all hang out and be absolute jerks. It was one big honky-tonk filled with good folks, assholes, bikers, good-ol' boys, sluts, and other assorted souls.

Campfires went for hours; from twilight until they were closed down by bitter-enders sometime before dawn. Many guys drank until they couldn't walk, then girls, wives, or anyone handy helped put them to bed. There were lots of promises, including many made to her by others than Mac, but little action. Instead of making serious moves, macho males ate *huevos rancheros, cabrito*, drank beer and booze, and passed out. Sometimes they forgot to pace themselves while drinking, and Terlingua was a marathon, not a sprint.

A touch on her shoulder announced Mac's presence. Aimee drew herself up out of her reverie and kissed him passionately.

"Hi, big boy. Today is the first day in the rest of our lives." Not an original line, but it conveyed what she wanted to say.

Mac was already dressed for the morning's chill. She rubbed his crotch with the flat of her hand. "If I died now, I'd die a happy woman," she said.

Mac chuckled and nodded at the cup in her hand. "I see you've finally converted. Next, I'll have you riding horses like a born-and-raised ranch hand. No more sore bottoms."

"You're the only horse I want, and you can make my bottom sore anytime." Aimee pressed herself into him, at the moment willing to follow him anywhere. It was amazing. Ten days ago she wouldn't have recognized his name. Now, he dominated her life.

He lifted her off the doorstep and guided her to the still-smoldering campfire. The sun's rays were creeping across the rocks and desert vegetation, evaporating the dew and restoring the ground to its daytime dusty condition. Distant mountains offered a kaleidoscope of colors, blues, red, pink, yellow, and brown. They emerged from gray to greet the sun while the animal life that feasted like skin bacteria during hours of darkness fled back underground. Mac turned Aimee toward the west, facing the skyline as one. He clamped her tightly to his chest, encompassing her with his arms.

"It's wide open spaces and no trees," he said. "The west. And I love it. Harsh, foreboding, dangerous, and beautiful. It uses people up and leaves their bones bleaching in the sand. Cruel, but always honest. Think you want a piece?"

"In a heartbeat. It's not mankind, it's nature bringing out the best in people. It's wonderful. Just like you."

The rocks changed color as they gave up their moisture in front of her. A lone hawk wheeled in the sky, hunting a morning meal in the scrub below. No one who saw this world could remain unaffected, she thought. Desert mornings were like births. Life was renewed, every day was spring. She had been renewed. Reborn. Not changed on the surface, not like winter snow giving way to spring green, but the deeper, hidden soul of life. Like the desert with its water deep underneath.

Maybe God loved her after all. For many years, she didn't think so. He punished her by letting her father die. She should have known what was happening and stopped it. She had failed the test again at school. All those failures, but he was giving her another chance.

With Mac. So strong, a truck couldn't crush him. Discarded by a woman who didn't know what she had. There for her, leading her out of the shadows of drugs and physical degradation into the light of a love-filled and meaningful life.

She turned around and kissed him again. There was no way she deserved her good fortune. But she could share it and maybe earn it with time. Aimee led him back to bed.

*****

After breakfast, Norm fired up his Coleman stove and greased the cast iron kettle. Cooking in aluminum supposedly didn't produce the same result, and Norm contended the cast iron somehow imparted a special enriching taste like a secret ingredient. Mac obtained the Styrofoam cup for their sample submission, and they carefully planned to have the chili ready exactly on time for the judging call. Doug Hamm was cooking alongside in his Taranchili booth, and the usual friendly bantering began anew.

Mac obtained his chiles at the Hatch Chile Festival in New Mexico, and told everyone his ingredients to be unsurpassed. But in every cook-off at least a half dozen submissions possessed a more or less equal chance of winning, and final judging was a crap shoot. That was what made cook-offs exciting; standards changed with each cook-off and set of judges. Everyone had their own pet opinion on what constituted good chili, and Mac's opinion did not always coincide with the majority of judges.

Mac listened to Aimee say they were going to win. But she didn't know anything about chili. It was just her day. She said it was perfect so far, and only right that Mac should take first place. But it was not to be. They made the semi-finals table, but no further. He told her it wasn't important, especially since Taranchili was eliminated in the first cut.

They went to the CASI cook-off at Arriba Terlingua to forget their loss. It was easy to do in the raucous activities. They sat with Norm on a hillside in front of Glen Pepper's pavilion to watch the various activities and shows. The sun was hot, and the beer flowed like water.

CASI's festivities lagged in the heat, and someone on the hillside started chanting, "Show us your tits!" Within moments, hundreds of yelling rednecks had joined in, and after one tall blonde biker girl flashed her chest toward the hillside, thousands took up the call. Soon the vast majority of females in the area below the stage laughingly lifted their T-shirts to explosive acclaim and cheers from their admirers.

Aimee hid her face while Mac cheered and hollered with the rest. No one picked on her, not the least because of Mac's commanding presence. He decided there wasn't a bra in camp, as tight jeans and T-shirts were almost a required uniform. A wet T-shirt contest was manifestly superfluous, but took place anyway. Some big-chested girl won after dispensing with her T-shirt altogether.

Rather than exposing Aimee to further ribald indecencies, Mac gave her a quick tour of several played-out quicksilver mines. They had been the scene of fantastic stories of greed, murder, theft, exploitation, and outright legalized robbery by unscrupulous lawyers.

Around the turn of the century, one mine owner had followed a deep cinnabar deposit onto another mine's property and extracted tons of high-grade ore while his lawyers fought one delaying action after another in Alpine courts. The case became studded with lies and red herrings by attorneys, until finally a counter shaft was dug that exposed the robber's operation in a dramatic underground breakthrough.

It was an exciting tale for some historian's best seller, and Texas proved its lawyers could lie as well as those in Colorado during the Stratton case. As usual, anything could happen on the frontier as long as someone was willing to take risks. Mac turned his thoughts to his operation and the discussion with Tom and Dave. Little had changed in a century.

Aimee and he had missed most of the campfire Friday night, and Mac would have to hurry to keep from missing it again. He didn't know how long his meeting with the Mexican drug lords would last and couldn't promise a time for his return. He borrowed Doug's Explorer and turned to Aimee as soon as they returned from Pepper's in mid-afternoon.

"I have to go to Lajitas for a few hours," he said. "Strictly business, and I'll be back for the campfire."

"A business meeting? Here?" she said.

"On the Rio Grande, at the Lajitas airport. Some guys are stopping to see me."

"Do you have to go?" she asked.

"Honey, I'll only be gone for a little while. I'll be back as soon as I can."

"I'll go with you and stay out of the way."

"No, it won't be like that, and there won't be any place for you to wait. You don't want to stand out by yourself in the desert, do you?" Mac kissed her softly but hurriedly. "I'll be back."

"I thought you said your meeting was at the airport. That's not out in the desert."

"It isn't, but it's just a landing strip without facilities." He hoped that was true. He couldn't remember what the airport looked like. "Please, trust me," he said. "I'll be right back."

He climbed into the Explorer, leaving Aimee waving good-bye and fighting back tears. The rearview mirror spoke volumes, not a word of which was comforting. She stood like a statue watching him leave until he disappeared over the hill beyond the Terlingua store.

Lajitas was little more than an airport, a few non-descript buildings, and a reconstructed Old West town for a tourist attraction.

A miniature Old Tucson, the fanciful street featured a bank, general store, sheriff's office, and other buildings. It was practically deserted, but November was hardly a peak tourist month.

This was truly an isolated corner of the world. There was no road on the Mexican side, and Lajitas was fifty miles from Presidio to the north and seventeen miles from Study Butte at the entrance to Big Bend. From there, the next town was Alpine, eighty miles north of Study Butte. The nearest Mexican village was Ojinaga, across the Rio Grande from Presidio. It was little more than a whorehouse catering to cowboys, and was famous as one of Pancho Villa's favorite spots during the Mexican Revolution.

Mac grunted to himself. The only differences between Juarez and Ojinaga were that El Paso was a lot bigger than Presidio, and *maquiladora* plants provided employment opportunities south of the border. Otherwise, Juarez was still a whorehouse.

Whorehouses and crib girls were long gone on the El Paso side of the river. The streets lined with narrow one-room apartments at sidewalk level could still be seen in South El Paso, but the crib girls who sold themselves in their doorways for fifty cents or a dollar had moved to Juarez. Prices had risen, but the girls were the same.

Mexico was a sinkhole of corruption feeding on American dollars as far as Mac was concerned. And when things got really bad, its denizens came across the river and stole everything they needed. Then corrupt American politicians came up with a free-trade zone scheme to move American jobs into Mexican border areas under the Maquiladora Act. Tijuana and Juarez were the major beneficiaries, and American plants moved in to take advantage of Mexican labor earning $1.79 per hour. Eastern investors and masses of Mexican laborers benefited while American workers suffered unemployment. Captains of industry stood in front of signs saying, "Hometown Motors" on TV and bragged about their cars made on the North American continent. Yeah..., in Mexico.

No wonder he couldn't make a living with the ranch. Between the easterners moving manufacturing facilities to Mexico and Canada, and the Japanese taking over everything else, a little guy like him didn't stand a chance.

It was a bad idea to think about politics and how the southwest was becoming Mexican. Mac's rage was building along with a piercing headache. He turned his attention to the upcoming meeting. There was a fifty percent chance he wouldn't survive it. It all depended on him presenting an image of power and usefulness. He wasn't Mexican, and Mexicans preferred to work only with their own kind. If they decided he could be easily replaced, he was history. Thinking about the odds, Mac calmed down. And his headache disappeared.

Chapter 35

Mac had noted the steady stream of light planes flying over Terlingua heading north for the last several days. Apparently, Big Bend was on a major drug-running flyway. The Lajitas airport was large enough for jets but stood only a few hundred yards on the US side of the Rio Grande. Drug traffickers would need to fly much farther into Texas to avoid DEA border controls. Nonetheless, the airstrip appeared to be enjoying a high level of activity.

Mac concentrated on the situation at hand. The twin-engine Beech he was expecting was not visible, and there was no activity around the small control tower and terminal. He parked between the terminal and several tied-down aircraft to wait. Mexicans were always late, and he hadn't bothered to arrive earlier than fifteen minutes before the appointed time. As expected, that moment came and went.

A half hour later Mac began speculating whether the Mexicans were going to show at all. There was hardly any choice but to wait. He didn't want to lose what he had built up with Aimee, but this meeting was critical.

Another thirty minutes crept by, but only two light planes landed during the long hour. Both disgorged couples who were met by people in vehicles arriving after Mac. He gritted his teeth, feeling as conspicuous as an elephant. Then he remembered that Lajitas was located at the mouth of Santa Elena Canyon, a favorite white-water rafting run for enthusiasts on the lower Rio Grande. Most likely the couples were going to shoot the rapids tomorrow, and the guides meeting them were from Far-Flung Adventures. It was a white-water rafting and canoeing outfit headquartered not far from the Terlingua store, and Santa Elena was one of its regular trips.

He should have planned an extra day and taken Aimee through the gorge. Supposedly the scenery was spectacular and the river wild and woolly. Or at least when the water was high. He wondered if this was the best time for white-water runs. That might depend on the Mexicans anyway. He had heard they controlled the river's volume with dams on the Rio Conchos flowing east from Chihuahua.

Thinking about white-water rafting with Aimee made him feel good, and time flew by more rapidly. With his thoughts on Aimee, Mac was startled to hear a larger plane taxiing down the runway. He hadn't seen or heard it approach, but it was a twin-engined Beech like Montana had described. Mac rolled out of Doug's Explorer and stretched to work out the kinks from his long wait. He walked through the small terminal to greet his guests on the hardstand. The eight passenger plane rolled to a stop, and its door opened, filled immediately by a huge Mexican wearing a *guayabera*. He lowered the steps and disappeared back into the plane, specifically taking no notice of Mac's presence.

Well, if the mountain wouldn't come to Mohammed, he'd go to the mountain.

Mac crossed the asphalt parking area and stuck his head in the aircraft's door. "Señor Mendoza?" he called out.

In the diffused cabin light, Mac could see the big Mexican staring at him with an Uzi on his lap. Three others eyed him with detached interest. The cockpit was hidden behind a curtain, and a pilot might have remained up front. It was a substantial delegation, more than he had expected. All were dressed casually, two being in their late thirties or early forties and one definitely in his late forties or early fifties.

The oldest, a light-colored balding man with a large mustache, motioned for him to come inside. Mac was pleased with himself for not bringing his PPK. There was nothing to be gained by going up against an Uzi, and if they searched him, finding a weapon would make him look unsure of himself.

He sat down at the small table across from the bald man, spreading his arms as if comfortable in his surroundings. Mac felt like a duck; calm and unruffled on the surface, but paddling like hell underneath. His headache returned as a dull, infrequent stabbing. He narrowed his eyes to make himself look more sinister. In this situation, appearances were a matter of life and death.

215

"You're Frazier?" the bald man asked.

"Yep, and you're Mendoza? You can speak Spanish if you'd like," Mac said in Spanish.

"I know," the man said. "What happened to your head?"

"Some guys tried to kill me. They're back in the food chain."

"Looks like they came close." The man nodded to the Uzi-toting bodyguard sitting behind Mac. The gunman repositioned himself, and Mac suppressed the urge to turn around and look.

The bald man waited until the bodyguard quit moving and switched to Spanish. "No matter, we're here to discuss business."

Mac grunted at the Mexican's Anglo-like approach in wasting no time. Normally, Mexicans waltzed around subjects for eons before coming to the point. He guessed Mendoza might not be Mexican, but since he couldn't differentiate between accents south of Chihuahua, there was no way to determine the drug lord's origin. Significantly, Mendoza hadn't introduced himself or any of his companions. Nor had Mac been frisked.

"So, who might I be doing business with?" Mac said. "I've already told you who I am, and you wouldn't be here except after checking me out with our mutual El Paso acquaintance. So how about some quid pro quo?"

"You think I could be *federales*, huh? Could be."

The bald man flashed an insincere, social smile without showing his teeth. He asked the little ferret-like man behind him for a piece of paper, then produced a gold pen and quickly scribbled his name. He pushed it across to Mac. "That's me. You take that to Montana, he'll verify it."

On the paper was *Jaime Mendoza* in surprisingly legible handwriting. Mac folded the small notebook sheet into a square and stuffed it into his shirt pocket. He was relieved. He would survive the meeting.

Mendoza gestured with his thumb toward the ferret-faced man, then the one on Mac's left. "This is Julio, he's Jesus, and my man with the Jewish equalizer is your worst enemy if you cross me. Now, what do you have to offer?"

Mac didn't bother to acknowledge the others except with a barely perceptible nod. He gestured with his hand as if throwing something onto the table.

"A secure pipeline from El Paso to Chicago. For anything. At present, I have excess capacity and am looking for more goods to carry."

"From El Paso? What about getting across the border?"

"I connect to the border over secure, private land. But not across. Right now, goods are brought in by coyotes with whom my connections are solid."

"There are no solid connections with coyotes. They sell themselves to the highest bidder." Mendoza studied Mac's face for a moment as if looking for some reaction to his words.

There wasn't any.

"No matter, we'll secure them or use our own people," Mendoza said. "Do you have some names?"

Mac mentioned three coyotes, including Villareal.

Ferret-face wrote down their names. The little Mex was obviously one of Mendoza's underlings, but the third man appeared more on Mendoza's level from his posture and demeanor.

"So what's your operation like?" Mendoza asked. "How many are involved?"

Mac described his operation, knowing full well Mendoza could duplicate his setup in other places. But there wasn't any choice, and the water tankers could hardly be kept secret after the first shipment. Mendoza seemed impressed, and Mac felt he was making a good impression.

"We'll try you out," Mendoza said after a pause.

He snapped his fingers and Ferret-face produced a paper with various phone numbers and names. Mendoza explained them to Mac and how his end would work. Mac's fee was set by shipment weight and type of commodity. He asked if Mac had any questions.

"Nope, but like any business deal, I would expect larger volumes and more favorable terms if everything works out to our mutual satisfaction. Currently, I have unused capacity, but I don't expect that condition to continue for long."

Mendoza nodded. "If this works out you'll receive greater volumes. You'll be contacted on Monday to confirm the first shipment. Of course, I expect exclusive rights to your services."

"With volume, I'll phase out the personnel traffic."

"No other shippers," Mendoza said.

"Pending adequate volume. If the volume doesn't develop, an exclusive may not be maintainable."

"No other shippers," Mendoza repeated.

There was no way Mac was going to give up this last bit of leverage. He held his head rigidly still, making no gesture that could be construed as agreement. He stared at Mendoza, waiting for him to speak again.

With a wave of his hand and a nod to his bodyguard, Mendoza terminated the conference. Mac stood up immediately and made his way out of the aircraft. Only the bodyguard moved, securing the steps and closing the door after Mac stepped down onto the hardpan.

This had been the most unusual negotiation of Mac's life. Not once had they shaken hands, or even spoken in a friendly manner. As much as he disliked Mexicans, evidently Mendoza distrusted Americans more. He had learned absolutely nothing about Mendoza's operation and very little about his new business partners.

The entire meeting hadn't taken fifteen minutes, and Mac stood inside the small terminal and watched the Beech depart on its way back south. The confrontation hadn't produced all he'd hoped, but probably all that was reasonable to expect. His operation was being placed on trial at forty kilos of coke per day; later, if things worked out, the volume could be expanded. He wasn't known or trusted yet by either Mendoza or his consignee in Chicago, but at least a starting commitment was there.

His only concern was the payment structure running through El Paso after delivery confirmation. Cash on the barrelhead was preferable, but he couldn't trust the tanker driver with such a transaction. His point of maximum leverage was when he possessed the freight, not after it was delivered. But Mendoza wouldn't agree to any payment before delivery, so he was stuck.

Initial shipments would be carried in suitcases by designated illegals each night, and supposedly neither the wetback nor his coyote would be aware of the cargo's value. Mac thought that was risky since luggage was often discarded when border patrols appeared. He assumed Mendoza was lying about how much the mules would know. At any rate, that wasn't his concern other than to check the luggage seal and verify the weight.

Curiously, no one in the airport appeared aware of Mendoza's landing or departure. He expected to be frisked or at least questioned by some Customs official on his return to the terminal area. Instead, he was totally ignored. It didn't seem logical that a plane could land from Mexico and be met by a waiting American without attracting attention. After all, he could be loading sacks of coke into Doug's pickup this very minute. This place was Mendoza's choice, maybe he controlled it.

A telephone call to Tippy was necessary, and Mac located a pay phone in the terminal's entrance. By some stroke of luck she was home, and he quickly informed her he'd be unavailable to work Monday evening. She accepted his change of plans without comment and agreed to cover the evening. Mac wanted to leave his time open to hear from Mendoza, but that was not information he shared.

The return drive went quickly enough, but Mac wished he had taken Aimee along. As it happened, she could have remained in the pickup, but he didn't know the meeting would take place in the plane. He hadn't wanted her to see or be seen by the Mexicans, and the only way to ensure that was to leave her back at camp.

It was amazing that such a beautiful girl could be so insecure. Aimee had everything going for her; looks, body, youth, education, a sweet personality, an adventuresome spirit, yet still feared people wouldn't like her or approve of her.

He reflected on her experience of living in the athletic dorm. That wasn't really her fault. Maybe she could have refused to have sex with the black players, but he wasn't there at the time and couldn't say what pressures she was under. Mac knew some football powers featured booster clubs of girls who escorted high school prospects on their campuses. The girls used sex to recruit the prospects. That was sheer prostitution, and at least she hadn't done that.

Her dive into drugs was understandable, but she didn't appear to be addicted. Aimee was no ozone ranger, although she sometimes seemed a little spacey. But she was having to adapt to a new way of life, and a little confusion was natural. Sensory overload, that's what it was. Hell, he'd have similar problems in New York.

At any rate, all she needed was TLC, someone to believe in her and help her get a fresh start. She deserved it, probably more than anyone he knew. At least now she would be receiving some benefit from the drug trade with him on the supply side.

His thinking about Aimee as a partner jolted him into reality. He was still married to Mary Lou, and Aimee thought he was single. That wasn't fair; he would have to come clean when he returned. She had trusted him with her story, he would have to trust her with his.

He wondered if her remarks about UTEP were true. They probably were. He had heard that the basketball coach found white families to sponsor his black players, and with their increased social access, the basketball players snapped up the local supply of interracially minded girls. But the football team was much larger. There simply weren't enough white girls around who were willing to service black athletes. And Doug was right. The community would never stand for a program like Aimee's was in. UTEP would have to settle for a third-rate team.

He remembered what a successful author said during a talk at UTEP. The author had been heckled by a drunk who'd shouted out, "Ninety percent of what you say is shit!"

The author had responded quietly, "But sir, ninety percent of everything *is* shit."

Mac couldn't agree more. If he could just lower it to eighty percent, he'd be happy.

*****

Aimee was waiting impatiently, and Mac deemed it better to postpone a confession concerning his marital status until a later date. Even though he admitted his error in not taking her along, his words did not have the effect he desired. During his late supper she sat quietly alongside as if expecting another ax to fall. Mac didn't know what else to do.

Gary P. Nunn and his band began playing in the open pavilion, and Aimee disappeared to dance in the dust. "London Homesick Blues" went on for hours while everyone sang or shouted the chorus until they were hoarse. The atmosphere, normally bright, clean and desolate, kept everyone perpetually stoned. Somewhere, bales of marijuana must have been burning but Mac reached for Jose Cuervo to help out.

He sat quietly at the campfire, nursing his tequila and seeing spirits dancing in the flames. The "bucking rock," an unstable boulder that unsuspecting souls attempted to use as a seat, periodically sent would-be riders pitching backward into the dark.

Carrie Forbes, Doug Hamm's youngest sister and the camp's best tequila drinker, went on a crying jag about how no one would drink with her. It was no wonder, Mac thought dimly. Carrie had opened a quart of tequila earlier and thrown away the cap. The first cowboy trying to match her had passed out within an hour, and now a second one was lying on the ground with his head in the fire. Norm benevolently pulled the unconscious body back from incineration, but spurned Carrie's overtures to join her in finishing the bottle so she could get laid. It promised to be another barren night for the feisty redhead who never failed to enliven the camp.

He hardly noticed the blonde amazon who parked herself on his right side with a Coors. She talked steadily with the guy next to her and punctuated her conversation by glancing over to Mac. In the dim light, she couldn't see his deformity, only his lean body and long legs.

Suddenly, she put a vise grip on his arm, and yelled into his ear. "If you've got six inches, I want to fuck you!"

In his mellowed-out state, Mac's reaction was mostly curiosity. He blinked, trying to separate the veils in his alcoholic haze. He wanted no part of her.

"Hell," he said, "I couldn't get six inches up even counting Norm there."

"Yeah? Horsepuckey. Lemme see."

The blonde began grabbing at Mac's belt buckle, but Aimee suddenly appeared behind them out of the darkness. Her hardened-steel voice rattled the entire circle of campers.

"Hands off my man."

The blonde looked up and took stock of Aimee.

Norm jumped in before either could say another word. "Whoa!" he yelled. "This is a friendly camp. No poachers allowed."

A long moment ensued while the two girls glared at each other.

"Sorry," the blonde finally said. "Didn't see any sign." She looked Mac up and down, noticing his head for the first time. "Looks like he'd fit you better anyway."

Aimee started to reply, but Norm shook his head.

The blonde rose and became lost in the gloom. Mac felt a surge of happiness that Aimee would fight for him. He stood up to invite her alongside.

The diabolical lawn chair chose this moment to fold up, and Mac went sprawling. He tried to get up but his legs wouldn't work. He had lost the marathon. Carrie wasn't the only girl to go without that night.

Chapter 36

Mac's headache returned Sunday morning with renewed intensity, accompanied this time by a hangover. Aimee was there to apply ice packs, treating him like a wounded hero back from the front lines. Mac was not slow to appreciate her efforts. She sponge-bathed his body with a damp towel, removing the hurt like St. Patrick banished the snakes from Ireland.

It was wonderful having someone who really cared. Whether Aimee loved him or not, she cared about him, and that was more than he got from Mary Lou or Tippy.

"I'm sorry I was mean last night," she said. "It wasn't my place to object to your meeting."

"That's okay."

"No, really, it won't happen again."

"When I'm being a jerk, I want you to tell me."

"But I don't want you to think I'm demanding."

"I think you're wonderful. Come here." He pulled her onto his chest and lay still. Her scent thrilled him with its freshness, like a newborn fawn in the meadow. He became utterly relaxed and dozed until he felt almost normal.

It sounded idyllic to remain with Aimee so she could banish his headaches to Never-Never Land, but Mac faced other obligations demanding his time. They packed up camp and departed for home before noon. Another Terlingua was history, the best ever in Mac's opinion.

They returned to the Bar-D in late afternoon, and he told Aimee he needed to check on his herd. True to her promise, she voiced no objection and busied herself with their clothes and gear from the trip. Wasting no time, he hustled over to check on Lupe and what had transpired in his absence.

Everything appeared unchanged as he crested the rise where he could first see her trailer. Lupe hurried out to unlock the rear gate before Mac thought she could hear his new Ranger negotiating the sandy track. He returned Lupe's smile and wave and drove straight to the trailer.

She caught up and was waiting for him as he hopped down from the pickup. Its oversize tires had caused him to install running boards, but he preferred to ignore them when getting out. As he turned toward Lupe, she jumped into his arms, wrapped her legs around him, and threatened to spill him onto the sand. Mac was stunned by her bodily assault, and her mouth fastened on his like a vacuum cleaner. He returned her hard kiss, but without opening his mouth.

He grinned and held her away so he could speak. "Whoa! Missed me, I see."

Lupe let go with her legs and dropped back to stand in front of him, sliding her hands down onto his arms. She kneaded his biceps as if testing his athletic build, demurely ignoring his gaze while catching her breath.

"Has everything been all right?" Mac asked. "Have you gotten along without me?"

Lupe nodded again without raising her head. "That woman, she bad for you."

Mac didn't realize Lupe knew about Aimee, and couldn't imagine why she drew such negativity. "Bad? What makes you say that?"

Lupe lapsed into Spanish. "She treats everyone like dirt except one coyote. I think she hates you. The talk is you killed her boyfriend Ricardo."

Mac understood now. Lupe was talking about Tippy. "Who says I killed her boyfriend?"

"A coyote." Lupe looked questioningly at Mac. "Is it true?"

Mac shrugged. "This is the first I've heard she was making it with Ricardo," he said. "I thought she was Ramirez's mistress."

"I heard that too, but she made most with Ricardo." Lupe followed Mac into the trailer telling him what she heard from several coyotes after Tippy departed. She began heating coffee without halting her profusion of words.

According to various coyotes, Tippy was a black widow. Any

man who visited her bed died. At first, they thought Ramirez killed Ricardo after discovering him with Tippy, but after seeing her continuing with Mac, they decided he was responsible for the disappearances.

Lupe's antipathy for Tippy was healthy, and Mac noted she identified with his interests. He listened carefully, greatly encouraged by her attitude and actions. Lupe was fast becoming his business wife without bedroom privileges.

Just thinking about Tippy made his head hurt again, or was it Lupe's chatter? He took the coffee Lupe offered and asked to see the manifests for the last several nights.

The volume was high, and Mac went outside to recover the money envelopes from the embedded safe. He stacked all four nights' receipts in his arms and returned to the trailer. Lupe relieved him of half, and they quickly sorted the envelopes by manifest.

Within minutes, Mac knew he had a problem. The tickets returned from Albuquerque were identical with what Lupe reported she passed out, but the money recorded by Tippy was short. The envelopes matched the money required by the manifests, so the discrepancy was between the tickets as recorded by Lupe and the manifests and money as handled by Tippy.

"It doesn't add up," he said. "Are you sure about these lists of tickets?"

Lupe bolted upright as if stung by his implied accusation and scowling face. "I not make wrong!" Lupe cried in English. "These right!"

She grabbed the lists of tickets, and went through each of them matching her count with that returned from Albuquerque. "See! See!" She pointed triumphantly to the lists. "He same as me!"

Mac wondered why Lupe was trying so hard to communicate in English when they usually spoke Spanish. Probably attempting to impress him with what she had learned.

"Let's match the tickets to the manifests," he said. "Maybe there's some glitch."

"Not in my work! Not my book!"

She paced at the end of the table, constantly leaning over to point out numbers in her journal and interfering with Mac's concentration. He slammed her journal on the table.

"Lupe, sit down!" he yelled. His headache was getting worse.

She dropped like a stone on the bench across from him. For a moment, Mac thought she might start crying, then realized she was more angry than scared.

Then he saw it. A manifest which Lupe listed as having accounted for twenty-eight tickets had only twenty-three names. The other manifest for that evening listed twenty-two names, and Lupe gave out twenty-two tickets. It was possible she miscounted between the manifests, so although Mac's main attention was drawn to the first, both manifests were suspect. At any rate, on that night five envelopes for twenty-five hundred dollars were missing.

The Albuquerque contact was paid on his ticket count, and the coyotes on their manifests. Tippy handled all transactions that evening. Mac had purposefully not told her that their Albuquerque contact was required to report ticket counts. His foresight in establishing checks and balances was paying off.

Looking at the payment ledger, Mac found his suspicions confirmed. Tippy recorded paying Albuquerque the amount indicated by her manifests—that is for five less people than he handled. Obviously, she sent the proper amount of money or the man would have complained. After all, he possessed the tickets and knew the number of people he handled.

The coyote bringing in the illegals was implicated because he constructed the bogus manifest. The black widow in the web's center was Tippy. She simply passed out five tickets for people who weren't listed, and the extra money went into her pocket less Albuquerque's cut. The coyote would have to be paid off, but Mac suspected she took care of him in trade. The only one she was cheating was Mac. The coyotes were right. Any man who slept with her got screwed in more ways than one.

Lupe watched Mac match the tickets, envelopes, manifests, and her reports, silently waiting for Mac to indicate what she should do. He shook his head for a moment, then cleared the table and spread the two suspect manifests in front of her folded arms.

"Do you know the coyotes who brought us these people?" he asked.

She glanced at the coyote codes in the headings and pointed at the short manifest first. "Sure. This one is Carlos Ortiz, the *cabron* who likes that witch. The other is Juan, a boy from Villa Ahumada who talks to me. I like him, *Patron*, I don't think he'd cheat us." She pushed the two sheets back over to Mac.

He noted that Lupe had returned to Spanish, and used "us" when referring to the operation. He smiled at her assumption of the two of them being a team.

"This Ortiz, what do you know of him," Mac asked his teen-aged partner in crime.

Lupe tossed her dark hair back from her face where it had fallen while studying the documents. "Not much, but he said he'd be back Monday."

"Tomorrow?"

"Yes. I heard him talking to the blonde bitch. She said she'd be here, too."

Yep, when Mac had telephoned from Lajitas, he'd told Tippy he'd be back tonight but would miss Monday. He felt a throbbing in his head and wished he had an ice pack.

Lupe noticed Mac's distress. She rose from her seat on the opposite bench and pushed her way onto his lap. She began to gently stroke his deformed head.

"I make you forget *la rubia*," she said.

"No, Lupe. There's nothing to forget about her."

"Then I be good to you anyway." She purred and nuzzled his neck.

Mac took her hands and leaned back so he could see her face.

"I promised not to take advantage of you, sweetie, and I would be if we did anything now." He was acutely aware of her age, most specifically, *under*age. "Let's wait until you're independent. By then, who knows? You may have found another boy closer to your own age that you prefer." Mac smiled, trying to lighten the sense of rejection.

Her already saucer-sized dark eyes enlarged, and again Mac thought she was going to cry. She placed an index finger on his lips.

"You're the only honorable man I've known in my life," she said. "I will wait until the time is right, *patron*."

Although the November night was turning cool, Lupe was wearing only a light blouse which buttoned in front. Her breasts jutted outward with adolescent firmness. Mac knew he could unbutton her blouse and do whatever, and for a brief moment, his headache disappeared.

227

Lupe began to smile at him, obviously feeling the rising hardness of his body as he thought about hers. She slid off his lap and patted Mac's enlarging crotch affectionately.

"Someday all of you will want me," she said.

Mac was suddenly embarrassed by her observation of his body's reaction. He swatted her rear good-naturedly.

"Behave yourself," he said.

Lupe giggled and took his coffee for a refill. She purposefully tantalized him by swinging her hips. Mac considered his options.

He needed this girl's loyalty above all else, and a physical relationship was enormously risky. She'd probably be completely devoted to him initially, but that could change in a heartbeat if she found out about Aimee at the ranch. That might destroy everything. There was simply no reason to put his entire life on red fifteen when the only payoff was grief.

Tippy was already past tense. Their physical intimacy had been terminated a few minutes ago, even assuming he let her live another twenty-four hours. Under no circumstances could he risk jeopardizing his relationship with Aimee by continuing with Tippy. Aimee was a pearl of great price, something he didn't want to lose over Tippy, Lupe or anyone else.

Except maybe Mary Lou. She still occupied a substantial portion of his thoughts, but was gradually being shunted aside by Aimee. It would take time to extinguish the torch he carried. Losing her had been his fault. He had been a jerk, driving her away to a squalid existence with a fat Mexican. If he couldn't set matters right with her, he'd make it up to Aimee, treating her like he should have treated Mary Lou.

Lupe brought him another cup of coffee and started to sit down.

He stood up and took hold of her by the shoulders.

"Lupe, you're extremely important to me, and I hope you know that." His head started throbbing with pain. "You're a young and beautiful girl who has all her life ahead of her. Maybe you're too young to understand, but I think of you as a very dear friend. I want us always to remain friends, no matter what."

Lupe's face darkened into a pout. "How can I be too young to understand that, *patron*? You've been very kind to me, and I'm much indebted to you. You don't need to worry, I'll always be your friend."

228

She stood looking at him with love and hurt in those saucer-sized eyes. Mac felt himself melting. He hadn't meant to hurt her, just establish the limits up front.

He didn't know what to do. He had become her family, a stable hold on life that she needed for building her self-image and values. Supposedly she had relatives in Chicago, but for better or worse, he had become the primary male figure in her life.

He drew her to him and crushed her in a hug. They stood together for a moment while his headache subsided. There was still at least an hour before the evening's cargo would start to arrive.

"Let's lie down for a little bit, I've got a headache," he said. Women were impossible, and he couldn't even handle this sweet little girl. He needed a rest.

She followed him into the bedroom, waiting until he got comfortable on her bed. Lying on his side, he took up almost the entire length. She climbed over his body and wrapped herself around him from behind. Much smaller than Mac, she laid her head on his back as if to protect him. She pressed herself against him, synchronizing her breathing with his. Mac relaxed, but did not fall asleep before the first group arrived.

Chapter 37

Life was really the pits. Mary Lou sat in her kitchen reading her economics text. The subject was gross national product and the effect of government spending—truly boring stuff fit only for academic gnomes and government misfits. Real life was enjoying the bright sunshine outside. That was where she should be, riding Twister to the ends of the earth.

She wondered if Mac had sold Twister or if she was being ridden by another girl. Both possibilities depressed her. Stuart would know, and she could phone him. He'd be at his office, waiting until the last possible minute to head home and face the wife and kids. Even on Sunday. Like all men, he used a woman for sex and avoided her the rest of the time.

Since the infamous lipstick night, she had rejected all attempts by Juan at reconciliation. In the morning he blamed her for his behavior, saying it was his right to have another woman when she refused him. Besides, they weren't married, and he could play the field if he wanted. Then he'd tried a different tack. His friends had talked him into it, and the girl took advantage of his drunken state. It made no difference. He had wanted her to service him while he was still covered with another woman's juices. And that showed an unpardonable lack of respect.

But it was tough being alone. She would have called him last week except for the actions of one of his drinking buddies. Scrawny Victor with bad teeth showed up Monday night wanting to talk. Thinking he was an emissary from Juan, she invited him inside the apartment while she unpacked her groceries. When she turned around at the kitchen counter, he pawed at her clothes and tried to kiss her. Then he got mad when she repelled his advances. But it was his attitude that really frosted the cake.

"Where do you get off being so high and mighty?" he yelled. "You ain't nothing but a slut! You fucking Juan, and he ain't got nothing. You fuck him, you kin fuck me. I got what you need, girlie. Go in your rear, come out your mouth."

His crude talk infuriated her. She marched to the front door and flung it open.

"Out!" she screamed. "Get the fuck out of here! Or I'll call the cops!"

He started to comply, then turned and grabbed her breasts. She slapped him as hard as she could.

The blow stunned Victor for a moment, and she pushed him through the doorway before he could recover his senses. He tripped and fell against the far railing.

She'd slammed the door and locked it immediately. Just in time. Victor began kicking the door and shouting obscenities. Mary Lou threatened him again with the police, but the stream of invective continued. Finally, Victor stomped away with a parting shot about cunt-headed bitches.

She stood there trembling. God, what the neighbors must think. That filthy-mouthed, ugly bastard. His teeth were mossy from tobacco stains and gapped like a ghoul's. What had Juan told him? Why did he think she was available?

She hadn't enticed him, with words, dress, or anything. Her jeans and shirt were absolutely normal, exposing nothing and flaunting nothing.

So why? Because she was white? Was she a slut because she slept with a Mexican? She would have expected such a reaction from Mac's fellow rednecks, but this was from a Mexican.

Victor's attitude was that if a girl went to bed with one Mexican, she couldn't refuse another. Like she had lost her right to say no. That was sheer bullshit. She was free, white, and twenty-one. She could say no to anybody, anytime.

Mary Lou hadn't talked to Juan since the confrontation with Victor. Nothing more had happened, and she was beginning to think Victor's actions weren't connected with Juan. It was possible he hadn't said anything. Maybe she shouldn't hold him accountable for his friends.

But first, she'd call Stuart. The finals at Terlingua were held yesterday, and she wondered if Mac cooked with Norm in the competition. Surely they couldn't have won, but with her luck, she wouldn't bet against it.

Dialing Stuart's office seemed weird, bringing back old times as if nothing had happened since July. But it had, and her heart jumped with a jolt of anxiety when he answered.

"Hi, Stuart, this is Mary Lou," she said. There was a distinct pause, and she envisioned him falling to the floor or dropping the receiver.

"Mary Lou, a voice from the past. To what do I owe this honor?"

She winced at the sarcasm, but his voice was cordial.

"Nothing in particular. Just wondered what happened at Terlingua. You know, if Mac went, and if he placed."

"He went, but I haven't heard the results of the cook-off."

"He go with Norm? I'm sorry about breaking up the team."

"Yeah. Norm and a couple of girls."

"Mac took a girl? He's got a girlfriend?"

"You bet. A gorgeous lady from the east. She's moved in with him at the ranch. Young and vibrant, never a dull moment."

"You're pulling my leg. That's not nice, Stuart. I never hurt you."

"No, cross my heart. Don't know how serious it is, but she's there."

"Riding my palomino?"

"Probably. She said something about riding a horse."

"Aw shit."

Mary Lou mumbled a limp thanks and hung up. She couldn't stop it. Her body shook as she began to cry.

So she was the loser instead of Mac. He had found love while she hadn't. Barefoot, pregnant, without a man, husband, father, or lover, nearly broke, and without a career, she was a pitiful excuse for a woman. Mary Lou felt her tightening shorts. The spread was coming, and she had already started showing.

She wiped her eyes and took a deep breath. Maybe Juan deserved another chance. After all, he was the only thing she had. Even Twister was serving a new mistress.

Juan's apartment key was still in her purse, and there was no time like the present to surprise him. She showered and did those things that made her especially presentable to a lover. Once again, she selected her sexiest clothes. There was no harm in facilitating a reconciliation with the right clothes and makeup. If Mac could find someone, so could she.

Juan's truck wasn't in his parking lot. Undeterred, she entered his apartment to wait. Mary Lou had made up her mind to rekindle the relationship. If she had to, she'd tell him about the baby. In the meantime, there was nothing to do but wait. She made the ultimate sacrifice. She turned on a football game to watch while she waited.

After an hour, the Chargers were bludgeoning the Broncos into abject submission, and there was no reason to endure further torture. Mary Lou began to roam around the apartment, looking for changes since her last visit. There was no sign of a new girlfriend.

She thought of the nightstand. After all, that was where everyone kept things they needed for bedroom activities. With a twinge of anticipation, she pulled out the drawer and looked inside. She was right. On top of some magazines was a vibrator. It looked like the one from her days with the professor, but she hadn't seen it for years. They all looked alike anyway. The magazines were girlie stuff, soft porn showing lots of boobs and genitalia. That was okay, too.

Underneath the magazines was a fat envelope, obviously containing pictures. She took them out and gasped.

They were her photos. The ones from her early days with Mac. All the porno shots they had so much fun making. The fat bastard had stolen them from the ranch. Probably showed them to all his friends. It was probably her vibrator, too. No wonder Victor had said the things he had.

She scooped up the photos and grabbed the vibrator. Hurriedly she went through the rest of the drawer. Fighting a rising panic that he might arrive at any moment, she found nothing else of hers. In less than a minute, she was out the door.

A block from Juan's apartment, she heaved a sigh of relief. It was her second escape. First from Mac and now from Juan. No, that wasn't right. It was her fifth. Her father, Tommy, the professor, Mac, and Juan. The men in her life. They all wanted something from her but weren't willing to give her anything in return.

Tomorrow she'd change her phone to an unlisted number. If that wasn't sufficient, she'd move to another apartment. Juan was now ancient history. Her baby would have to get along without a father. She'd supply men from time to time for role models, but on her terms instead of theirs. Her baby, boy or girl, was henceforth the center of her life, and future lovers would have to give a lot to get a little.

Chapter 38

Monday morning passed rapidly as Mac watched Aimee take possession of his house and bedroom as her own. She seemed to have recovered from the mood caused by his meeting at Lajitas, and his being away last evening didn't bother her a bit. They had made love like there was no tomorrow. Mac marveled at how his headache pain evaporated in Aimee's presence, but when he mentioned her effect, she gave him the classic physiological explanation.

"That's because your blood was going to your head before and causing pain from too much pressure. When I'm around it goes to a location where we both get a lot of benefit."

He chuckled, but more likely, the reasons were emotional, which manifested themselves physically through headache pain. It subsided as he lost himself in Aimee's presence, with or without sex. She soothed the raging beast in him, calmed him, and blew the pain away with tender kisses. Sunlight and the day's heat brought the pain back, but Mac no longer became angry over his affliction. Aimee would make it go away in the evening.

What bothered him most about his headaches was that he felt so good while killing Mexicans. A psychiatrist would probably stamp him with some horrible label and declare him insane. Mac worried about that, and knew temporary insanity didn't fit because of his premeditation. Maybe his actions weren't legal, but they were right. His head confirmed the righteousness of his cause by ceasing to hurt when he did battle. It was warfare, he was a warrior, defending himself and his kind.

Tonight promised to bring more of those warlike actions, for the first time against an Anglo and a woman. He thought about Tippy, and the contrast between Aimee and her green-eyed fellow female was startling. Tippy was a more classical beauty, but Aimee was sexier. At least to Mac. That was because Aimee jumped his bones willingly, even eagerly. With Tippy, it was part of her job. Tippy couldn't be trusted, and he debated whether or not his only option was to eliminate her. It was a daunting prospect, and one he wasn't quite ready to face.

And then there was Mary Lou. Lying with Lupe in her trailer yesterday evening, he had thought mostly about Mary Lou. He didn't want to lose Aimee, but he wanted Mary Lou to be happy. And there was no way she could be happy with a Mexican. She deserved some of the money that was rolling in, and it could keep her from ruining her life. If only she'd call.

But Aimee had made him forget all about Mary Lou when he returned to the ranch. She even made him forget about Tippy.

Tippy. His mind kept coming back to Tippy. She was a problem he had to resolve. For Aimee, Lupe, and himself.

Montana had phoned early in the morning to say that trial shipments would begin Wednesday. Mac was now free this evening, and he immediately decided to handle the skimming problem without delay. He would be at the well tonight instead of Tippy.

Shortly before noon, Stuart called to remind him of their meeting in Las Cruces. It concerned his application to drill additional wells in the Mesilla Bolson and would divert his attention from Tippy for a few hours. The water issue was a barnburner, and like everyone else, he didn't want El Paso tapping into New Mexico's supply. Aimee asked to go along, and Mac was proud that she wanted to attend a public hearing at his side. She'd show his Las Cruces acquaintances that his injury hadn't destroyed his ability to attract women. And if the meeting became too heated, she'd be there to soothe his pain. He helped her into his truck feeling as light-hearted as on his best day with Mary Lou.

Before they reached Interstate 10, Aimee commented on the diesel pumps scattered along the road to irrigate fields from the valley's network of canals. Sometimes she was like a little kid, seeing things for the first time and causing Mac to view familiar surroundings from a fresh perspective. Then she saw a house, ostensibly in the center of a pond.

"What's a house doing in the middle of that lake?" she exclaimed.

"They have water rights, that's all," Mac said. "The lawn is irrigated like a field, and you don't see it because it's under four or five inches of water."

"What happens to the water?"

"Evaporates, or is absorbed by the ground. Takes a day or two, and you'll see a green lawn."

"Pretty lazy way of watering," Aimee said. "I assume they don't have a basement."

"There are some at higher elevations, but not here in the valley. There'd be more except most of El Paso is built on caliche, and it's like concrete lying a few feet under the surface. Makes a great foundation, but basements are too expensive to dig."

They turned onto the freeway at Vinton and headed north. The Texas state trooper and his souped-up Mustang were in the Visitors' Center clocking opposing traffic. Mac punched the Ranger and darted into New Mexico.

"Didn't need my 'don't give me a ticket' decal this time," Mac said.

Aimee puzzled over his comment. "Say what?"

"I donate every year to the Texas State Troopers' Association. Get a decal for my money. It's behind me in the rear window. Don't know if it really works, but I'm yet to get a ticket from a state trooper."

"Sounds like the ranch is safe from tigers because one's never shown up."

Aimee pointed to a long bridge on the service road over a harmless-looking dry wash. "Why such a big bridge? There's no water."

"Not now there isn't, but wait 'til it rains. The ground doesn't absorb water, and the area is subject to flash floods."

Mac directed Aimee's attention to the mountains stretching from the Anthony Gap to the Organs. They were part of the Franklin Mountains that started in El Paso and ran north to become the Front Range in Colorado.

"If those mountains get a couple of inches in a short time, that arroyo back there could see a ten foot wall of water coming down it. And it might not even rain here. That's the danger. People camp in an arroyo, never feel a drop of rain, then are swept away in a flash flood that originated miles away."

"I never thought the desert was dangerous that way. What a riot to drown in the desert."

"Not funny when you see what water can do."

"Is that what those long earthen dams are for? I thought they were reservoirs or watering holes for cattle." Aimee pointed to one of the large flood control dams built by the Bureau of Land Management between the highway and mountains.

"Yep. Ninety-nine days out of a hundred they're bone dry. But when it rains, they keep this road in place."

Mac sped pass Vado and hoped for an easterly breeze. No such luck. As he came abreast of the line of dairies west of the highway, it seemed that every cow on the feed lots had her tail raised.

Aimee held her nose. "How can people live there?" she cried.

A number of modern and expensive homes were located on the service road alongside the dairies. With a westerly like Mac and Aimee were experiencing, the stench in those houses had to be well-nigh overwhelming.

"Guess it smells like money to them," Mac said. "Now you know why I keep my cattle away from the ranch house."

"No kidding. It's awful."

Aimee was quiet the rest of the way into Las Cruces. It helped to keep one's mouth tightly closed around the dairies, which she hadn't done.

There was time to kill and Mac was hungry. He decided to take in lunch at the Great American Food & Beverage Restaurant on Lohman. It was a place like Bennigan's or Applebee's except for the two railroad dining cars in its parking lot, and with the similarity in names, people confused it with the Great American Land & Cattle Company steakhouse in Vinton.

A few minutes later, Stuart arrived with two of Doña Ana's county commissioners. Mac commented on their unusual synchronicity while they pushed two tables together. Stuart was well-acquainted with the proprietress, a wispy blonde named Ginger, and she made her presence known as soon as she spotted him with the politicos. One of Las Cruces's more notable business women, Ginger was politically connected to the governor.

Stuart and Mac rose from their hard wooden chairs to greet their hostess, Stuart making his usual exaggerated greeting amid a profusion of politeness. Ginger had just returned from a diet and exercise spa that she called a "fat farm." Listening to her account of life on the farm, Mac couldn't understand why the size-four Ginger threw away her money on such excursions. He shrugged and supposed she needed a rest from Las Cruces and the attention she received in her red Corvette. A dynamo like Stuart, she was the most eligible bachelorette in town.

Ginger soon dashed away to handle some crisis in the kitchen, and the men sat down to order. They were almost ready when Mac looked up and saw another blonde approaching. It was Tippy. God damn! Mac's head gave him a jolt of pain. Tippy was a nightmare that wouldn't go away. Controlling his anger for allowing this situation to occur, Mac quickly stood up to head off a confrontation.

"Tippy!" he said. "What's happenin'?"

He wanted to groan. His excessively jovial greeting wouldn't have fooled a child.

Tippy looked stunning in an Irish green dress that accentuated her green eyes. Her long hair streamed seductively, and she tossed it around with elegant flips of her head.

"Saw your Ranger outside, and thought I'd drop in." She eyed Aimee while waiting for an introduction, then turned to Stuart when one wasn't offered.

"Hi, Stuart," she said. "You guys are out in force today."

"Tippy, you know Commissioners Macias and De Castro?" Stuart led with the introductions, trying to take some heat off Mac.

"No, I don't believe I do." She shook their hands graciously as each re-introduced himself. Pausing only a second, she turned back to Mac. He responded almost involuntarily to her unspoken request.

"And this is Aimee Barnes, Stuart's ex-sister-in-law from North Carolina. It's her first time out west." Mac gestured in Aimee's direction, praying she wouldn't say the wrong thing. He didn't want either woman to meet or even know about each other, yet here they were, going eyeball to eyeball.

"Nice to meet you," Tippy said. "Have you been seeing much of the country?"

"Some," Aimee replied. "I went to the Terlingua cook-off last week and had a blast."

Mac's worst fears had been realized. Tippy knew Mac had gone to Terlingua, so obviously Aimee was his current interest. Mac desperately attempted to find some way to end the conversation, but Commissioner Macias stepped in and made the situation worse.

"Miss Gallagher, we'd be honored if you'd join us for lunch," he said.

There was nothing Mac could do. He hoped against hope that Tippy was late for some appointment and would refuse the oily politician's offer. She didn't.

"Thank you. That's very kind of you," she said.

Macias rapidly shifted places, and offered Tippy the chair across from Aimee. Stuart was pushed to the far end.

"Having a beautiful woman at your side is worth a dozen stares, and half of them turn into votes," Macias said.

Tippy sat down, brushing Macias with her silky hair and touching Mac's knee with hers. By merely sitting down between them, she seemed to take possession of both men.

Nicely done, Mac said to himself. He gnashed his teeth. Politicians would be the death of him one way or the other. The girls were at his half of the table, both within touching distance. And Stuart was too far away to help, dammit.

"How long do you expect to be out here?" Tippy asked Aimee.

"I don't know. It's pretty indefinite."

"Well, you must let me show you around. Where are you staying?"

"At the Bar-D. Mac's been real good about introducing me to western life."

"Oh, I'm sure he has."

Tippy turned slowly to Mac and smiled. "You didn't tell me you had such a lovely house guest. You've been holding out on me."

Aimee stared at Mac as if seeking an explanation.

"Tippy and I are business associates in some local investments," he said.

Commissioner Macias raised his eyebrows. "Oh, really? What kind of investments?"

"Land and water," Mac said. "Ms. Gallagher has a number of Mexican clients for whom she makes investments in the area."

"Yes, and we've done quite well so far, haven't we, darling?" Tippy said. She affectionately patted Mac's leg before he could forestall her action, and her "darling" sounded like something from Zsa Zsa Gabor.

A sinking feeling knotted Mac's stomach. This was terrible and getting worse.

For the moment, Tippy let him off the hook by diverting her attention to Macias and chatting about real estate. It was a mystery how she could fabricate stories so readily, but Macias was thoroughly captivated by her charm. She lightly touched the politician's arm to emphasize her friendliness and femininity, and another conquest was hers anytime she wished.

Mac's role as Tippy's partner declined steadily as she talked, and Macias obviously believed he wasn't a major player. It was common knowledge from the water hearings that Mac's ranch hadn't been doing well, and Macias knew he was in hock up to his ears.

Tippy was in her element, dominating the table with superior airs and cowing poor Aimee into silence. When Mac tried to advise Aimee on what to order, Tippy corrected him and told Aimee to try the spinach salad that Ginger featured as her leading special. When Commissioner De Castro spoke to Aimee, Tippy usurped her reply, supplying the appropriate answer as a second question. Aimee couldn't get a word in edgewise, and withdrew into herself.

That suited Tippy enormously, but the non-verbal communication was worse than the verbal. She took every opportunity to make little gestures designed to display her intimacy with Mac. Her body language was unmistakable, and more than once, Mac thought Aimee might bolt for the door.

Mac did what he could to bring Aimee into the conversation. Tippy didn't ride, and Aimee could talk about Twister. So he brought up the subject of horses. It was a catastrophe. Tippy interrupted to say that Mac was an excellent rider with lean legs that were much stronger than one might think. Nobody could miss the implication unless blinded by her charm like Macias was.

A lull developed in Tippy's social seminar while the waitress removed their plates. Mac seized the opportunity to set up his evening. His head was flirting with stabbing pains, and demanded a victory over Tippy, no matter how small.

"We won't be needing you at this evening's meeting," Mac said. "I'll handle it alone."

"Really?" Tippy looked genuinely surprised. "It's no trouble for me to be there."

"Yeah, in fact I'd rather you weren't there. The property's not being kept up as well as it should, and I'll need to talk with the caretaker."

He had purposely intimated he wanted to be alone with Lupe, and Tippy would take that as a sign things weren't going well with Aimee. She would think she had gained the upper hand. She reacted as expected, unable to suppress a smile.

"Well, if you don't think I need to be there..." she said.

"No, I don't."

*****

Mac rated lunch as an unmitigated disaster of the first magnitude, and the hearing on his applications to drill irrigation wells didn't go much better. Figuratively speaking, attorneys from El Paso muddied the water, and the meeting rained uncertainty. The New Mexico State Water Commission tabled his applications along with others to avoid giving the current suit by El Paso additional credence in federal district court.

It was all El Paso's fault. The city had purchased land in New Mexico with water rights, but intended to pipe the water across the state line into Texas. New Mexico was fighting hard to keep its water in the state. It wasn't New Mexico's fault that El Paso was expanding recklessly when its resources couldn't support geometric population growth. Stemming unbridled growth was the only workable approach to maintain a quality existence for current residents. Stealing another state's water was unconscionable!

Mac remembered a time when Norm had lunched with him in Las Cruces, and he had introduced the El Paso native to several of his Cruces acquaintances. The water issue had just hit the papers and feelings were running high. One of the pecan growers from Mesquite evinced a certain standoffishness, and Norm tried cracking a joke. "Don't worry about me, guys; I don't drink water." Not only did no one laugh, but room temperature dropped to absolute zero. Yeah, water wasn't a joking matter.

Now Mac's plans for agricultural expansion on the Bar-D were firmly on ice until El Paso's suit was settled. That might take years. Even into the next century.

Mac knew ranchers in Otero County who owned land appropriated by the federal government in World War II. They still hadn't received compensation, but that's the way things went. Japanese interned in California were paid reparations of twenty thousand dollars per person while law-abiding Americans who fought in the war lost their land and got nothing.

Now the government was striking him. The Bar-D was in New Mexico, he paid real estate taxes in New Mexico, but couldn't sink a well to reach water on his own land. All because a city in another state needed water to flush turds down its sewers.

Well, at least he had Aimee. On the drive back to the ranch, she listened to him complain about the water situation. She offered little comment, and it was apparent the confrontation with Tippy had shaken her badly. His efforts to divert her attention weren't working, and he didn't know how to provide effective reassurance. Talking about Tippy would indicate she was important to Mac, whereas his silence might be taken as evasion. Either way, he would lose. Mac decided to let the matter drop unless Aimee brought it up.

The only positive thing to come out of lunch was Tippy's agreement for him to handle the illegals this evening. He would have an unencumbered opportunity to deal with Ortiz, then settle accounts later with Tippy. She evidently didn't suspect he had discovered her little scam, but she'd know before morning. The fox was in the henhouse, and the chickens were sleeping.

Lunch also confirmed one other thing. Tippy knew too much and was dangerous. Since she couldn't be controlled, she had to be eliminated. There was no longer any choice. He mentally steeled himself for what was an inevitable moment a few hours hence.

After supper, Mac excused himself, reminding Aimee of his meeting in Cruces. She had been quiet since lunch and not responded to his touch.

He casually mentioned Tippy liked to put other women down by playing up to their men, and that Aimee shouldn't take her so seriously. Mac bit the bullet and offered to talk about Tippy when he returned. Aimee didn't seem especially interested, and he decided it was something that would work out with a little time. In a couple of days, he'd say Tippy had left town and they were no longer business associates. That should help since Aimee wouldn't have to worry about running into Tippy again.

He kissed Aimee passionately on his way out, telling her to put on something sexy for his return. He hoped she would, but she only responded with, "We'll see."

Chapter 39

This time there was no kiss from Lupe as Mac stepped out from Rover. He assumed she was just nervous and distracted. Ortiz was due this evening, and she wasn't sure of Mac's intentions. In the trailer, she made a pest of herself, buzzing around Mac like a honeybee searching for nectar and continually asking if he wanted anything. He finally settled for an ice pack to subdue the headache that had started at lunch. The hearings had worsened the pain, and Lupe's constant chatter didn't help.

For almost an hour, he lay on her bed while she gently moved the ice around his forehead. Water dripped onto Lupe's pillow, but his pain subsided to a dull ache. Thinking about Aimee's love and Lupe's care almost lulled him to sleep. He was barely awake when the first coyote pounded on the trailer's door. Immediately, his headache got worse, but Mac ignored it for the job at hand.

He altered his normal routine and processed each group as they arrived. Ortiz was late, and Mac purposely glanced at the coyote's manifest with only a cursory interest. He didn't need a second look. The additions at the bottom stuck out like John Hancock's signature. Apparently, Ortiz hadn't been tipped off and was forced to add the names enroute. They were hurriedly scrawled, almost illegibly, and in a different handwriting than the rest.

Mac told Ortiz to stick around after the tanker departed, an unnecessary order since no one could leave until the pay codes were distributed. He settled up with the other coyotes and left Ortiz for last.

The skinny Mexican hadn't impressed Mac with his intelligence or energy on previous occasions, and there was no obvious reason why Tippy would choose him as a partner. Only of medium height, Ortiz was somewhere between twenty-five and thirty years old, with

244

shaggy black hair and pinched, pock-marked cheeks. He slouched and shuffled as if attempting to avoid attention, and would be invisible in a group of chile-pickers.

"Tippy wanted me to bring you to her place," Mac said to the silently waiting Ortiz. "You can leave your van here, I'll bring you back."

He handed the extremely dark Mexican his pay code and collection address, and told Lupe he'd be returning shortly. Purposely intended to deceive others, Mac's comments to Lupe were always the opposite from what he meant. She understood he wouldn't be back that night.

The Mexican climbed into Rover's passenger seat, and Mac drove out through the rear gate. He headed south instead of north.

"Got to take the long way," Mac said. "Miss Gallagher wants some chiles I bought."

Ortiz nodded without comment. He seemed completely at ease, maybe because he had received his pay code and instructions. Mac noticed Ortiz possessed a lazy eye, adding to his appearance of disinterest and indolence. It was difficult to imagine Ortiz being loved by his mother.

Mac drove up the arroyo leading to his mine, stopping with his headlights illuminating a half-dozen *ristras* hanging on a rack by the portal. In the gloom and glare the blood-red chiles looked black, like so many devil fingers clawing at the gathering breeze.

"Come on, pack a hand," Mac said. He hopped out with the Jeep's engine still running.

Ortiz stepped onto the sand and approached the chiles on Mac's right. Squinting at the chiles in the harsh light, he didn't see the homemade blackjack in Mac's hand.

A single hard rap collapsed the skinny Mexican like a sack of potatoes. Mac grinned with satisfaction. His headache had evaporated with the blow.

He moved Rover to its normal hiding place down the arroyo, then returned to unlock the mine. Mac easily hefted Ortiz's dead weight over his shoulder and carried the unconscious coyote inside. The chile rack was heavier, but it too went through the entrance without difficulty. Mac's adrenaline was working overtime. It took but a moment to strip Tippy's associate of his worldly possessions and handcuff him to the chile rack.

This was not to be a gentle discussion. Mac chuckled at Ortiz's posture. Except for the missing cloth over his private parts, Ortiz made a good artist's model for Christ on the cross.

Working rapidly, Mac restored the mine's entrance to its previous camouflaged condition. In spite of the evening's chill, he broke a sweat and cursed the need to keep this location secret. His headache reappeared with the physical exertion, getting worse as he overheated in the dust. By the time Mac finished, Ortiz was stirring and making noises.

Mac splashed the Mexican with cold water to hasten events along. Tippy would be getting apprehensive, and he didn't want to keep her waiting.

Ortiz opened his eyes and stared at Mac with obvious fear. "Whatcha doing, man?" he said. "I ain't done nothing."

"Except steal. That's your way of life." Mac turned a rickety wooden chair around in front of Ortiz, then sat down so he was straddling the back. He examined the knife he found strapped inside Ortiz's boot, flipping it casually to gain Ortiz's attention.

"Who's idea was it? Yours or Miss Gallagher's?"

"Ah don't know what you talkin' about."

"Too bad," Mac said. "I follow Moslem customs in punishment for crimes. You know, you lose a hand for stealing once, both for twice. Only… I've modified it a little. You lose one ball for stealing, one for lying."

He stood up and kicked the chair backwards. Talking a measured step toward Ortiz, he grasped the Mexican's genitals in his left hand.

Mac's head was throbbing, and sharp, stabbing pain came in flashes. He needed to get this over quickly and calm down before he burst something.

"Your dick's kinda small. Maybe I'll take it instead." Mac smiled through the pain, purposely making his appearance grotesque to the scruffy *cholo*.

"No, man, don't!" Ortiz yelled. He lashed his head from side to side. "I don't know nothing!"

"Tell me about the five extras," Mac said. The Mexican's body odor offended him, and there was a positively rancid stink coming from the parts in his hand.

"What extras?" The coyote sweated profusely as the temperature rose within the confined area. He thrashed his legs in panic, raising dust which hung around Mac's feet.

"Wrong answer," Mac said.

He stepped back slightly to improve the light and studied his holdings. The Mexican's testicles were drawn up tightly as if resisting Mac's grasp. He pulled down on the larger one, then pinched it away from its brother.

"Whatcha doing, man?" Ortiz said. "Come on, I don't know nuthin'."

Mac sliced the scrotum open with his knife like when he turned calves into steers. Only this time, he didn't have to pull the testicle down—it spurted by itself from the split sack to hang by its ducts.

Ortiz screamed like a wounded cat, splattering Mac with saliva. He kicked out and jerked his body against the chile rack.

Ignoring the inhuman sounds, Mac cut the connecting tubes. More shrieks threatened to burst his eardrums, and he held the severed testicle up for Ortiz's inspection. The terrified Mexican recoiled at the sight, and Mac casually dropped the dangling organ into the sand.

The mutilated coyote closed his eyes and babbled incoherently. Mac doused him a second time with cold water. He held the bloody sack tightly to stem the crimson flow, and began again as Ortiz's groaning abated.

"Now," Mac said. "You've lost one, but you don't want to lose the other. If you do, you'll never be a man again. Tell me about the extra five people."

Mac increased the intensity of his voice with each word in his last sentence, progressing from friendly concern to nasty and threatening. He squeezed the remaining testicle to punctuate his statement, and Ortiz's body buckled in fear and pain.

"It wasn't me, man! It was her!" Ortiz's dark face was glistening in sweat as his head lolled from side to side.

"Why? What was in it for you?"

"Ricardo was my cousin," he rasped between short and shallow breaths.

Mac nodded. He understood why Tippy had chosen this pitiful specimen to hit back.

"Tell me the whole story. We've got time." He pulled Ortiz's tadpole maker out as far as it would stretch and stroked it with his knife like stropping a straight razor. "Otherwise..."

The story bubbled out between coughs, sobs, and pleas for mercy. It was all Tippy's idea. When she heard he was Ricardo's cousin, she drove him to Cruces and took him to bed. He had nothing personal against Mac, but she gave him no choice. After they had sex, she said she would tell Mac he raped her if he didn't do his part. He didn't get any of the money, and only had sex with her twice. The second time was the night she kept the money for his five unlisted illegals. They were going to short Mac again tonight, but he was there instead of Tippy. The Mexican swore on the Virgin Mary and his mother's grave that was all he knew.

It seemed improbable to Mac, but anything was possible where Tippy was concerned. He tossed Ortiz's knife in the dirt and took out his blackjack.

"So you got to fuck her," Mac said.

"She forced me. It wasn't my fault."

"Where? Where'd she do this to you?"

"Aw, man, in her house. Where else?"

"You mean my house. You fucked another man's woman in his own house?"

"Ah didn't know, man!"

"Well, I hope you enjoyed it. That was your last white girl."

He dropped what remained of Ortiz's genitals as the pent-up blood gushed forth. With a terrific blow Mac whacked Ortiz across his left temple, exactly where his own skull had been cracked in the summer. Ortiz went out like a light. Internal bleeding would kill him in a few minutes if the shock hadn't done it already.

"Correction, that was your last girl, period," Mac said.

His head was throbbing, but the pain was livable. He still faced a long night with the worst to come. This whole business was making him sick.

"Nothing personal," he said to the dying Mexican. Mac noticed a dung beetle mounting the fallen gonad. Ortiz was on his way back into the food chain already. The lime pit would soon claim another.

Chapter 40

Tippy's front courtyard was bathed in light, displaying the entry to its best advantage with hacienda-style hospitality. Mac parked Rover behind her Mazda in its usual place, taking his time to turn off the radio and lights. He walked jauntily to the door as if expecting a loving greeting from his mistress. His headache had subsided after depositing Ortiz in the lime pit, and in spite of the uncontrolled throbbing in his left temple, Mac felt ready to deal with Tippy. As long as his pain didn't affect his vision or balance, he'd be able to do what was necessary.

Eliminating all traces of Ortiz's demise at the mine had been cathartic. The Mexican's wallet had contained a paper with Tippy's phone number in her handwriting, adding physical evidence to verify his story. Revenge by relatives was a time-honored Mexican tradition and explained Ortiz's involvement. Mac maintained the fiction of not knowing what happened to Garcia and the missing coyotes precisely to avoid a blood feud. Mexicans had large families, and with six dead already, there could be dozens of greasers ready to carve his name in bullets if they knew the truth.

Garcia must have meant more to Tippy than she let on. Although sex for Tippy was a mechanism for controlling men, that didn't mean she wasn't capable of getting involved. Garcia had been tall and suave for a Mexican, and Mac recalled that Garcia's endowment had been impressive. Whatever he had, she had been willing to cheat on Ramirez for a piece of it.

It hurt Mac to admit it, but Garcia had been the most handsome man he knew in Tippy's life, Anglo or Mexican. Most men currently around Tippy were downright ugly. He had been handsome once, but not any longer. Every time Aimee touched his head he feared she

249

might wake up and realize how deformed and ugly he really was. The same was true for Lupe, but he doubted that she viewed him as a love object.

He felt the billy in his jacket pocket. He had learned its value, and decided to dispatch Tippy the same way as Ortiz. He knew there was no other choice. Tippy would eventually have him killed. Losing Ortiz meant she'd just find someone else. Mac didn't like the idea of snuffing a woman, but it was a matter of self-preservation.

He unlatched the steel gate and quietly let himself in the front door. His hope to surprise her vanished when she appeared in the atrium almost immediately. She must have been sitting up and waiting.

Tippy looked spectacular in a bright green nightgown probably purchased from Frederick's Of Hollywood. He hadn't seen it before, and it was one of those sexy, funky styles with a tied bodice and slits down the sides like an Ao Dai. The color was perfect for Tippy.

She hesitated a moment for Mac to appreciate the gift he was about to receive, then walked toward him like Miss America coming down a Las Vegas runway. Tippy stretched herself against his chest, gently took his cheeks between her hands, and pulled his face down to hers. Her kiss was soft at first, then became harder and more demanding as she wiggled her body into his. Mac stood breathlessly as his senses were assailed by her sexuality.

"Missed you," she said, as she leaned back for a moment. She reached below with her hand and began massaging his groin.

In spite of himself, Mac was becoming aroused. The last thing he wanted was to think with his dick instead of his mind. She was attempting to re-assert her control through sex.

Now. He told himself. *Do it now before she talks you out of it*.

But he vacillated. Maybe he should give her one more time like a condemned prisoner getting a last meal. Then he remembered Aimee, and that this woman was his enemy.

Unbelievable. She was so beautiful. Yet so evil.

The argument raged in his mind and confused him. Something delayed was something denied, and time was working against him.

She unzipped his fly and took him out while he floundered in uncertainty. His knees began to buckle, and he needed to steady himself.

"Let's sit down for a moment," he said.

She smiled knowingly and ushered him into her living room. Tippy spun around and pushed Mac onto her flowered, aqua-colored couch. Pulling up her nightgown, she straddled him. As expected, there was nothing under the silk. He wanted to resist, but the heat that engulfed his dick addled his brain. The nightgown disappeared over Tippy's head, and she buried Mac's face in her cleavage.

Mac fought for supremacy and rationalized his acquiescence to her desires. He would enjoy himself one last time and then snuff her. She wasn't in control, he was. He could decide to do this or not. And why not?

But there was a reason, and he knew it. He wanted to be faithful to Aimee and build a relationship based on trust and open communication. Mac focused on Aimee, and his mind switched off the sexual urge and replaced it with increased headache pain.

Tippy leaned back and cupped her breasts, expertly rotating her pelvis in slow circles and grinding into Mac to maximize contact and sensitivity. Then she let herself go, flinging her long hair around to brush Mac's face. Tippy moaned loudly and rolled her eyes to the ceiling. She thrust forward and backward from her waist, augmenting her moans with shivering squeals of ecstasy.

This time it wasn't working. Her overwhelming eroticism maintained Mac's full arousal, but he felt detached. His attitude was one of disdain, watching this woman make love to some man on her couch. Tippy was doing her number, and the man's identity was irrelevant.

He remained motionless in his slumped position, both hands flat on the couch to either side. Mac studied Tippy's face, waiting for her to look at him and notice his lack of involvement. It took a while, but finally she saw his face and slowed her movements to a subtle rhythmic undulation.

"What's wrong?" she said. Her voice was husky and contained a note of surprise.

Mac continued to stare without speaking. Tippy halted her motion and placed her hands on his chest.

"Don't tell me you prefer that Carolina redneck. She hasn't a clue to what it's all about."

"Is this what you did to Ortiz?" Mac said.

Tippy tightened down involuntarily, her face flushing at his accusation. Mac almost laughed aloud thinking about how a woman spoke the truth when impaled by a man. In any other situation, Tippy would have handled his question without a flicker of emotion. She started to rise, but he grabbed her hips and clamped her in place. "Well?"

Her face contorted into a ferocious mass of hate. "You bastard!"

She swung a roundhouse right at his chin, but Mac was faster. He caught the blow on his left arm, spraining Tippy's wrist. She cried out in pain, and he flung her off his body. Tippy clawed awkwardly at Mac as she bounced off the cushions, but the force of his shove sent her sprawling on the floor.

In an instant Mac was straddling her, pressing her arms into the soft silvery carpet. He glanced down, suddenly realizing he had landed too high on her torso. His open fly left him dangerously exposed. Mac jerked his pelvis backwards just as Tippy lunged forward to bite.

"You bitch!" he yelled. Mac slugged her hard across the mouth, snapping her head sideways on the floor.

He rolled her onto her stomach before she could retaliate. Her hair caught underneath his knee and prevented her head from following the rest of her body. She screamed in agony, and only the sound told Mac her neck hadn't broken. He wrestled her arms together behind her back, handcuffing her with some difficulty as her hair became entangled beyond belief. She yelled and screeched her objection to every movement.

His head responded to her shrieks with lightning bolts of pain. Mac yanked her to the couch and slapped her twice to halt the noise. Tippy's mouth was bleeding, and the fear in her eyes exceeded that of any coyote Mac dispatched earlier.

"You got it wrong!" Tippy screamed. "It wasn't me!"

Mac stuffed himself back inside his Levi's and zipped up his fly. She had left a wet circle on the edges he would have to clean later. He stood over her and glowered. Naked except for the handcuffs, she struggled to sit up on her couch. Tippy started crying, but Mac couldn't tell if it was from pain or to highlight her helpless condition.

"My wrist's broken!" she wailed. "God, it hurts!" Her face was already scarlet, and when she spoke, small flecks of blood splattered onto her chest and legs.

"Sorry about that," Mac said. He felt no sympathy for her at all. His eyes were clear, but his head was throbbing worse than before. Flashes of pain reverberated through his forehead when Tippy yelled, and he knew a splitting headache was only moments away.

"So talk," he said.

"Ortiz made me do it!" she cried. "He's Ricardo's cousin, and came here to kill me. Said I had Ricky snuffed."

"And you said?"

"I told him I didn't know what happened to Rick. He disappeared before I met you."

"He believed that? Bullshit."

"No, not at first." She licked the blood from her lips and swallowed. "Can't you take these handcuffs off? My right arm is killing me."

"It's not your arm you need to worry about. So how did you convince him? Or did you try to bite his dick off, too?"

"I would have, but he was going to carve me into little pieces."

Tippy tried to plead with her eyes, but it wasn't working.

"Yeah, Mexicans always carry knives. What was his like?"

"A switchblade." Tippy realized this question was a test. She began to perk up since Mac was giving her a chance to prove her side of the story. "It had a black handle and was maybe five inches long. About the size of his cock."

Mac eyed her steadily. The knife description was accurate, and he had noted Ortiz's equipment was typical for a Mexican. He nodded almost involuntarily.

"So you gave him a piece of ass and part of the take to save your life. Bullshit. Not if he thought we blew Garcia away. He'd fuck you silly, play connect the dots on your body, and rip off everything in the house."

"That's not how it happened."

"Obviously."

"I told him I was pregnant with Ricky's kid."

"Pregnant? You?" Mac snorted, almost breaking into peals of laughter. The pain in his head held his mirth in check. Ortiz had not mentioned Tippy was pregnant, and he obviously hadn't known.

"It's true." Tippy's voice became almost reverent. "I'm pregnant. That's the only thing that saved me. That's why the skimming. He said we had to provide for Rick's kid. It saved you, too. He was going to kill you, but I convinced him he needed you to make money."

Tippy was making a desperate effort to regain control of the situation with lies.

"Yeah," Mac said. "Then he fucked you to prove he was boss."

"Something like that. You don't believe me, do you?"

"No."

"Call my doctor; he'll verify my condition. Or you can use the home pregnancy test I have in my bathroom. That'll do it, too."

Mac leaned over and jerked Tippy to her feet. She started to cry again. As far as he was concerned she could cry the Johnstown flood; it wouldn't make any difference.

"Mac, for God's sake, please don't hurt me! Think of the baby!"

"If there is one."

Tippy tried to lean into him. His clothes contrasted sharply against her nakedness, and Mac noted she seemed surprisingly small and fragile. He held her away from his body like leading a captive to execution. He propelled her down the hallway toward the master bedroom, roughly steering her by pushing and pulling on her hair. She staggered a few steps in her bare feet for each of his forward strides, trying to keep her balance and avoid being stomped by his cowboy boots. Without an ounce of gentleness, he thrust her into the large bathroom adjoining her bedroom.

"Where's the test?" he said.

Tippy gestured with her head in the direction of the cupboard door. "In the linen closet."

Mac found the small box alongside her tampons while Tippy sat down on the toilet.

"I pee on it, and it turns pink if I'm pregnant," she said.

He read the instructions. The paper supposedly turned pink if a woman was pregnant, blue otherwise. Mac felt a pang of uncertainty that she might be telling the truth. At least about being pregnant. Not that it changed anything. She still orchestrated the whole scheme and recruited Ortiz into being a willing participant. He held out a strip of testing paper to Tippy.

"Stupido, how'm I gonna hold it with handcuffs? Hold it yourself. You know where."

Mac glared at her, then thrust the paper between Tippy's legs. She

254

smiled evilly, and Mac felt the warm urine spray over his hand. He pulled his hand up as if it were on a hot stove. The paper was pink.

"Okay, so you're pregnant by some greaser," he said.

Mac rinsed his hand under the faucet and dried himself with one of her blue towels. He kept telling himself her condition made no difference, she still had to go. It just upped his numbers. The world needed another Mexican baby about as much as six sacks of elephant shit.

Tippy sat quietly on the toilet and watched him. "So now what?" she asked.

He looked around at her tiled bathroom. This was a good place to control the blood. She had left a few drops in the living room and hallway, but he could clean those up easily. The house was already in his name, and after he disposed of her body in the lime pit, donations to the Salvation Army would take care of her clothes and other belongings.

He thought about her family, then remembered she told him she hadn't seen them since leaving home. Most likely no one would miss her for years. Except Castillo, and he didn't like her anyway. She'd just be another unexplained disappearance.

It was time for the inevitable. His headache was stabbing his forehead with pain and peppering his eyes with tiny stars. He took out the billy.

"Well, it doesn't change what has to happen."

He reached for her hair. The full realization of Mac's intentions thundered into Tippy's consciousness and threw her into absolute terror.

She catapulted herself off the toilet seat, landing hard on her knees and burying her face in Mac's legs. Hysterically she sobbed into his jeans, slobbering blood from her mouth.

"Oh God! Don't kill me! I'll be good! I promise I'll never go against you again! I'm yours forever! Please don't kill me!"

Mac pulled up Tippy's head by her disheveled blonde hair to get a good swing. Her usually sparkling tresses were wet and oily, and he noted with disgust the blood she left on his pants. They'd have to be washed thoroughly before returning to the Bar-D.

Tippy whipped her head about wildly. "No! No! You got it all wrong! Don't! You can't! You can't!"

He let her head drop to get a better hold on her slippery hair. Sobbing and coughing, Tippy pressed her forehead into the tile and fell into a fetal position. Mac cursed himself for his weakness in dispatching a woman. All it would take was one good whack. He grabbed her hair again to finish what he had started. He pulled it back from her left side, grasping it in a knot above her head.

"No! No! Mac, No!" In utter panic she shrieked continuously. She violently thrashed her head around and Mac lost his grip again.

"You can't! It's your baby! You can't kill your own baby!"

Chapter 41

Mac's head cut loose with a terrific barrage of pain. He pulled Tippy into a sitting position against the bathtub for support.

"What? What did you say?"

"It's your baby!" she sputtered again. "I'm almost six weeks along. It's your baby."

"My baby?"

The enormity of the situation hit Mac like a truck. Six weeks? Tippy was a liar, a whore, and a thief, but this had a certain ring of truth.

"My baby? How can it be my baby?"

"How in the hell do you think? The normal way."

"I mean, I thought you were on the pill."

"Well, it failed."

"So it could be anybody's."

"There wasn't anybody else. Not until Carlos."

"Carlos?"

"Ortiz. Last week. Did you kill him, too?"

It made sense. She would've told Ortiz if it was Garcia's kid, or any other Mexican. But Ortiz didn't know she was pregnant. So the baby was Anglo. And the only Anglo around was Mac. She probably intended to use the kid to claim his property. She wouldn't have told him unless it was a matter of life and death—hers.

All this half-conscious thought took place in a second while his head registered 9.0 on the Richter Scale. Now she was guilty of new crimes!

He dropped the blackjack and slapped her as hard as he could. A gush of blood spurted out of her nose.

"You fucked some filthy Mexican with my child inside you?"

257

His temper shot out of control as his head throbbed wildly. He battered her head against the bathtub and hit her again.

"Whore! Cunt! Slut!"

His head exploded as Tippy wailed and screeched like some terrified animal. Mac dropped to his knees and smashed her face again with his fist. He swung blindly at her breasts, landing blows with both hands. He wanted to destroy that matchless body that mocked him with its beauty.

His fists tore into her ribs and stomach, then struck bone on her hips and legs as she drew up her knees to protect herself. Mac howled in rage, and stood up when he saw her exposed cleft. Pink rimmed with blond. That was the root of all evil! He savagely kicked her where he could do the most damage. His boot lifted her off the floor and slammed her into the bathtub.

Mac covered his ears to blot out Tippy's unholy scream. His head shattered into thousands of sharp icicles of pain, piercing his eyes and ears, even pounding into the base of his skull. He rocked back and forth, searching for the strength to beat her into submission, dismember her into unrecognizable parts, and stop the stream of abject abuse spewing forth from the devil's own mouth. His baby! It wasn't enough for this whore to plot his demise, she had to steal his child! His head was killing him, the room was spinning, and Mac felt himself falling.

He caught himself on a towel rack and dropped to his knees beside her. Nausea threatened to overwhelm him. He rested his forehead on the cool bathtub rim and tried to think. Nothing made any sense. The bitch deserved to die. But what if the child was a boy? Tippy was his life support system. What the hell was he doing?

He was damned. God would never forgive him. A few worthless Mexicans were one thing, killing his own flesh and blood was another. For a long moment he knelt there, letting the bathtub cool his brow.

Tippy's screams subsided into sobbing, and Mac patted her shoulder in a gesture of compassion.

She squealed and shuddered uncontrollably. Her hair was matted against the tub, and her nakedness seemed strangely hideous and obscene. This beautiful creature had been transformed into a mass of oozing fluids and repugnant sounds, made worse by the handcuffs which still defiled her naked body in its unnatural posture.

He pulled her to him, and cradled her head.

"It's okay, I won't hurt you anymore," Mac said. He twisted his body around and sat beside her against the bathtub. His head was still playing the Anvil Chorus.

"I didn't mean that," he whispered.

"You bastard!" She sobbed. "You bastard! You tried to kill your own baby."

"It's okay," he said. "You're all right."

"No, I'm not!" she yelled. "My hand's broken, my face is ruined, and I hurt like hell!"

"We'll fix everything. There's no permanent damage."

She shook her head against him. "Please, get these goddamn cuffs off! God, it hurts!"

Mac fished out his key and unlocked her handcuffs. Tippy immediately crossed her arms against her chest and covered her breasts. Her legs were flat on the tile floor and held tightly together. She was shivering, and tears were dripping from her blood-streaked and puffy face. He got up and ran cold water over a towel.

Tippy remained sitting against the bathtub while he wiped her blood.

"Hold on," he said, "I'll be right back."

Mac grabbed two washcloths and turned for the kitchen. He slipped on the wet bathroom floor and crashed into the door frame. His shoulder would have complained, but the pain in his head masked all other feeling.

He returned with two icepacks that he applied to Tippy's nose and mouth. She hadn't moved an inch while he was gone. Blood ran down her chest and abdomen to disappear between her legs. He looked at her wrist, which was rapidly swelling. He gently tested it, and decided it was sprained instead of broken. Tippy was still sobbing, taking no notice of his actions or presence.

The floor was covered with urine. It was obviously Tippy's. He couldn't remember when, but he must have scared the piss out of her. The usually immaculate bathroom stank from urine, sweat, and fear. Coated with blood, it looked like a battlefield. Mac's own clothes looked like he had run through a shower.

The linen closet was still open from when Mac retrieved the home pregnancy strips. A large, printed beach towel dominated the bottom shelf. Blue and silver for the Dallas Cowboys, it looked expensive and hardly fit Tippy's dominantly feminine tastes. Mac momentarily wondered if Tippy had been a Dallas Cowboy Cheerleader.

He bundled her into the towel and carried her onto her bed. She lay back to stop the flow of blood from her nose, but otherwise, made no movement to help. Mac tore a pillowcase into strips and carefully wrapped her injured wrist. His headache subsided into a manageable series of jolting pains.

Tippy lay on her bed like a corpse. She held an icepack to the left side of her face and made no attempt to cover herself. Her beautiful figure was blanketed by angry red blotches, and her knees wore crimson welts as pads. Mac spread her legs to clean between them, and she offered no complaint or resistance. Blood was trickling from a nasty scrape, and her blonde hair did nothing to hide the massive welt in her most private area. Tippy opened her eyes to glare at Mac as he pushed her legs back together.

"What happened to Carlos?" she asked.

"He's gone," Mac said.

"Gone? Gone where?" She was having difficulty speaking, and her chest heaved when she made the effort.

"Gone where he'll never come back."

"You were going to kill me."

"But I didn't. Now it's your turn to prove I wasn't wrong to save you. And you'd better be a hell of a mother."

"You're one to talk. Good fathers don't try to kill their kids or beat up their mothers."

"You deserved it. Every bit of it. Thank your lucky stars you're carrying my kid."

Mac rose from the bed and went into the maid's room to wash his jeans in the sink. His shirt was even bloodier, but cold water removed the splashes of blood along with the sweat and urine. He threw everything in Tippy's dryer and walked back to her bedroom wearing only his socks.

She was still lying on top of her bed, unable or unwilling to do anything for herself. He carefully lifted her limp body and pulled down the spread and top sheet. Tippy looked like a little girl who had been pummeled in a landslide. They were all in a landslide, Mac grunted to himself, Tippy's had just come a little sooner than most. And it could have been worse.

His headache continued to ripple his forehead with sheets of lightning, and Mac desperately wanted Aimee to soothe his pain. He remembered to wash himself clean of Tippy's fluids. The guest bathroom was handy, and he used it to avoid the mess in Tippy's. There was a risk that Aimee might smell another woman's scent when he returned, but Mac couldn't take the obvious solution of showering. That would make him smell fresh and clean. He'd shower at the Bar-D when he got home. He decided to leave Rover's canopy down, allowing the desert wind and dust to obliterate any remaining traces.

His jeans weren't quite dry when he checked about twenty minutes later, but Mac declared them sufficiently far along for his purposes. Ready to leave, he peeked into Tippy's bedroom and noted she was curled up under the bedspread.

"I'm going," he called.

"Good riddance," she replied.

Mac walked around the bed to face her. "I'll see you tomorrow. We'll treat tonight as never happening."

"Yeah, right."

He leaned down and spoke two inches away from her face. "If you're good, I'll be terrific, if you're bad I'll be worse than you can imagine. It's your choice. Tomorrow."

Interstate 10 was lightning fast, but it was always a racetrack at night unless there was some event at NMSU's Pan-American Center. Mac's headache receded to dull stabs, about the level he normally experienced when working the ranch during daytime. Somewhere in the recesses of his brain, a voice told him that leaving Tippy alive was going to be fatal to his health. It couldn't be helped. Killing a woman had been beyond his current capabilities, and Tippy was the only woman he had ever hit.

He had done the right thing, but horribly complicated his life. After his kid was born, Tippy would have to die. That would be tricky, as she would be expecting such a move. Mac couldn't imagine how he'd do it, but it was the only way to have both Aimee and his child. He'd also have to shield her from his side venture. When they accumulated a sufficient nest egg to be financially secure, he'd close down the well's activities and become legit again.

The ranch was his main interest, but with excess cash available, Stuart and he could go into partnership on some other business. Maybe pecan orchards, an amusement park, or a restaurant. That would be good—a restaurant. Aimee could act as hostess, and wouldn't have to worry about details or losing her job.

The drive from Cruces was invigorating, and with Rover open to the cool November night, Mac became intoxicated in the fresh desert air. The sky was cloudless, and stars seemed to hang about twenty feet above his Jeep. His clothes finished drying in the low humidity, and the prospect of seeing Aimee in a few minutes made his knees weak with anticipation. Mac hoped she would still be awake, but if not, he would cuddle up and try to possess her without disturbing her sleep.

The ranch was dark as Mac pulled up in the area that passed for utility parking between the house and garage. He quietly pushed the kitchen door open and slid inside to sneak down the hallway. The starlight was enough for him to find his way, and he reached his bed without making a sound above a soft footfall.

The bed looked flat and unused. That was weird. She must have decided to sleep in the guest bedroom since he hadn't come home before she retired. That was silly. She didn't need an invitation. His bedroom was hers from now on. He tiptoed back to where she had slept before Terlingua and peeked in. That bed was unoccupied, too.

Mac switched on the light. The room was clean and tidy, completely without Aimee's things. He ran back to the master bedroom, a sense of fear gnawing at his innards. Same thing. There was nothing of Aimee's to be seen. He raced through the house turning on every light in a terrifying sense of panic.

Aimee was gone.

The kitchen answered his questions. On the cork board, Aimee had pinned a note. Mac tore it down and read furiously.

"Dear Mac.

I'm sorry to leave you this way, but it's for the best. I don't want to interfere with your happiness. It's clear that Tippy is the main woman in your life, and I can't compete with her. So let's leave it at that. You are a dear person, and I love you. But I could never be enough. One way or another, you would choose Tippy. I'm just making it easier for you this way because I love you. Thanks for all the help and kindness you gave me.

Love, Aimee."

Mac grabbed the phone and dialed Stuart. He answered on the fifth ring. Apparently, he had been asleep.

"Stuart!" Mac yelled. "Aimee's gone! Is she there?"

"Huh? Gone? No." Stuart sounded like he wasn't dealing with a full deck.

"Well, where did she go?"

"Dunno. She called this evening and said she was flying to California. I thought you were with her."

"Hell, no! California? Who does she know there?"

"Dunno. You know her better than I do."

Mac hung up the receiver without saying good-bye. A glance at the kitchen clock told him it was almost two o'clock in the morning. He couldn't believe it. There was nothing he could do. The El Paso airport didn't have any flights until the American red-eye to Dallas at three forty-five. She probably took Southwest. Those bastards flew almost every hour to San Diego or Los Angeles during the day. She could have made the last flight easily. And he had no idea where to find her.

He sat down on the floor against the kitchen cabinet. His house seemed utterly empty. The silence reigning throughout the brightly lit rooms closed in on him like a fog.

For the first time since he was a little kid, Mac began to cry. Once the tears started, they flowed unabated. He had nothing left. No emotions, no love, no fear, no hate, no nothing. Only his headache remained.

Chapter 42

Nothing looked better in the morning, and Mac's headache was back. He slept on top of his bed, not feeling sufficiently worthy to sleep under the covers. Life had gone out of his house. For some reason the structure was cursed, and its inhabitants were doomed to loveless, meaningless existences. As current owner and resident, Mac writhed under the curse's full weight like a hiker buried to his chin by a landslide. He had chased both Mary Lou and Aimee away. Mary Lou into the arms of a Mexcrement, and Aimee to God-knows-wherever.

He had initially been bitter over Mary Lou, then decided that their breakup was caused by a combination of bad timing and errors in communication. But Aimee's departure was a tragedy. Aimee had taken Tippy's lunchtime antics to heart and assumed there was a prior claim on his affection. Her insecurities had overwhelmed her. In spite of his true feelings, Mac couldn't protect Aimee from herself.

He sat at the kitchen table watching the sun's rays creep across the scrub mesquite beyond the road. He loved this land, barren and unforgiving, challenging man to conquer it and extract its riches. The Mexicans failed miserably. Only his hardy breed of Scotch-Irish warriors were able to overcome its hazards and extract a hard-won living. Now Mexicans were returning in enormous numbers, rendering Amulot proprietors like himself impotent through procreation, and enjoying the bounty won at such cost by Anglo pioneers.

Why Anglo women would consider Mexicans for lovers defied his imagination. They lived off their women in a maternalistic society, playing at being great macho heroes by fathering as many brats as possible. In reality they were simply slobs cashing welfare checks. The women carried the burden, becoming crones, fat and ugly, before they reached middle age.

But they had families, something Mac didn't. What good was industry and creativity without succeeding generations to enjoy it? Anglos were a dying race being milked for their productivity before being genetically exterminated.

Stuart had already thrown away his heritage. After another generation of intermarriage with Mexicans, there wouldn't be any more Anglo Prescotts. They'd be a Mexican family with a few Anglo ancestors hidden as skeletons in their closet, one of whom would be Stuart.

The landslide had already trapped Stuart. He was buried under a deluge of brown, losing his heritage and way of life for nothing. His wife used only a tiny piece of him to create progeny, then treated the rest of Stuart as a rubbish heap. Stuart was like Justinian, the last Latin Emperor of Constantinople. After him came mongrel emperors, claiming to be Romans. It was the same for Amulots. They were dying out and leaving an "American" legacy to be abused by waves of brown, black, and yellow immigrants seeking entitlements. A landslide of immigration was burying them all; Stuart had just been submerged a little sooner.

Maybe Mexicans weren't as lazy as popularly thought, but ambition was practically unknown. A Mexican waiter could work thirty years in a restaurant and never once think of advancement. Why should he better himself? His status was measured by numbers of descendants, not figures in his bank account. And the women were no different. They could work fifty years as a maid but be entirely content with a family of twelve kids. Sooner or later, all the economic benefits of Anglo industry would fall to them anyway. Existence brought rights, and if they couldn't provide for themselves, Anglos would do it for them.

Running illegals was patently wrong, but Mac saw it only as a temporary means to an end. Trying to lift himself out of his funk, he pulled out the well's books and began totaling his profits. He had amassed over five hundred thousand dollars, enough to pay off his note on the ranch and add a fair amount of stock. And that didn't count the funds he'd acquired by confiscating Ramirez's assets!

Ramirez. A name from the past. According to Castillo, the long-departed transport mogul's wife was still waiting patiently for his return, scrimping by as best she could. Mac didn't feel sorry for her in the least. If she was that stupid, she could wait forever. After all, she had ignored the existence of his mistress, and her inability to take control of her own life was simply another manifestation of that pitiful Hispanic macho culture.

Meanwhile, he had lots of money, but no way to enjoy it. It was all in cash, and if he was going to put the ranch in order, he needed first to launder his large amount of greenbacks.

He decided to approach Stuart with his dilemma. Cash flows were due to increase substantially when drug shipments began, even if he discontinued transporting illegals. Something had to be done, and soon. He threw his ledger into a grocery sack and headed for Stuart's house.

$$*****$$

"That's the story," Mac said. Of course it wasn't. He had left out Tippy's pregnancy.

Stuart listened intently, and made himself an accessory after the fact." Quite a crisis," Stuart said. "Both an opportunity and a danger. I assume you're thinking of a role for me."

"I need help laundering cash and putting my dirty money to good use. You're not only my best friend, you're the best businessman I know."

"I can't bail you out if we're both in the same cell."

"True. Masking your participation would be top priority. So what do you think?"

"I think you're crazy as usual, but we might be able to work out some sort of accommodation. Maybe selling tiny building lots on some portion of your ranch through a phantom corporation. Set up monthly cash payments by individuals who default on their land contracts so the property reverts to you. That way we could explain the money flow, nobody would complain, and we wouldn't need to formally subdivide and meet the requirements for real estate developments. Then you'd have the money legitimately and be able to invest in the ranch or other ventures."

"That's exactly what I need," Mac said. "See, I knew you'd come through. You've done these land sales before, how about setting it up for me?"

Stuart sucked in his breath before answering. "Okay, but officially I know nothing about the well, and all the ersatz land buyers are easterners from out-of-state."

"Or Mexicans from across the border."

"That would be even better."

"Great! And the risk disappears."

"The risk comes from you transporting illegals. If one gets caught and exposes your operation, you'll go to jail for a long time. You'd be better off drowning them and facing murder charges."

"Yeah, I need to decrease my exposure to coyotes and border crossers. They don't feel any obligation to keep my identity secret."

"You need a front man at the well. How about your shady Hispanic ambulance-chaser or a truck driver who wants to settle down?"

"Possibly, but I'm already converting to something inanimate and more valuable."

Stuart nodded. "So Montana came through?"

"Yep. I'm starting test runs later this week."

"You know I don't like it. Illegals are a victimless crime. You're innocently breaking the law while drugs are truly evil. Your security would improve, but you'd be selling your soul."

"But I'll just be moving coke and pot. You've done both yourself and haven't felt like a master criminal." His comment was perhaps unfair, but Stuart had broken his cherry with both drugs in bygone days.

"There's a difference between using and distributing," Stuart said.

"Hey, it's gonna get in, one way or the other. And we're not making people use it who don't want to. Remember De Lorean's cocaine deal and the arguments used to defend him. Besides, we can run it until we make some stake and close it down."

He sensed Stuart softening. "Let's agree to not get greedy and stop when we've made some number like five mil," Mac said.

"Think you can do that?"

"Sure. I'm not stupid, and if I was greedy, I would have done this long ago instead of punching cows. Look at it this way; it's not our fault the price of beef is down as well as chiles and onions. We do a few unnatural acts to put things right. We've got to keep up America's agricultural capacity for the future."

"I see," Stuart said. "This is a patriotic act."

"Better than adding illegals to welfare rolls and social services."

The deal was cut with a toast of two beers, and Mac left Stuart to set up the land sales company. Selling small lots to eastern speculators had made Stuart wealthy, and Mac knew the paper shuffle was in good hands. The easterners would never make any money off their purchases, but who cared? Anyone who lived east of the Mississippi or west of the Sierras wasn't a real man anyway.

But certain loose ends worried him. Tippy for one, and as Stuart continually said, Mexicans who could identify him as running the operation. It was time for Tippy to bear the main burden of risk by being the visible boss. She could ostensibly run the show while he and Lupe carefully monitored her activities.

Things were falling into place with one major exception, and that factor ate away at Mac as he drove. There was no woman in his life with whom he could enjoy the fruits of his labors.

He hoped his son or daughter would provide the meaning he sought if no woman became available. It would be fun to raise a boy in the ways and traditions of his ancestors. If it was a girl, he'd give her everything she needed to become the first woman president. But he wished he had a wife, a mate, a partner with whom to share his life.

Chapter 43

Mac swung into Tippy's driveway, not surprised to note the outside looked exactly like when he left earlier that morning. The only difference was the light. Two in the morning was a lot darker than two in the afternoon.

He entered through the front door, but saw no sign of Tippy in the main part of her house. Detouring left into the kitchen to turn on the coffee-maker, he scanned the counters for signs of activity. There weren't any, and the cheese plate he had seen on the butcher block last night hadn't moved. Taking the long route through Tippy's dining and living rooms, Mac made his way to her bedroom. As expected, she was keeping to her bed and nursing her injuries.

"You're back," Tippy said, as if speaking to a leak in the ceiling.

"And how's my esteemed business partner and mother-to-be of my child today?"

"Recovering from being hit by a Mac truck. I should have gotten his license number."

At another time Tippy's comment might have been witty, but in her current condition the witticism bombed with a dull thud. Mac's head immediately began to register about 3.2 on the Richter Scale.

Tippy was wearing an aquamarine silk nightgown which contrasted beautifully with her blonde hair. He noted her hair was washed and combed, but not up to its usual standard of radiance. A line of nasty bruises drooped from the left corner of her mouth like a Fu Manchu mustache. Her nose seemed puffy, but otherwise, her face looked fairly decent.

"You look pretty good to me," Mac said.

"It's makeup."

He studied her face, checking it closely in spite of her

unwillingness to hold still. She was right about the makeup. Her left cheek was badly bruised, and her nose was possibly broken.

"You've done a good job. Let's go hear the El Paso Orchestra and show you off."

"Fat chance," she said. "My boobs and ribs hurt so much I can't move."

Mac gently untied the nightgown and opened it down to Tippy's waist. She offered no resistance, and Mac immediately saw why. He had turned her superb chest into a profusion of discolored patterns. Black, blue, brown, and red, all of which would be turning a ghastly yellow in a few days. He couldn't remember doing so much damage, but her torso looked like it had gone fifteen rounds with Mike Tyson. He wondered if he had permanently damaged anything that might affect her nursing ability. Her breasts were badly bruised and swollen.

Without indicating his intent, Mac flipped the covers down to expose Tippy's legs. She remained motionless and voiced no objection while he pulled her nightgown up and bunched it on her chest. Tippy was wearing blue nylon panties, and he carefully slipped them down and examined her. They concealed a horrible red and blue bruise. There were nasty looking contusions all around on her abdomen and legs, and both Tippy's knees were blackened and swollen. Mac couldn't imagine beating her so badly, but the evidence was there before him.

"Yeah, I see. Sorry," he said. His words sounded lame, even to him.

"*Now* you're sorry. Last night you wanted to kill me." Tippy rolled carefully onto her side and drew up her legs.

"Then I discovered you possessed hidden assets. Now I'm ready to turn the operation over to you."

Tippy looked at him suspiciously. "Pardon me? What did you say?"

"You know, handle the nightly shipments, et cetera. Become a real partner. That way you won't be tempted to steal from yourself, especially now that I'm expanding."

"Expanding? How expanding?"

"Handling white powder and weed. It can move just as well as people in tankers, and it's a whole lot safer and more profitable."

She studied his face for confirmation of his intent. "You're crazy. La Cosa Nostra will eat you for breakfast."

"Why should they? The Mexicans have agreed already, and I'm a serious businessman making product available to whoever wants it."

Tippy waited several long seconds to comment, never once lifting her eyes from his.

"Minimum a grand a night, and this house for starters. Above the grand, fifty percent of your cut."

Mac threw his head back and snorted a short laugh. "Fifty percent? Lady, look at yourself. Right now you're not worth fifty dollars for a whole night."

"It's for your kid. He needs insurance."

"Five percent in trust for the kid, ten percent for you, after expenses."

"You're a generous bastard, aren't you?"

"It'll make you a rich woman."

"And I suppose you want bedroom privileges."

"Of course. How else can I maintain that closeness partners need?"

"Of course." Tippy slowly slid her legs over the side of her bed and placed them on the floor. Mac rounded the bed to help her stand up. She didn't thank him for his assistance.

She ambled slowly toward the bathroom. "Order in some pizza. I'm starving. And forget the privileges. You kicked the door shut last night."

The pizza was excellent, better than Mac thought a mixture of sausage and pepperoni could be. Tippy softened slowly, and the baby growing inside her forged an indelible bond between them. Even so, Mac knew Tippy negotiated with hidden agendas.

His new operations manager would probably be laid up for a week, but Mac satisfied himself no bones were broken. He would have to keep her under close observation. Mac couldn't help thinking she might have another stooge to send against him. Women could easily double and triple head, and in Tippy's case, she could take the entire Russian Navy in a single night.

She was back in bed when Mac let himself out. Already it was dark, and Lupe would be worrying. He had stayed longer than intended.

Driving south toward La Union, his head starting throbbing again as he thought about Mexicans. They weren't all bad. His vaqueros worked steadily although without vigor, and he had no cause to complain. And Lupe tended to restore his humanity after he finished handling human beings like they were so many trapped squirrels.

His fence light was on by the front gate, and Mac drove straight in from the county road. A test shipment of grass was due in with Villareal, the same coyote he had talked to the first night. These early shipments would be small as agreed at Lajitas, and Mac was going to take advantage of the gradual buildup to commit his personnel before they could object. The tanker drivers were the most likely to raise a fuss, but possession of controlled substances was not subject to greater penalties than transporting illegals.

Only Villareal and Mac knew drugs would be transported tonight, but Mac found Lupe in a state of high anxiety. He had not stopped to see her during the day, and she didn't know whether he was alive or dead. Worst of all, he had forgotten about Ortiz's van still parked in front of the trailer. Its keys were in Rover's glove compartment, and Mac hurriedly drove it a half mile into his range. He left it in one of the many dry arroyos cutting through the escarpment's edge, a narrow one that featured more brush than most. The van wasn't hidden, but the coyotes couldn't see it from their usual route.

Mac arrived back at the trailer out of breath from his half-mile jog and fighting a renewed headache. He doubted it came from his relatively minor exertion; more likely it reflected stress from anticipating problems later in the evening. Lupe wasn't in a much better mood, but pointedly asked no questions about Ortiz. Worse, she inquired about Tippy.

"*Patron*," she said. "I don't want to know anything about the Ortiz *cabron*, but what did you do concerning Señorita Rubia?"

"Rubia?" Her question didn't register at first, then Mac realized Lupe was referring to Tippy. Rubia in Spanish meant blonde in the female gender.

"Oh, she received her just punishment."

"Which was?" Lupe scurried around the trailer, setting out sandwiches and drinks for the illegals. She avoided Mac's gaze.

"Why do you ask?" he said.

"She stole from you. Her punishment sets a precedent for future cases like her."

Mac was astounded that this unlettered teenager could formulate a concept so perfectly fitting the situation. He assumed she learned it from the criminals she had known.

"Her body paid the price," he said. "She will feel pain and discomfort for many days."

Lupe looked at him suspiciously. "You fuck her?" she said in English.

"No." Mac glared at her. "If I had, it would be none of your business. But no. Her skin is much darker now."

"You beat her, huh? You like it?"

"Yes and no. She got what she deserved, but I didn't enjoy it. I don't like beating women."

"You beat me if I steal?"

"Maybe. It'd depend on the circumstances." Mac didn't like this conversation one bit.

"But I good most time, *patron*, bad very little. She bad all time."

Lupe's English was fractured, but her point was clear enough. Evidently, she expected to be punished for any transgression, probably by a beating.

"You beat me, I not do again. Beat her, she do double."

"Well, I think she's learned her lesson. Besides, I have you to keep her honest. You'll do that, won't you?"

"Yes. Always." Lupe switched back into Spanish. "I'll have to watch her very closely and not let her know I'm doing it. You didn't tell her how we caught her, did you?"

"Absolutely not. When she recovers, I'm going to use her more often here in place of me. I'll need you more than ever."

"She'll be working more? Not less?"

"Yep. I'll be doing other things to improve our business and don't have a choice for the time being. As long as you're here, it'll work. I'm depending on you."

At first, Lupe seemed surprised and disgusted by Mac's actions, then warmed to her increased importance. She sat down at the table where they had perused the manifests.

"I'll act for you," she said. "You can trust me."

He leaned across the table and kissed her on the cheek. His surprise gesture of affection caught her unawares, and she was unable to respond before Mac resumed his seat.

"I know I can. Otherwise I'd get rid of this whole business."

No sooner had Mac said that when he heard a vehicle crunch into the yard. The first group had arrived. Lupe remained seated as if dazed by Mac's show of affection and the whole conversation.

Villareal didn't show up until after the tanker pulled in and began loading. The Acapulco gold was in five large suitcases, and Mac instructed him to hand them down to the people in the tanker after everyone was in. No one questioned their contents, least of all the tanker driver.

Mac pulled the driver aside after he topped off his trailer with water.

"We loaded five extra suitcases," Mac said. "They don't go with the others to the normal drop. After getting rid of the wetbacks, go to this address." He gave the driver an address near the Albuquerque airport.

"Ask for Al Sharp. He'll take the suitcases and give you a receipt. Bring that back to me on your return, and there's an extra two hundred for you."

The pot-bellied Anglo driver looked at Mac as if watching North Vietnamese troops approach the wire.

"Five hundred," he said.

"Three, and the receipt comes back in one day."

The driver nodded and waddled to his cab. Score one convert, Mac grinned to himself. He figured the others would probably go along equally fast. This was the road to riches.

Chapter 44

Stuart rudely broke Mac's slumber the following morning with a wake-up call.

"Sun's up, buddy. Time for you to be, too."

Mac agreed, and couldn't understand why he'd slept so long. "What'cha got? Can I dump all this cash now?"

"Soon. I'm incorporating Canutillo Land Company, and it'll provide what we need."

"In whose names?"

"The registered agent is my attorney, all common stock will be held by us, and the required officers are two of my married half-sisters. They agreed for five grand a year."

"What in the world did you tell them?"

"That other businessmen were watching me closely. This would prevent my competition from knowing up front that I was involved. Sounded good, even to me."

"So when do we start?"

"Got to get the papers back first, but the grand for capital is already in the bank. You need to sign your signature card. And we're the Board."

Mac marveled at Stuart's efficiency. They'd be legally depositing large sums within a week. His euphoric brain took a short holiday.

"Want to see the operation tonight?" Mac asked.

"Are you crazy? Of course not. And neither do you. How soon can you be out?"

"Maybe within a week. My manager's laid up. She needs a few days to recuperate."

"She? A split-tail? Now I know you're crazy. Mexicans will eat her alive."

"Not likely. She'd screw a snake if someone would hold its head. Her favorite trick is the old knife-in-the-back."

"Sounds like a pleasant person. Who is she? Can you trust her?"

"No, but the system I have in place should keep her fairly straight. It's Tippy."

"You got shit for brains, dummy. She's the worst risk I've seen since investing in S&Ls. What the hell are you thinking?"

"It's not what you think. She'll be okay. And remember, the person in that job is taking all the risk."

"Bullshit. That lady eats nails, and they come out packaged in Styrofoam with pink ribbons and bows."

"Maybe, but I'll talk to you about it later." Mac wanted out of this discussion. "By the way, we have a van to return to Juarez."

"That, at least, is no problem, *amigo*. It's the first thing you've said that isn't."

They skipped further comments on Tippy and the well, and returned to discussing how the land deals would work. A section of Mac's ranch would be subdivided into tiny lots for investors, selling for a thousand dollars a lot. Closing and processing fees would be a hundred, and the time payment fee was another hundred. The down payment was a hundred, followed by an equal amount each month. The plan was to have all purchasers randomly default on their land contracts between the second and twelfth month. According to the contract, the lot would revert to Mac's ownership and could then be resold.

"But if I'm the owner, how can the company sell my land?" Mac trusted Stuart but didn't understand the mechanism.

"The company takes the section on consignment, and receives a fourth of all payments as a management fee. You get three-fourths directly, then you and I split the other twenty-five percent later."

Mac liked it, the scheme was beautiful. "No problems with government?"

"Not that I can't handle. A little *mordida* goes a long way, even north of the border."

Obviously Mac's fears were unfounded.

At noon when he stopped by the trailer, Mac found the tanker driver waiting for his bonus. Lupe didn't know about the deal, and the trucker looked like he worked himself into a snit.

"Last time I do this!" the driver bellowed from the trailer door.

"Chill out. Start-ups always have a few glitches. I trust you had no trouble?"

"Went like shit through a short nigger."

The driver counted the bills Mac handed him. His attitude changed immediately.

"Sorry about bitching. If you get any more of these special shipments, I'll be glad to handle them."

"The receipt, please," Mac said.

"Oh, yeah." The trucker's protruding belly made it difficult for him to dig into his pants pocket. He retrieved a blue slip of paper and handed it to Mac.

"Wait."

Mac walked into the trailer and held the receipt up to a light. It bore the watermark he was expecting. While the trucker watched from the trailer's step, Mac dunked the paper into a glass of water on the kitchen counter. It turned red.

"Fancy paper, huh?" the driver said. "Wanted to make sure I didn't fake it."

"One can't be too careful in this business. Had to know the luggage arrived at its proper destination." Mac smiled guardedly at the man still standing on the step. "You did good. We're in business together."

Lupe watched without commenting until the trucker was gone.

"What was all that about?" she asked. "He was here for an hour and kept telling me I owed him three hundred dollars."

"You did, but you didn't know it. In the future, I'll leave money for you to handle guys like that. See? I told you that you'd be my girl here. You're getting more important every day."

"What about the paper?"

One thing about Lupe; she sure wasn't stupid. Mac showed her the watermark in the shape of a bear. The color test she had already seen.

"If the bear isn't there or the paper doesn't turn red, don't pay anybody," he said. "Every so often we'll change paper to turn different colors, but I'll tell you first. I'll also phone in the amount and what the receipt should say. Okay?"

"Sounds easy enough. What if the receipt isn't like you tell me?"

"Don't pay the man. Call me instead."

Lupe faced Mac squarely and set her jaw. "And if they insist?"

"Pay them. Then call me." He decided to take a chance on her loyalty. "It'll be handled later. It won't happen more than once. You don't see Ortiz around anymore do you?"

Lupe nodded. "Things are getting more serious, aren't they, *patron*."

"Always were. When in doubt, you don't know nothin'."

"As you say, I never did." Lupe smiled and walked back into the trailer.

*****

The next few days passed uneventfully while Mac divided his time between Stuart and his new corporation, Lupe at the trailer during noontimes and evenings, and Tippy in the afternoon.

Mac thought she was making a remarkable recovery, although her bruises turned a sickening shade of yellow as expected. She said they looked worse than they felt, and Mac took her comments at face value. Her formerly matchless breasts were ugly shades of black, blue, and yellow, as though they had contacted some localized form of hepatitis that was devouring the darker discolorations. He couldn't imagine how they felt inside. Presumably like his head.

Over the weekend, Tippy regained some of her former spirit. She moved around slowly, but no longer like a hospital patient pushing an IV pole. She still couldn't wear a bikini, but her face looked normal under heavy makeup. On Tuesday, she announced she was ready to assume control of the operation at the well.

"Feeling our oats, are we?" Mac said, as Tippy spun around to show him her agility. He had spent every afternoon with her, helping her exercise and generally playing concerned husband. He hoped she took his actions as conciliatory atonements, but in truth, he was just burning time. The ranch held too many reminders of Aimee and Mary Lou.

"Still a little sore in spots, but it's all working."

"Like a Swiss watch or a Mexican bus?"

"That's for me to know and for you to find out."

Mac stood up slowly from Tippy's couch and took hold of her

shoulders. She looked upwards with a twinge of fear, then eased into friendliness as his eyes glazed over with lust. He leaned down and kissed her passionately. She responded after a short hesitation.

"I've missed you," he said. It was only partially a lie. He preferred Aimee by a wide margin, but longed for the uninhibited eroticism of this sexual athlete. "What say we take up where we left off before I went galactic?"

He reached below and discovered she wasn't ready. But it didn't take her long to change that. She moved to his touch, and in a moment her efforts produced a wide-on. Mac walked backward to the couch and sat down, pulling her onto his lap. She opened her mouth for a round of tongue wrestling, then opened the rest of herself to his enjoyment. Only afterward did she speak in sounds other than moans and gasps.

"That's what you should have done a week ago, you dumb ass," she said. "See what you would have missed if I hadn't talked you out of doing me?"

"I won't miss it anymore. Not unless you cut me off."

"Humph. Can't expect a child to be happy when his father isn't. Besides, you're easy."

Somehow, Tippy always managed to have the last word and spoil his mood.

*****

For three weeks the operation ran like a well-oiled machine. Tippy was magnificently cold to coyotes and truckers, demanding respect with her imperial demeanor. More important was the lack of glitches in financial matters. Both groups gave her credit for making sure their money showed up, but in reality, she handled only coyotes. The drug shipments involved no evening monetary transactions at the well, and Lupe paid the truckers after checking their receipts when they returned.

Lupe grumbled over Tippy's showboating until Mac explained how the system worked. The most visible or best known person took credit when things went right. But when things went wrong, that individual was first in line for health adjustments. In this business, that was Tippy.

Truckers could divert some cargo, but Mac doubted it would happen. Once they no longer carried illegals, drivers would be required to dump their overlying water load at delivery. If they stopped enroute to off-load, they'd have to dump the water to reach the drugs, then refill before reaching their destination. That was possible to accomplish, but risky. Accomplices would be necessary, and they might talk. With word getting around about the disappearance of previous management and some coyotes, bucking the system looked like a sure way to get snuffed.

Actually, unless a driver was clearly the thief, Tippy would get blamed for any shortage. She didn't know exactly how much came in from Mexico and went out in the tanker. The coyote would certainly claim he delivered every ounce. Without being able to prove she loaded the coyote's amount into the tanker, the Mexicans would demand her scalp. Maybe his, too, Mac thought glumly. An additional control procedure was needed to protect himself, even if it entailed increased cargo handling and time of processing.

One solution was to have Mendoza seal the containers before sending them north. If a container arrived with a seal broken or missing, a coyote's ass was on the griddle. If a problem was discovered in Albuquerque, Chicago, or wherever else Mac delivered, then the driver was implicated. Or Tippy. This meant drivers had to be given a container count and allowed to inspect all seals at time of loading. Not exactly what Mac wanted. He had hoped to keep tanker drivers ignorant of their cargo's size and value. There was too much incentive to disappear with a large shipment. The only deterrent was fear, and Mac decided to require complete family data on each driver from Larkin.

Until seals could be arranged, Mac ordered Tippy to inspect and count each shipment to keep the accompanying coyote and trucker honest. That added time at the well which increased their risks, but it couldn't be helped. The illegals were deposited first into the tanker, then Tippy, Lupe, the coyote, and driver took inventory together. Only after all parties were satisfied could loading proceed. Hopefully, it would keep everyone honest.

That was the key—keeping everyone honest. Management theorists like McGregor and Bernard would be spinning in their graves if they heard Mac talking. But they were theorists, and this was real life. Even more than real life, it could be real death. He had to have safeguards. Tippy might be able to co-op a coyote or trucker, but she'd never convince Lupe to go along. The system might not be the best, but it could work. A theft might still occur, but he'd know where and by whom.

The first week with the inspection procedure went smoothly enough to allay Mac's apprehensions. He found a four-part pre-numbered invoice form at a stationery store to use as an inventory control document. After recording containers and contents in code on the invoices, each participant received a copy: the coyote, trucker, Tippy, and Lupe. Both Tippy's and Lupe's came to Mac, although Tippy thought Lupe's copy was kept at the trailer. Lupe seemed satisfied with her role. So did Tippy. She took Mac's changes in stride without complaint. This was good. Tippy was the person most at risk.

Chapter 45

The next step was to set up a meeting with Mendoza to discuss sealing shipments. Montana arranged it within a few minutes of Mac's call, this time in Juarez. The possibility of surveillance by Mexican and American DEA agents didn't increase Mac's enthusiasm, but Montana assured him Mendoza would handle security professionally. That was another thing bothering Mac. Montana was costing him five grand a month for a few phone calls.

It was noon when Mac nudged his Ranger across the viaduct into Mexico at the Bridge Of The Americas. The wide concrete structure arched over the pitiful irrigation canal called the Rio Grande, and Mac noted there was little southbound traffic. As usual, the northbound lanes were packed back to the bridge with a mass of trucks and various vehicles waiting processing by American Customs.

Chamizal Park on his right was deserted, and Mac was reminded of how bizarre El Paso really was. In 1845, Chamizal had been on Mexico's side of the river, but later it became American when the Rio Grande changed course. President Johnson gave it back to soothe Mexican pride during the 1960s, and his action was hailed as a great peace-keeping gesture. Big deal. A little over three hundred acres of useless land became a monument and park to inter-American cooperation.

But El Paso was an unusual town. The city was divided into east and west by the Franklin Mountains which couldn't be crossed except in the narrow strip of the pass itself or fifteen miles to the north on Trans-Mountain Road. The east side was further divided by Fort Bliss, Biggs Field, and El Paso International Airport into a northeast strip and eastern wedge. Then the wedge was divided again by Interstate 10, commonly called the Berlin Wall, into northern and southern sectors. North of Route 10 was Anglo, south was Mexican.

Developers working east had burdened El Paso with their own brand of humor. The streets in one large section were named for professional golfers. It wasn't so bad living on Arnold Palmer or Jack Nicklaus, but who wanted to live on some obscure Robert Wynn or Russ Randall? Further east were celebrities and other sports figures. People like Cheryl Ladd, Jerry Lewis, Don Meredith, and Tracy Austin. And hometown boy Lee Trevino was a major thoroughfare.

Mac thought living on Cheryl Ladd would be a kick, especially if he got bedroom privileges. Maybe the street names gave Mexicans a sense of becoming American. There was an undercurrent of patriotism in the city in spite of LULAC's "Spanish firstism." The symphony under Abraham Chavez always started its concerts by playing the Star Spangled Banner.

The sloppily dressed little Mexican border official waved Mac through the imposing gateway without speaking. He appeared joined to his concrete post, and signaled to Mac with his fingers. His motion was so limited that his forearm never moved. Mac decided an industrial time and motion expert could learn copious quantities of coprolite from these people.

He continued south past the Electric Q, a large disco hall where liberal American girls came to find Mexican studs and get their brains fucked out. The parking lot would have been slippery with condoms if the Mexicans used them. But they didn't. Not when the girls were American. They couldn't be held accountable for wild oats across the border.

Some El Pasoans frequented Juarez to follow the dogs or hang out in bookie joints. Betting on horses was big business, and Juarez covered all major US tracks. Even more important were the tourists. They flooded in, expecting bargain prices, especially for booze, not realizing that El Paso's were just as low.

But the biggest draw in Juarez was still sex. Prostitution was rampant, but Juarez also featured things like dog and pony shows. Locals joked about the term "dog and pony show" to describe sales presentations. The ones in Juarez were real. Watching some stunning chick take on a Black Lab or donkey gave the term new meaning. The girls that humped animals were supposedly Miss Universe caliber, but Mac couldn't verify that from personal experience. Like many local Anglos, he was yet to avail himself of most Juarez attractions.

He snaked his way to the Pronaf, artfully dodging boys at each corner who attempted to clean his windshield. The fluids they used approached the consistency of olive oil, and unwary travelers frequently paid for its removal after being victimized by some aggressive eight year-old. Various vendors offering cigarettes and souvenirs would enliven the return trip, but Mac had long ago learned the art of looking in the wrong direction.

The Pronaf's large parking area was almost empty, and Mac took one of the spots near the Archaeological Museum. The lot was free, but he paid a dollar to the man in green who approached as he locked the truck.

He walked across Abraham Lincoln and entered the large State Exhibition Hall. He followed the one-way signs taking him through the many rooms showing products from each Mexican state. After the halfway point, he began to wonder when he'd be approached. Then Mac saw a familiar face, his old Uzi-toting friend from Lajitas. The large, Indian-looking Mexican went through a side doorway marked "private." Mac followed as if he were a Hall official.

The room was an office containing three desks, none of which looked used on a regular basis. Mendoza stood as Mac entered. He greeted Mac warmly with an extended hand, breaking the mood he'd established at Lajitas. Mac guessed he had passed the trial period with flying colors. Only ferret-faced Julio was with the drug lord this time, and Mac decided the ugly little man doubled as a secretary and accountant.

The meeting was short but sweet, and Mendoza promised to develop a program to seal or otherwise make the containers and bundles of dope tamper-proof. He appreciated Mac's position, and the seals would make acceptance of shipments easier at their ultimate destinations. There were many cities he wanted Mac to cover, from Salt Lake City to Cleveland. Coke would start arriving in quantity, and of course, Mac's revenue increased accordingly.

There was little else to discuss. They were like two sharks agreeing to divide a tuna without biting each other. Mendoza had probably heard about the missing personnel by now, and Mac held no illusions concerning the Mexican's lethal inclinations.

Watching Mendoza exit through the opposite door, Mac was impressed that the drug lord possessed sufficient wherewithal to use a government facility as a meeting location. Mafia dons didn't use the New Jersey capitol building for meetings. Or maybe they did and Mac just didn't know it. Nonetheless, there was no question about Mendoza's thorough security. The Hall was a huge and complex building by Mexican standards, and with each using different entrances and exits, no one could connect the drug lord with the *gringo*.

After a few minutes he re-entered the exhibition rooms and followed the visitor's route to the front exit. His Ranger was still in its space across the street, and Mac walked casually to his vehicle like any tourist seeing the sights. The little man in green was gone. Then it hit him—the guy had been another of Mendoza's men. The drug lord controlled his environment and people, leaving nothing to chance. Mac had been on his turf and under his protection the entire time.

With nothing further to do south of the border, Mac headed north. Rather than returning to La Union, Mac stopped by Sioux Street for a late lunch and to sort things out. The restaurant off Montana was practically deserted, but uncleared tables indicated he had missed a busy noontime. The dark atmosphere and heavy wooden tables looked friendly and inviting rather than foreboding, and Mac expected the dim light would relax his eyes and subdue his headache after being on Mexican turf. In general, his headaches had seemed less intense in the past two weeks, and hopefully, that signified internal pressures were finally receding.

His major concern was the operation and its expected longevity. There was no way it could last forever, and he wanted to make his bundle and get out before unforeseen forces trapped him in a landslide. He wasn't greedy. Sipping his unsweetened iced tea, Mac addressed his problem down the road.

Tippy was the key, and maybe he could swap the well and operation to her for his kid. She wouldn't want the child except to control him, and this way, they could both get what they wanted. It sounded like a superb idea. He'd make the trade next summer after Tippy whelped, and then when things went sour, Tippy could sit in jail instead of him.

All he had to do was eliminate the paper trail. Castillo could put the well in Tippy's name and take care of the taxes without her knowledge. Mac hadn't yet filed the change of ownership, so he'd simply instruct Castillo to pass the title from Ramirez to Tippy. Backdated appropriately, no one would question Ramirez's gift to his mistress, and Mac's name would never surface. Tippy's house could be worked the same way.

The ranch's telephone number was off-limits to everyone but Lupe, and there weren't any long distance records to worry about. He had always phoned Castillo and Tippy from Stuart's office or the trailer, and those were local Las Cruces lines.

The faxes were the only loose ends. He'd destroy his copies and the records from Lupe's machine showing transmissions to the Bar-D. They were local calls, but the fax automatically printed status reports for verification. As far as Mac knew, they were the only documentary proof of a link between the trailer and his ranch.

In the meantime, he'd make it look like he'd worked for her from the very beginning. Most of the coyotes and tanker drivers already believed Tippy was in charge, and he'd have Lupe confirm their impressions when asked. Castillo and Lupe knew better, but he was a lawyer, and she would eventually disappear to Chicago or some point in the north.

If necessary, he'd turn state's evidence. He'd say he did everything for love. No one would doubt him when they looked at Tippy, especially considering his affliction and his wife leaving him for another man. And his money was all legal. None of it could be traced to drug origins, and it was safe from seizure. Yep, he was learning. With a little effort, he could insulate himself just like Mendoza did.

His lunch, a self-made salad from Sioux Street's salad bar, was excellent.

*****

Canutillo Land went into high gear following Stuart's receipt of its incorporation papers, and to Mac's astonishment, Stuart showed a distinct talent for generating an endless number of phony Hispanic names to purchase lots. Their bank accounts grew rapidly with daily deposits from bogus sales, and the corporation seemed to mint money in small denominations.

Part of his plan was working, and with drug shipments increasing, Mac had already turned to winding down traffic in illegals. He had limited the number of wetbacks first to thirty, then twenty, then a dozen. In one way, that decreased security. The remaining illegals would surely guess what was in the extra luggage, and as Stuart pointed out earlier, handling drugs by themselves was safer. He was ready, and a week after his Juarez meeting with Mendoza, told Tippy to inform the coyotes she was terminating the operation.

Castillo contacted the Juarez connections who assembled the convoys of illegals and notified them. Mac was surprised everyone took the shutdown so calmly, but his ingratiatingly smiling lawyer said the Mexican contractors would simply increase their operations out of Zaragosa to compensate.

According to Castillo, the tanker transport operation originated in response to El Paso's initiative for a free border zone. The well was located beyond where the proposal drew INS's border control, thereby circumventing the idea's objective before politicians finished posturing about its great effect in eliminating illegal entries. Zaragosa was also outside the free border zone, but its illegals went east in boxcars, a slower but cheaper mode of transportation. Mac's system had been a Cadillac, more expensive than most, faster, and used primarily for better-paying clients.

*****

"Big change," Tippy said when the first tanker pulled out without a single wetback inside.

"Yup. And it's time for a raise. You've earned it."

Mac thrust a stack of cocobucks into Tippy's hand as she watched the tanker disappear. She stood in the parking lot, almost on the very spot where Ramirez had died. Mac imagined if she shuffled her feet, she'd be stirring dust containing molecules of his blood.

Tippy gave a whoop for joy. She threw herself in Mac's arms. "Let's go celebrate."

Mac glanced back at Lupe standing in the trailer's doorway, staring but saying nothing. There was no mistaking her look of disapproval, but he couldn't disengage himself and console her. She had been enduring Tippy's snide remarks and put-downs since Tippy's assumption of management, and Mac guessed it was only her feelings for him that kept her around. All in all, he couldn't have wished for a more virtuous and industrious daughter.

Nonetheless, he couldn't help himself—he left with Tippy.

287

Chapter 46

Before Mac's pickup reached the county road, she had unzipped his fly and attacked with relish. The bouncing made her sport all the more exciting, and Mac didn't last 'til Interstate 10.

They drove straight to Tippy's house instead of pulling into Fast Eddie's to celebrate. Tippy's excitement was infectious, and as the Ranger rolled to a stop, they both jumped out and raced for the door. Seconds later they were in her bedroom, their clothes having magically fallen off in the atrium and hallway, forming a trail from door to bed.

For the first time since Aimee, Mac felt truly excited by a woman's eagerness to make love. Every indication and movement she made said she wanted him. Maybe pregnancy had turned Tippy into a more loving and caring woman. Mac wasn't willing to bet on it, but wasn't about to question her motives either. Not now, at least.

She pushed him onto his back, and ravenously brought him to full height. Her body shown pearly white in the indirect light, and all trace of her injuries had vanished. Mac stroked her satiny skin, feeling its smoothness, and lusting after its contrast of pink and white.

Tippy even paid him a compliment, remarking on his size and saying he was her largest man ever. Mac doubted that, but her words had their desired effect. He kissed her in response, feeling desired. And she didn't stop there. She said he was beautiful, the best formed man she had seen, one who could drive a woman crazy at the mere sight of his giant maypole. It was bullshit, but Mac wanted to believe. He stretched up and turned off the lights, leaving only the hallway to illuminate the lovers in a romantic twilight.

Tippy assumed her favorite position on top in a frenzy of lust. Her stunning body seemed possessed by the goddess Tippy believed

288

herself to be. Mac gripped the edges of her bed, and held on while she undulated frantically. She was wetter than usual and gasped in ecstasy when she rode down to take his full length. Mac's head began to swim as she glued herself to his body. The sex act had become a life unto its own.

She moaned and quivered like a loose sheet of aluminum. Mac's view was awesome, but the dim light was playing tricks on his eyes. His hands looked black, and Tippy's wetness spread over his tummy like a black tide. He reached behind him and flicked on the reading lamp.

His hands weren't black, they were red! Dumbly, Mac examined his hands to confirm they were covered with blood. Tippy abruptly stopped moving and hid her face in her hands.

"Oh, my God!" she cried repeatedly.

He sat up and took Tippy into his arms as his head exploded is a paroxysm of pain. Mac carried her into the bathroom and set her on the toilet. Her legs were bloody like his groin, and tears ran out from beneath her hands. He knelt and tried to wipe away the blood with a hand towel. Her sobs came in short bursts, jolting her chest and body. Mac's head reverberated from blasts of pain. A team of horses were thundering down a rocky road. But he could not mistake the terrible wrenching in his gut, this time outstripping the pain above.

"Leave me, please," Tippy said. She pushed ineffectually at his hands for him to stop.

Mac stood up and backed out of the room, quietly closing the door. He stood in the middle of Tippy's bedroom for a moment, trying to get a hold on his emotions. He didn't love Tippy, but desperately wanted the baby she was carrying. It was his hold on life, his ticket to immortality. He killed Mexicans without a qualm, but here he was in shock just thinking about his unborn child in danger.

He stripped the bed and washed the sheets and himself in the maid's room. He returned to Tippy's bedroom and made up her bed with clean sheets, just finishing when she opened the bathroom door.

She walked like a zombie into the bedroom, halting after three tentative steps.

"I lost it," she said.

Her words pierced his chest like a red-hot spear, searing his heart with a jolt of pain. His face flushed, but for some reason, the throbbing in his head ceased altogether. His head felt fuzzy and numb as if gearing up for a violent seizure. He stepped forward and took Tippy into his arms.

"That's okay," he said. It wasn't, but he couldn't say otherwise. He rubbed her neck and stroked the long straight strands of hair flowing down her back. "There's plenty of time for more."

She didn't respond and stared dumbly at her bed. He held her against his breast, but she stood like a statue with her hands at her sides.

Mac wondered how she thought this might change their relationship. With absolute certainty it would, but Mac couldn't predict its effect. He hadn't expected Mary Lou or Aimee to leave him, and knew his understanding of female behavior left much to be desired.

He eased Tippy into bed and lay beside her. She acted dazed and in shock, avoiding his eyes and not saying a word. For a fleeting moment he wondered if he would survive to see the dawn. He had never spent the night or been asleep in Tippy's presence before. But this time, he couldn't go home. He cradled her in his arms, and she fell asleep within minutes. For Mac, sleep came much later.

The first gray light of morning filtered in through Tippy's jalousies to strike Mac's eyelids like damp balls of cotton. He awoke to discover Tippy still nestled on his chest, her body curled in a fetal posture against him. They hadn't moved all night, and he had survived. He drifted back into a half-sleep, keenly aware of the pressure of her body. For an hour, he argued with himself whether or not it was time to get up. Finally she stirred, wiping the dab of saliva she had deposited on his chest with her hand. He opened his eyes to find her staring at him.

Mac spoke first. "Would you like some coffee?"

Tippy nodded without speaking. Mac couldn't be sure of the emotion he saw in her eyes. It was a mixture of fear, hate, uncertainty, exhaustion, and even an appeal for compassion. He gently lifted her off his chest, and swung his legs out of bed. Without bothering to cover himself, he strode down the hall into the kitchen to turn on the coffee-maker.

She was wearing a light yellow nightgown and sitting up when he returned. Still in the buff, Mac lay on the bed with his feet

290

extending over the side, propping himself up with an elbow. He stroked Tippy's left arm and waited for her to speak.

"Well, now what?" she asked with an air of resignation.

Mac swallowed and tried to compose his thoughts. "We go on like before. Losing the baby doesn't change our arrangement."

"But you don't need me anymore."

"No," he said. "But I want you. Like I said, nothing's changed."

"Yes, it has."

"Okay, something has changed. But it doesn't have to affect our relationship."

"A relationship, you call it? You tried to kill me before. How do I know I'm not expendable again?"

"That was business, and you had chosen the wrong side. As long as you stay on my side and don't fuck Mexicans, you have nothing to worry about."

"Promise?"

"Absolutely."

"Then prove it." Tippy abruptly gained strength and turned to face him. "Get rid of that little whore you keep at the trailer."

Mac was taken aback by her aggressive turn. "Why? We need her. Neither you nor I are going to keep up that place."

"Get someone else then. I don't care who, just make sure he's a male."

"Look, I'm not screwing her if that's what's bothering you."

"I don't care. Get rid of her."

Mac felt trapped watching Tippy grow stronger in front of him. There was no reason to terminate Lupe except for her loyalty to him.

"I don't want to," he said. "She's done a good job, and you have no reason to dislike her."

"I've seen the way she looks at you."

"She's a kid, for Christ's sake! I fed her when she was starving. She's like a daughter or niece. Get off this!"

"You promised, and I'm asking for proof of your intentions. That's not too much in light of your past behavior."

Mac heaved a huge sigh. "Okay, I'll talk to her. I'm not promising to do anything right away, but I'll think about it. Okay?"

"It's me or her."

"Jesus, won't you ever quit? I told you I'd think about it."

Mac backed off the bed and stepped into his jeans. He left his shorts on the floor, deciding haste was more appropriate than proper dressing.

"Your coffee should be about ready. I'll see you tonight."

He strode to the doorway, then turned to face Tippy. "You know, the baby was as much mine as yours. Don't you think I mourn its loss, too?"

"Who knows? You didn't feel it in your body. You're not the one who has to see a doctor today."

"Well, I do mourn it. You're more worried about losing leverage than losing a baby."

Tippy eyed Mac fiercely. "Don't let the door hit you in the ass on your way out."

"Believe me, it won't."

Chapter 47

In the evening, Mac stopped by the trailer to check on Lupe. She was quick to open the gate as usual, but her usual good mood was absent.

"Did you sleep with her?" she asked sharply.

His eyes blinked involuntarily at her accusation.

"Yeah, but we didn't make love." Mac decided since he hadn't ejaculated he was technically being truthful. "It got to be too late to drive back."

That didn't sound right, and even weakened his first statement. He walked with Lupe to the trailer. She seemed to ease up a bit, and accept his explanation for the time being. She changed the subject, but was obviously begging to hear the particulars from last night.

"We're not going to need the safe anymore?"

"No border crossers." Mac sat down at the dinette. "How about some coffee?"

Lupe poured a cup and placed it before him, then plopped down in her customary spot on the opposite bench. Mac didn't use cream or sugar, and sipped the hot java without waiting for it to cool. He felt the steady pressure of Lupe's gaze, and stared into the dark liquid to avoid her. As usual the coffee tasted good.

Lupe broke the silence. "Do you find me pretty?"

"Of course. Why do you ask?" Her question was a bolt from the blue, completely without context. By any standard, Lupe was very pretty with beautiful light brown skin and huge doe-like eyes.

"You have done so much for me, *patron*, I am afraid to ask for a favor." Lupe bowed her head and stared at the tabletop.

"Anything. You know that. You're very important to me."

"Very important?"

293

"Very important. Without you, I couldn't keep people like Tippy in line."

Lupe stood up and took Mac's hand. "Come here. I have something to show you."

"What?"

Mac rose from his seat, but couldn't imagine what Lupe wanted him to see.

"Come with me," she said.

She led Mac down the short hallway to the bedroom, then pushed him toward her bed. He sat on the edge and folded his hands.

"What is it you want to show me?"

He assumed she had received a letter or something from her family. Lupe often visited the La Union post office either mailing a letter or checking general delivery when he took her shopping. For a moment, he feared she was going away. He didn't want her to leave, not the least because Tippy would interpret Lupe's departure as confirming her dominance and authority.

Lupe put her hands on his shoulders as if to steady herself while she spoke. "I do everything I can to make you happy, *patron*."

"I know you do, Lupe, and I appreciate it."

"But you are still unhappy. And I cannot be happy."

"Sure you can. You make your own happiness."

"I cannot be happy until I make you happy. You promised me a favor. I want to make love to you."

Mac stared at her, wishing she hadn't said that. He didn't know what to say.

"But..."

She took a deep breath. "Otherwise I cannot stay."

Dumbfounded by her unexpected demand, Mac couldn't think of an adequate response. Women, even underage teenagers were impossible. He liked her and owed her a lot, but didn't want to complicate their relationship. Why did she have to do this? Whoring was a thing of the past. He had taught her respect. She didn't need to sell herself to men anymore. She was better than that.

Her street-wise eyes melted into the wide, innocent buttons of a baby as she pleaded for him to grant her wish.

"Please. I will do anything if you make love to me."

She was putting him in a corner. To refuse would be a

devastating rejection. A few seconds before he had reminded himself he couldn't allow her to leave. Now he was facing an ultimatum. He nodded slowly, unsure how his response would be taken.

Lupe leaned forward and kissed him. Mac allowed her to push him flat onto her bed. His passivity spurred her on, and she knelt astride him to pull her sweater over her head. She wore no bra, a condition Mac had failed to notice. He wondered if that was usual. He couldn't remember because he had never looked at her as a potential bed partner. She was a kid, underage, and a Mexican.

But she slid down his legs to unbuckle his belt—not the action of an underage kid. On the other hand, her breasts were firm mounds, jutting out provocatively, but not yet developed in shape. Nor did her nipples protrude.

He felt her unzip his jeans and take him out. She shook him like a rag doll that couldn't stand up by itself. Lupe giggled as she stroked him with both hands. Mac's dislike of Mexicans and their culture vanished.

Mac wondered if Mexican girls matured earlier than whites. Probably, because they seemed to age faster. Lupe was from southern Mexico, the state of Oaxaca, a particularly hot province.

Lupe stepped from the bed and pulled off his boots and jeans. Mac remembered he hadn't worn shorts that morning. His pelvic area disappeared under her dark hair, and Mac felt himself being consumed with gusto. Lupe's expertise was lacking, but her enthusiasm made up for deficiencies in technique. She struggled out of her jeans, and Mac soon saw her small brown rear waving in the air as if trying to capture his attention. He started to sit up to stop her, but she pushed him back and straddled him.

Dammit! It was the same as Tippy had done the previous evening. He was surrounded by women, all of whom wanted to be on top! The frustration of dealing with Tippy boiled over into anger against all demanding women. If he had to do this, then by God, he'd do it his way!

With a forceful twist, Mac rolled Lupe onto her back and assumed the superior position himself. She probably didn't weight much over a hundred pounds and was easy to maneuver. Little Lupe lifted her feet toward the ceiling, and Mac drove into her. She gasped and moaned, and his headache submerged under the elemental desire to copulate. He turned into a savage, making her pay for her desire, and exploded with all the ferocity he could muster. Then he collapsed on top of her, sweating profusely in the small room.

Lupe lay motionless for several minutes, keeping her legs locked behind Mac's back. She gently stroked his ribs with her hands.

"That was wonderful, *patron*. I knew you'd be terrific lover."

Mac wanted to laugh, but coughed instead. He had been trying to teach her a lesson, but she had taken his abuse as sexual ardor. Well, he wasn't going to tell her any different; she deserved that. He felt her squeeze him, communicating in the most intimate fashion. He began to grow again in response. His headache disappeared.

"Again, lover, again," she breathed.

Mac looked at this adolescent waif beneath him, egging him on to another bout. He felt strangely attached to her and knew he wanted to please her. And it was so rewarding since she appreciated everything he did. Lupe wanted him unconditionally.

Mac began again, slowly, gently, and with all the tender loving care he could muster. He wanted to show her what making love was all about. The first time had been raw sex, probably no different than all her other experiences.

He imagined her as Aimee and concentrated on building that gentle physical intimacy that had restored Aimee's passion for normal sex. It seemed to work, and Lupe said the most exciting things. How good it felt, how wonderful he was, how everything.

Afterwards came the guilt. He rolled off with a horrible feeling he shouldn't have touched her. But that was wrong, too. She needed his attention to savor whatever afterglow was present.

He turned on his side and started massaging her body. Lying there, gently stroking Lupe's thin brown thighs, Mac felt cursed. She was a child, with a child's body, and someone who didn't yet know her own mind. He should have protected her from himself, helped her grow into a strong, self-respecting woman.

"You have to stay the night," Lupe said. "I've never slept with a man, and it is only right that you be my first." She pushed Mac onto his back and straddled him as she had done earlier. "I want to sleep on your chest, held and protected from everything."

She re-inserted him, and Mac was dimly aware of how ready she was. He wanted to finish this, and give her the climax she deserved.

Mac couldn't help himself—he wanted her to experience the ultimate he could offer. She moved slowly and tenderly, and Mac gave himself over to her.

There was no shipment due that evening, and Mac decided to give Lupe her wish. But there was little sleep, as Lupe made the most of her time with him. Soon Lupe experienced what she was seeking.

"That was my first time," Lupe said afterward, not bothering to explain. "Thank you, *patron*. You have made me into a woman."

Mac's conflicts receded, and he felt happy for her. He retrieved a wet cloth from the bathroom, and bathed her as lovingly as possible. His heart went out to this waif, and he decided to show her love and respect, both physical and spiritual. He pleasured her, and she did the same to him. Morning came too soon.

"Will you be back tonight, *patron*?" Lupe asked after making breakfast.

Lupe hadn't bothered to wash when they got up. Mac approved, and hoped it wasn't just a holdover habit from her former life. He hated it when women immediately got up and washed themselves thoroughly as if they were trying to rid themselves of all traces of him.

"Yes, but it'll be the same as the other night."

Lupe misunderstood and pouted instantly. Mac quickly corrected her impression.

"I'm not going to Cruces afterward," he said.

Her face brightened with anticipation. "You'll stay here?"

"No, Lupe. I think we should consider last night as a one-time happening. That was what you wanted, wasn't it?"

She dropped her head and looked at the floor without speaking.

"You said you'd do anything for me if I made love to you," he said. "Let's be realistic. There are thousands of boys your own age who'd kill to do what I just did. You'll find one and be exquisitely happy. You don't want some stove-in ugly cowboy."

Lupe turned her head away, but not before Mac saw tears slide down her cheeks. Christ, he felt like a heel. He kissed the top of her head and rapidly walked to his truck. He started the pickup without looking back, but Lupe was standing by the open gate when he pulled out into the circular driveway. He drove through while she gave him a tiny wave with her fingers.

What a jerk he was. What had he just done? Hit and run like a Mexican. But then, he knew better. He had shown her how to love, and that love was what she deserved. Still, it had been wrong. And he had ridden bareback all the way, protecting neither of them.

It was this whole setup. It destroyed his sense of values and morality. He had been selfish, putting his own welfare above hers. Whether Lupe believed it or not, going to Chicago was the best thing she could do. He should have refused her demands and let her leave.

Chapter 48

The next two weeks were uneventful, and the nightly shipments passed through without incident. Lupe was unusually quiet, as was Tippy. Mac figured both woman and girl were mad at him, and it was best to keep a low profile.

He told Tippy that Lupe could stay until she left of her own volition. His bedroom privileges were withdrawn immediately.

He buoyed himself by checking his nest egg of cash in the mine. It was growing enormously, and Mac doubted the land sales operation would be able to launder money fast enough to keep up. It was a nice problem to have.

To Mac's surprise, Stuart recognized the identical problem and proposed a solution.

"You need to get into a maquiladora," Stuart said while relaxing at the Bar-D. Ermie was giving him a hard time over her holiday budget, and for the last week, Stuart had spent every evening with Mac. "Buy into some small manufacturing operation on contract with a major producer. Or process coupons or something."

"Like a rag shop?"

"Whatever. It really doesn't make any difference. What you need is a plant in Mexico so we can trade in dollars and pesos."

Mac's interest grew immediately. "I'm listening."

"The maquiladora agreement allows American companies to ship raw materials and semi-finished goods to designated Mexican border areas, convert them to finished products in contract facilities, and repatriate the finished goods and leftover scrap to the US without paying duty."

"That I already knew. How does that allow me to convert funds and make money?"

"Hear me out," Stuart said. "We deposit your cash in Juarez banks, convert it to pesos, and use it to pay the Mexican labor and plant expenses. The banks over there are dying for dollars, and give super-high interest rates."

"But I'm not interested in pesos. We can keep pesos a month and lose half our money. There's no stability."

"No, dummy! That's just to get rid of your cocobucks. Our affiliated American company will pay us immediately in dollars deposited in an El Paso bank. So your cash goes to Mexico, we make a profit in peso trading and manufacturing, and are paid legitimately here in the US."

"Taxes. What about taxes?"

"We operate the Mexican facility at a loss on paper. That's why companies do this. It's a made-to-order tax shelter on top of producing at lower cost."

"You mean we raise expenses by paying ourselves big bucks over there. In dollars. We give ourselves dollar accounts."

"Exactly. But not salaries. It's called expense reimbursement, and we can shift that money into gold or whatever without the least problem. Not even pay taxes. How about it?"

Mac raised his eyebrows and looked out the window. He knew Stuart too well.

"We already own one, don't we? Or almost, at least. What type?"

"A coupon redemption shop. You'll have your pick of eighty nasty-looking females."

It took only three days to cut the deal and set up appropriate banking arrangements. The setup was just how business had always been done on the border. El Pasoans had worked profitable deals with Pancho Villa while he raided Columbus and slaughtered *gringos*. The maquiladora program was a federal boondoggle, making lots of money for companies by avoiding high-priced American labor. The tax advantages were pure pork, and there was no reason he shouldn't cut off a small piece for himself. It might be cheating, but it was legal.

*****

The weather turned cold in preparation for Christmas, sinking overnight into the thirties. In spite of his pyramiding fortune, there

300

was no one with whom Mac could share his holidays. He hadn't heard from either Mary Lou or Aimee and didn't know their addresses. He'd take Lupe to Stuart's for dinner and opening presents, but his season promised to be barren.

Tippy was out for obvious reasons, and she could buy her own damn presents. Even though his headaches were becoming milder, Tippy was still dangerous to his health.

Nonetheless, Mac had tried one last time to thaw the ice. It was a serious overture toward regaining bedroom privileges, but Tippy started playing games. Mac knew it was her way to force him onto her turf, and he wasn't willing to sacrifice his self-respect.

They were going over the books in her house while having a drink, and he became increasingly friendly to set the stage. Tippy seemed to respond, and after an hour of playful yuks and touching, Mac kidded her about how the numbers looked better when she was pregnant.

"You'd like to start another kid, huh?" she said, leaning back in her dining room chair.

"Sure. I'm the last of my family. Two or three would be better."

"With me? After all we've been through?"

"Why not? We're compatible. Even better, we don't harbor illusions about each other."

Tippy stood up, sashayed to Mac's chair, and brought her chest close to his face. He turned to meet her, swiveling with difficulty on the luxurious carpet. Stepping between Mac's legs, Tippy vigorously rubbed his crotch and whipped her long hair around his head. She was wearing jeans and a loose-knit silver sweater that was not covering a bra. Without warning, she yanked up her sweater and thrust her left boob into Mac's face.

"Want to chew on that, big boy?" she said.

Mac managed a "sure" and twisted his head to capture her pouting pink nipple. Tippy immediately stepped backward, pulling her breast out of Mac's mouth with an audible *pop*. She whipped her sweater down with both hands to cover herself.

"Well, you can't." Her eyes glinted evilly and, as Mac recognized from prior experience, with sexual excitement.

He restrained his anger, knowing she expected him to jump up and attack. She would fight back, scratching and flailing to punish

301

him for his impertinence. Then, if he followed her script, he would force himself upon her so she could submit with total abandon. That was what she wanted—a physical confrontation ending in her bedroom with fierce and unrelenting love-making. He'd have his bedroom privileges back, but they would have come on her terms.

Mac smiled and relaxed in his chair.

"Sorry you feel that way," he said. "It might have been incomparably beautiful."

Tippy shivered and stared speechlessly. There was no way she could mistake his words. He had rejected her as a sex partner, clearly indicating she was too much trouble.

Tippy started to say something, but apparently decided against it. She gave an exaggerated shrug and resumed her seat. She turned away and looked out at her back yard.

"It's up to you," she said.

Mac knew it was. From now on.

*****

"You did the right thing," Stuart said over his usual Coors at the ranch after Mac related the incident. "Tippy was always bad news, regardless of her looks and talents."

"Yeah," Mac said. "Her price is too high for me, but she has her uses."

"Not in bed, *amigo*. She not only screws your ears off, she takes your balls, too."

"That's not what I mean." Mac smiled, watching Lupe clean his microwave in the kitchen, wondering if she could understand their softly spoken words. "You know Macias. Noticed any difference in him?"

Stuart thought for a moment. The effusive Hispanic commissioner for Anapra and Sunland Park hadn't been much in evidence lately.

"No, not particularly."

"Then you've missed it. How did he vote on our sub-division application last week?"

"You're right! He voted to approve without a murmur. Always before he opposed me."

"Tippy did that for us, and it didn't cost a cent." Mac rolled his eyes and grinned. "Well, not quite. I had to put up with an earful. Seems our macho hero is the proud owner of an implant. Once he's pumped up he stays that way until the release valve is tripped."

"And she didn't know how to work the valve."

"Exactly. He fooled her by going first to the bathroom, and she didn't know it was artificial. She couldn't tell when it was over and spent hours working to make things happen."

Stuart chuckled. "I can imagine. Probably thought she had lost her touch or wasn't attractive enough. At any rate, you're playing with fire. She'll use him against you."

"Eventually, but not now. She's worried I might dump her at any moment."

"She's replaceable with just about anybody."

Stuart noticed Mac watching Lupe and changed the subject.

"Looks like you've finally decided Hispanic women are okay."

Mac turned and shook his head. "No way. She's just a kid, a teenager."

"Yeah, and England moved the age of consent from twelve to thirteen in 1875. You're still living in the nineteenth century, you'll have no trouble."

"Stuart, she's illegal!"

"Right, and so's the well. Since when have you become so pious?"

Mac threw up his hands. Lupe was looking over at him, smiling like he was the love of her life.

He had driven Lupe into El Paso for a fun day of shopping the previous day. Earlier in the fall everyone had assumed she was his maid, but now they guessed she was his daughter.

Sometimes Lupe was a grownup woman, but in shopping, she was a typical teenager. Buying on an unlimited budget had been an adventure, and she acquired a new wardrobe that would be the envy of many girls on El Paso's aristocratic Rim Road.

Her English was improving, too. Lupe spent most of her lonesome hours reading books or watching the color television Mac installed before Thanksgiving. She generally spoke in English with Mac, and he occasionally brought her back to the ranch after lunch to help maintain the house. She loved his house, but tended to organize

Mac's things so he couldn't find them. They never spoke about their time together in her trailer, but Mac was under no illusions those events had been forgotten.

"Okay," he said to Stuart. "No offense, but let's just say I prefer white girls."

"I hope you find one, buckwheat, but there aren't that many around here. You got to take the best of what's available."

"Maybe I'll go find Mary Lou."

"I said *the best*. Ask yourself what you want from the mother of your sons. Then find one with those qualities."

Mac agreed with a nod. It sounded good in theory, but his looks were reality. He needed someone who could accept him in spite of his appearance. Mary Lou had loved him once, maybe she could again. He should contact her, but didn't know her address.

"Where's Mary Lou living now?" he asked.

"Beats me. Try the phone book."

"What about your sheriff's department contact? He probably knows."

Stuart was staring at him like his marbles were rolling out, and Mac decided a rationalization was required.

"I'll need her address to file for divorce."

It was Stuart's turn to nod. He called Akers. Jed supplied the apartment complex but didn't know which unit was Mary Lou's.

"Ha, the vaunted Prescott information network doesn't know everything," Mac said.

"Not today anyway. But whatever you do, don't go there personally."

That was precisely what Mac did the following evening. Mary Lou's complex was behind a Pic-Quik store on Missouri, and finding her apartment was easy. Mac checked the matrix of mailboxes, and Mary Lou Frazier was typed neatly in the slot for C-7. It was in the second stairwell he tried, on the top floor to the right. He could see light through a smoky glass window alongside the door, and Mac pushed the square button below the peephole. His usual dull headache began sending fresh rivulets of pain across his forehead.

The door opened wide and Mary Lou stood gazing at Mac in surprise. She started to say "What's the—" but halted in mid-sentence. Her expression turned into a scowl. "Mac. What the fuck are you doing here?"

Mac was too stunned to answer. His runaway wife looked a mess, harassed and haggard. She had gained at least twenty-five pounds, most of it in her thickening midsection and legs. Standing in slippers, she epitomized a frumpy housewife. Her stretch pants indicated a condition he hadn't thought possible, and she looked tired, droopy, and unappetizing. Her hair straggled in all directions from a bad perm, and she was wearing too much makeup. He was astounded at the change.

"You're pregnant," he said.

"Brilliant deduction, Sherlock, but no thanks to you. Now if you don't mind..."

She started to close the door, but Mac stepped over her threshold and stopped it with his foot. He pushed it open again as she struggled against him.

"Please," he said. "It would help if we could talk."

"I can't help you." Her tone was more disinterested than angry. She stopped wrestling with the door and held it halfway open. Mac removed his foot.

"Don't you want—"

"I don't want anything from you. All you do is fuck up my life. So beat it before I call the police."

"I never hurt you. I love you." The words were out before he knew what he was saying.

"Bullshit! That's why you got Juan kicked off the force."

"Not me. I—"

"Well, I hope you're happy. He's gone."

"Who then—"

"None of your damn business. Look, I'm busy. What did you come here for?"

"To see you. And how you were getting along."

"Well, now you've seen me, and now you know. Satisfied?"

"Can I do anything for you? I mean, this can't be easy." He pointed to her enlarging belly.

Mary Lou took a deep breath and exhaled. "You should have said that a year ago. Now, it's too late."

"It's never too late."

"It is for me. You want someone with whom you can ride naked across the desert. Make love to all night, and show off to your friends.

305

I'm not that person anymore. Look at me. I'm pregnant, fat, my face is breaking out, and I don't feel well."

"I'll get something for you."

"Get me ten thousand dollars and leave me alone."

"What?"

"Ah, forget it. Go take care of your new girlfriend." Mary Lou was getting angry.

"But she's—"

"I don't want to hear it. Just leave. Get the fuck out of here."

The door slammed in Mac's face. Wow, was Mary Lou bitter! This was the woman with whom he had shared five years of his life, and she couldn't give him the time of day. There was nothing here for him, even less than nothing.

With a profound sadness, he knew Mary Lou was lost to him forever. Then his spirits lifted. He realized his headache was gone.

Chapter 49

Five days before Christmas, the shipment was especially heavy in coke, and in spite of a blistering headache, Mac helped oversee the high-dollar transaction. Everything took place without incident, but Mac was waiting for the day of his first hijack. His organization lacked the muscle to prevent a serious effort. He drove back to the ranch thankful that day hadn't appeared.

Funny, the kitchen door was unlocked. Mac snapped on the kitchen and living room lights, looked around and saw nothing unusual. For a fleeting moment he sensed a twinge of fear, wondering if some coyote's relative or mafia hit man was lurking in the shadows. He scornfully laughed off the feeling, and concluded he had failed to lock the door when he hurried out earlier.

He reached into the fridge and retrieved a Coors. Instant Christmas spirit in a can. It was too much to expect, but a beer usually helped him relax.

A tentative female voice spoke behind him.

"Hi, Mac."

His heart jumped a foot, and he almost dropped the beer. That voice… It couldn't be...

Mac turned to drink in the image of the lady standing in the archway separating his kitchen and living room. She looked absolutely gorgeous in tight jeans and a beige pullover, steadying herself with her hand on the wall. The face he beheld was his own personal goddess of love.

"Aimee!"

He flew across the half-dozen feet that separated them and swept her into his arms. Her eyes closed as he overwhelmed her with kisses, giving her no chance to respond. Maybe she was just passing through, maybe she had stopped to say she was getting married. There were a thousand things she might say that he didn't want to hear.

He pulled her into the living room.

"Mac, please," she said. "I—"

"God, I'm glad to see you. I love you. I hope you're back for good."

Those statements had emanated from his unconscious, telling both Aimee and himself how he felt. They plopped together on the couch.

Aimee looked at her hands held tightly in his. The pause was pregnant with silence. Mac dared not say anything more until hearing her response.

She answered in a barely audible voice without looking up. "If you want me."

Mac crooked his left index finger under her chin and lifted Aimee's face to meet his. Her eyes flitted between the floor and his face.

"Absolutely."

Aimee's eyes started to mist over, and Mac leaned forward with a gentle kiss. She responded by slowly opening her mouth. Then she grabbed his face and smothered him with wet kisses.

"Oh, Mac!" she cried. "I've missed you so."

There was an urgency Mac hadn't felt before as Aimee fumbled with his belt buckle.

In a moment, she wrapped her long fingers around him and tugged as she stood up. Mac struggled to shed his Levi's, pulling his boots off before Aimee yanked him to his feet. Her strength astounded him. Hopping twice, he managed to discard the denim from around his ankles as she towed him down the hallway.

When they rested Mac nuzzled her neck, kissing the tears that flowed freely down both cheeks to wet her ears and neck. "I love you, Aimee," he said. "I love you."

"Oh, Mac, I'm so stupid. How can you forgive me?"

"No, you're not. Everything's all right now. We're together."

She faced him directly. "You're a good man, Charlie Brown. The best I've ever known. I don't deserve you."

"It's me who doesn't deserve you," he said. "But I want you all the same."

"And I want you." She paused as if uncertain whether to continue. Mac steeled himself for the worst.

"Can you be happy with me? You have that lady in Las Cruces who makes me look like day-old bread mold. Compared to her, I'm zilch." Aimee's eyes filled and dropped fresh tears.

It was time to fight for her love, and what he said would be critical. Mac let his heart speak instead of his head.

"You're not zilch, and that woman means nothing to me. She's a manipulating bitch, not fit to hold your coat. I don't have anything to do with her outside of business."

Aimee took a deep breath and started making circles in the hair on his chest.

"Can I be enough for you? Can you be happy with just me?"

"You bet. Happier than I've ever been before. Happier than any man has a right to be."

Her tears started to flow again. "But I've been so bad. All those black football players. And the drugs. Sometimes I don't even know who I am."

"I know who you are, and that's all that matters. It'll be us two against the world, from this moment forward. Everything else is in the past. Let's agree to just be ourselves together."

"I'll try if that's what you want."

"That's my girl!" He kissed her quickly, put one leg over her hips, and cradled her in his arms. Wrapped inside him, she was protected from all dangers. Aimee's breathing became more regular, and Mac felt his heart swelling from pride and love.

This was all he ever wanted. The peace and sense of belonging from being loved. Mary Lou hadn't loved him, he understood that now. She loved making love, but didn't love the man himself. It was different with Aimee. With her there was a meeting of souls, a melding of hearts that he hadn't experienced with any other woman.

Reality intervened as Mac tried to sleep. He had nothing to offer Aimee. He wasn't free, and his business life wasn't honorable. To make an honest woman out of her he'd have to fix both situations. Operations had to cease. There was no way he could continue running drugs with Aimee around.

And he was a murderer. He couldn't undo what was done, but he could change. One way or another, he had to exorcise his dark side.

She believed in him, never questioning he might be anyone other than a good person. It was time to pony up and be the man she thought he was.

Sleep came slowly, but his life had come together. The God of the Amulots had given him a second chance. Everything bad was behind him. Mary Lou, Tippy, all the people who made his life so difficult… He was holding his chosen mate, and his dynasty would come. Three, or maybe five kids. It would be wonderful to take his rightful place in the march of generations. And his headache was gone. Aimee had done that, too.

*****

The morning was a blur of activity. Mac would have preferred to remain in bed with Aimee the entire day, but that wasn't possible.

She slept curled around him with her head on his chest, holding on to his body for dear life. He attempted to extricate himself without waking her up, but her eyes popped open at his initial effort. She followed him into the bathroom to watch as he shaved, then joined him in the kitchen before he finished the scrambled eggs. Aimee wrapped her arms around him from behind and pressed her nude body into his. Their simple sharing seemed more important than making love.

A million questions raced through his mind, but they were risky. Some could needlessly damage her self-confidence, and others might bring answers he didn't want to hear. Aimee was a fragile flower of exquisite beauty, but prone to wither under the slightest heat. Well, such pyrotechnics weren't going to come from him. Quite the contrary, he intended to carefully nurture her as a bud coming into bloom, giving her all the love he could muster.

When Mac asked Aimee what she wanted to do that day, her answer said it all. She hugged him and buzzed his ear. The words came from deep within her heart.

"I'd rather spend time with you than do anything else," she said.

His chest swelled from pride, but what he had before him couldn't involve her. Reluctantly, Mac told Aimee she'd have to remain home.

"Then I'll use our time apart to ensure we won't waste our time together. I'm here for you, not for anyone else."

310

How anyone could withstand such a loving creature was beyond him.

Leaving the ranch had never been so difficult, because now it contained Aimee. Mac kissed her at the kitchen door and marched away to Rover. Looking back, he saw her framed in the doorway as God made her. Whoever or whatever God was, He had done his work well.

Close to ten o'clock, Mac arrived at Stuart's company office in Anthony. He strode in smiling like the Cheshire Cat.

Stuart looked up. "You seem awful happy. Who is she?"

"Aimee. She's back, hopefully for good."

"Congratulations, guy. Too bad you can't keep her by tying the knot."

"Yeah, well, that's just a minor detail. It shouldn't be too hard to get a divorce with Mary Lou cleaning that deputy's pipes and getting pregnant."

Stuart just grunted. He had seen other divorces turn bitter in more cut-and-dried situations than Mac's.

"But that's only one of the things I have to do," Mac said. "I'm going back to being legit. I'm terminating my water hauling operation."

Stuart smiled broadly. "Glad to hear it. Never did like being involved. Maybe now we'll avoid jail."

"You'll shut down the land sales company? There's still a lot of cash to launder."

"We'll do it slowly. How soon are you closing down?"

"Not certain. Closing down will be like two porcupines making love—it has to be done very carefully. The cash needs to go faster than coupon processing can absorb it. Any ideas?"

"Well, I've always wanted to get rid of my C-stores. How about me swapping you three of them for notes. You can bleed cash in through store receipts and pay off my notes. Okay?"

Mac whooped at the idea. "Shoot, yeah. That'll kill two birds with one stone."

"How so two?"

"I'll run the ranch, and Aimee can manage the stores. She'll love it."

Stuart smiled and offered his hand. "Okay, then. Consider it done."

Mac grabbed Stuart's hand and shook it vigorously.

"We'll need to go to the mine to see how much I have," Mac said.

"That where you stashed your cash?"

"Yeah. It's better than any bank."

"Well, any time that's convenient. Meanwhile, I'll get the papers drawn up on my Canutillo, Anthony, and La Union convenience stores. How about one twenty-five apiece?"

"Sounds good to me." Mac looked away in the distance. "Maybe next week on the mine. For now, I've got lots of loose ends to tie up."

"I'll bet. Better wear a jock strap complete with cup. Body armor, too. Call me if you need any help," he said, trusting that Mac wouldn't call.

"I got myself into this, I'll get myself out."

"Hopefully standing up."

Chapter 50

Mac stalled again in doing what he knew had to be done. He decided to wait until the New Year to close down the well operation, since he wanted to focus on Aimee over the holiday season. It would be tricky, and the closing needed to be planned well. He would need an excuse, and a good one. He had to deflect Mendoza's wrath to someone else, and his prime candidate was Tippy. That would take some doing.

Aimee was bustling around the kitchen with dinner almost ready when he returned. It felt wonderful to have someone waiting for him, someone who truly cared for him, loved him, and wanted to spend time with him above all else.

He was fortunate she hadn't questioned his marital status. Divorce was tough. It was a public admission of failure, not becoming to a man at all. He didn't want to face Mary Lou, say bad things about her, or even let people know she was pregnant. But sooner or later, it would be necessary.

It was Aimee's very lack of pressure that made him want to do right. She asked for nothing except his love and attention, and material things or appearances were of no consequence. The ranch had been important to Mary Lou, but Aimee hadn't once asked for a tour of Mac's holdings. Nor had she evinced any interest in his financial condition.

For the first time in eons, Mac spent most of an evening watching television. Aimee plastered herself on him, and during a brain-deadening series of sitcoms, talked about her trip to California. She had left New Mexico because she thought Tippy possessed a prior claim on Mac, both privately and publicly.

"What happened to her?" Aimee asked.

"She's still in Las Cruces doing her thing."

Aimee looked away at the floor. "She was pregnant, you know."

"Yes, I know. She miscarried a couple of weeks after you left."

The silence was deafening, and Mac knew he had to say something.

"She had a Mexican boyfriend who disappeared after he found out she was pregnant."

"I thought Mexicans were big on having kids."

"They are, but not in paying for them. Tippy could be very demanding."

Aimee stroked Mac's chest. "You have to forgive me. I thought it was yours."

"Tippy's not my type in spite of how she carried on. She was just pulling your chain."

"She did a good job."

"You shouldn't have left. You had no competition. There was only you."

"Convince me," Aimee whispered.

He set about to do just that. Afterward, Mac thought of those typically stupid statements politicians make, "Together we can make a difference," or "With your help, we shall succeed." What they meant was, "Vote for me, and I'll maybe make it worth your while." This time, such statements weren't just platitudes. Together, and with mutual help and support, Aimee and he could work miracles.

*****

Stuart disturbed their reverie the following morning with papers for Mac to sign. Aimee cooked breakfast while Mac and Stuart concluded their business. She had learned to make *huevos rancheros*, Mac's favorite breakfast, and she showed off her culinary skill in the kitchen by placing colorful works of art in front of both men.

Mac grinned and interrupted Aimee's domestic endeavors. "Before you sit down, honey, we need your signature."

"On what?"

"Bank papers and the like. You need to be on a local checking account and able to handle things when I'm out of town."

Mac held a pen out for Aimee to take, and pushed several papers in her direction. She took the pen and signed where Mac pointed without looking at the documents.

314

"Thanks," he said. "Now, how would you like to have your own business?"

"After you finish your breakfast." Aimee pointed to her cooling plates.

Mac nodded. He dug in and almost inhaled her masterpiece. Even so, Stuart finished first.

"This is a win-win situation," Stuart said. "I didn't know you were getting the best cook in the valley."

"Now you know why I love her." Mac turned to Aimee sipping her coffee. "Time for good things to happen to you."

"Good things have already happened to me," she said. "I'm content."

"Well, you deserve more. As of a few minutes ago, you're the proud owner of three convenience stores. Stuart and I needed to square away some of our partnerships for tax purposes. With me tied up in running the ranch, the C-stores need somebody else."

Mac smiled and pushed the papers over to Aimee. "They're yours. Sort of an early Christmas present."

"Mine? But I didn't ask for anything. I don't even know anything about convenience stores. And I can't let you just hand me three stores. I haven't done anything to earn them, and don't have the money to buy them."

Aimee's words came in a torrent, and for a second, Mac thought he might have gone too far. Aimee seemed put upon by his unexpected action and maybe a little scared.

Mac waved his hand. "Don't worry, you'll learn. And if it makes you feel better, you can pay me a consulting fee of ten percent of your profits. How's that?"

Aimee scooted over and pushed herself onto Mac's lap. She hugged and kissed him on the cheek. "Oh, Mac, you don't have to do this. I'm not going anywhere."

"I know, but I want to. And it'll be good for both of us. Everybody needs something they can call their own, and this way, we'll both have things to do by ourselves in addition to what we do together."

She kissed him fervently, ignoring Stuart's presence. "I'll make you proud of me," she said finally.

In honor of their new partnership, Stuart suggested they fly to

Vegas and take in some shows. Aimee wouldn't have it. Her time in California had underscored her desire for family and happiness during the holidays. She belonged here with Mac, and wanted nothing more than to kick back and enjoy the peace and quiet.

She loved Mac with all her heart, and there was nothing about him she would change. Like two ospreys wounded by hunters, they nursed each other back to health and mated for life. All their bad times were in the past, those times alone and unloved, all gone forever. There was no greater joy than waking in Mac's warm bed, feeling his ever-present morning stiffness, and starting her day like she'd ended her night.

*****

For the first time in his life, Christmas Day felt truly like Christmas to Stuart. He sat in his favorite chair with a cup of eggnog, savoring his good fortune and that of Mac's. He was surrounded by family and friends, all of whom loved or respected him, and it was wonderful. Thanks mostly to Mac's new venture, he had surprised Ermie with his generosity and placated his children's desires for soon-to-be-broken toys and soon-to-be-discarded items.

Aimee and Mac arrived before noon to share in the family's traditional Christmas dinner, and his world was filled with happiness. In particular, Stuart was reminded of the saying; "All the world loves a lover." Certainly it was doubly true in this case. There was something between Aimee and Mac that lit up the room. They radiated warmth and joy, exciting the kids even more than the toys.

Maybe it was the way Aimee's presence rendered Mac's countenance almost handsome. That took some doing, but today Mac was smiling and following Aimee's every move with a look that transformed him into a benign and friendly cowboy. Stuart knew their togetherness went far beyond a satisfying sex life. They drew emotional strength from each other in a true synergistic love match.

He wished his relationship with Ermie was as intense. Aimee was Mac's partner in all things, while Ermie was his maid and the nanny for his kids. He was the breadwinner, the man of the house. He made the decisions, and she obeyed. Well, more or less, depending on her ability to manipulate him.

Watching his friends cavort in happiness, Stuart sensed he had missed something in life. What they so joyously and innocently flaunted were emotions he hadn't experienced. No woman had ever loved him like that, not Ermie, not Aimee's sister, not any of his earlier flings. He was just the husband, father, and provider for a large extended family.

A knock-down, drag-out love affair was probably out of reach. Women considered him attractive only for his economic assets and stability. Part of that was due to his less than average height, but being a businessman also contributed to his wimpy persona. Stuart was boring in comparison to Mac, trying hard, but never able to break out of his drab existence. He began to feel maudlin, telling himself Ermie probably respected him, even possibly was fond of him, but didn't love him beyond that.

Then Aimee approached, and he felt blessed by her affection. She refreshed his eggnog with a large lump of French vanilla ice cream and kissed his cheek.

"Thanks for everything," she murmured in his ear. "None of this would have happened without you."

Mac's favorite song, "Landslide," came to mind, and Stuart felt a momentary panic. He looked at Aimee's beaming face and saw it lying crushed and bleeding amid the dusty rocks of a slide. Life couldn't get better than this, it could only go down. He had helped bring happiness into Aimee's life, but she had climbed to a height above him and was beyond his control.

Then the emotion passed, and Stuart once again resided in the present.

"You're welcome," he said. "Just make me happy by being happy."

Chapter 51

After Christmas Aimee prepared herself to inspect her stores and battle new dragons. It was time for her to join the world of adults, put the playground of college and drugs behind her, and show what she could do. Her doubts were almost incapacitating, but had to be overcome. Otherwise, she was not worthy of Mac's love.

Mac had offered to help her get started, but Aimee refused his assistance. Stuart could teach her the ropes, and she'd accept help from him and no one else. What she learned would be brought home as a present to Mac, establishing her value as a person, and proving his faith in her was not misplaced.

She asked a plethora of questions at each store, mostly directed to Stuart out of earshot from her newly acquired employees. Conceptually, the business appeared simple. Gasoline sales provided a base of revenue covering fixed and operating expenses, and margins on in-store sales generated profit. Stuart explained how jobbers maintained inventory levels on her shelves, but mentioned she needed strict controls to prevent them from cheating.

The average inside sale was below three dollars, and counting nickels and dimes was mandatory. Money orders were a big business at the beginning of each month, mostly being purchased by Mexicans to pay their rent. The primary selling points were speed of service and location convenience rather than price. Several large twenty-four hour supermarkets competed with lower prices and longer operating hours, but they weren't as close to the market. There was a niche the C-stores filled, but management could never be complacent.

"So what's the biggest problem I'll have?" Aimee asked. Her enthusiasm was growing in leaps and bounds. Seeing and touching something she owned was tremendously exciting.

"Personnel," Stuart said. "Both your employees and suppliers."

"Why suppliers? They keep my inventory levels up, and I pay them. What do I care what their personnel is like?"

Stuart smiled at Aimee's overlooking what was obvious to him. It was the law of human behavior: if you don't understand a person's actions, look for the financial angle. Suppliers were a case in point. They were willing to carry in their goods, unpack cartons and containers, stock shelves, and dispose of the boxes and unneeded cases. Supposedly, they relieved store managers of these inventory management chores to control displays and shelf location, but that overlooked the financial angle.

"Because they steal," Stuart said. "Theft is a major concern. Suppliers do the most, followed by employees and customers."

"How? I thought customers stole the most."

"Hardly. As suppliers put their items on shelves, they take others off. Like putting on cheap chips and taking off expensive hair spray. Then they carry out the empty cartons, but they're not empty. If you count what's delivered, it's all there, but other items come up short in physical inventory each month. Or when the pop or milk vendor brings in cases, you count the cases. Only you can't see the bottles or cans in the middle, and assume they're there. But they're not. Instead of nine gallons of milk, you get eight. And that's if you watch. I know a case where a chips vendor wheeled more stuff out than he brought in for two whole months."

"But won't his company know? They can't possibly condone such practices."

"They don't see it. Often the delivery man can sell what he steals from you to the next store on his route. You'll even be offered extras from time to time. They won't be on his company's invoice, just something the route driver picked up and wants to sell to cover his cost. Only he has no cost."

"Then I'll call his supervisor and have my stores taken off his route." Aimee bristled in a burst of righteous indignation.

"Sure you will." Stuart nodded slowly, then shook his head. "The supervisors are all ex-drivers, and the biggest crooks of all. You'd be better advised to keep suppliers out of your stores. Have them make deliveries to the door, or require all cartons to be flat before taken outside. Even then, you'll have to count everything yourself."

Stuart paused for a moment while Aimee stared in disbelief.

"I'm sorry to make it sound like everyone's crooked, but so far, I've only mentioned actual theft. They also cheat on pricing. Some delivery invoices are so complicated they take a PhD to figure out. You can see the quantities, but prices are hidden so you can't check the driver's math."

Stuart retrieved a chips supplier invoice from the Anthony store's packet of documents.

"Look at this one. You can hardly decipher his writing." Stuart pointed to the scribbles inside tiny, pre-printed boxes for quantities. "The tiny numbers in red are prices for various quantities, and the facing page gives the extensions. Before we went on computer and began extending every invoice in my office, this particular vendor overcharged us an average of thirteen dollars per invoice. All errors were in his favor."

Aimee examined the black and red invoice. It was horribly complicated. The lines and numbers almost gave her an instant headache. She didn't want to look at the document—and realized that was the point.

"When we went on our present computer system, our purchases dropped by almost two thousand dollars per store per month," Stuart said. "That paid for our computer system and the gal to input vendor invoices with a whole lot left for profit."

"I can't believe people are so venal," Aimee said. "This is institutionalized theft."

"Yeah, but now we're getting to the good part. With the store manager's collusion, they have a license to clean out the store. Catching the manager is like nailing a crooked casino dealer in Vegas. You have to watch the numbers, look for things outside the averages, then catch him in the act."

"But I don't know anything about computers. I won't know what's right or wrong."

"You will from this system. It was programmed by a local hot-shot and it generates great statistics on store operations."

Aimee changed the subject to the physical stores themselves. All three appeared in excellent condition, with large canopies that extended the store roofs over double rows of gas pumps. But the primary color was orange, and Aimee didn't think it was very friendly.

Stuart explained that orange was the traditional Scotch-Irish color, but she was free to change it to anything she wished.

"Is Mac Scotch-Irish or Amulot?" she asked. The only thing she knew about Mac's family was that his mother and father were dead. She had heard Mac use the terms "Scotch-Irish" and "Amulot" at Terlingua, but didn't understand what they meant.

"Both. The two terms mean the same, and you're a quarter yourself," Stuart said. "I know that from your sister. A quarter Scotch-Irish, half English, and quarter Huguenot French. The best mix possible for an all-American girl."

"Why is that better than others?"

"This country's your heritage. The majority of patriots in the Revolutionary War were Amulots, Americans of Ulster and Protestant Scottish or Irish lineage. So were the founding fathers. Amulots won this land by right of conquest from its aboriginal inhabitants, then subdued it through hard work. All other claims are merely whimperings by defeated peoples or subversions of the truth by johnny-come-latelys. The Indians ought to be happy we didn't totally exterminate them."

"You're supposed to call them Native Americans," Aimee said.

"Bullshit! So they got here first by ten thousand years or so. You were born in the United States. Aren't you a native? If your ancestors came here three hundred years ago, does that make you less of a native than someone whose forefathers arrived a thousand years ago? Should Ainu be called Native Japanese? They were in Japan before the Japanese arrived. How about the Israelis? Does Palestine belong to them because they were there two thousand years ago? The Palestinians only arrived in the seventh century. Or the Comanches. They came from Utah to Texas in the seventeen hundreds, exterminating the local tribes. Does that give them a better claim than Amulots who arrived less than a hundred years later? Regardless of what thumb-sucking bed-wetting liberals say, calling Indians by any term other than aborigines doesn't make much sense."

"I didn't mean to get you so riled up," Aimee said. She gave Stuart a kiss on the cheek.

Stuart beamed. "If that's my reward every time I make a speech, I'll go into politics."

"No, Stuart, you're a doer. Like Mac says, if you can't do it, teach it. If you can't teach, then teach the teachers. If you can't teach the teachers, administrate. If you can't administrate, then run for political office. You have a long way to fail before you get there."

"Maybe, but there are lots of ways to fail."

"You haven't failed at anything yet."

"Not in business, not yet. But it can happen."

"Aw, come on. What can go wrong?"

"All those things I don't expect. We get to believing our own press clippings and close our eyes. Then get caught in landslides."

"Landslides?"

"Powerful landscape-altering events or movements. The Indians were buried in a landslide of Scotch-Irish, now we're being buried in a landslide of non-whites. As individuals it happens, too. Each of us gets caught up in events beyond our control, and we either succumb or get rescued by others. You and Mac were lucky. You helped pull each other out."

She squeezed his arm. "I know. And we'll never get buried again."

*****

Learning the convenience store business was a walk through an alligator pond, but under Stuart's tutelage, Aimee caught on fast. Her unbridled enthusiasm also generated ideas like politicians' promises, some good, some bad. For example, she wanted to establish lighter work schedules and higher pay rates.

"Not a good idea," Stuart said. "The going wage for this type of work is minimum, and offering more money will only raise costs. Remember, the average annual family income in El Paso is only twelve thousand dollars, and in Anthony, it's even less."

"But I'll get better workers."

"No, you won't. Store clerks are young and only working until they acquire a more marketable skill, get married, or otherwise find a better job doing something else. You'll never be able to attract clerks with money. If they show promise and enthusiasm, make them assistant store managers or managers. Then pay them more. But only with promotion."

"But they deserve more. It's hard work."

"If you get reasonable employees for the wage you offer, you're paying the right amount. If they could find better work or better pay, they'd leave or not work for you in the first place. That's the law of the marketplace."

"I'd still like to do what I can. Is there a way to know how much I could raise wages without impacting profits?"

"Sure, but I can tell you the answer. Zero. Zip. Nada. This industry's based on minimum wage help. Any increase in wage rates comes directly out of profits."

"Show me."

Stuart sat at his CRT and demonstrated how higher pay for clerks impacted profits. Aimee was astounded the computer system could generate pro forma numbers so rapidly, and the figures dissuaded her immediately. She could inaugurate better working hours and conditions, elegant uniforms, and a more generous policy with respect to in-store purchases, but wages were best left alone.

"What do I do when the government raises the minimum wage?" she asked.

"First, you stretch. Cut hours for clerks and get managers to work longer. Get rid of part-timers and casual help, school kids, and the like. Remember, it's not just the wages. Fringe benefits and taxes go up since they're based on wages. Then, raise prices to cover the mandated cost increase. Hit the volume items first, cigarettes, chips, and pop."

"But I'll lose sales."

"Only if you raise prices before your competition. You're all in the same boat. Everyone will have to cut personnel and raise prices to survive."

"So raising the minimum wage reduces employment."

"Yep. Fewer people are employed and they have to work harder."

Aimee couldn't believe there were so many gray areas, particularly in dealing with store managers. They were classified as supervisors and expected to work a minimum of forty-five hours for forty hours pay. They didn't receive overtime, but lacked hiring and firing rights. Nor did they set wages. Under current labor laws they were clearly abused, yet formed the backbone of her organization.

The next day, Aimee decided to allow managers overtime pay

until Stuart threw cold water on her initiative. He telephoned and asked to see her as soon as possible without stating why.

"You have a crisis," Stuart said when she walked into his Anthony office. "Personnel type. The Anthony store manager is stealing."

Aimee felt like Stuart had slugged her in the stomach. She sat down and composed herself before speaking. She had driven in immediately from the ranch after receiving Stuart's phone call. The store manager was an Hispanic boy in his late twenties who had gone out of his way to be friendly.

"How do you know?" she asked.

Stuart pushed several store reports toward Aimee as she scooted her chair to his desk. According to the daily sheets, their ice cream jobber was receiving half his money in cash on delivery at the store, but ice cream department sales from register tapes seemed small in comparison with the purchases.

"Call the jobber," Stuart said. "Tell him you're checking suppliers to set a policy on paid-outs and get his opinion. The number's on top of his invoice next to the purchases sheet."

"What about the other two stores? Do we make paid-outs there, too?"

"Different jobber. Anthony's the only store using Valley Dairies. It was my first store, and I went with Valley because they furnished ice cream freezers as part of their service. When I built the other two stores, I bought my own freezers and contracted with a cheaper distributor out of El Paso."

Aimee picked up Stuart's telephone and dialed. She was immediately connected with Valley Dairies' owner, and a few questions established her store manager's culpability beyond all doubt. She replaced the receiver in its cradle and turned to face Stuart.

"He doesn't want his drivers carrying cash. None of his current customers make paid-outs, and he recommended I stay with that policy. Our manager is falsifying his reports and pocketing the money."

Aimee didn't remember the young man's name and looked again at the sheets. Ramirez, Rafael Ramirez, a typical Hispanic name.

"Do you know this Ramirez well?" she asked Stuart.

324

"No, he's only been manager for a few months. But he lives in one of my trailer parks, so I'll probably have to evict him after this."

Stuart went out to his secretary's area and returned after rummaging through the personnel files. He held a manila folder in his hand and starting reading its contents. "I'll be glad when you take over all these, but I understand that Rome wasn't built in a day."

"Does he have kids?"

"Yeah, four. He's twenty-seven, wife's name Lucy." Stuart opened one eye wide and squinted with the other. "I talked to him. Told me his older brother was a big-time crook who got rubbed out in some mob war, so he had a lot to prove. Even moved here from Cruces to be near the store. I thought he was a good hire."

"I feel bad about his wife and kids," Aimee said.

"Can't do that. They're not your problem. He took his chances and put them at risk. It wouldn't be the first time the innocent suffer along with the guilty. Want to prosecute for embezzlement?"

Aimee shook her head. "No, it doesn't involve that much money. And if he went to jail, who would feed his wife and kids?"

"It's your call, but just getting fired for stealing is no penalty at all. That's the way they think around here. If you're not tough, they take advantage of you. And if you don't press a criminal case, you'll probably have to pay unemployment."

"But we're firing for cause. Even I know you don't pay unemployment then."

"You have to prove it. And evidence that would convince a jury doesn't necessarily cut any ice with the unemployment commission. Not prosecuting for theft will be taken as a de facto admission of not having sufficient cause."

"So what do I do? Sounds like I'm forced to swear out a complaint."

"You could threaten a criminal action and let him resign. Then you won't have to prove anything, and won't have to pay unemployment."

Aimee nodded. Business was far more complicated than she had imagined. She wanted to be charitable to the man's family, but instead, she was letting a crook go unpunished to save herself time, grief, and money. She felt dirty somehow.

"Look," Stuart said. "Every industry or occupation has its

325

crooks, but that doesn't mean you have to be one. Think about it. Stockbrokers who churn client holdings for commissions, insurance agents who sell whole life policies, professors who trade grades for student evaluations, businessmen who exploit workers, and employees who steal from employers. Everyone makes their own choice."

Aimee didn't know what to say. She had done illegal things herself, but the drugs only affected her, and the sex was always with consenting adults. At least Mac wasn't a crook, and although Stuart probably clipped some corners, he made up for it with his generosity. Well, all her reprehensible actions were in the past and would stay that way.

In the afternoon Stuart handled Ramirez, and Aimee assumed active management of the Anthony store. The second shift clerk was a heavyset Hispanic girl named Rosa, and the assistant manager who handled weekends also helped during the evening drive-time rush. Rosa was in her mid-twenties and still single, a condition Aimee attributed to her rather homely appearance and no-nonsense attitude. She was also an inveterate gossip and spent every spare minute telling Aimee the life history of each person who came into the store. After the first hour, Aimee decided she knew more about the local residents than she cared to.

The first shift clerk was Raul Chacon, a tall, thin fellow from La Mesa who clearly resented her authority. About the same age as Rosa, Raul acted as if working for Aimee threatened his *machismo*. If so, that was his problem, and Aimee discovered herself hardening toward him. She guessed such attitudes went with the territory, but she didn't like to see herself becoming less sensitive to others' needs.

"You may lose all your male employees," Stuart said when Aimee voiced her concern.

"Why? Can't they work for a woman?"

"Not a young one they'd rather see under them. And I mean lying underneath them in bed. It's all about power, and they want to be powerful."

"What about the females?"

"It goes both ways. Some, particularly the better-looking ones, prefer to work for a man because they want to be proud of their boss as a powerful male. Also, they may think they can use their looks to get ahead. Others would rather work for a female. Some will be proud of a female being successful, but more will be glad they don't have to fend off their boss's advances."

If she had to have an all-female organization that was no problem to her. In the east, most C-store clerks were Pakistani, and on her travels, she noticed the small motels were run by Indians. At least her stores would require American citizenship. That might be violating some EEOC regulation, but she'd do it anyway. Americans needed and deserved to be employed instead of foreigners.

Aimee re-established integrity with suppliers from her first day at Anthony. It meant paying more taxes, but she would not have it otherwise. Stuart chided her by saying he'd see how long she'd resist the siren songs from soft drink and chips suppliers for kick-backs and under-the-table deals. Forever, as far as she was concerned.

As with all good things, there was a downside. Aimee now had less time to spend with Mac. He was happy with both her new-found confidence and business enthusiasm, but displeased with the long hours she set for herself. Until she found a replacement, she planned to open her Anthony store at six, work the breakfast, lunch, and evening busy hours, then close the store at ten-thirty.

She promised her heavy schedule wouldn't continue forever, and would look for a new manager after New Year's. For now, however, managing a store was the fastest and best way to learn the business. Mac would have to understand and be patient. This was something she needed to do for herself, and she'd make it up to him later. They would have plenty of time to enjoy themselves before they started a family. Mac talked of four or five kids, and that sounded good to her.

The only thing that concerned her was that Stuart said the convenience stores were often targets for armed robberies. She didn't carry a gun, and wouldn't know how to use one anyway. Mac said he'd train her, but guns scared her. She decided to keep as little money as possible in the register and put up no resistance in a robbery. One could not go through life worrying about what might never happen.

Chapter 52

The time had come to announce that the well was dry. The trailer came into view as Mac turned toward the escarpment and flood control dam. Lupe was waiting beside the main gate when he crested the first shelf above the valley floor. Mac thought she would be pleased with his decision to stop running drugs. She hadn't liked doing that from the beginning and absolutely detested Tippy's management.

Mac's excitement loosened his tongue before reaching his usual place at her dinette table. He stood at the kitchen counter, seeing a new radiance in Lupe's eyes even before he spoke. Evidently, she was anticipating his announcement.

"Lupe, I'm closing down the operation," he said.

Lupe dropped like a stone to the dinette bench. Her eyes began to fill with water. "Why? What have I done wrong?" she said.

"You haven't done anything wrong. It doesn't have anything to do with you."

She burst into tears. Mac was appalled. Four months earlier, Lupe had been a hardened, homeless prostitute working her way north. Now she was a little girl, sobbing her heart out over losing a job that could have sent her to jail for her child-bearing years.

"What's going to happen to me?" Lupe wailed. She threw herself in Mac's arms.

He tried to hold her arms to keep a sense of distance, but succeeded only in appearing unsympathetic and uncomforting.

"You'll go to your relatives in Chicago like you intended when you first arrived. I'll give you the money and pay you for the time you've worked here."

"But I want to stay with you! I love you!"

Mac's head jerked. "Whoa," he sputtered.

He pushed her head away from his chest so he could face her directly.

"Lupe, you're a beautiful young girl with all your life ahead of you. You don't want me. This was a bad deal, against the law. You need to forget me and all this. Go to school in Chicago, find some nice boy, get married, and raise a family."

"You don't care about me."

"Yes I do. I think of you as my daughter. But I haven't been fair to you, getting you involved in this and keeping you shut away from everyone. You need a proper family, school, friends, and all that."

"Let me come live with you. I won't be any trouble. I can go to school here."

"No, it wouldn't work out. We've already gone beyond a father-daughter relationship, and that wasn't right either. You need to build a life for yourself without me."

Mac thought fast, trying to find things that would convince Lupe her departure was best. Everything that came to mind sounded like phony rationalization.

After a long moment, he noticed she was nodding almost imperceptibly.

"So when do I leave?" she said.

"I'll call the airlines. How about tomorrow?"

"How about today?"

Lupe was punishing him for some reason, but her mien was making this easier. "Let's see if there's a flight," he said.

Mac picked up the telephone book and found American Airlines. He dialed the 800 number and wasn't even put on hold. The reservations lady said there was space available on the 1:49 direct flight to Chicago. Lupe nodded her acceptance, and Mac booked a first class seat.

A quick trip to the mine produced a sack of hundred dollar bills that Mac stuffed into a carry-on bag he gave her. He promised to ship the remainder of her belongings when she gave him an address.

When Lupe emerged from her bedroom, he decided he had dodged a bullet. She was wearing one of her Christmas dresses, looking self-possessed and almost legal. Not quite an adult, she was more than a maid or an inexperienced teenager. There was too much

329

knowledge in her eyes. He was sorry to see her go, and would miss her.

They drove to El Paso International in almost complete silence. Lupe's demeanor was decidedly frosty until she was ready to board the plane. She seemed to have something to say but couldn't say it.

They let the other passengers board first, and stood facing each other in front of the gate. The waiting stewardess, a tall, dark-haired Anglo, held her collected boarding passes impatiently. She glared intently at Mac as if he was some sort of criminal cavorting with an underage Mexican. That was exactly how Mac felt.

"Thank you for everything," Lupe said. "You've given me more than you know. I will name my first child after you."

"That's not necessary, Lupe. You're a fine girl, and I'm glad to have met you and been able to help."

Lupe quickly stretched up and kissed Mac on the cheek.

"Yes it is," she whispered. "You're my *patron*, the lord of my *hacienda*, and it's your right."

The stewardess was tapping the carpet with her left foot and making "tsk-tsking" sounds. Mac wanted to say something, but couldn't think of anything appropriate.

Lupe turned and handed her boarding pass to the unsmiling girl. She handed Mac a card and entered the ramp. She waved at Mac only once. Then she disappeared.

Mac didn't open the card until seated in his Ranger. It was a friendship card in Spanish that Lupe must have purchased while he was buying her ticket. He slowly read the note she had written.

"You're going to be the father of my first son," it said. "The boy will be worthy of his father and make you proud. From a giant will come another giant. All my love, Lupe."

*****

Lupe's note threw Mac into turmoil, but he had business to conduct. Montana required a personal contact, and Mac handled him on the way back from the airport. They went for a walk together, and Mac said a contact in the Las Cruces police department had mentioned he was under investigation. The informant was supposedly someone in Cruces, so Mac was closing the operation down temporarily. Montana listened without comment, merely stating he would pass on the information as appropriate.

An icy chill descended on their conversation when Mac mentioned he would have no need for Montana's legal services in the near term. That comment was a risk, but Mac couldn't stomach paying crooked lawyers more money than absolutely necessary. Depending on his communications security, Montana might or might not inform Mendoza that Mac had terminated his services. The inference was clear. Mac had shut down his operation permanently instead of temporarily.

Mac's precipitous and unilateral action wouldn't cause Mendoza a monetary loss, but might embarrass the macho Mexican with respect to his American buyers. Mac had no way of knowing what promises Mendoza had made or how the loss of Mac's pipeline jeopardized the smooth running of Mendoza's empire. Montana wouldn't tell Mac anything, that was for sure.

He assumed drug lords like Mendoza lost segments of their operations to police actions from time to time and took such dislocations in stride. Mac felt certain the Mexican cartel used traffic lanes other than his tankers. On the other hand, the volume had been immense, and the security outstanding. Not once had there been a loss.

The other necessary telephone calls went easily enough when Mac returned to the trailer. He told each contact the operation was temporarily suspended because of border patrol activity. Castillo sounded relieved and made no mention of the future. He hoped Mac would understand if demands on his time rendered him unavailable for any private work. Mac laughed and said he understood.

The only problem remaining was Tippy. She would hit back at him one way or the other. If she learned Aimee was back, she'd strike there and attempt to drive her away. She also might influence Macias between the sheets to kill Mac's well applications.

Stuart had been right. He shouldn't have expanded Tippy's role or directed her to work on Macias. She was now in a position to hurt him, and Mac possessed no counter-balancing mechanism to use against her. Killing her was out of the question. He hadn't been able to do it before, and he was less able to do it now with Aimee around. But, maybe money would talk, either with Tippy or with Macias.

331

Mac pushed Rover hard to Cruces to avoid thinking about the impending confrontation. The county mounties weren't in evidence, and Mac guessed his transit time from Anthony might be a personal record.

Tippy sat quietly while he explained the operation's shutdown.

"Okay, Mac, so that's that," she said.

"Yep."

"No severance?"

"Consider yourself duly compensated. You have the house, your car, and the funds you've stashed so far. This makes us quit."

"Then we have nothing more to say. You may leave." With a wave of her hand, Tippy regally terminated the audience.

Mac blinked at her cold dismissal. He turned on his heel and strode to the door. He stopped momentarily, carefully removing Tippy's house key from his key ring. He dropped it on the terra cotta tile in the atrium and walked out without looking back. The ringing of his key pealed like Tchaikovsky's triumphant church bells in his 1812 Overture. It had ended, and he would never return. At least one source of his headaches had been expunged. But she had taken the news all too calmly.

Chapter 53

Five days later, Aimee was on her knees stocking a soap delivery when she felt the presence of another individual beside her. A pair of beautiful green eyes sparkled down at her over a broad smile. She had seen the long-haired blonde only once before, but recognized her instantly. It was Tippy, wearing a dark green dress and looking like she'd stepped off the cover of *Vogue*. An immediate pang of jealousy skewered Aimee's solar plexus, but she rose and smiled a greeting in return.

"Tippy, isn't it? I met you in Las Cruces one time at lunch." She extended her hand.

Tippy shook it politely. "Yes, Tippy Gallagher, and you're Aimee. Sorry, I've forgotten your last name."

"Barnes," Aimee said. "How are you? I understand you and Mac aren't in business together anymore."

"Yes, I haven't seen him in quite a while. How's he doing?"

"Terrific." Aimee couldn't refrain from gloating. "The ranch is doing real well, and he sometimes helps me with my stores."

"Oh. This is your store now?" Tippy raised her eyebrows, and Aimee recognized the gesture signifying doubt.

"Yep. You like it? I also own one in Canutillo and one in La Union."

"Well, you're quite the entrepreneur. Can we expect to hear wedding bells soon?"

Aimee tilted her head and frowned. "I doubt it. Things don't move that fast with Mac, and he only filed for divorce yesterday."

Tippy gasped in genuine surprise. "I didn't know he was married."

"Yes, but I've never met her. They've been separated a long time."

Mac had finally come clean concerning his marital status. His action was a positive step, regardless of how belated. She'd known about his situation from the beginning, but hearing it from him made all the difference in the world. Now she was pleased to discover she knew something about Mac that Tippy didn't.

"So how does Mac help out? Here at the store, I mean."

Aimee led Tippy around the aisle to her mini-delicatessen's table area. She motioned for Tippy to join her at one table near the baseball card display.

"Oh, he comes down and helps me close up. You know, collect the cash and make out reports." She leaned forward to whisper. "Around here it wouldn't be a good idea for me to handle a lot of cash by myself late at night. As a woman you can understand that."

"Oh, absolutely," Tippy said. "In these parts an Anglo girl needs protection after dark. But what happened to Rafael, the guy who used to manage this store?"

"Gone. We caught him stealing."

"Really? I thought he was one of the few honest men left."

"You knew him?"

"Indirectly. I knew his brother."

Aimee's interest soared immediately.

"I thought his brother was supposed to be a gangster or something."

"Could have been, but he was nice to me. Here in the southwest, men treat men one way and women another. So when will Mac come by?"

"About nine-thirty to ten. Stop by if you're in the area, I'm sure Mac would love to see you." Aimee wasn't sure that was true, but it didn't hurt to be polite. The store was a public place, and Tippy could show up any time she wished.

"I'll be busy tonight," Tippy said, rising to leave. "Just say hello for me, and that I'm glad things have worked out."

Aimee watched Tippy leave, noticing that she neglected to make a purchase. Tippy reeked of money from the gold bracelets, rings, and chains that adorned her body in good taste. The most beautiful woman in the Rio Grande valley had just paid her a visit. Most likely Tippy was staking out the competition for Mac, but in any case, the visit had been overly friendly. Tippy had something in mind, and Aimee didn't like it.

Tippy was evidently wealthy or had a rich boyfriend. Her car was a new Mercedes, one of the most expensive ones. It was like watching a commercial on TV. The gorgeous, expensive woman gracefully got in her car and drove away without glancing back at the hoi polloi.

It wasn't logical for any man to resist her, but Mac had. Alongside Tippy, Aimee felt unsophisticated and homely, even backward like a country hick. No man would choose her over Tippy unless he really loved her. But she had Mac and Tippy didn't.

Tippy had made her feel like an outsider even in her own store. But it was her store, and Tippy was on her turf. She resolved to improve the store's appearance and carry classier merchandise. In New Mexico she couldn't sell beer and gas together at the same store. Well, she'd put up a liquor store next door, or perhaps build an adjoining restaurant and really create an uptown operation. That would show Tippy she wasn't just some redneck bed bunny.

She went back to her work, purposely reminding herself that she was rich beyond her fondest dreams. She had her three stores and Mac. What more could she want? Tippy was probably one of those women who could never be satisfied and always had to win out over others. Why should she ruin her life by competing against people like that?

Aimee practically raced home after the noontime rush, but Mac was somewhere out on the Bar-D range. To her intense disappointment, Mac didn't show up before she had to return to Anthony for the evening rush. That was a shame. It would have been wonderful to spend the afternoon in bed. Her thoughts remained focused on sex, and she decided to surprise Mac that evening by not wearing panties. He loved it when she flaunted her sexuality, and this would be a perfect time.

Rosa was particularly talkative during the evening, especially when Aimee brought up the need for fancier uniforms. The current store smocks were drab, and Aimee wanted dresses with aprons for the girls and shirts and ties for the guys. Rosa preferred jeans for comfort, but Aimee argued for a more professional image. At the very least, unisex shirts with a new Swift-Stop logo and stylish slacks would be a definite improvement.

Deciding on a new logo was another issue she had discussed

with Stuart. She favored using lightning bolts for the "S"s in Swift-Stop, but Stuart had pointed out the similarity between her design and the SS of Nazi Germany. As long as the "S"s were not put together, she thought her idea would work. Besides, she proposed to use New Mexico's Zia in place of the dash to give the name a distinctly local flair.

In the morning, she'd finalize the logo for all sorts of novelties, pens, coolers, hats, coffee cups, et cetera for sale in the store. Then she'd draw up a mascot named Swifty for promotion and advertising. Those were the fun parts of the business, and areas where she could impress Mac with her ingenuity.

As the evening wore on, she became increasingly anxious for Mac to arrive. She needed him, his strength and his love. A business could never substitute for a loved one, and by nine, her heart jumped every time a car pulled in at the store.

Then she saw Mac drive up in Rover. She felt a wonderful, exciting sensation of joyous anticipation. Her love had arrived. Everything was beautiful, and her world was at peace.

*****

Last year had been his best year ever, and Stuart was working late as usual. It had been dicey at times, but the outcome was well-nigh perfect. His businesses had prospered, and his involvement with Mac had proven highly profitable. Even his drinking was under control, and his health was never better. He'd go over the books with Mac and divvy up the profits. He had invited Aimee and Mac to his house for dinner, but Aimee said they had other plans. He grinned to himself, guessing what that meant.

They deserved to bask in their happiness. Mac's year had been uncommonly tough—almost terminal. And not just physically. He had been on the ropes financially, morally, and legally. He was okay now, thank God, and if his luck held for a few years, his illegal activities would be buried with the passage of time.

Aimee deserved her good fortune without qualification or limitation. Her college experience had been dreadful, but, with Mac's help, she was putting that and her stint with drugs firmly behind her.

At long last Mac had filed for divorce from Mary Lou, and his idea to put the stores in Aimee's name kept them from being subject to the property settlement. The lawyers hadn't started yet to run up their bills and make their clients' lives miserable, but Stuart knew it was just a matter of time. He prayed that Aimee wouldn't be involved, but knew Mary Lou would drag her in as certainly as night followed day.

Mac had stopped by and given him Lupe's card. Stuart wasn't surprised, but Mac steadfastly said he and Lupe had been together only a single time, and then only because she had given him an ultimatum. Okay, but one time was all it took to make a girl pregnant. So now Stuart had to arrange to support Lupe and her child without Aimee finding out. That was no problem, she'd be just another expense item in his business ledgers.

He was reviewing contracts for the coupon processing business when his telephone rang. Stuart hesitated to pick up the receiver, then decided it might be Ermie. Stuart glanced at the clock on his desk and noted it was after ten-thirty. Very late. He should have been home two hours ago. He tossed the papers onto his desk and reached for the phone.

The voice wasn't Ermie's. It was Manuel Gomez, the Anthony chief of police. Manny was an old acquaintance who played golf every year in Stuart's foursome at the Anthony Invitational. This time his call was not social, and there were no opening pleasantries.

"Stuart, there's been a shooting at your store on Doniphan," Gomez said. "You want to come down here. I need your help in the worst way."

Gomez was an easygoing professional policeman with almost twenty years of service to Anthony, but better known for his political acumen than his law enforcement skills. He and Stuart had scratched each other's back for most of their adult lives, but this was the first time the chief was desperate for Stuart's assistance.

"It's not my store anymore, Manny," Stuart said. "I sold it to Aimee Barnes. You need to phone her. She lives with Mac Frazier at the Bar-D."

"Do me a favor and get here. I don't know the Barnes woman, and I need your help."

"Okay. Let me call Ermie, and I'll be right down."

It suddenly struck Stuart that Gomez had said "shooting." He assumed the chief meant a robbery.

337

"By the way, you said a shooting. Was anybody hurt?"

"Yeah, tell you when I see you." The chief rang off without another word.

Wow, it was serious. Stuart swept the pile of contracts into his drawer and ran out to his car. He forgot to telephone his wife.

*****

Patrolman Hernandez waved Stuart through the police line and into the C-store parking area.

"The chief's inside," Hernandez said.

He offered Hernandez his hand in greeting, but the distracted patrolman ignored the customary courtesy. The mob of people, cordon of police cars and patrolmen, and garish flashes from the cruisers' lights had changed his former property into a disaster movie sound stage. Stuart followed the stocky Hernandez into the store. The cash register was open, but otherwise the inside looked completely normal. A siren was wailing in the background.

Gomez stopped him as he approached the storeroom door.

"It's pretty gruesome, Stuart," the heavyset Hispanic said. "Hold on to yourself."

"No problem. Nothing can be that bad." Stuart had seen all sorts of farm and traffic accidents over his years in the valley.

The left side of the storage area was lined with heavy-duty shelves containing boxes of merchandise. Cases of pop and larger items were stacked in the middle. The right wall was cinderblock and separated the storeroom from a tiny office and lavatory. Blood was splattered around pockmarks on the cinderblock wall, and three bodies were lying in various awkward postures of death in front of the red splashes.

Stuart's face flushed with an unbearable heat, and he grabbed Gomez's arm to keep from falling. His head spun in disbelief. The horror before him surpassed his worst nightmare, and he fought to regain control. A good minute passed before Stuart was out of danger of fainting.

He recognized all three individuals, Mac, Aimee, and the store clerk Rosa. Mac was on the left, coated in red from a large number of bullet holes. Aimee lay close to Mac, her torso twisted in Mac's direction. Someone had methodically blasted their faces into ghastly fragments of gore. Aimee's right cheek and eye were horribly mutilated by exiting rounds, and her shattered jaw hung from grotesque shreds of tattered muscle. It was as if she had turned to see Mac one last time before her face was destroyed by successive bullets. Mac's weakened skull had blown apart, and his brains, blood, and hair mingled with Aimee's on the floor between them.

The deaths were appallingly obscene. Aimee was dressed in a skirt and sweater, and both had ridden up to eliminate any semblance of modesty. Like Mac, she had been shot several times in the chest. Her legs were spread apart, and even at a glance, Stuart could see she wore no panties. She must have been raped. The day had been unseasonably warm but not too warm for panties.

Blood was everywhere, and the bodies, particularly those of Aimee and Mac, were almost floating in a red lake. Stuart changed his mind; Aimee couldn't have been raped after being murdered—the rapist would have been covered in blood. It'd probably been done before she was killed, and Mac made to watch. Then they must have been lined up against the wall and shot down like in Chicago's St. Valentine's Day Massacre.

The stink of blood, urine, and feces was revolting, all the worse because it came from people he loved. Stuart excused himself to go outside and throw up.

Chief Gomez followed him into the parking lot and waited quietly for Stuart to compose himself. Not having eaten supper, Stuart had little to lose.

"Did you know the Anglo girl?" the Chief asked. "We couldn't find any identification."

"Aimee Barnes," Stuart said. "She owned the store." He coughed uncontrollably as he tried to speak.

"Sorry, Stuart. I know it's not pretty."

"Do you have to leave her exposed like that? Is nothing sacred?" Stuart was feeling both sick and angry.

"Until all the photos are taken, we can't move them."

"God, what happened?"

"Near as we can tell, it was a robbery, but evidently the perpetrators were known to the victims. The cash register's empty, but unless the victims knew the robbers, there wouldn't have been a reason to blow anyone away. Neither girl's purse nor Mac's wallet was found, but of course I recognized both Mac and Rosa Alderete."

"I'm surprised you recognized Mac. Somebody tried to blow his face away."

"Yeah. Did a pretty good job, too. Same with the Barnes girl. She must have been beautiful."

"Looks like it got her raped." Stuart was breathing rapidly to clear his head.

"Probably, but we'll know for sure from the autopsy. From the way they were killed, I think Mac and the Barnes girl knew the robbers. It's rare to see someone murdered with such malice. Poor Rosa was really in the wrong place at the wrong time."

"Mac has no family, Manny. I'll take care of arrangements. Aimee Barnes was my first wife's youngest sister, so I'll probably be involved there, too."

"I thought Mac was married."

Crap, Stuart had forgotten about Mary Lou. "Yeah, but he already filed for divorce."

"Well, that doesn't mean anything. She's still spouse of record. She at the ranch?"

"No, living with a guy in Cruces and carrying his child." Stuart cursed Mac for his procrastination.

"Manny, Mac and Aimee Barnes were living together at the Bar-D, and there wasn't any contact with Mary Lou. Give me a chance to get Aimee's things from the ranch before Mary Lou takes over."

"I'll have to notify her as soon as possible."

"You don't know where she lives, and that means you can't release Mac's name."

Gomez took out his notebook. "Gimme your first wife's name and address. Least I can do is notify her."

Stuart glared at the chief.

"It's only right, Stuart. Eventually she'll learn when it happened, and we'll have no good reason for not telling her immediately." The chief's eyes were pleading. "Come on, you want me to help you."

Stuart nodded and rattled off the name, address, and telephone number. He staggered over to his car. "Mac and Aimee were my friends, Manny. Keep me informed of everything you find out."

"Go home and get some rest. I'll keep you posted. In the morning you can give me a list of Mac's enemies, acquaintances, business dealings, et cetera. I'm going to need your help on this, and you're the only person I know who's intimately acquainted with two of the victims."

"I won't let you down. Just keep the media away."

Stuart spotted the Channel Four News van bouncing to a stop on Doniphan. Thank God the store was fifteen miles from El Paso. It was time to make tracks.

Gomez was slightly taller than Stuart, but a damn sight heavier. Like most Hispanics in the valley, he wore a mustache and his face showed the ravages of adolescent acne. But Manny was brighter than most, and relatively honest. He could be swayed, but not at the cost of his personal integrity. Stuart would have to figure something out to keep the chief in line.

There was no justice in the world. Wheeling south on Doniphan, Stuart knew he'd have to set matters right himself. Mac was the last of his family, and without an heir except for Lupe's unborn child. Instead of driving home, Stuart gunned his car toward the Bar-D.

The screen's hidden key got him into the house, and the papers he sought were in Mac's desk. He wasn't on the property for fifteen minutes, and neither of Mac's hands was around. With an immense sigh of relief, he turned back onto the highway from the ranch road without his incursion being discovered. Now it was too late. No one would know he had been to the Bar-D. The TV people could stake out the ranch all they wanted, but they wouldn't see him. The next several days would be damage control, then there would be time for revenge.

Not for a millisecond did Stuart believe it was a robbery.

Chapter 54

Eliminating several of his agreements with Mac gave Stuart a lien on the Bar-D and outright ownership of all its northern range. The C-stores were legally owned by Aimee, and Mary Lou had no chance at them. They'd fall to him unless Aimee's family could pay off her notes. The most serious problem lay in what Mac might have in his mine. It needed to be cleaned out immediately.

After discussing Mac's activities and acquaintances with Manny Gomez during the morning, Stuart retreated into seclusion. He hadn't mentioned the well or Mac's involvement with illegals and drugs, nor his ex-girlfriend, Tippy. He wanted Gomez to conclude that Mac recognized at least one of the robbers, probably blurting his name, thus causing his own death and that of the girls.

Stuart was sure he knew what happened. Aimee had phoned yesterday and told him of Tippy's visit, and even mentioned her connection to the departed manager, Ramirez. Somehow, Tippy had heard about Mac and Aimee and probably dropped in to case the layout. The bitch was responsible for the atrocities Stuart viewed in the storeroom. Most likely she wanted to kick-start the well operation and take over Mac's contacts. In gangster-land style, she'd eliminated all threats to her security from the Bar-D's direction. He'd have to be careful himself since Tippy knew Mac and he were close.

His biggest problem was that he couldn't enlist any help. Not from Chief Gomez, not from Jed Akers, not from anyone. No one could know he was involved with Mac running drugs, or even that he was aware of Mac's criminal activities. Always before when he did something ticklish, he relied on friends for help. This time he would have to do everything himself.

He wondered how Mac and Aimee died. Mac would have known

they were all doomed. From their positions, Mac and Aimee were comforting each other when they died. At least that much was good. They had gone together, in each other's arms. Aimee might not have been scared at all.

He spent the evening at home, frustrated by his conversations with Gomez. Ermie was colder and more unresponsive than usual, busying herself in trivial matters and ignoring him. Stuart was isolated with his grief. The murders weren't something they could discuss, and with Aimee's sister arriving in a few hours, Ermie felt dragged into Stuart's first marriage.

The next day was no different. Ermie took the kids to visit her mother to give Stuart some space. He spent the morning putting his paper house in order to euchre Mary Lou out of as much property as possible.

By mid-afternoon his spirits were in the toilet. He needed a woman or a drink or both. A woman wasn't available, but a bottle was. He downed a drink, then another, then another. Oblivion came before sleep.

Dawn brought another workday and a terrific hangover. He drove to Las Cruces to make the tin mine disappear. At New Mexico State, a friendly graduate assistant took him almost directly to the USGS charts he needed. The Rio Grande valley had been extensively surveyed in the past, and many of the maps were old. There were a number with various dates that included Mac's holdings. The Bar-D's buildings were accurately shown and annotated on some, as well as Stuart's own properties.

Within a half hour after arriving in Cruces, his NMSU foray was crowned with success. A topographic map dating from 1940 showed a "mine" symbol on Mac's property. About seven hundred yards south of Mac's northern section line and somewhat west of the eastern escarpment, it was the only such mark on any of the maps Stuart examined. That chart disappeared.

Next came the mine itself. Stuart hadn't been there since before the operation started, and its contents stunned him. They were more befitting a cave filled with pirate treasure than an abandoned tin mine in the desert. Stuart found over two million dollars in cash and over two hundred pounds of gold Krugerrands in addition to his own gold and silver stash. He couldn't imagine how Mac had squirreled the gold and frankly didn't want to know. The well operation's books were there, and he learned of the payments to Tippy, the coyotes, truckers, and other personnel north and south. It was all in black and white, and could send a bunch of people to jail.

Including himself, Stuart realized. Mac had made notes on his land sales and the coupon processing business, firmly implicating Stuart as a co-conspirator. His participation in the money laundering was established beyond all doubt, and he was at risk as much as anyone. But he hadn't killed Mac and Aimee, and someone in these books had.

The best candidate was Tippy even if he hadn't known she'd cased the store. But Stuart knew she couldn't and wouldn't have done the deed by herself. Not that finding someone to help was a problem for her. Accomplices would have been easy to recruit, or maybe supplied free of charge by Mac's old buddy Mendoza.

He remembered Aimee said Tippy drove a new Mercedes and was expensively dressed. Yeah, Mendoza was probably involved, and Tippy's juicy twat would be working overtime keeping his attention. Even without Tippy's favors, Mendoza was an obvious participant. Mac had caused Mendoza to lose face, and that alone might have been enough for the Mexican drug lord to support Tippy's action.

This was not good. If Tippy found out he was involved, Mendoza could send any number of *pistoleros* to hunt him down and fill him full of holes like Mac. He needed to eliminate all traces of his complicity.

Stuart also found anon-descript suitcase filled with a number of personal articles, jewelry, billfolds, watches, and other items a man might carry. Identification in the billfolds showed three to be Mexican nationals, but only a single name meant anything to Stuart. Ramirez. So Mac *had* killed his ex-store manager's older brother. That sealed the connection. No wonder Tippy knew about Aimee at the store and chose that site to take revenge.

The interior of the mine was impressively equipped with all the comforts of home. Stuart could hide out there for weeks if necessary, and the extensive provisions indicated Mac had prepared for such a possibility. He had also stashed several boxes of dynamite in the mine, for some purpose that Stuart could only guess. Even detonators were present, along with coils of wire, crimping tools, and timers.

The whole thing was bizarre, but so was Mac's involvement in illegal activities in the first place.

It took three trips in his Blazer to empty the mine of its treasures, but the first thing Stuart did was burn the books Mac kept on his financial dealings. So he committed another criminal act, this time obstructing justice. Whatever that was. There would be no justice for Aimee or Rosa. They were innocents trampled in the grass when elephants fought.

The watches and jewelry went to a pawn shop in El Paso, and Stuart destroyed the remainder of the mine's personal items. With his actions, all physical evidence linking Mac and himself with the deceased Mexicans was scattered and untraceable. Why Mac hadn't gotten rid of this stuff earlier was unfathomable, but Mac hadn't gotten his divorce either.

Facing his best friend's guilt in killing people without a compelling reason was difficult, but Stuart believed Mac had been temporarily deranged from his head injuries. Part of the problem was the general lawlessness of their border environment. It seemed everybody acted beyond the law at times, and those who were most successful were also the biggest crooks. Like the old saying; "Life is like a cesspool—the really big chunks rise to the top."

The pawn broker accepting Mac's merchandise was a case in point. He imported Mexican silver coins for melting, paying a fraction of the coins' metal value but much more than they were worth as coins in Mexico. They were legal to import into the US, but illegal to export from Mexico. So they were smuggled into El Paso, then the dealer drove onto the Bridge of the Americas, did a U-turn just out of sight from the American side—but before reaching Mexican controls—and came through US Customs, legally declaring the coins.

So everybody was working a scam of some sort. Mac had just gone a little overboard, and got caught in a landslide—one he hadn't seen coming. He should have worked his way up rather than running for the roses on his first outing. He was an amateur in a professional's game, and his sentimentality was his undoing.

Perhaps Mac's greatest sin was putting Aimee at risk. That broke the unwritten code of western honor and was almost unpardonable. It was also another reason Stuart believed Tippy orchestrated the deaths of Mac and Aimee. No man would have done that. Certainly not a westerner. Mac's only defense was that he would have expected his enemies to observe the code and not harm Aimee. But the code only applied to male killers, not females.

No doubt Mac would have sacrificed himself to save Aimee if given a chance. Only yesterday a lady jeweler from Juarez delivered a beautiful hand-made diamond ring Mac had ordered for Aimee. It was to be her engagement ring, one of a kind, and Stuart paid for the ring with the intent of giving it to Aimee's sister as proof of Mac's intentions. For five thousand dollars he had acquired a ring that would retail at over three or four times his cost, but such things were common among those with the right contacts.

Six days later, Chief Gomez furnished Stuart with the autopsy reports.

The shots to Mac's and Aimee's faces came from a nine millimeter handgun and were inflicted while the victims already lay on the floor. They were coup de grâce shots, clearly indicating an execution rather than a robbery gone bad. Even more telling evidence came from Mac's body. His genitals were badly bruised, evidently as the result of blows before he'd died.

Aimee hadn't earned the same treatment, but was still singled out for worse abuse than poor Rosa. Her face had been completely ravaged by someone bent on destroying her beauty. There was no sign of rape or even sexual molestation, although a small amount of semen was found in Aimee's vagina. The examiner concluded it was the result of earlier sexual activity, possibly the previous night.

The missing panties were still a mystery. There were no lines on Aimee's body indicating their earlier presence, and the examiner thought she simply wasn't wearing any that evening. Other than her blouse and skirt, Aimee was wearing cotton socks and boat shoes, apparently attempting to be comfortable while working on her feet in the store.

Mac had taken seventeen rounds, Aimee twelve, and Rosa three. Only two distinct weapons were identified, although there could have been more since all bullets were heavily damaged. The killers had taken time to reload in order to further desecrate their victims. As Chief Gomez pointed out, these murders were with malice.

Stuart found himself becoming angry over the extent of the

autopsies. They violated the victims' privacy, especially with respect to Aimee and her sexual activity. He read about the size and condition of her vagina, that she was not pregnant, and that her pubic hair was blond but slightly darker than that on her head. Who in the hell needed to know all that? This was a kind, loving human being. What did the size of her vagina have to do with anything? What difference did it make if she had sex the night before she was killed?

It wasn't going to happen to him. When it came time for him to depart, he'd walk into the desert and let the vultures feed. Anything was better than an autopsy report going into some stranger's file to be read by other strangers.

The report he held in his hands was another thing to hide from his first wife. She was already a basket case threatening to destroy his current marriage. She blamed Stuart for letting Aimee get involved in something that caused her sister's death. And Ermie agreed with her. The two women had made common cause against him, and Stuart's only refuge was his office.

Most importantly, the autopsies confirmed Stuart's opinion about who was responsible for his friends' deaths. Only Tippy would have kicked Mac in the balls and destroyed Aimee's radiant beauty. She probably lifted Aimee's skirt to see what interested Mac and discovered the lack of underclothes. An unexpected bonus satisfying her curiosity, no doubt.

"What other evidence have you uncovered?" Stuart asked Gomez.

"Not much. There weren't any witnesses, there wasn't any video camera in the store, and the only thing anyone saw was a large, dark sedan pulling away before the bodies were discovered."

"No one heard the shots?"

"Yeah, several people in nearby houses. But it was dark, and nobody rushed outside to see what was going on. There were so many shots, some of the witnesses thought they were firecrackers. One bang is a shot, thirty must be fireworks."

"So where's your investigation going?"

"We're looking for suspects among people who didn't like Mac. Also people who didn't like Mac and the Barnes girl."

It was time to bite the bullet and divert the chief's attention. Stuart knew what to offer.

"Mac was my closest business associate, and I brought Aimee

out here and introduced her to him. I don't want their reputations sullied, and any investigation naturally finds some dirt. It would mean a lot to me if the case was considered a robbery."

"Say what? You involved in this?" The chief rose up and looked at Stuart suspiciously.

"No, absolutely not. I just don't think digging into Mac's past would do anyone any good. Especially Mac and Aimee. As you know, he had already filed for divorce from Mary Lou, and that automatically makes her a suspect. I know everybody, and these are good people who don't deserve suspicion, long investigations, and devastating local gossip and speculation."

Chief Gomez smiled. "You know who did it, don't you?"

Stuart scoffed. "I'm a local, and all locals speculate."

"But you know more than other locals."

"If I do, I'll take appropriate action."

"Appropriate action is telling me what you know."

"Appropriate action is helping you do your job. I'm willing to do that. That's why I think you should decide this was a robbery and look for robbery suspects. Beef up your police force, improve your investigative techniques through better training and equipment, and increase security in Anthony to lower crime."

"What the hell are you talking about? All that costs money, and you know what our tax base is like."

Stuart had counted Mac's stash the previous day, and combined with their company's bank accounts, Mac's liquid assets amounted to over four million dollars.

"Tell you what," Stuart said. "I'll establish a trust fund of three million dollars in the names of the three victims for the purpose of improving our police department. Like I said, I'm willing to help you do your job."

The Chief whistled, then smiled wickedly. "Okay, it was a robbery gone bad. I'm not interested in importing organized crime and frightening the populace with stories of mob executions and so forth."

"Neither am I. El Paso can keep those honors. We want a nice place to live without those problems. Let's both praise and bury Mac."

"I can handle that. The public doesn't need to know someone smashed Mac's balls before shooting him."

"No. And I won't embarrass you by adding to your body count. Not in Anthony, I won't."

"Thanks for small favors. When can we announce your gift honoring the three victims?"

"Any time you wish. I'll have the money for you within a month."

Chapter 55

"You bastard! What are you up to?"

Stuart held the receiver away from his ear and speculated on the identity of his caller. It had to be Mary Lou, since his police gift had not yet been announced.

"Mary Lou," he said. "How nice to hear from you. I trust you're bucking up well under these tragic circumstances."

"Tragic, my ass! Mac was begging for someone to fill him full of holes, and you know it. I want to know about this lien you have on my ranch and the property you're supposed to own which should be mine."

"By all means. Mac and I were in business together. I underwrote a lot of his activities, and what you see is the result."

"Bullshit! You're stealing it from me!"

"Gee, I would have thought you'd be concerned with the police investigation into Mac's and his girlfriend's death. You didn't stand to get much in a divorce, but now you get it all. That and revenge usually make for a good motive and attract suspicion."

"They've already been here, and I have an ironclad alibi, so forget your insinuations."

"How about the deputy who's roto-rootering your plumbing? He have a good alibi?"

"Fuck you and the horse you rode in on."

"How's the pregnancy? I understand a Mexican squirt gun got you."

"Yeah? Well, I understand your cock rotted off from all the Mexicans you've fucked."

"Time has not softened your tongue, I see. I hope your deputy knows how to run a ranch so you can pay me off."

350

"That cocksucker's long gone. And thanks for arranging to get him fired. So it's just you and me, motherfucker. And I'll pay you off if I have to work south El Paso."

"I thought you *were* working there."

The receiver at the other end went down with a bang. Stuart broke out with a belly laugh. He figured the Bar-D wouldn't last a year. What Mac built, Mary Lou would fritter away. Hopefully, sooner rather than later. She had deserted his friend when he needed her most. In many ways this whole thing was her fault, and somehow she had come out a big winner.

*****

The telephone call to Stuart had been extremely unsatisfactory, and Mary Lou cursed herself for letting it get out of hand. She had no friends, and it was stupid to piss off the most powerful man in Doña Ana County. New Mexico was a community property state, but she and Mac had signed a prenup specifically exempting the Bar-D. Mac had inherited it and the prenup requirement had been included in his father's will. So whether or not her signature was on the papers concerning the Bar-D, she couldn't claim that Mac's contracts with Stuart were invalid.

She re-dialed Stuart's number. This time she played nice. She invited Stuart to the memorial service she had arranged for Mac. He immediately accepted, and thanked her for the invite. Following the service, Mac was to be cremated. Not that there was much of Mac to be cremated anyway. His skull and brains were sponged off the stockroom floor, and the autopsy had removed his internal organs. Some body parts had been zippered back inside his chest cavity, but they may or may not have belonged to Mac. It was a barbaric ritual.

She gave Mac's urn to Stuart the day after the cremation, asking him to place it wherever Mac would have wished. That was something Mac had never mentioned, and if anyone, Stuart would know Mac's desires. At any rate, it eliminated an odious duty for her. She didn't have the money for a monument in a local cemetery, and she asked Stuart to take care of that also. He promised he would.

The ranch belonged to her now, at least for the moment, and Mary Lou lost no time in cleansing it of all traces of Mac's girlfriend. She didn't have many belongings, either in clothes or personal items, and Mary Lou speedily boxed up what she found. Surprisingly, there were no birth control pills in the medicine cabinet, or any evidence of any birth control being used like condoms, a diaphragm or even spermicide. Evidently, Mac and the girl were trying to have a baby.

Well, she definitely was having one. Juan had been extremely dark, with black eyes and hair. It the child took after him, she'd have trouble attracting whites again. If necessary, she'd say she was raped to eliminate the stigma.

On the other hand, she was no longer certain Juan was the father. When she went in for her checkup the previous month, the doctor had said her baby was abnormally well-developed for the conception date she had assumed. He suggested it might have been as much as five weeks earlier. She and Mac had sex the morning of the roll-over, so it was possible the child in her belly was Mac's. Lord, she hoped it was. Stuart would do anything then to keep the Frazier line going, and life would become a lot easier.

As she cleaned up the ranch, Mary Lou decided she shouldn't have been so nasty to Stuart. One caught a lot more flies with honey than with vinegar. They had gotten along well at the hospital until The Whole Enchilada Festival.

She thought about Stuart as she scanned through a pile of Mac's mail. It included a friendship card from a girl named Lupe in Chicago. Mary Lou hadn't thought Mac knew anyone in Chicago. It was as good an excuse as any to talk with Stuart.

He came on the line immediately and was pleasant as usual. Mary Lou responded in her friendliest tone.

"I've been going through Mac's mail," she said. "Who's this girl, Lupe?"

"Lupe? What's her last name?" Stuart asked.

"Looks like Garza, but her writing isn't very good."

"I'm not sure. What are you looking at?"

"Nothing important. Just a card."

"From where? What's the address?"

More questions. Mary Lou was becoming exasperated. "What am I, your computer dating service? From Chicago."

"Oh, now I remember. That was a maid Mac hired. She moved

to Chicago around the beginning of January. Why? Is it something important?"

"No. I was just curious."

"Well, I'm sure you don't have to worry about her. Mac didn't stir Mexican honey pots."

"I don't know. You have to bite into a sour apple to find out it's sour."

"Are you saying you bit into a sour apple lately?"

"Hey, let's just say I made a mistake. But only one. It looks like Mac screwed everything that walked." She was guessing, and wanted to hear Stuart's reaction.

"Actually, as far as I know, he was absolutely faithful to you until you moved out," Stuart said.

That jarred her, but it was probably true. Mac had never given her cause to be jealous.

"Well, tell that to the slut he got killed. She picked the wrong guy to ply her trade."

Stuart's voice hardened instantly. "Regardless of what you think of Mac, she was my first wife's younger sister, and a really sweet kid. Her death was a real tragedy. Think about it. Five months earlier, it could have been you."

Mary Lou sucked in her breath to absorb Stuart's body blow. He was right. She hadn't known the girl and shouldn't have said what she did.

"Sorry, my apologies. I didn't know. You may not believe this, but I loved Mac. I just couldn't play the dutiful wife when he became abusive. And it hurt to hear he was happy with someone else."

"Yeah, marriages are sometimes tough," Stuart said. "Apology accepted."

"By the way, I boxed up some stuff that belonged to your sister-in-law," Mary Lou said. You can have them if you'd like. I'll leave them outside on the patio if you don't want to see me."

"That won't be necessary. I'll stop by tomorrow morning if that'd be convenient. And give me the card from the maid, and I'll let her know Mac is among the departed."

"I'll be here. You can even have a cup of coffee and listen to a pregnant widow's blues. Just promise not to automatically take Mac's side on everything."

"Fair enough. No matter how thin you slice a piece of bread, there's always two sides. And we do have to deal with each other, like it or not. We might as well agree to like it."

Mary Lou nodded to herself and felt optimistic for the first time in months. Stuart really wasn't a bad guy. Maybe they could form a friendship based on common interest. Who knew, they might even become friends with benefits.

Chapter 56—Valentine's Day

Stuart had destroyed Mac's papers acquiring the acreage from Ramirez when he discovered they were still unfiled in Las Cruces. The whole setup was weird. Tippy was listed as the owner according to the property records in Cruces, and the papers were dated the same as Mac's. Castillo had signed everything using his power of attorney from Ramirez. It was the same for Tippy's house. There was no physical evidence linking either Mac or himself to Tippy or the property with the well. Mac had prepared for this eventuality.

Stuart surveyed the scene and gathered his thoughts. As much as he was extracting revenge for Mac and Aimee, he was protecting Mary Lou and himself. It was important to cauterize this festering wound on the Bar-D's northern perimeter. Mendoza needed to be diverted from the area, the Mexican drug operation terminated, and their names erased from any possible connection or retaliatory action.

But it wasn't just similar business interests with Mary Lou anymore. He had changed his mind about her. He still hadn't forgiven her for leaving Mac the way she had, but understood her point of view. And she had apologized over her remark about Aimee.

In some ways their lives were similar. Neither had a really close friend, he had lost Mac, and Mary Lou had been secluded on the ranch. Now her pregnancy isolated her even more. It was hard for her being alone and friendless, but he was equally alone in his marriage. Ermie and he hadn't made love since long before Mac's dog was killed, and the situation was probably permanent. She rolled away when he came to bed, and the loneliness was suffocating.

It must have been that way with Mary Lou after she and Mac became estranged. Then came the accident, and Mac went over the edge. The timing was perfect for Beltran to step in and take advantage of Mary Lou's vulnerability for a quick piece. Unfortunately, it'd ruined her life.

Over the past two weeks he had spent most of his evenings at the Bar-D, for the first time truly communicating with a woman. Mary Lou listened to him, and he listened to her. In the beginning they talked about Mac, but increasingly they shared thoughts about themselves. Her pregnancy allowed them to become close without being pressured into a sexual relationship. She was more than halfway through, and fortunately had escaped morning sickness and the usual complaints by pregnant women. Nonetheless, she was not having an easy time. Her pregnancy temporarily ruined her best assets.

Things changed last night. Mary Lou broke down when talking about how no white man would want her if the baby were Mexican, and he tried to comfort her. Her tears and hunger were real. Before they knew it, they were in each other's arms and kissing. Two lonesome souls, seeking love and affection. And he wanted her, pregnant or not.

It almost happened. Things got pretty hot between them, but he chickened out. He had yet to cheat on Ermie, and the sense of guilt stopped him. Maybe he was a jerk because he wasn't getting any at home, but this was a big step. Mac hadn't done it until after Mary Lou left him, and he couldn't do it either. And Mary Lou was no one-time happening between strangers who would never see each other again.

She took his refusal in good grace, better than he had a right to expect. When he said he couldn't continue, she respected his wishes. She agreed some things could not be pushed, and she would wait until he was ready.

"If we start this," Stuart had said, "It can't be just an affair."

"But you can't get divorced."

"No, I can't imagine that. So where does that leave us?"

"As two very close friends with benefits. It's a time-honored practice that you, as the *patron* of the county, should have a wife and a lover. No one would think less of you; in fact it would be quite the opposite. And no one would say anything against me either, with you standing by my side."

The image had appealed to Stuart, and Mary Lou was probably correct in her assessment as to how their relationship would go over.

He saw the potential. "We could be partners like Mac and I were, and you would gain stature in the community."

Mary Lou had kissed Stuart where Ermie never had, and Stuart knew he wouldn't refuse her a second time. Ermie didn't care, and didn't want him. As long as he provided for the family, Ermie was content. And the kids didn't care if he was unhappy. They only cared about themselves, their friends, and the size of their allowances.

He made his decision. The next time he'd be ready. She could be his mistress, and he'd divide his time between home and the Bar-D. Having someone like Mary Lou pursue his body would give him the sexual power he'd always wanted. Others would respect him as a man, not merely as someone good at making money. They'd respect him even more if they knew about what he was going to do tonight.

*****

All his preparations had gone well, and it seemed appropriate that the end would come on St. Valentine's Day.

Now, it all had come down to him and this radio transmitter. He stared at the green button, telling himself he could do this. The people inside the trailer were all criminals of the worst stripe, and he was doing humanity a favor in eliminating them. Included was his best friend's nemesis—the bitch who had kicked Mac in the balls before plugging him between the eyes. He might even be offing Mendoza, since the older bald Mexican fit Mac's description of the drug lord.

Tippy was inside the trailer, and her life was in Stuart's hands. He wished he was closer, and able to the expression on her face as she died. He hated her more than he had ever hated anyone.

He didn't give her another second. Stuart stabbed the button down hard.

The effect was unbelievable. The trailer disintegrated in all directions as a terrific ball of flame rose from the spreading gasoline. Tippy's Mercedes flipped upside down and started burning alongside the flaming wreckage of the van and another vehicle. The tanker toppled onto its side, and it too began burning in a spreading pool of diesel fuel. The well and pump disappeared in a huge cloud of dust, and the fire from the sheds cast an eerie light over the whole surrealistic scene.

Nobody came out of the trailer. Flattened and burning brightly, it was little more than a funeral pyre for those within. Stuart shrugged, thinking how the authorities would have difficulty determining who perished in the fire. He tried to make out bodies, but nothing was recognizable. That long blonde hair had undoubtedly frizzled into charred specks with the first licking flame. He hoped Tippy was still alive for a few more moments, perishing in terrible agony, watching and feeling her flesh roast in the flames, the fire consuming her soul and purifying the earth.

After all, Tippy believed herself to be an Aztec god's consort. Too bad for him. Her god would be sleeping alone tonight. He should have known better than to pick a mere mortal. Regardless of how beautiful she had been, she was a cinder now. Boiled, cooked, and charred beyond recognition. It couldn't have happened to a nicer person.

Stuart cradled the transmitter and walked back down the hill to his Blazer. It was over. He had almost doubled Mac's number. Mac had done in six and his score was eleven. He fired up the Blazer and headed south.

The light from the fires was dimming as Stuart turned east on the county road that led past the Bar-D. A landslide had brought everyone down. He pressed hard on the accelerator, hoping Patty Duncan was still at Great American. Perhaps she would sing him another song. This time for the future—his and Mary Lou's.

www.ingramcontent.com/pod-product-compliance
Lightning Source LLC
Chambersburg PA
CBHW072341020726
47506CB00004B/957